ALL

THE

EVER

AFTERS

ALL THE EVER AFTERS

The Untold Story of Cinderella's Stepmother

Danielle Teller

WILLIAM MORROW
An Imprint of HarperCollins*Publishers*

HarperCollins books may be purchased for educational, business, or sales promotional use. For information please e-mail the Special Markets Department at SPsales@har percollins.com.

FIRST EDITION

Designed by Leah Carlson-Stanisic

Borders created by Leah Carlson-Stanisic from artwork by Jamie Ekans/Shutterstock, Inc.

Library of Congress Cataloging-in-Publication Data

Names: Teller, Danielle, author.
Title: All the ever afters : the untold story of Cinderella's stepmother / Danielle Teller.
Description: First edition. | New York, NY : William Morrow, 2018.
Identifiers: LCCN 2017043121| ISBN 9780062798206 (hardback) | ISBN 9780062798077 (trade pb)
Subjects: LCSH: Cinderella (Tale)—Adaptations. | Stepmothers—Fiction. | BISAC: FICTION / Fairy Tales, Folk Tales, Legends & Mythology. | FICTION / Historical. | FICTION / Literary.
Classification: LCC PS3620.E447 A79 2018 | DDC 813/.6—dc23
LC record available at https://lccn.loc.gov/2017043121

ISBN 978-0-06-285638-8 (international edition)

18 19 20 21 22 LSC 10 9 8 7 6 5 4 3 2 1

In memory of Anne Shreenan Dyck,
the best mom in the whole world

ALL

THE

EVER

AFTERS

Prologue

THE ROYAL COURT

Suppers at the royal court have become entirely too oppressive. It isn't just that they are interminable, or that we must adhere to the newest fashions, the face powder, our hair tortured into great bejeweled rams' horns, the silks with sleeves so tight that it's impossible to raise one's spoon to one's carefully tinctured lips— No, the worst is the gossip, the sinister buzz of wasps ready to slip their poisonous stingers into whatever tender flesh lies exposed.

This evening I was ordered to sit next to the Earl of Bryston, a pompous halfwit who has rarely been to court. He presides over some godforsaken swamp in the north, and he seems to believe that his family's long history of loyalty to the crown gives him the right to opine on the behaviors of the royal family.

"My lady," he said, plucking at cuffs so voluminous that they draped into his soup, "I understand that your noble daughters are not yet wed?"

"No, my lord," I answered as briefly as courtesy would allow.

"And yet, I have heard that they once vied for the attention of

Prince Henry himself?" The earl dabbed his crimson lips daintily. "That they tried to alienate his affection from Princess Elfilda?"

"You seem amused, my lord." He could not have mistaken the coldness in my response. "I fear that much of what you have heard is not true."

"Ah, well, it is an incredible tale!" He smiled broadly. "The beautiful downtrodden maiden who ascends to the royal palace, the jealous stepsisters, the glass slipper that would not fit . . ."

"My lord, I cannot credit such a tale."

"Come, my lady! You know that the whole kingdom is enthralled by our radiant and benevolent princess! I have heard a great deal about you and your daughters." He looked at me knowingly.

"Compelling fiction often obscures the humble truth."

"I do hope that you will tell me about the slipper," he said, ignoring my reluctance. He broke a piece of bread, leaving a trail of crumbs across the table. "My wife is frantic to know the particulars! They say that the prince let every maiden try the shoe, even your daughters!" He laughed.

"It is droll to imagine them receiving attention from a prince?"

"Well . . ." His shrug was eloquent.

"They are ugly, and Elfilda is beautiful."

The earl frowned and pursed his lips. It is genteel to imply nasty insults, not to speak them directly.

"My lord, I may have heard some of the rumors to which you allude. To my mind, these stories insinuate a plague of blindness. Prince Henry would have to be blind not to recognize the object of his admiration or to distinguish an ugly girl from one of unsurpassed beauty. My daughters would need to be blind to their reflections in mirrors and on the faces of those who behold them—" My voice rose, so I paused and began again blandly. "They would also need to be blind to the truth that men persuade themselves that beautiful women possess virtue and good character, whereas no amount of virtue can make an ugly woman beautiful."

"My lady, Princess Elfilda is a dazzling star who shines in the royal firmament, where she belongs." He did not attempt to conceal his disdain. "That she invites you and your daughters to dine here at the palace is a testament to her compassion, forgiveness, and generosity."

"Indeed, my lord," I murmured. "Indeed that is so."

I am only of interest to the Earl of Bryston and his ilk because of my stepdaughter. Princess Elfilda is the most celebrated woman in the kingdom, perhaps in all of history. Commoners line the streets for endless hours, even in dark and sleet, hoping to glimpse her face through the window of her gilded carriage. When the princess has her gown cut in a new way or adopts a different hairstyle, every female creature in the city imitates her appearance. Last autumn she wore a choker of pearls to church on Michaelmas, and the next day every noblewoman's throat was wound snugly with pearls or other jewels. By Christmastide even the peasant girls wore chokers of beads or ribbon, whatever material they could find to replicate the fashion.

Princess Elfilda's popularity derives in large part from her astonishing beauty, but there is something else about her nature that attracts the masses. Her habitual muteness and the gentle hesitancy of those rare words that do fall from her lips make her seem bashful, as does her manner of ducking her head and looking up through sweeping lashes. Apart from her collections of baubles and kennel of favorite dogs, she appears to have no passions or vices, and when she attends royal functions, her gaze drifts to invisible spectacles that only she can apprehend. Her elusive character is a blank parchment upon which any story may be written, and every girl who dreams of becoming a princess can imagine herself in Princess Elfilda's famously tiny shoes.

I know more of the princess's history than anyone else alive, and the true tale is not as fantastical as the one sung by troubadours. Nobody is interested in the story of a flesh-and-blood nobleman's daughter, one who wet her bed, complained of boredom, fought with her kin, and turned up her nose at winter greens just like any mortal child. Nor do I have any desire to diminish the adulation for the princess, which makes both the admiring and admired so content.

I do not set out to write the princess's history, but my own, the only tale I have the authority to tell. My quill may resurrect ghosts to keep me company during the long days at the castle, and if it cannot, at least my mind will be occupied and my hands busy. As for fables about good and evil and songs about glass slippers, I shall leave those to the minstrels. They can invent their own tales about Cinderella.

THE MANOR HOUSE

I hardly remember my own mother. I have a memory of arms surrounding me and pushing my head into a soft bosom that smelled of kitchen smoke, lye, and some light acrid scent that I can no longer identify. This memory evokes comfort, but also childish impatience and distaste for yielding flesh.

I do remember her singing; she had a pretty voice. She had heavy auburn hair that she would sometimes allow me to braid.

I was told that she died in agony while my brother tried and failed to enter this world. She labored for three long days as the baby died inside her. Then she too was called to God's side. I do not know where I was as she lay those three days on the birthing bed that became her deathbed. Maybe I was sent away to a neighboring home. Maybe my mind recoiled so violently at the scene of her death that the memory ripped free. I wonder sometimes if the thoughts that flock my nightmares are abandoned memories coming home to roost.

Several years after my mother died, I was sent to work at the manor house. I would have been sent there eventually, because my father was only a half-virgater, poorer than most, and I was the youngest of three children. My brother and my father did what they could with our land, but they also owed work in other parts of the manor's holdings. I was certainly not going to have a dowry, and there was no need for two girls to tend to our cottage. Under more fortunate circumstances, I might have remained at home several years longer to help my mother with the baby, but as it was, I left home with half of my milk teeth. I was a sturdy child, big for my age and strong. My father must have believed that I would fare well at the manor house.

On the day I was to leave home, I lay in the loft long after everyone else had risen. I kept my eyes shut, listening as my sister made the fire and chided the hens that got in her way.

My father said, "You should wake Agnes." Still, I did not move.

"Agnes!" my sister scolded. "Get up and say good-bye to Father and Thomas!" Reluctantly, I rose and lowered myself from the loft. My father's gaze was grave but unapologetic. He opened his arms to signal that he wished me to approach and embrace him.

"Remember that your mother will be watching from heaven," he said gruffly. "Be godly and good. We shall see you on May Day." He released me and turned toward the door.

"Bye, Nessie," my brother said softly, "we shall miss you."

I watched them dissolve into the morning twilight mist as they left to harness the oxen.

"Let's get you a warm bowl of pottage before you go," my sister said. She stirred the steaming pot on the hearth briskly. When she looked up, tears glistened in her eyes. "Oh, this green wood smokes too much," she said. "It makes my eyes sting."

The walk from our cottage in Over End to the church in Nether

End was as familiar as a lullaby, but I had never been beyond the church. The crouching woods of Aviceford Manor's demesne lay beyond the river that divided the church from the manor's holdings. On the Sabbath, it was my habit to steal a moment before Mass to visit the riverbank, where I would scour the sand for pretty stones. Even in winter, as long as the snow was not too deep, I would risk a scolding to slip over the embankment. Once near the river, however, I cast only a rare glance into the dark underbrush on the far bank. I knew of fairies who dwelt in rotting mossy trunks, fairies who stole babies from hearthsides at night and left changelings in their places. I was too big for the fairies to snatch, but I did not care to glimpse a scurrying shadow in the woods, sly yellow eyes gleaming.

Once safely inside the church, I would sit beneath a high lancet window facing the trees, holding a smooth stone in my hand and following the dance of dust motes animated by wavering sunlight. There I would remember that fairies are not real.

On that day in early spring, the swollen river swallowed the banks nearly whole, and bare branches scratched at low clouds. Though it had rained heavily the night before, the sky still hung close and dark, pregnant with water. It settled itself over me, making it difficult to breathe.

I counted twenty-two wet logs beneath my feet as I crossed the slippery bridge. Once on the other side, entering the mouth of the forest, my breath eased a little. The trees on either side were quite ordinary, and the wet road remained familiar underfoot. The mud sucked greedily, pulling a shoe right off, and my stockinged foot squelched deep into the muck. After that, much to my irritation, my shoe slipped from my slick foot every time my attention wandered.

I carried with me a small bag containing my other gown, my cloak, the wooden cross my father had made for me, warm stockings my sister had mended, and my collection of stones. Stones are a foolish thing to carry through the countryside, but I was attached to my collection, which I had curated over the course of years. For every stone that I kept, I rejected twenty. Each had to be unique, and it had to harmonize with the others in the collection besides. My favorite place to hunt for stones was at the river, where the water wore them smooth, and the damp brought out color and patterns in the rock. My most treasured stone was oval and flat like a flagstone. The green face was shot through with gold lines, like silken threads in a tapestry. I would hold that stone in the palm of my hand to soothe myself when I had trouble sleeping at night.

Where the woods thinned, yellow coltsfoot pushed through dead grass and leaves, the coarse, genial blooms undimmed by midday blackness. The woods gave way to meadowland, and as the road began to climb, orchards. I knew that my father sometimes worked in these orchards and nearby fields, and I marveled at the distance he had to travel for his week-work.

I struggled to keep my shoe on my foot as I climbed toward the manor house, and this distracted me enough that the appearance of a gate in front of me took me by surprise. I had expected a grand building, but I was unprepared for the scale of the surrounding wall. The wooden gate was reinforced with bands and studs of iron, and it stood at least twice as high and three times as wide as the doors of the church. To my relief, the gate rested ajar, and I pushed with my shoulder to open it farther.

The stench of pigs was first to greet me, and then the confusing sight of several squat structures, some of wood and some of stone. The ponderous sky chose that moment to release its burden; thick sheets of rain obscured my view and battered me with fat, tiny fists. I ran to the nearest building to escape, realizing as I approached that it was a stable. If the horses objected to my intrusion, their noise was drowned by the hammering of rain on the slate roof.

I huddled in a corner, away from the draught, watching the drops gather and fall from the ends of my hair, yearning for our warm hearth and my sister's chatter. I would only be allowed to leave the manor on saints' days and other holidays, and I would never again wake up snug against my sister's warm back. A prickling behind my eyes and tightness in my throat told me to think of other things. I could make out the glossy flanks of horses in the dim light; sometimes a shadowy eye gleamed over the edge of a stall. The air was pungent, but I was comforted by the smell, which I associated with the warmth of their sturdy bodies. I never learned to ride, but I think that I would have enjoyed it.

I never understood why Elfilda—Ella, we called her then, before she became a princess—was so afraid of horses. Her father insisted that she learn to ride. At some point, it was left to me to enforce this dictate. Ella fought the poor stableboy like a cat when he tried to lift her onto the back of a palfrey. When I took the reins and slapped her pale hands sharply, she desisted long enough for the boy to lead her on a slow walk. She never did learn to ride properly, however. It is probably just as well, since hawking makes her cry for the dead bunnies, and hunting is even worse. When the royal court hunts, she feigns illness, though by now her husband must have realized that she will never join them. She takes refuge with her dogs in the kennel, or with us, until the horses are stabled and the meat hung out of sight.

When the rain slowed, I made my way back outside. The sky had brightened a little, and I took in the scene around me. I could see now that there were two gates, the one I had passed through and a second gate farther on, surrounded by tall hedges. Over the hedges, I could make out what I assumed to be the roof of the manor house.

The gate swung briskly open, and a man and a boy appeared. I had not passed a single soul on the road, and I was pleased to see two of my own kind. They wore plain jerkins and hats to shade their faces, and the boy carried a gardener's scythe in his belt. I hastened toward them, my bag bouncing on my back.

The man turned his furrowed face, his pale eyes nearly vanishing beneath wrinkles when he smiled.

"Ho, missy!" He tipped his hat. "What brings a drowned mouse like you out of the woods?"

"My father heard from the bailiff that the manor house is in need of a new laundry girl."

"Is that so? And you think a wee girl like you will be useful to the laundress?"

"I am not small!" I pointed to the boy standing sulkily beside him. "I am taller than him!"

The man laughed. "True enough, true enough. Well, I don't know much about laundry, but it does not surprise me that Miss Elisabeth is in need of another new laundry girl. She has a sharp tongue, that one."

My heart sank again, but I said nothing.

"My name is John, and this here is Benedict. He is going to help me to prune some trees in the orchard, aren't you, Benedict my boy?" The boy scowled, and John jostled him. "You will have to excuse the bad manners of my young apprentice; he is an odd boy who does not like to climb trees. What might we call you, missy?"

"Agnes, sir."

"Well, Agnes, I am very pleased to meet you. If you run along to the house, the chamberlain will find Miss Elisabeth for you. Go to the back door, past the herb garden. That is the kitchen entrance, and someone there can point you to Mr. Geoffrey. If Mr. Geoffrey is in a good mood, he might let you have a spot of bacon and some ale while you dry out." John winked as he turned back toward the orchard. "Take what you can get when you can get it, Agnes, and you will fare all right here."

His parting comment did not settle my nerves, but the mention of bacon made my mouth water. The rain had stopped entirely. With a deep breath, I entered the gate through which John and Benedict had appeared and saw Aviceford Manor for the first time.

The sky continued to play games with me: The same moment that the house came into view, the sun leapt from behind a cloud, beaming sudden life into the red sandstone walls of the manor. Rows of glazed windows shone golden, diamond panes glinting. The only glass windows I knew were the narrow lancet windows at church; this house boasted grand mullioned windows, recessed under decorative arches. To my young eyes, the house might have been a castle. The massive main building was flanked by crenelated turrets, ornamented with three stories of lacey cusping and delicate, clover-shaped quatrefoil windows. Lion head corbels guarded the vaulted entrance; above them squatted fanciful spiky-eared gargoyles, their wide mouths holding trumpetlike water spouts.

I could not see the rats, scuttling in the shadows, or hear the crunching of termites, feasting on rafters and braces. I could not feel the ivy, ripping at stone, turning towers into sand. I knew nothing yet of the cloying sickness of relations in that house. To me, the manor was simply beautiful. I was, after all, a child.

2

THE LAUNDRY

For those unfamiliar with Aviceford Manor, it is the smallest of three manors that lie within the grand landholding of Ellis Abbey. The Abbess Elfilda (yes, the godmother of Princess Elfilda) appointed Emont Vis-de-Loup, youngest son of Lord Henry Vis-de-Loup, 4th Baron of Wilston, to act as manorial lord at Aviceford. Emont would inherit little from his family, and he could never hope to be a tenant-in-chief like his father, but the manor provided him with a comfortable living even after the abbey took its share.

Emont was unmarried, and gossipers in the village liked to say that he saved his affection for barrels of ale and bottles of wine. This shifted more than the usual burden of manorial supervision to the chamberlain. Geoffrey Poke had been well ensconced at the top of the servants' hierarchy when Emont became lord, and the combination of Geoffrey's craving for authority and Emont's disinterest allowed the chamberlain to expand the power of his position. By the time I met him, he had become an iron-fisted autocrat who did not brook even the most trifling opposition from his inferiors.

As I first stood before him in the hallway by the buttery, I might have been a disappointingly small wood pigeon he was considering having plucked for dinner. He slowly circled, examining me from my sodden hair to my humiliatingly exposed foot—I had been obliged to leave my muddy stocking outside along with my shoes.

Abruptly, he said, "What is your father's name, and where does he live?" His voice was thin and nasal.

"William, sir. William Rolfe. We live in Over End."

"Over End, Aviceford Village?"

"Yes, sir."

"What are you, fourteen years old?"

"Ten, sir. Nearly eleven."

He lifted his eyebrows. "What use are you?"

"I am a hard worker, sir. I am strong, and my mother taught me well."

"What would your mother know about laundry?" He brought his hatchet face close to mine. "You smell like pigs' dung."

I stared at his fat lower lip, peculiarly fleshy in his narrow face, glistening with spit. His mouth was so crowded with teeth that his lips did not fully close. I wanted to back away from his unpleasant breath.

Geoffrey continued to stare at me, moistening his lips again with his tongue. He made a grunting noise in the back of his throat. "I suppose you will do," he said finally, moving away. "The laundry has been piling up since the last girl left, and I am running out of linens. I shall take you to Elisabeth."

I had been thinking of bacon since my conversation with John. As the tall chamberlain led me away from the kitchen, I felt like a savory morsel had been snatched from my hand. "Sir?" I said. "I have had nothing to eat since daybreak."

He looked at me with irritation. "Dinner has already been cleared. If you are lucky, you might get some supper."

As we traversed a narrow passageway of stones, their surfaces cracked and rough as ancient cowhide, I noticed the chamberlain's awkward gait. The sole of his left shoe was several times the thickness of the right, and the blunt toe angled in a strange direction. What grotesque deformity hid beneath the oiled covering?

The hall tapered away in front of us into the gloom, disappearing into the black maw of an open doorway. Geoffrey jabbed a long finger toward the entrance. "There is the laundry room. Go find Elisabeth." He limped away, leaving me alone in the passage.

I peered from the doorway into darkness. Weak light from a solitary window near the ceiling illuminated a shallow, stone-lined pool of water on the floor, but the rest of the room lay in shadow. Gradually, the shadows assumed recognizable forms. An enormous wooden bucking tub squatted near the pool, raised on four stout feet. Along the back wall was a cold fireplace, ashes spilling over the edge of the hearth, wood strewn in disorderly piles. A mountain of linens towered in the corner. There was no laundress.

When I considered returning to the chamberlain, my stomach clenched sickeningly. I would wait for the laundress to return. I looked for a seat, and as there was none, I perched on a smooth stone at the lip of the pool. The stones formed a low wall around what presumably functioned as a laundry basin. I decided to put on my clean stockings while I waited. I was hungry and damp, but at least I would have warm feet.

As I bent forward to peel off my single wet stocking, a deep sighing breath broke the silence of the room, like a rock thrown into a still pond. I froze, the hairs rising on my arms.

A stirring in the heap of linens should have returned me to my senses, but instead, I panicked. I scrambled backward, splashing loudly into the slack pool. The water must have been standing unused for a great length of time to have accumulated such a thick layer of slime, and my disturbance released an evil stench. A shrill screech filled the room, echoing, as the laundress rose from the pile of soiled linens and bore down upon me.

"Get out of there!" Her massive bosom heaved. "Get out, you little brat! What are you doing?"

Slipping on the slime-covered stones, I did my best to oblige. "My name is Agnes, miss, and I am the new laundry girl."

The look she gave me was impenetrable. She placed incongruously doll-like hands on her ample hips. When she began again, her tone was measured. "If you are the new laundry girl, we had better see what you can do. Considering how much work you have," she jerked her head toward the pile of laundry, "you had better get started right away, hadn't you?"

"Yes, miss." I shivered. The room was cold, and I was dripping wet.

"It is cold in here, but lucky for you, your first job will be to build a fire." She stepped into the shaft of sunlight, and for the first time, I saw her properly. She was as plump as a Christmas goose; I marveled at her girth. Yellow curls escaped from the edge of her dirty bonnet. Her face might have been pretty if her delicate features had not been enfolded in doughy flesh. "What are you waiting for?" she asked sharply.

I hunched my shoulders and slid over to the fireplace to sweep the hearth, keeping my head down. Weeks' worth of ashes choked the fireplace. I filled the bucket with as many cinders as would fit, clearing some space, and I built a small bed for the fire using twigs and straw. Next to the fireplace, I found a good flint and a supply of char cloth, and the fire was soon lit. I then began to organize the haphazard piles of wood and kindling on the floor.

"Never mind that," said the laundress. "Get the ashes ready."

I looked at her, confused.

"Spread the ashes on the bucking cloth, you idiot!"

I had never used a bucking tub before. Gingerly, I reached up and sprinkled black soot on the cloth that stretched taut over the opening.

"Afraid of straining your wee delicate arms, princess? Dump those ashes and fetch water from the rain barrel." She handed me an ancient, blackened kettle.

My footsteps echoed dully as I retraced my steps through the narrow hallway, past the cramped and lightless buttery and into the back foyer. Late-afternoon sunlight streamed through the windows, dazzling my eyes and coalescing in bright pools on the flagstones. I could see that a coating of ashes clung to my wet frock; brushing at them only made dark smears.

As I approached the heavy doors of the kitchen, which hung ajar, an invisible wall of sound and scent—clanging pots, muffled shouts, the aroma of roasting chicken and baking bread—arrested my feet in midstride. I inhaled greedily, which only goaded my hunger into sinking its claws deeper.

Outside, my shoes were hardly drier than I had left them, but I knocked off the mud as best I could and put them back on. A path snaked along the rear wall of the manor, leading to the gardens and dovecote. As the stone slabs were slippery with rain and moss, I walked alongside, in the coarse and dripping seedling grasses, swinging the empty kettle to make raindrops scatter from drooping stalks of dogtail.

Over the low wall surrounding the herb garden, I recognized the back of John's leather jerkin and his frayed hat. He yanked up fistfuls of young mint and comfrey, which ran amok, covering the soil in a riotous froth of green. Doubtless he was beating the shoots back to make room for herbs that still slumbered in the earth.

"Little mouse!" he said with a laugh. "You have turned from a pretty little white mousie to a black one; did you meet a witch?"

I grimaced, and his smile softened.

"Cheer up, little mouse. Miss Elisabeth is hard-hearted, but she is a practical woman. You look like a clever girl who can find a way to work with her. Keep your chin up."

I nodded and carried on. Nothing was served by arguing.

A rain barrel was located at the far side of the herb garden, where it could be used for watering. I plunged the kettle deep into the clean, chill water. The cold was both painful and delicious, and I pushed my arms deeper, leaning against the barrel. Light rippled across the surface of the water, and as it calmed, I could see my reflection peering back at me. If my heart had not been so heavy, I would have laughed. My face was almost entirely black; only my serious brown eyes were recognizable to me. I released the kettle with one hand to splash water on my face.

John was nowhere to be seen as I struggled back toward the house, holding the kettle with both hands, trying to keep it from knocking against my shins. Once again, I paused at the entrance to the laundry room, allowing my eyes to adjust to the dimness.

The laundress had stretched herself out on the pile of dirty linens, and I hoped that she had fallen asleep. She stirred as soon as I entered the room, however, and sat up.

"What took you so long? You will not sleep tonight at this rate." She adjusted her cap primly. "Put the kettle on the fire. You will need to keep fetching water and heating it until the tub is full. If you are lucky, you might be done before the compline bell, but I doubt it." She rose, smoothing her skirt. "I am going to supper."

"But, miss, I have not eaten since daybreak!"

"Then you had better hurry." She crossed to the door with a surprisingly light step. "When you finish here, you will sleep in the kitchen. There will be a trundle next to the larder." Her shadow, which had eclipsed the doorway, disappeared.

I confess that I felt very sorry for myself in that moment. After she left, I sat by the fire and had a cry. It was the first time that I had been away from my family, and my sister's absence was a hole through my chest. I had never been thankful enough for Lottie's bowls of filling pottage, or for the comfort of nestling against her solid back, rocking with each sleeping breath. I yearned for home, but even as I watched my tears splash into the feathery ashes, I was aware of another feeling. Deep beneath my piteous thoughts curled something else, something hard and vengeful.

My arms tired from carrying loads of water and lifting the heavy kettle over the tub. Light faded and then departed from the window. Though it became more difficult to see, I did not much miss the cheerless light. The firelight was not enough, but it was hearty.

I was preoccupied when John came into the room, and I started when he coughed.

"Sorry, mousie, I did not mean to frighten you. I just brought you a little supper."

As he set a cloth-covered bundle and clay bottle on the floor, I had a giddy impulse to run to him and throw my arms around his narrow chest, like I used to do to my father when I was a tot. Instead, I said, "How can I thank you, sir?"

"Ah, Agnes, it's nothing. And everybody here calls me John. I saw Elisabeth in the kitchen and figured that you might be needing a bite of food to keep you going. I brought you some cold chicken with onion and a bit of bread, as well as a spot of ale. One thing you will like about working at the manor is the food!"

"God bless you, and thank you, thank you, thank you!"

He looked amused by my effusiveness. "I am going to bed. The menservants sleep in the outbuildings, but the laundress and laundry girl sleep in the kitchen."

"Miss Elisabeth said that there will be a pallet near the larder."

He must have heard my discouragement, for he sighed and said, "I came to the manor when I was near your age. Elisabeth was even younger. I remember how she ran away. Came back with a black eye and probably worse. Her father had too many mouths to feed. It can be hard here for a child, I grant you. Some people let it get to them. Don't you do that. You do your best to get by, and one day you will be head laundress, and you will have a laundry girl working for you."

His words were no comfort, but I said, "Yes, sir."

"Good night, Agnes."

"Good night, sir."

I fell on the tray when he left and ate with relish. Chicken was a rare treat; the food and John's kindness lifted my spirits. Though my arms were sore and my body drained, the remaining hours of work did not seem as onerous as the first. I kept my mind occupied with fantasies about manor food and the approach of May Day, when I would have the whole day free to celebrate at the parish church.

After banking the fire, I gathered my bag and made my way to the kitchen. The passageway was dark as pitch, but pale moonlight from windows in the back foyer guided me to the kitchen doors. The room appeared too grand to be a kitchen; its lofty height seemed more fitting for a cathedral. Shafts of moonlight illuminated lingering blue smoke near the vaulted ceiling. Scattered streaks from a skylight pierced the gently roiling smoke, like the Holy Ghost descending.

Embers glowed in a fireplace massive enough to contain a whole ox, silhouetting a heap of blankets on the floor that must have contained my new enemy. Even her bulk was dwarfed by the size of the hearthstone. She had told me to look for my bed by the larder, which I deduced was the dark entrance yawning in the back wall. It did not surprise me to see how far it was from the fire. I circled the trestle tables and found in one of their shadows the straw mat that the laundress had left for me. A thin blanket had been placed atop the pallet.

I removed my cloak and collection of stones from my bag, dropping the sac at one end of the mat for use as a pillow. Though I wanted to collapse from exhaustion, I first aligned my stones in a row across the head of my bed, a tiny wall of soldiers to guard me in my sleep. I then wrapped myself as well as I could in my cloak and blanket, and I sank into the sleep of the dead.

THE ROYAL COURT

Solitude is the commodity in shortest supply at the palace, but Princess Elfilda has succeeded in carving out a generous portion for herself. She has always been happiest in her own company. It pleases her to have familiar faces nearby, but she does not enjoy social intercourse. If she could do away with ladies-in-waiting entirely, she would, but as that is not possible, she has relegated them to a suite separate from her own. My daughters are among those ladies, and though their duties are light, they are not allowed to stray from the retinue. It pains me that I so seldom have the pleasure of their company.

Today is a joyful day, because they came walking with me, my daughters, Charlotte and Matilda. The king and queen have left for the summer palace, and with most of the royal family and courtiers absent, it feels like a holiday.

"Mother!" Matilda called when she found me in the nearly deserted garden; she ran to me and threw her arms around my shoulders in an enthusiastic embrace. Even as I staggered to keep my balance, I reveled in the solidity of her body, the vital warmth and heft of her precious flesh and blood and bones.

Charlotte followed in a more stately fashion, reproaching her sister. "You should never run, Tilly. Stop acting like a baby. God be with you, Mother." She kissed my cheek fondly. "You look lovely. This style suits you. Your waist is as tiny as a maiden's."

"And my brow is as wrinkled as an old crone's."

"Ha!" Matilda kissed my other cheek. "You are as fair as this spring day."

"If by fair you mean argent."

"You are insufferable, Mother," Matilda said. "There is hardly a gray hair on your head."

The girls each took one of my arms. They are both a fingersbreadth taller than me, broad shouldered and sturdy. They leaned in close and gripped tightly, ushering me down the path like a couple of palace guards removing an unruly petitioner from the throne room. The sensation was surprisingly pleasant; I floated through the garden on strong currents of their affection.

The palace grounds are impressive but austere. There are no flowers, only fancy topiaries, fountains, and statues. The groomed footpaths take straight lines and cross at sharp angles, their geometry unsoftened by shade and ungraced by the prolific disorder of nature. I feel exposed there, exposed to the harsh sun and to the many pairs of eyes that gaze from palace windows and passing coaches.

As we skirted the central fountain, the sun's rays burned through a straggling skein of cloud and spread a hard glitter over the onyx pool. We turned toward a side trail that meanders through a copse of trees, a corner of the grounds that had been allowed to retain a glimmer of the wild.

"It's such a relief to be rid of Lady Margaret," Matilda said. She referred to the mistress of the robes, an imperious woman who kept a strict watch over the ladies-in-waiting.

"Even Cinderella is more cheerful now that the shrew is away."

"You should refer to your stepsister as Princess Elfilda," I admonished, "and please don't let anyone hear you calling names. We have enough trouble."

Matilda stuck out her tongue and rolled her eyes comically. "Well, Lady Margaret is a shrew, and everyone knows it, including Princess Oblivious."

"Ella isn't oblivious," Charlotte said. "She just doesn't care about gossip and intrigue."

"*Princess* Ella to you."

This time it was Charlotte's turn to stick out her tongue at her sister.

"In any event," Matilda continued, "I didn't mean oblivious in the sense of stupid; we all know that she is quick-witted when it comes to lessons and music. I only meant that she wouldn't know a backstabber if she witnessed her wiping blood from a dagger on the back of a corpse."

"Exceedingly colorful image, dearheart. How worried ought I be?" I asked.

Charlotte sighed. "Nobody is in danger of being stabbed with a dagger. Tilly is being dramatic. It is only that everybody wants something. Cecily Barrett's fine bosom is on display for Prince Henry at every possible opportunity, and he can't help but feast his eyes——and who knows what else. Ella——pardon me, Princess

Elfilda——is so innocent, she doesn't even notice; she has chosen Cecily as her favorite because she takes an interest in the dogs. Cecily doesn't give a fig about dogs. She only pretends to care to gain some advantage."

"Cecily isn't even as bad as some of the others," Matilda said. "That Hamelin girl has got her sticky fingers in the coffer. She buys clothing and collectables for Ella, who has no idea about the price of goods. Then she wonders why her allowance is all used up halfway through the year."

"What about you?" I asked. "Has the situation improved at all?"

Charlotte pulled me closer and planted another kiss on my cheek. "Don't fret about us, sweet Mother. We are so fortunate to be here."

We walked in silence for a few moments. The dappled shade of trees gave us relief from the glare of sun and afforded us temporary privacy. Long shadows of trunks banded the path ahead with shades of dove gray and gold.

"I can't help but worry," I said. "I hear whispers about you."

"They are nothing more than that. Whispers."

"Oh, but you must tell Mother about your great toe!" Matilda said with bitter amusement.

"Do hold your tongue, Tilly!"

"What is this about your toe?"

"Nothing, idle gossip," Charlotte said.

"Come on, tell her!"

"You tell her if you are so eager! You are such a troublemaker."

"Well, the other day several of the ladies cornered us and insisted that we remove our shoes," Matilda said. "'Whatever for?' we asked. 'We have heard that you are missing parts of your feet,' they replied. I thought they were daft. But they told us there's a story circulating about Prince Henry using Ella's abandoned little shoe to track her down after she ran away from the ball. They said that Lottie and I pretended to be Ella. Both of us! Hoping that he would marry one of us." Matilda laughed, and I felt Charlotte flinch. "They said Lottie was so convinced the prince would mistake her for Ella that she cut off her great toe to fit into the slipper. And when she failed, I decided that it would be an excellent idea to cut off my heel and shove my mangled foot into the bloody shoe, sure that Prince Henry would look at me and say, 'You are the beautiful creature I danced with all last night!'" Matilda's voice had grown thick with the threat of tears, and she ended with a little gasp that was halfway between a laugh and a sob.

Charlotte gripped my arm with all of the ferocity that she kept from her voice. "We mustn't repeat such nonsense, Tilly. We should just be grateful that our stepsister married well and that we are here."

"But who would make up such scandalous lies?" Helplessness drove the claws of my anger inward. I wanted to make myself a living barrier between those vile women and my daughters, to protect them as I could when they were children.

"It is merely the way rumors grow," Charlotte said, stroking my back. "These ladies ingratiate themselves with Ella, and they wheedle for bitty morsels of gossip. She means no harm. You know how Ella is; she reports the particulars faithfully without always understanding the larger picture. Remember when she was a wee girl, and she told us that Frère Joachim had brought a whip to punish her if she was naughty? You were furious, but it turned out that the 'whip' was only a bulrush that he had brought inside for his lesson. Ella didn't understand that he was jesting. I suppose she had never seen a real whip."

Indeed, I am sure that Princess Elfilda has not seen a whip or a switch to this day. Children of noblemen are not casually beaten in the way that is so customary for poor children.

THE LORD OF THE MANOR

On my second day at the manor, I woke to the sound of men bickering. Three pairs of legs clad in rough woolen stockings were visible to me under the table; these belonged to kitchen scullions engaged in a heated argument over who would split the wood and who would set the fire. I squinted into the bright sunlight and stood up gingerly. I had overslept. My back and arms ached, and the cold had seeped into my bones. I would need a thicker blanket if I was going to continue to sleep alone and so far from the fire.

The scullions paid me no heed. One gestured emphatically as he made his case, slicing through interruptions with sharp chopping motions. A much older scullion leaned listlessly on the table, a passive expression on his face. It was disgraceful that the boys would not give the older man the lightest task. He looked as though he might be ill.

The laundress was nowhere in sight, and her bedding had been removed. I wondered why she had not woken me. It was surely not out of kindness that she let me sleep.

I put my two favorite stones in my pocket and returned the re-

mainder to the sac along with my cloak; I then looked in the larder
for a place to store my bedding. The room was windowless and
dank. Appetizing and rancid smells mingled to create an aroma
that befuddled the nose and stomach. Two thick slabs of meat dangled from the ceiling, and a side of beef lay bleeding on a broad
stone thrall. The shelves held crocks of lumpish gray meat buried in gelatinous lard, meat that one day would dance and sizzle
deliciously over the fire after its heavy coat of lard melted away.
Carrots and gourds, last year's vegetables, partially filled floppy
baskets. I snatched a carrot from one of the baskets and placed the
softening tuber in my pocket. I had learned that meals might not
come regularly, and I was not going to let an opportunity pass to
put food in my stomach.

The lowest shelves hung two handsbreadths off of the floor, and
though I imagined cockroaches or worse made a home under the
shelves, the room was kept clean and free of dirt and dust. This
seemed like the most private place to store my belongings, and
the sleeping mat would fit there as well.

After stashing my effects, I made my way back to the laundry.
The laundress was waiting for me, this time on a broad chair that
had not been present the day before. In the dim light, she looked
like a gargantuan spider placidly appraising her next meal.

"Well, well, the princess awakes. I trust that you slept peace-
fully?"

I said nothing, unsure how to prevent her from pouncing.

"Do you know what we do to encourage punctuality?"

"No, miss." My voice was hardly above a whisper.

"Ten lashes," she said lightly, almost cheerfully. "But in your
case, since you are new, we shall make it only five. I think that
will help you to remember next time. I borrowed this whip from

the stable." She raised her right arm, and I saw the short leather horsewhip uncoil from her hand.

"Turn and lift your dress."

A fire roared to life in my belly. I could take my punishment, but whips are for beasts.

"Hurry, now!" she said sweetly, cocking her head as though she were offering me a treat.

I turned toward the wall. The heat flared, licking around my heart. I held my dress over my head, and when the first blow landed, I was relieved. It was not as heavy as my father's lashes. He would make us cut green switches from a hazel tree in our croft to use for our own beatings. Before that thought was fully formed, burning agony seared my back. Pain tore through my breast, my head, my limbs, dwarfing the heat in my belly. I gasped. Pain still mounted when the second blow landed. Then the third. White light filled my vision even when I closed my eyes. Four. Five. On the fifth lash, I collapsed to my knees.

"Get up," the laundress said evenly.

When I did not move, she said, "I shall have to whip you again if you are slothful as well as tardy."

I rose and lowered my dress as carefully as I could. The fabric scorched my back.

"Take this back to the stable. They may need it for the other animals." She tossed the whip at my feet, and I bent slowly to retrieve it. The pain was beginning to recede, making room for my anger. I walked stiffly, trying to keep the cloth from touching my back.

I was tempted to walk out the door, through the orchards, meadow, and woods, and keep walking all the way home. I was old enough to know, however, that my family could not keep me, and I had nowhere else to go.

✺

In the stable, I found a boy repairing a saddle. He looked up, blinking. The stable seemed smaller in the sunlight than it had in the dark of the rainstorm. I had hoped to find the building unoccupied. My cheeks warmed; I wanted to hide the whip behind my back. Instead, I mumbled, "I am returning this for Miss Elisabeth," and I placed the whip beside him. The boy appeared uninterested; he yawned and resumed his work. Beatings were commonplace.

"Are there horse blankets needing mending?" I asked.

He looked up again. "Sure. There's always blankets in need of mending. Who are you?"

"Agnes. The new laundry girl."

He shrugged. "Don't know why you want to, but the blankets are hanging on the pegs." He motioned with his head. "Take any one. They all have holes."

I selected a blue blanket that appeared newer than the rest, and, without thinking, slung it over my shoulder. I failed to swallow a short cry of pain as the blanket slapped against my back. I slinked away, letting my "Good morning!" trail behind me, where it may have gone unheard.

Before returning to the laundry, I ran to the kitchen to deposit the blanket. The room had become a bustling hub of activity. Menservants busied themselves stirring pots, hanging cauldrons, chopping vegetables, baking bread, crushing spices, straining sauces, feeding the fire. Only the head cook stood still, barking orders that sometimes drowned in bangs, clangs, and crashes as the other servants hustled around him like a stream divided by a rock. Echoes from the vaulted roof amplified the din. The sticky swelter of the kitchen was worsened by the sun's rays streaming through the skylights, and the fires were banked high. Steaming moisture coated the gray stone walls of the vast room. The massive, sagging beam that spanned the breadth of the kitchen seemed to float in the haze; headless pink carcasses dangled from iron hooks screwed into its underside. Near the larder, a man butchered what appeared to be a goat. He leaned on his cleaver, red-faced and sweating, a slash of blood across his tunic. I passed him without being noticed, stashed the horse blanket with my other belongings, and hastened to the laundry.

It did not seem as though the laundress had moved since I left her, but she must have, for she now held a loaf of bread in her tiny, dimpled hand. She tore delicately at the soft-crusted loaf, chewing slowly and deliberately. "I am glad to see that you are learning to be prompt." She paused for another bite. "You will need to start every day by dawn if you expect to keep up with the laundry. As long as you get your work done and don't complain, I shan't have to correct you." She smiled. "You are late today, but you can begin by draining the water from the bucking tub into the laundry pool. Unfortunately, the basin is too dirty to use for dollying, so you will have to clean it first." She brushed crumbs from her lap. "The chamber pots are beside the basin. Pour the piss into the bucket once you are finished hauling water. I shall return the pots."

I wondered why she chose to return the pots. It was amply evident that she intended for me to do all of the work; why would she reserve this task for herself? Perhaps she wanted to see the belongings that the guests left in their chambers. I had overheard the kitchen staff complaining about so many mouths to feed today.

Elisabeth readjusted her bulk in the chair. "If you don't want to be up so late, you had better get busy. You have a lot of catching up to do."

"Yes, miss." I kept my eyes fixed on the wobbling flesh beneath her chin. My back still burned, and my heart was leaden, but I would not let her see me cry.

After the laundress left, I took the flaccid carrot from my pocket and ate it while I planned. If I could manage the bucking at the same time as I worked on the other tasks, it would save time. I needed a clean place to put the laundry from the bucking tub, though, so I would need to scrub the pool first. I cursed the laundress again. If the basin had been in continuous use, it would not be filled with slime. Emptying and refilling the pool would take hours if I had to carry the dirty water one pail at a time all of the way outside.

I looked at the window high in the wall. It was unglazed and loosely shuttered; spiders had weaved a dense curtain of lacy web. If only I could throw the dirty water out of the window, the pool would soon be empty.

I rummaged through the laundry until I had an armful of light stockings and handkerchiefs, and then I tied them securely together in a chain. The bucket handle creaked as I attached it to one end of my improvised rope. It would be difficult to remove the knots later, but I did not mind paying that price if this scheme saved me time.

After placing the bucket in the laundry basin, I climbed carefully onto the bucking tub. Tautening fabric across my back caused me to gasp as I pulled myself up. Bracing my feet against opposite lips of the barrel, I teetered into an upright position. From that vantage point, I could see that the window had a broad sill. It was a long leap, but worth an attempt.

I tied the rope to my wrist so that I would not drop it, and then I jumped from the barrel, grabbing the windowsill with both hands. I used all of the strength in my sore arms to haul myself to the window, my feet scrabbling against the stone wall. The pain in my back was searing, and I scraped my forearms and knees as I struggled to take a seat on the sill. Despite my discomfort, I was pleased with my success. When I knocked the rotting shutters open, the shawl of spiderwebs tore asunder and flapped in ragged streamers in the clean breeze that blew through the west-facing window. I could see the orchards from my perch. The plum trees were in bloom, a girlish blush of rose next to the barren apple trees. Soon those old crones would also cover themselves in pink and white blooms, a brief vanity before bearing fruit.

The sun had just passed its zenith, and I turned my face toward its warming rays, closing my eyes. I could hear the chirrup of a lonely frog. The sun drew bright squiggles on the inside of my eyelids and banished the cold from my bones. My mother was up there, in heaven. I wondered if she saw me. She would probably tell me to get to work.

I tugged on the rope attached to the bucket handle until it tipped over in the basin below. Then, with a swift pull, I lifted the bucket of water toward me. With two hands, I could manage. A green splash sloshed from the bucket as it grated over the sill. Balancing the bucket at the edge of the outer windowsill, I tipped the foul water onto the new grass below. I then lowered the bucket to the basin and drew up another full pail.

The basin was soon empty enough for a good scrubbing. I was about to hop down from the window when John called up to me.

"You really are a mouse, crawling up into the windows! Does Miss Elisabeth know what you are up to?" He set the empty wheelbarrow on its feet and tipped his hat back until I could see his squinting eyes.

I shook my head and placed my finger to my lips, hoping that he would lower his voice.

"Are you coming for dinner? I was just heading in myself. After the master has finished dining, the servants gather in the kitchen. Join us!"

I smiled at him and waved. Food would be very welcome. After jumping down, I emptied some water from the bucking tub into the basin and scrubbed it thoroughly. It would be better to starve than face any more discipline from the laundress. I gave the basin a final rinse and sopped up the dirty wash water with a rag, filling the bucket. I brought the pail with me, planning to discard the water outside on my way to dinner.

Toward the back foyer, the chorus of voices and clatter of dishes from the kitchen grew louder. Hopefully I was not too late for food. I quickened my pace, but just as I crossed the entrance to a short passageway that opened between the buttery and the pantry, an incoherent bellow caused me to freeze. I looked down the dark corridor but saw only a shaft of light from a partly open door that I knew led to the great hall. There was silence for a moment, and then from the depths of the passageway, the rise and fall of a man's voice, ranting, muttering, raging, then muttering again. Realizing that I should not be eavesdropping, I continued toward the kitchen. Before I had taken many steps, the voice roared "Geoffrey!" three times with increasing vehemence, and I heard a door slam with a reverberating bang.

It seemed to me very bad luck that I was alone in the hallway when Geoffrey Poke quickly limped out of the kitchen, scowling, aiming for the corridor by the pantry. He carried a carafe and cups on a tray, and in his haste, one of the cups tottered over the edge and smashed on the stone floor. He cursed, and his scowl deepened further when he looked at me. "Clean it!" he grunted through his teeth as he clomped past me. He disappeared down the passageway.

I picked up the ceramic shards carefully, gathering them in my skirt. From beyond the pantry came murmuring, and the rant began again, only to be cut short by violent coughing. The coughing too ended abruptly. After a moment, the door creaked open, and the chamberlain's uneven step echoed down the hallway. The lash wounds on my back prickled as I heard him round the corner behind me. I turned and stood, holding the broken cup in the folds of my dress.

The chamberlain's hands were now empty, and he rubbed his palms forcefully over his sparse, greasy hair. He looked like someone whose best cow had been seized by the tax collector.

Geoffrey's eyes darted to the bucket beside me, and his expression lightened. "I have a job for you," he said. His lips thinned, baring more of his crowded yellow teeth.

I waited to hear what new trial he had devised.

"In the great hall, you will find your *master*," he drew out the word scornfully, "sprawled upon the floor, lounging in a pool of his own vomit. You will clean Sir Emont, the floor, the chair, and anything else befouled by his stinking spew."

I was shocked by his disrespect for the lord of the manor.

"He won't remember that we sent a dirty runt like you to clean his mess. He won't remember anything when he wakes in the dead of night with a mouth full of sawdust and a hatchet through his head."

After a momentary panic, I realized that he was speaking of a headache.

"When you finish, report to me." He limped back toward the kitchen.

Any satisfaction I had felt about making progress on the laundry evaporated. I did not want to go down that hallway to a part of
the house where I knew I did not belong. It was wrong of Geoffrey
to send me there. A laundry girl could not tend to the lord of the
manor. The situation amused Geoffrey, though whether it was my
discomfort or Sir Emont's debasement that pleased him, I could
not tell.

With a sigh, I returned to the laundry room to find a rag and a
brush, and then I fetched fresh water from the rain barrel. I had to
do as I was told.

I crept down the dark corridor leading to the great hall and opened
the door into the screens passage, the area under the minstrels'
gallery that divided the service quarters from the living quarters.
The back of the decorative wood screen was rough and plain, and
bright light sliced through the arches facing the great hall, making
the shadow at my feet a straight, sharp edge. I took a deep breath
before stepping across it into the light.

The room was cavernous, with the same high-pitched roof as
the kitchen. A long row of giant arch-braced trusses made of dark
oak lined the ceiling. Their right lines had been softened by orna-
mental curls and long sweeping curves, but that made them no less
imposing. The ceiling itself had been painted with a pattern of red
and gold lozenges surrounded by a band of stars that encircled the
whole of the hall, blurred by peeling plaster and a coating of dust
and soot. Brilliant sunshine spilled from grand mullioned windows, dulling the firelight that writhed and flickered on a hearth
larger than the sleeping loft of my father's cottage. The massive
overmantel was engraved with four different coats of arms, and

it was supported by lions carved from the same blue-gray stone, gazing with fierce pride at something only they could see.

The great hall was occupied by a single individual. He was not sprawled on the floor, as described by the chamberlain, but he was slumped forward and unmoving at the end of one of the trestle tables nearest the fire. As I approached, the rancid smell of vomit stung my nose and caused my empty stomach to churn.

Emont's leonine head was cradled in the crook of his elbow. He had the apple cheeks of a boy, but a regal forehead. His sparse whiskers were in need of a shave. Hair spilled over the embroidered sleeve of his white shirt, the ends curling in a puddle of maroon vomit, and his mouth hung slack. The table had been cleared after the meal, but several carafes remained, along with cups that must have belonged to other guests. The lord of the manor still held a cup in his hand, ready to toast the empty benches. He snorted, startling me, and then sank back into a soft, rhythmic snore.

Dark red stains spread over the underside of Emont's sleeve, making it look as though his arm was bleeding. He had obviously been drinking wine. I would need to move him in order to clean the mess. I sighed again and set my bucket of water on the table next to his elbow. A giant baby, vomiting on himself and falling asleep.

I did not want him to wake and find me there, but I did not see how I could move him on my own.

"Sir?" I said tentatively, next to his ear. The fumes were sickening.

He did not stir.

"Sir?" I said again, shaking his shoulder lightly.

He snorted but did not wake up. I decided to start cleaning; maybe the cold water would rouse him enough to move. I started with his hair, taking the ends in my hand and rinsing them with a dripping brush. His hair felt silken against my fingers, and the firelight burnished its red and gold hues.

I smoothed his damp hair carefully over his doublet so that it would not fall forward again, and I lifted his heavy head by pushing the flat of my hand against his forehead. This, or the damp cold rag over his mouth, finally caused him to stir.

"Hmmmph!" He pulled his head back from my hand and looked up at me from under drooping lids. He had a weak, dimpled chin and a small round nose that would have been pretty on a girl, but his broad face was as bland as pottage. His head wobbled, and I feared that he would fall forward again, so I reached for his shoulders. He seized my wrist so suddenly that a startled cry escaped my mouth. His grip was surprisingly firm.

"Who are you?" He spoke slowly, as though it took great concentration to form the words.

I wanted to squirm away and hide. "Agnes, sir."

"What are you doing here, Agnes?"

"I have come to clean up, sir."

His eyes drifted to the table, and then down to his soiled doublet. He snorted, and the ghost of a smile crossed his lips. "This is most unfortunate for you, isn't it?" He squeezed his eyes shut as if pained. I wondered if he felt embarrassment. He certainly did not seem as discomfited as I felt.

"Why don't you move aside, sir, and I shall get this finished."

He slid down the bench toward the fire, using his hands to steady himself. I quickly washed the table, bench, and floor. When I stood again, he was watching me blearily. The bloodshot whites of his eyes made the peculiar violet-blue of his irises more vivid.

I stacked the cups from the table and placed them on the tray that the chamberlain had left behind.

"Leave the carafe!"

"Yes, sir." I placed the full carafe and a clean cup beside him. Nervously, I said, "Sir, I should clean you up a little." The wet cloth dangled from my hand.

He grabbed the rag and dabbed ineffectually at the front of his doublet and the sleeve of his shirt. "Don't worry, the laundress will get these."

I blushed deeply. He was obviously confused.

"Just help me with the belt and buttons. I am no good with buttons."

I should have made an excuse and left to find the chamberlain, but he seemed so helpless, swatting intently at his waist and fumbling with the buckle. I felt a pang of pity, maybe even tenderness. I helped him with his buckle, followed by the rows of buttons on his doublet and shirt. He thanked me earnestly and struggled to remove his clothing. I quickly picked up my bucket and the tray of cups, made a hasty curtsy, and escaped while his head was still bent, before he could ask me to help any further.

After reporting to Geoffrey and begging one of the scullions to find me some food, I returned to the laundry room for another long night. The laundress did not come again, though I noticed that she had taken the chamber pots away.

When it was time for bed, I lined up my stones. It was too dark to tell whether there was blood on the back of my dress. The pain would cause me to sleep on my belly that night.

Gratefully, I pulled the heavy horse blanket over me. The scent of the stable was comforting. From the darkest corners of the room came the soft scratching and scrabbling of rodents, but I told myself that my stones would protect me from them. Children's thoughts incline toward magic and superstition, and mine were no exception.

THE LORD'S CHAMBERS

Those first days at the manor formed the pattern for my next four years as a laundry girl. In some ways my life improved, but in other ways it did not. I worked harder—and longer—than at any other time in my life. Even when I started the brewery as a young mother, I did not experience the kind of exhaustion, the bone-deep weariness that I did at the manor. There were times when I did not think that I could lift the kettle one more time, though necessity drove me to lift it anyway. I was habitually dark with ashes, and the harsh soap caused blisters on my hands.

I did discover efficiencies that allowed me to keep up with the endless round of laundry. John found a ladder for me so that I could dump dirty water more easily out of the window, and he placed a rain barrel just outside so that I could lower the bucket for fresh water during the rainy seasons. I learned how to keep all of the laundry stages operating at once, so that no time was wasted in idleness. I also learned which fabrics required the most thorough bucking and which did not, and I batched my laundry accordingly.

While I was never truly happy during those years, small comforts cheered me. I looked forward to Mass every week in the manor's chapel, where I was transfixed by the stained-glass window behind the altar. I paid no attention to the priest's Latin murmurs and chants but allowed myself to be transported by the jeweled perfection above his head.

The window depicted the Holy Spirit in the form of a dove, diving from heaven on rays of golden light, luminous golden swords that pierced the head and breast of a kneeling Virgin Mary. The Virgin was so white, paler than death, or snow, a sapphire cloak over her shoulders and honeyed hair tumbling to her waist. A book had fallen to the floor, leaves fluttering, and the Virgin clasped her hands to her heart. She was not looking at the dove. Her downcast eyes, profoundly sorrowful, seemed blind. I would close my own eyes and imagine swords of light; the urgent beating of great wings; a turbulence of draught and feathers, sharp claws sinking into my wrist, foreign, soft, insistent writhing against my breast.

I found ways to improve my creature comforts at the manor. I kept (and mended) the horse blankets until I met my family again at the parish church on May Day, when I asked my sister for a blanket from home. She ran to fetch it right away, my sweet, stern Lottie. I added straw to my pallet and placed a sock filled with oak ash near my bed to keep the rats and mice away.

I looked for allies in the kitchen, and the most elderly scullion, William, became a valuable acquaintance. He seemed lonely, and I think that he enjoyed my chatter and occasional sour remark. He would smile widely in appreciation, exposing the gaps in his rotting teeth, and pat my arm softly with his chapped and calloused hands. When I did not appear at meals, he was careful to set aside food for me in a basket in the larder. If there was meat, he saved me a generous portion, and he always managed to secure a piece of bread, even when there was none for the other servants to eat. It bothers me to this day that I did not have the means to repay him for his kindness.

Neither John nor William could protect me from the laundress, who was an unpredictable bully. On the best days, she helped me with the fire or folding linens and chatted. She told me about her time as a laundry girl, how hard she had worked and how often she had been thrashed by the laundress. Elisabeth claimed that she had less appetite for the whip than her own overseer, that I was fortunate. It was true that she had whipped me only thrice in four years, and though she sometimes whacked me with the dolly stick, that was far more bearable.

Elisabeth's favorite subject was her former sweetheart, a young swain who had died many years before in a fire at the mill. By her account, he was the most handsome, strong, courageous, clever, and pious man ever to have walked God's green earth. She said that she had been the prettiest girl in Aviceford, and I believed her, for despite sagging jowls and the coarsening of age, evidence of fine features remained, as well as clear gray eyes and masses of ill-kempt fair curls. Beauty notwithstanding, she would likely not have married her beau without a dowry. I was tempted to say that his death was providential; otherwise, she would have suffered through his marriage to the second-prettiest girl in the village. I knew what was good for me, so I held my tongue.

Most days, Elisabeth ignored me, but on the worst days she toyed with me, making arbitrary demands, forcing me to work through meals or stay up through the night. She might decide at suppertime that all of the bedsheets needed to be washed and pressed by morning, or that the whites were not clean enough, and I had to start again.

It puzzled me that Elisabeth remained in the manor's employ when she did so little work. There was too much laundry for one person; on holidays I would usually fall behind if the laundress refused to help, but the chamberlain never intervened. Since there was no lady of the house to supervise the servants, and since Emont took no interest in the management of domestic affairs, Geoffrey Poke acted as the final authority. He was not a person to whom I could appeal for justice, particularly following some turns of event that solidified his dislike for me.

Geoffrey himself heralded the first incident. He appeared in the laundry late one night, giving me a terrible fright. I was in the habit of being alone, as the laundress usually only came to drop off washing or chamber pots, or to nap in the afternoon. I did not hear him approach, as I had been thrashing the clothing vigorously with a dolly stick. I looked up to find a looming, skeletal figure holding a flickering candle. The flame illuminated Geoffrey's countenance fitfully, creating deep shadows where his eyes should have been.

I could tell that the chamberlain was furious. He uncurled his long fingers, dragged his palm across his shining pate, and clenched his fist again. "Come with me," he said.

I did not ask why. I removed the apron that I had learned to wear over my dress to keep it clean from ashes, and I used the inside to wipe my hands and face.

The chamberlain said nothing as he led me down the corridor. The clomp and drag of his feet filled the silence. As he did not hold the candle aloft, I was forced to wade through thick shadow behind him, lifting my feet carefully so that I would not stumble on an uneven flagstone. When we turned down the passage to the great hall, I assumed that this was going to be a repetition of my last encounter with the manorial lord. I wondered why I had not been told to bring a bucket.

To my surprise, the great hall was empty. The fire had died to embers, and the room was dimly lit by guttering candles in sconces bolted to the wall. Flickering shadows from iron fleur-de-lis crenelations made jagged teeth across the floor.

Geoffrey crossed to the dais and climbed stairs to an entrance that I knew must lead to the manorial lord's private quarters. I followed stupidly, unable to conceive of a reason why I might be brought there. We traversed another cold, dark passageway, approaching a door surrounded by a halo of light. The chamberlain knocked and pushed forward without waiting for a response. The heavy door creaked reluctantly open. Geoffrey's stooped shoulders obscured my view of the room, but I could tell that a fire was lit, and an emerald and gold canopy confirmed that we were indeed entering a bedchamber.

Coldly, the chamberlain said, "I got the girl like you asked." He pulled me out of the dark doorway and gave me a shove into the room, causing me to lurch and nearly fall into a short man with a bulbous nose and a red cap. He took a quick step back, squinting and blinking.

With a shiver, I recognized the man as the apothecary from Waithe, the town nearest Aviceford. When wealthier villagers became ill, the apothecary was called, as there was no physician within many miles of the village. Our family could not afford the apothecary, but I had seen him at the home of the reeve, when the reeve's wife fell sick with childbed fever. The poor woman died despite the astringent poultices and medicinals concocted by the apothecary. I shared sickbed vigil with some other girls whose families could spare them from home, and the sad reeve paid me a few coins when it was all over. I was glad for the money, but I did no more to earn it than mop the good wife's brow.

A violent fit of coughing came from the bed, and I realized that the chamberlain had been addressing the patient, not the apothecary. Emont was propped on his elbows, facing the firelight, his broad chest heaving violently with each cough. When he recovered from the fit, he looked at us vacantly. His face glistened with a film of sweat, and his eyes were glassy.

Geoffrey said, "I don't know what you want with the girl, my lord." He flung the last word like slop to a pig. "The chamber servants, including myself, are more than capable of caring for you. The laundry girl does not belong here."

Emont shook his shaggy head, then moaned and slumped onto his back. Geoffrey's eyes narrowed, and his thin top lip tightened in a snarl. He spun and clomped away, pausing to spit on the floor before leaving the room.

I approached Emont, who lay with his eyes closed. The flush of fever and his rapid breathing made him look like a ruddy-cheeked boy who had been playing in the snow. The apothecary removed a cup from Emont's hand and brought it close to his face so he could peer inside. "You must make sure that he drinks his medicine." He squinted at me again, frowning.

I nodded. I did not want to be there, and a wave of anxiety washed over me when I thought about the laundress. I should have been more frightened about being left in charge of a sick nobleman, but for some reason, I was not.

The apothecary carried his brown leather bag to the fireside, where he riffled through its contents, lifting out one bottle and then another for close inspection. When he found the medicine he was seeking, he brought it to me. "Give him a half-filled cup of this horehound and coriander elixir three times each day. He needs to finish what is in this cup before he sleeps. If his fever does not break within two days, you should send for a surgeon, as he will need to be bled."

I wondered how far a messenger would need to travel to find a surgeon. I fervently hoped that Emont would recover quickly, not least because I needed to get back to work. I took the bottle of medicine from the apothecary and thanked him.

After the apothecary left, I drew a stool to the bedside. The floor had been strewn with meadowsweet and lavender, and the herbs crushed under the feet of the stool released fresh fragrance. Emont appeared to be in the shallows of a fitful sleep. His eyes flicked erratically beneath purple-veined lids, and his breathing was ragged. He did not wear his nightcap, and his damp, greasy hair splayed out on the pillow like a ratty halo. I had never seen a feather bed before, and I pressed lightly on the edge of the mattress, feeling its softness. How glorious it would be to sleep in such a bed every night.

Emont did not wake even during his coughing spells, and I grew stiff from sitting still. I leaned my forehead on the corner of the mattress and dozed. When I opened my eyes again, the room was dark and cold, and my neck was sore. The fire had died to an orange glow, and the candle was half spent. All was silent except for the distant hoot of an owl. As I stirred the embers, they sparked and smoked, so I put fresh wood down, coaxing the flames back to life. Although I was unsure of the hour, I thought that it must be time to rouse the master for his medicine. I shook him gently, and his eyelids fluttered. He coughed and turned onto his side.

"Sir, you must wake and take your medicine. Wake now."

He opened his eyes, still coughing, and looked at me, confused. "What is it?" His voice was croupy and weak.

"I am Agnes, sir, and I have your medicine."

For some time, he stared at me blankly. Then, narrowing his eyes, he said, "You despise me too, don't you?" His cough was a wet rattle. "Contempt. I see it."

"Sir, I am sure that no good Christian holds you in contempt. Now it is time to take your medicine, sir."

He nodded docilely. He drank from the cup that I handed him, and though he grimaced, he finished the draught. He lay back and closed his eyes.

"I hate this place," he rasped, coughing again. "Would that my father had never bargained with that woman." He made no more sound, and soon fell back asleep.

I nursed Emont for two days, after which his fever subsided. He continued to speak and sometimes cry out in his delirium, and I was never sure whether he was aware of my presence or not. When his eyes did focus on me, he seemed content to have me there. Though much of what he said made no sense, I suspected that his unhappiness ran deep. I was too young to understand how a wealthy man could be sad, but I perceived bleakness in him.

Elisabeth did no laundry while I was gone. Upon my return, she ordered me to work through the night to catch up, and when she found me asleep in the morning by a dying fire, she beat me with a dolly stick.

A fortnight later, when Emont requested my aid again, Elisabeth was in the laundry with me.

"What does the master want with this gormless girl?" she snapped at the chamberlain.

"Shut your gob," Geoffrey replied.

"You can't take her from me. I've only got the one."

"Are you telling me what I can and cannot do?"

Elisabeth seemed to catch herself. She pressed a hand over her eyes, and when she lifted it, her brow was smooth and her lips curved in a coy smile. "I never tell you what you *cannot* do, now do I?" Her tone was one I had not heard before.

To my astonishment, Geoffrey smiled too. "The girl will be back before you notice her gone," he said.

Elisabeth's laugh was edged with frost.

I followed Geoffrey back to Emont's chamber. The shutters were closed, and the light from a low fire imparted a desultory, reddish glow. An iron candelabrum hung from a ceiling beam, and though it was daytime, the candles were lit, slumped and melted, lowering stubby fingers of wax drip by drip. The master slouched in a chair by the hearth and motioned me over when I entered. I curtsied and waited expectantly, but his head remained bowed. He tapped an empty cup against the armrest; the metallic clank rang loud in the silence.

"Geoffrey," he said without turning his head. "Leave my wine. You may go."

The chamberlain set a flagon on the floor beside Emont. "The laundress needs the girl back tonight," he said.

Emont mumbled something unintelligible and waved the chamberlain away. Geoffrey pressed his lips together; a crooked tooth poked out, which made him look more like a grizzled old hound than the tyrant I feared. He slammed the door, which made me jump, but Emont did not react. He turned his head slowly to look at me. His eyes were sunken, and the shadows made his gaze baleful. He extended the hand that had been curled in his lap, and I saw the glint of a blade.

"Can you help me?" He held out the knife. The handle was made of smooth bone with a gold tip. A silver cross had been inlaid where the handle was widest.

"Sir?" My thoughts darted like rabbits, trying to divine his meaning.

"Oh, ah, if you would be so good as to trim my nails. I can manage the left hand but not the right."

I had not been aware of holding my breath, but it came out in a rush. "I should open the shutters so I can see." I bustled to the window. Though the day was overcast, I was momentarily blinded by the flood of light.

In ordinary sunlight, the room and its inhabitant looked shabby and forlorn. Dark patches of soot on the walls and ceiling appeared to be centuries old, as did the faded tapestry and drapes. Wine had been spilled on the bedclothes. I wondered if they had been changed since I last stripped the bed. Emont's fine silk robe bore stains, and his stockings were crumpled around his ankles. Scraggly whiskers fuzzed his cheeks and hid the dimple in his chin; his long hair was tangled and matted.

The fire flared and spat when I fed it a log sticky with pine sap.

"Let me have the knife," I said. After the words left my mouth, I feared that I had been rude, but Emont held the knife out obediently. I never trimmed my fingernails; mine broke or I bit them off. I decided to approach the task like whittling, aiming the blade away from the fingers. I took his hand, which was small for a man, soft and pale as pastry dough. It looked dainty in my rough, blistered paw.

"No," Emont said. "Not like that. Use the knife to curve." He placed his other hand on top of mine to demonstrate. His palm was warm.

The sharp blade peeled the nail away like bark from a tree. When I had finished cutting the nails on his right hand, I said, "Should I help with shaving, sir? Or perhaps your hair?"

"I could use some tidying, couldn't I?" He raked his hair with his fingers. "Perhaps you could assist, thank you." He filled his cup with the wine Geoffrey had left and took a great swallow. He coughed and then said, "You have eyes like a cow."

"Sir?"

"Your eyes. They are soft and brown and solemn. Just like a cow."

"Oh." I wasn't sure how to respond.

"Not that I am comparing you to a cow. You seem like a clever girl."

"Cows can be clever too, sir."

He seemed to find my statement amusing, though I had meant it sincerely. Emont laughed heartily before draining the rest of his cup. "Get on, then," he said. "Make me beautiful."

I brushed his hair first, as I was confident that I could do it well. Untangling snarls and smoothing his curls made me homesick, not only because it reminded me of brushing my sister's hair, but because it had been so long since I had felt a tender touch. Loneliness lodged in my throat like a piece of gristle.

I fetched a bowl of water and the razor. Emont closed his eyes and tipped back his heavy head while I scraped at his whiskers. A contented smile made his appearance more youthful. "You have the touch of an angel, Agnes," he murmured.

After I patted his cheeks dry, Emont thanked me distractedly and poured himself another cup of wine. He propped his stock-inged feet against the hearth. "Shut the window before you go," he said.

I walked slowly back to the laundry. Nothing good awaited me there.

Elisabeth was stirring the fire; a shower of orange sparks turned to gray ghosts. "The sun is already setting," she said. "You had better hustle. I wouldn't like to have to punish you." She held the poker aloft and waggled it, as though mocking the threat implied by the gesture.

"The master asked after you," I said.

The laundress's expression went blank.

"He wanted to know how I like my position." I paused. "He said I looked tired and asked if I was overburdened. I told him you had been feeling poorly and so hadn't been able to do your duty of late."

Elisabeth lowered the poker in a leisurely fashion, but I could see her jaw working as she clenched and unclenched her teeth.

"I am to report back to him. He is a most considerate master."

The laundress did her part with the laundry that night, and she never beat me again for the offense of being called into the master's service. I wish that the same ruse could have fooled Geoffrey, but he knew the master intimately. Geoffrey understood that Emont had only the murkiest idea of how the manor was run and that Emont depended on him completely to maintain a facade of re-spectability. Moreover, love of drink breeds a sort of blindness to other people, and Geoffrey knew that our master would not take a real interest in my life. The chamberlain sharply resented my incursion into his territory, but he did not feel threatened by me. He knew that his power over Emont far exceeded any small influence that I might have.

A second event that increased Geoffrey's dislike for me might have yielded an advantage had I known how to use it. This happened on a day when there was a large party of visitors, and I had a heaping basket of white linens to clean. The guests and Emont were presumably at dinner in the great hall, but the laundress had not brought the chamber pots as usual. I was frustrated with the stains, and I decided to fetch the chamber pots myself.

I had by that time visited the sleeping quarters and solar on several occasions when my help was requested by Emont, and I knew how to access that part of the house while avoiding the great hall. I went out the back entrance near the kitchen and circled the manor house, past the garden and dovecote. I squeezed through a thicket of holly bushes that crowded the windowless base of the west wall and there mounted a neglected staircase that led to the second story. I had to tread carefully on the weather-worn steps as the mortar was crumbling and stones sometimes came loose underfoot. The oak door at the top of the stairs was never barred; it opened onto a landing that looked down on the great hall. Three long tables had been covered with white linens and set with silver; the guests in their finery were colorful and raucous, out of place in somber Aviceford Manor. As I ducked down the corridor, I heard an explosion of laughter and wondered what grown men and women found so funny.

I made quickly for Emont's sleeping chamber, because that was the room I knew the best. When I opened the door, I saw two figures moving on the feather bed, and an unpleasant sensation trick-led down my spine. The laundress was entirely unclothed, swaying on all fours, like a child pretending to be a horse. Her pendulous moonlike breasts were blotched with red; they swung heavily as her head reared back, yanked by the chamberlain, who had one hand wrapped in the nest of blond curls at the nape of her neck. Elisabeth held her eyes closed and bared her teeth in a grimace.

The chamberlain was a more unsettling sight still, as he was clothed from the waist up like an aristocrat dressed gaily for a hunt. He wore a velvet and gold doublet with a fur collar and a hat with a long curving feather that bobbed violently by his ear. With each low grunt, his naked hips and sagging bottom thrust ener-getically at the laundress's jiggling rear, which he observed with intense concentration.

I might have escaped unnoticed had Elisabeth not turned her head to the doorway at that moment, just as I pulled it shut. Her face was half veiled by tangled hair, but I caught her look of unal-loyed hatred before she disappeared behind the reassuringly solid surface of the closing door.

THE ROYAL COURT

I am to be a grandmother! I suppose that I should say "step-grandmother." Princess Elfilda sent for me this morning, bidding me to visit her chambers. The royal family remains at the summer palace, but Ella claimed ill health and stayed behind. She dislikes travel, but her excuse was not fabricated; she has been feeling poorly, and now we know the cause.

When I arrived, Ella was still in bed, wearing a billowing silk chemise. With gold hair tumbling loose over her slender shoulders and porcelain hands clasped in her lap, she looked like a little girl again. Two of her hounds sprawled beside her; they raised their heads and pricked their ears suspiciously but didn't bark. Dog hair fuzzed the blankets and the kennel scent was not entirely masked by lavender oil. The queen has tried to break Ella of the habit of bringing dogs indoors, but the king takes the beautiful princess's side in everything.

"Good morning, Your Highness," I said. "The rose has returned to your cheeks. I trust that you are feeling better?"

Ella flushed pinker. "I am, thank you." She unclasped her jeweled fingers and spread them over her belly. "I am with child!" she said abruptly, as though the words had been straining to escape her lips. She watched me carefully with her lambent violet-blue eyes.

"Why, how wonderful, Your Highness! How far along?"

A slow smile spread over Ella's face, and she reclined against the pillows at her back. "I am not certain——four or five months."

"So long! Why did you not tell me sooner?"

She ducked her head. "I feared that speaking too soon would invite bad fortune."

Ella has already been married for two years, and the whole kingdom is impatient for a royal child. Although the baby will be far down the ladder of succession to the throne, Ella is so adored by the people that her every sneeze provokes fits of wonderment and delight. Her child will doubtless be the object of equally feverish idolatry.

"Does the prince know? The king and queen?"

"Not yet. They will return from the country soon enough."

I stepped toward the bed, intending to sit on the edge of the mattress; one of the hounds bared its teeth and growled.

"Down, Bo!" Ella lightly swatted the dog's neck, and it settled its chin on its paws. I stopped several paces from the bed.

"You are truly feeling well, Your Highness?"

"Yes, I am."

"There is little peril of losing the baby now. You are blessed this time."

The prior year, Ella had presumably miscarried. She had been sick, with vomiting, and she confided to me that her monthly bleeds had ceased. Then one morning, I was called to her chambers to find her in bed like today, but pale and trembling. She pulled back the covers to reveal blood-soaked linens; the nightgown she wore was stained scarlet from the waist downward. She swore me to secrecy, and I arranged for the bedclothes to be smuggled to the laundry without the knowledge of the ladies-in-waiting. I sponged her clean and helped burn her nightgown in the fireplace. There was little call for such furtiveness——miscarriages are commonplace, after all——but the princess has always been uncomfortable with matters of the flesh. I told no one of the incident, not even Charlotte or Matilda.

"Are you sure that the danger has passed?" Ella twisted a lock of hair through her fingers and brushed the ends against her cheek, as she used to do when she was a child. I have always found the gesture annoying.

"Nothing is certain, Your Highness, but it is highly auspicious that you are so many months along and healthy. Have you felt the baby quicken?"

"No . . ." Ella frowned. "How does it feel?"

"You will know soon." I smiled at her concerned look. "It is a lovely fluttering."

"How much did the birthing hurt?"

I thought about how to respond. I wanted neither to frighten nor mislead her. "It is bearable, Your Highness, and it ends in the greatest joy you can know."

Ella looked unsure but asked no more questions. She cradled the head of one of the hounds with both of her hands and kissed its nose repeatedly, making little cooing sounds. Then she smiled and said, "I hope it will be a boy!"

Charlotte and Matilda will be delighted to know that their step-sister is with child. I hope that they will be given some role in the upbringing of their niece or nephew; sadly, this is likely to be the nearest experience they will have to motherhood. It is not only their lack of beauty that prevents marriage: Though we live like aristocrats, we are penniless and depend upon the generosity of the king for every scrap of clothing and food. I have no dowry to settle on my daughters. Being aunts would give them joy and a much needed wholesome pursuit away from palace intrigue.

As I reflect on my recent writing about Elisabeth, I wonder whether she ever miscarried or gave birth in secret. I would guess that she had congress with the chamberlain for years, and she was not yet too old for childbearing when I arrived at Aviceford Manor. With her large girth, a pregnancy may have gone unnoticed, and I do recall at least one mysterious absence, when she left the manor for more than a week.

Perhaps the devil's bargain she made, trading her chastity for comforts Geoffrey Poke could supply, seemed like a good bargain to Elisabeth. Nothing, however, could make up for the pain of giving away a child.

The laundress gave me ample reason to hate her, and I used to think that she had been born without a single virtuous bone in her whole body. Now that I am older and have seen so much more of mankind, I no longer believe that people are born without virtue. It gets beaten out. Misfortune threshes our souls as a flail threshes wheat, and the lightest parts of ourselves are scattered to the wind.

THE MESSENGER

I was fourteen when there came an opportunity for me to escape the manor house, at least for a short time. I was by then desperate for any change. I had grown increasingly lonely, not only because I felt my isolation more keenly as I grew older, but because I lost my only friend. John was killed one snowy winter morning by the collapse of a barn roof. He had been the person I sought the moment I entered the kitchen for meals, the audience for stories I rehearsed in my mind, my guide for navigating the alliances and enmities of other servants. He taught me how best to stay out of the chamberlain's way and where to stash the apples he brought me from the orchard. Most of all, John pulled me back from my tendency toward melancholy. Whenever tears threatened, he had some witty words or humorous antic at the ready. I did not know how much I relied on him until he was gone.

After John died, I fell into a deep sorrow. I received news of the barn collapse from Elisabeth. I do not think that she relished my pain; even she seemed sad about John's death. For the first time since my arrival at the manor, I broke down and sobbed in front of the laundress. She said nothing to me, but let me exhaust myself, and when I returned to the bucking tub with sore eyes peering from swollen slits and a trail of snot and tears down the front of my gown, she did not chastise me.

From that day, my time at the manor was almost unbearable. I sat alone at supper and listened to my heart thunder as I lay awake each night. I had no appetite, and the frocks that had become too tight across my growing bosom and hips hung loose once more. I sleepwalked through my duties in the laundry, hardly bothering to acknowledge the laundress on the rare occasions when she was chatty. I felt invisible.

On saints' days and other holidays I was allowed to leave the manor, and I saw my family then, usually at church. It should have made me feel better, but somehow it made me feel even more alone. Everyone in my family had married, and Lottie already had two babes, though one of them died in the cradle. My father married a widow from the village, a sharp-tongued gossip. My brother and his wife still lived at Father's house, and Lottie lived in Nether End, nearer the church. Without a dowry, Lottie had been unable to do better than a villein as poor as our father, and while her husband was a godly man, I doubt that she loved him.

Elisabeth was a constant reminder to me of what my life would become if I did not find a husband. She never spoke of the bed-chamber scene I had witnessed, but it became evident to me that she had chosen harlotry over the drudgery of being a laundress. Even at the age of fourteen, I understood that slothfulness could not account fully for such a choice; she must also have been driven by despair, the same shadowy desolation that closed on me. Blistered hands, an aching back, endless toil, unremitting loneliness shaped my days and nights and every day to come, a gloomy blur of sameness that stretched nowhere except to its own pointless end.

As I teetered on the brink of marriageable age, I was too conflicted to truly mourn my lack of prospects. Even wedlock, while preferable to life at the manor, did not represent escape. The best that I could hope for was the life my sister lived, a smoke-filled house of dirt and straw, an empty belly, dead babies. I was a mouse trapped in a corner, looking for a crack to flee through but despairing of finding one.

It is said that clouds may turn forth a silver lining, and indeed, if Elisabeth had been less spiteful, I might never have found out about the opportunity at all. She taunted me one hot afternoon in August, as I was kneeling on the lip of the laundry basin scrubbing shirts. Sweat slid from under the band of my bonnet, trickling to the tip of my nose or the edge of my jaw before splashing into the tepid pool. Elisabeth had come to recline in the relative cool of the dark laundry room; she lay on a pile of linens, wearing only her chemise, fanning herself with the lid of a rush basket.

"I heard something from Geoffrey."

I swatted at a fly that droned in erratic circles around my head and then returned to scrubbing, not caring what she had to say.

"I heard that Abbess Elfilda requested a girl to help with her mother."

Her tone of voice told me that she was up to no good, but she had piqued my interest. I took her bait. "What do you mean, miss?"

"I mean that the mother of the abbess had a lady's maid who took ill. It will take some time to get a new one, and so the abbess asked for a loan of a girl from our manor. I told Geoffrey that of course we couldn't spare you."

My mouth felt dry. "I am not sure that I understand, miss."

"I mean, you dimwit, that you might have gone to the abbey to play lady's maid for the old woman. But you shan't." Her fleshy underarm jiggled like a pale fish on a hook as she fanned herself. "They'll find a girl from one of the other manors. Anyway, we have only you." She wrinkled her nose. "Cothay Manor has a goose girl and chambermaids for the lady, besides two laundry girls. The abbess only wants to take from our manor because she knows the souse won't complain. Besides, Geoffrey says she wants to punish us for poor revenues. God's bones, we can barely keep up as it is."

I struggled to control my voice. "When did the message arrive, miss?"

"This terce. The abbess's messenger is still in the kitchen, waiting for supper. A dark-skinned devil."

I returned to scrubbing, trying to ignore the roaring in my head. I could not stand that the possibility for liberation had miraculously appeared, only to be snatched away by the person I most wanted to escape. Although I was no longer a child—in fact, I stood a full head taller than Elisabeth, and I was as strong as any boy—the laundress made me feel powerless.

Sharp pain sliced neatly through my self-pity. I had scraped my knuckles against the rough stone at the edge of the basin. For a moment my fingers went limp; I watched as the new pink furrows I had dug began to slowly fill with red. Sitting back on my heels, I sucked the blood away. It tasted of metal, like the blade of a knife.

Pain calmed the ferment in my mind. There had to be a way to circumvent Elisabeth; I could not sit idly by as she closed the door to my escape. I had to find some way to approach Emont. Even if I failed, I would have the comfort of knowing that I did not just lie down and let Elisabeth wipe her feet on me. I went back to work, nurturing the seeds of my new resolve.

When suppertime arrived, I spread the ashes on the bucking cloth, wiped my hands, and walked slowly toward the kitchen. The usual chaos awaited me there. The serving staff was just finishing with the lord's supper in the great hall, and many of the other servants were gathering at the trestle tables in the kitchen for their own suppers. It was hotter in the kitchen than in the laundry, and the men were red-faced and sweating. We were not supposed to eat the leftovers from the master's table, but as Emont employed no almoner to supervise the table scraps, and as tonight there were no guests, the serving boys brought back a plate of sturgeon with pear and raisins and a pigeon pie. On the kitchen tables were trays of pork roast, carrots, turnips, and ceramic jugs of ale.

The abbess's messenger was seated near the door, enthusiastically tearing into a piece of pork. I had noticed him before when he had stopped in for meals at Aviceford Manor. He looked different from anyone I had ever seen; his skin was chestnut, as though he spent every day of his life in the sun, but his face was smooth, not rough and wrinkled. He always seemed to be in good humor, joking with the kitchen staff. He carried himself with confident grace, but he did not behave haughtily toward the servants, even though they were beneath his station.

On an impulse, I walked over and stood in front of him on the opposite side of the table. When he looked up, I curtsied. "Greetings, good sir. I am Agnes." I did not have a plan for what to say next.

The messenger leaned back, stretching his long legs in front of him, and he beamed at me. His teeth were white and straight as a string of pearls, and his smile could have lit a cathedral. "Good evening, Agnes. My name is Fernan. I am pleased to make your acquaintance." He spoke with a slight accent, the result, I would later learn, of a childhood in Aquitaine.

"I have heard that you brought a message about a position at the abbey."

He arched his black eyebrows. "Why does a laundry girl know the content of a message intended for her master?"

"How do you know that I am the laundry girl?"

"Either you are a laundry girl or you have been cleaning chimneys, cinder wench!" He laughed, and I blushed deeply. I had forgotten to wipe my face before coming to supper.

"Did you already deliver the message to the lord, then?" Despite my embarrassment, I looked him steadily in the eye. I knew from what the laundress had told me that the message had been delivered to the chamberlain instead.

His smile wavered. He opened his mouth to say something, and then closed it again. It was my turn to raise my eyebrows, which made him laugh again. "I suppose that I did not deliver the message directly to the intended recipient, no, but not everyone reads his own letters." Fernan waved genially at the bench in front of me. "Sit, sit! Join me. I have a weakness for cheeky lasses."

"I cannot sit here, sir. This table is for the highest rank." He should have known that. He was making fun of me. Already, I was getting sidelong looks from the menservants gathering at the table. When the chamberlain arrived, I would be in trouble.

"Nonsense! You are my guest."

"Really, I cannot." His flippancy irritated me. "I have a favor to ask of you." I was surprised by my own temerity.

"What might that favor be?"

"Can you speak with Sir Emont about his response to your message before you leave? Can you call on him after supper?"

Fernan wiped his sweaty brow with his sleeve. "I think that I can guess the reason for this strange request, and I don't object to helping you. I still need Sir Emont's signature on the response that I have drafted." He patted the satchel by his side. "However, your master is not likely to go against Geoffrey's recommendation."

"I know, sir. But I would appreciate it all the same."

He shrugged his shoulders and smiled. "Very well! I wish you luck, laundry girl."

My heart pounded as I walked to my usual seat near the other end of the kitchen. I used to eat with John and old William, the scullion who rewarded my chatter with treats that he secreted away during the course of his day in the kitchen. Poor, frail William got no break from his labors, and by the time I was fourteen, he had died of brain fever, the result of overwork. My supper seat was now between a chitty-faced, sullen youth who ignored me and an oily scullion who pressed his skinny leg against mine at every opportunity. As usual, we made no conversation. I was too nervous to eat, but I had to bide my time until all of the servants were finished in the great hall. I pushed my food around my bowl, watching the traffic through the kitchen doors carefully, because if I waited too long, the chamberlain would be finished with his own supper and roaming again. When I judged it to be safe, I bade my tablemates a good night and slipped out of the kitchen. Fernan was still at supper; as I passed behind his broad back, his animated story provoked a roar of laughter from his neighbors.

My life would have turned out very differently had I not found Emont still sitting in the great hall that evening. The red sun lay low on the horizon, lighting the room with a fiery glow. As I passed the series of diamond-paned windows, the warp of the glazing made the sun look like a rosy apple bobbing in a rain barrel. Emont stared into his cup, paying no attention to the sunset. I approached from the front so that I would not startle him, but it still took a moment for him to notice me.

"Agnes. Why are you here? You're filthy."

I blushed for the second time that evening. I had forgotten about the soot on my face. "I have heard, sir, that Abbess Elfilda needs me to fill in for her mother's lady's maid until they can find a suitable replacement from the castle."

He narrowed his eyes. "So Geoffrey told me. He also told me that he cannot spare you."

I gathered my courage. "Sir, might not a refusal to send me to the abbey anger the abbess further?"

"Further?"

"Oh . . . It is not my place to say, sir . . . I should not have come to you. It is only that the laundress seemed so afeard that if I did not go to the abbey, Mother Elfilda would punish us. She said small remittances from Aviceford displease the abbess, and she will be furious if we refuse this request as well. I only came because the laundress was so troubled. I mean no impertinence, sir."

Emont scowled. He took a long draught from his cup and set it heavily on the table.

"Sir, if you had sent me, I would have been diligent and godly, but I can see that I should not have bothered you with things that I cannot understand. I am most contrite." I curtsied and lowered my gaze, waiting for him to dismiss me.

Emont might not have had much stomach for arguing with Geoffrey, but I could tell that my words had reached their target.

He groaned with irritation and released me with a gruff command. I flew from the room, seeking familiar, safe territory before the chamberlain could overtake me.

I learned of my success in the very early morning when the tip of Fernan's boot jostled my elbow. I had been sleeping prone on the kitchen floor, and it took some moments for the sticky cobwebs of slumber to clear from my head.

"Up you get!" he whispered. "We have a long road ahead!"

When I realized that he was taking me to the abbey, my heart leapt into my throat, but I was careful not to show my excitement. Fernan turned his back while I took off my nightcap and pulled a dress over my chemise. I silently gathered my few belongings, including the stone collection, and placed them in my bag. The morning was mercifully cooler than the day before, but there was no need for a cloak. I pinned my plaits together and covered my head with the gray coif that I reserved for rare trips outside the manor.

As we left the kitchen, I cast a glance at the bulky form of the laundress, who lay sprawled in her scant underclothes, glistening with sweat in the weak light of dawn that filtered through the skylights. I prayed that I might not meet her again.

6

ELLIS ABBEY

Fernan led me silently to the stable. His demeanor was less friendly than the night before, but I didn't care. Everything made me want to sing for joy: the rosy dawn giving way to the brilliant light of day, the dew that soaked my shoes, the sweet scent of woodbine. I stopped at the rain barrel to rinse my face and ran to catch up to Fernan, who strode ahead. He walked with a springy lope, leaving dark imprints in glittering patches of sunlit dew. It pleased me that I could copy his long stride, for I nearly matched his height. I imagined that we were a pair of wolves slinking over the dappled grass.

The stableboy had already saddled Fernan's rounsey, a silvery gray mare named Perla. I was to ride pillion behind Fernan, and there was a moment of awkwardness when it became apparent that I did not know how to mount a horse. There was no resemblance to a graceful wolf in the way I struggled to get my leg over the horse's back. Through some combination of Fernan pulling and the boy pushing, I was finally settled with my bag in front of me, gripping the back of Fernan's saddle.

Fortunately, Perla was a good ambler, and though Fernan told me that I rode like a bag of barley, I was soon able to relax my grip and take in my surroundings. Fernan rarely spoke, and I tried to ignore his broad back in front of me; something about the way his thin tunic rolled across his shoulders and clung to his skin as the morning grew warmer made me uncomfortable.

August is a busy month in the countryside. Fruit pickers swarmed the orchards, and the boughs of trees trembled under the weight of climbers. Women and children milled among the stands carrying baskets, yelling objections when they were struck by apples falling from above. The fields too were humming with industry, as every available pair of hands had been conscripted for the wheat and rye harvest. Teams of reapers crept alongside golden palisades of grain, felling stalks with flashing sickles, while binders followed behind, gathering swaths into bundles. The weather had cooperated that year, remaining dry and unusually hot for the whole week, and while the harvesters no doubt cursed the heat, they would be grateful for an easy harvest. I knew that my father and brother would be somewhere among the workers in the fields, but I could not make them out that day.

The dry weather sped our travel, and we were soon beyond the boundaries of Aviceford Manor's demesne. As the sun climbed steeply overhead, we entered a small market town, which Fernan told me was called Old Hilgate. It was a rank and cheerless place, with rickety market stalls made of wood and cob, some of them three stories high, crowding the narrow, rutted street. Perla had to pick her way through streaks of rubbish strewn from doors and windows, and entrances to side alleys were choked with barrels, broken crates, and other detritus. Few townsfolk roamed the streets, because it was not a market day, and shops were closed.

Fernan told me that on market day, the town would be transformed as people from the countryside and manors poured in. The shops were thrown open, the streets teemed with bustling crowds, and the alehouse filled to overflowing. Music and banter enlivened the now quiet marketplace as goods were bought and sold, gossip exchanged, news delivered, flirtations traded. "Even a serious girl like you might find it to your liking," Fernan said. Though I couldn't see his face, I knew that he was smiling.

When we reached the market cross, Fernan pulled Perla to a halt. "We should stop here to eat," he said, pointing to a squat building; a garlanded alestake jutted from the thatch roof. "The ale is usually watery, but the food is not too bad." He held out his hand to me, but I did not immediately understand that he meant for me to dismount. He heaved a sigh, and turning in his saddle, grasped me around the waist. I yelped with surprise as he hoisted me from my perch and slid me halfway down Perla's flank before dropping me to the ground. I landed unharmed, though his grip had been disagreeably firm. More than anything, my dignity was bruised.

"I do not enjoy being treated like a child!"

"Then dismount like a lady next time. Do me a favor and hold the reins."

I took the reins grudgingly while he jumped down and strode into the alehouse to find someone to feed and water the horse. He brought back an urchin with a dirty face and a runny nose, and we left Perla in his care.

The alehouse, which was smoky and poorly lit by a few tallow candles and a halfhearted fire, was furnished with four long tables, all empty except for a clutter of flagons at the farthest ends. The straw on the floor was moldering and matted down, littered with food scraps that had been left untroubled for some time.

We took seats nearest the only window, hoping that a breeze would diminish the stink of tallow and rot, and a stout alewife came to take our order. Her surly expression softened as Fernan chaffed her good-naturedly. The ale she served us was indeed watered down and had a bitter taste, but the meat pie was decent, as was the applemoyse. Given the uncleanliness of the alehouse and the poor quality of the ale, it did not surprise me to discover that the alewife's daughter did the cooking. She should have done the cleaning as well.

Fernan jollied me as he did the alewife, and I soon forgave him for shoving me from the horse. As we finished our dinner, I asked him how he had learned to read and write. I had never known anyone but priests and noblemen to be lettered, and I felt the prickings of envy. Fernan did not object to answering my question; indeed, he seemed to relish the sound of his own voice.

"I learned to read Latin when I was a child in Aquitaine. I grew up on the fringes of the court of Edward of Woodstock, Prince of Wales . . . He was Prince of Aquitaine too, of course."

I knew nothing of Aquitaine or princes, so I held my tongue.

"When my father was a young knight living in Castile, he was conscripted into service by the prince. As he told it to me, my father took no notice of the quarrel over the Castilian crown, as he had not a drop of Castilian blood in his body. He was a heathen from Granada."

My spine stiffened at the word "heathen."

"My father was a mercenary. He was a skilled knight, and he served the prince well. Edward of Woodstock was a fierce warrior—as well as a fine leader—and my father admired him." Fernan paused and glanced out the window. The sunlight made his amber eyes glow bright. When he looked back down at his cup, his eyes seemed an ordinary dull brown, like tiny lanterns that had been extinguished.

"My father pledged fealty to the prince. He followed Edward to Aquitaine and converted to Christianity. That is how I came to be born in Aquitaine. My father taught me horsemanship and swordsmanship, and the prince allowed me to be educated with boys in his court." He grinned at me, perhaps aware of both my awe and my defensiveness about my ignorance. "That, laundry girl," he said, "is how I learned to read and write."

"What of your mother?"

"I never knew her. My father told me that she was godly and fair."

"Have you any brothers or sisters?"

"Nay, none."

"How did you come to England?"

"My father died of consumption. When the prince moved back to England, he brought me with him and left me under the authority of Mother Elfilda, his father's second cousin."

"Why are you not a knight?"

Fernan smiled and leaned back against the wall, swinging his legs onto the bench. "Is this an inquisition? You should tell me about how you came to be a laundry girl at Aviceford Manor."

"I was the second daughter, my mother died, my father couldn't keep me. I needed to eat."

"You might consider embellishing your story just a trifle for the sake of the listener."

"I don't like embellishment. Why are you not a knight?"

"Being a knight is not just about being able to ride a horse and fight, Agnes. The English consider me to be lowborn."

"Even though your father was a knight?"

"He was not an *English* knight."

"I see. Well then, how did you become a messenger?"

"Mother Elfilda decided that since I can read, write, ride, and handle a sword, I would make an excellent messenger. And I am good, if I dare say so. I like it too. The work pays well, because of the danger. And I meet so many pretty girls."

"Don't tease." My voice sounded severe to my own ears. "What danger?"

"I could get saddle sores."

"A tender arse is indeed a handicap."

"Whatever happened to 'yes, *sir*' and 'no, *sir*'?"

"I am a lady's maid now. And you are not so much older than me . . . *Sir.*"

He laughed, baring his gleaming teeth. "You are not as staid as you pretend!"

I opened my mouth to ask another question, but he cut me off, saying, "We should be going. We have hours yet to ride, and you don't seem to run out of questions!" When he slapped tenpence on the board, my expression must have betrayed my thoughts, for he laughed again, saying, "I told you that I am well paid!"

We rode the rest of the way mostly in silence, and I was content to be left to my own happy thoughts. God had opened a window for me, and I flew forth like an arrow, growing dizzy with my rise. Already the manor seemed like a dark blot far beneath me.

As we neared the abbey, the trees grew thicker and more wild. Ellis Abbey was built on Ellismere Island, which was not truly an island, for it attached to the shore of the lake by a thin isthmus.

The island was thickly forested, an empty wilderness except for the abbey and a hunting lodge owned by the king.

We were nearly upon the abbey when it came into view. The entire compound was enclosed by a massive stone wall that could have served as fortification for a castle; beyond the enclosure, alabaster spires soared to the sky like pale fingers stretching toward heaven. The lake was a dark mirror, a reflection of the blue sky and soft clouds, and it seemed that the Kingdom of God was everywhere around us, just beyond reach.

My heart quickened as we passed through the shadow of the open gate. Over the crown of the arch, three words were carved deeply into the moss-blackened stone.

"What is written there?" I asked.

"It says, 'Welcome, Cinder Girl!'"

I didn't gratify him with a laugh, and he couldn't see my smile.

The abbey was built so that the first view encountered by a visitor was of a road, perfectly straight, flanked by rows of magnificent elm trees. At the end of the road, framed by the elms, was the ghostly face of the church. High walls and a vaulted stone roof were supported by swooping flying buttresses, giving the appearance of a white bird about to take flight. The outside wall of the nave was adorned with a rose window and steeply pointed lancets alternating with decorative arcading. The church did not seem high-wrought, but airy and graceful, aspiring skyward.

We did not take the road toward the church, but turned aside, toward the stable. We passed a rose garden and a fishpond, and then a field of brilliant purple lavender. My most fevered imaginings could not have matched the beauty of the place.

Fernan left Perla with the stableboy and ushered me with my small bundle toward the dormitory, a long building that enclosed one side of the cloister behind the church. "You had better clean yourself while I inquire about whether Mother Elfilda might receive you," he said.

I had washed my face in the rain barrel that morning, but no matter, I was not going to argue. Fernan left me at the entrance of the dormitory and told me to wait while he sent one of the sisters to help me. I sat on the stoop, inhaling the sweet, hot scent of summer, watching bees drone drunkenly from one clover to the next. The queasy fluttering in my stomach settled; I was too happy to be worried.

I took the stones out of my bundle and held the most treasured ones in my hand. I thought of myself as grown up, but I had yet to put all childish things aside. I had not added to the collection since the day I left home, as any association with the manor would only tarnish it. While the green stone was always my favorite, on this day the white stone seemed almost as precious. It was small and many-faceted, and it glittered in the sunlight. The stone, in its simplicity and inconsequence, seemed as much an inspiration to modesty and purity as the abbey itself.

I nearly fell backward when a nun opened the door behind me; my pebbles clattered on the flagstones as I hastened to kneel.

"Get up, then. I've come to give you a bath. I am Sister Marjorie." Her voice rasped like dry leaves. "Follow me."

I scrambled to gather my belongings and followed the shuffling nun into a sunlit arcade. The stone floor was worn to a smooth polish in the most trafficked areas; to one side stood a wall of columns, clusters of slender, dark marble stems surrounding fluted central pillars. Slanting shafts of light created shadow doubles of the columns on the floor separated by bright arches. Sister Marjorie's white veil glowed when she passed through the luminous half-moons.

The sound of falling water came from the cloister, and I glimpsed a fountain and a profusion of flowers before we entered the dormitory. I wondered why such a magical place would be deserted.

Sister Marjorie led me slowly from one end of the long dorter to the other. She was so short that from the back, she would have looked like a child were it not for the stoop of her shoulders. Besides mattresses lining each wall, the enormous room was empty of furniture and clean as a pin. The floor was strewn with fresh rushes, the walls were free of black woodsmoke stains, and sweet air blew from open windows. Trees growing near the casements dappled everything with light and pearl gray shadow that shimmered when the wind blew. The dormitory seemed a comfortably cool place to sleep, though I would discover in winter that the cold could bite, for there was no fireplace.

At the far end of the dorter was the warming room; fires were allowed there, but none was lit on such a warm summer day. The windows were mere slits near the ceiling, better suited to letting smoke and steam escape than allowing sunlight to enter. Whitewashed walls, the scent of rosewater, and two fat, gleaming copper tubs made the room inviting despite the dim light. One of the tubs was still filled with unheated gray water; on the surface, a film of soap scum made lazy swirls.

"Leave your dress on the floor. I shall bring you a clean frock." The nun handed me a lump of soap and padded slowly to a linen chest.

With a shiver of pleasure, I remembered that I would not have to do the laundry. I said a silent prayer of thanks, for I could scarcely believe my good fortune. I tossed aside my clothing and climbed into the tub; I was too tall to fit properly, and with my knees folded near my ears, I must have looked like a giant cricket.

A few rays of sunlight angled steeply across the warming room, plucking golden notes from the burnished belly of the empty copper tub next to mine. I watched as a spider lowered itself toward the tub on a wisp of thread. It became transfixed in the path of a sunbeam and froze, spinning perilously, so I reached over and broke its web with my finger, lowering it safely to the floorboards. "Godspeed!" I whispered as it darted into the shadows.

Sister Marjorie returned carrying a scrub brush and a gray woolen gown very like her own habit. I did not like the idea of being scrubbed or having to wear such a hot, itchy frock, but I was too happy to really mind. Frail as she appeared, the nun was plenty strong enough to scour me to a bright pink. She informed me that weekly baths were expected at the abbey. This was not as bad as it might sound, for in the winter, though the water in the tub did not stay hot for long, the warming room was cozy with a cheerful fire. Also, once the sisters trusted me to clean myself properly, I was allowed to scrub myself.

Sister Marjorie spoke little; she did not even ask my name. I imagined that at her age, her thoughts were drawn toward the world to come. I dressed in the clean linen chemise from my bundle and the gray frock, which was as disagreeable as it looked. The elderly sister then took me back through the dorter and into the cloister.

The cloister was no longer deserted. A dozen nuns sat upon stone benches or strolled silently along the paths that separated four flower gardens. The paths met in the center of the cloister, where a three-tiered fountain splashed water into a quatrefoil basin of polished black stone. The gardens were full of color at that time of year, flush with pink roses, yellowwort, purple foxglove, mauve centaury.

The ebb and flow of gray-clad vestals in the cloister would become familiar to me in time. Their days, like the phases of the moon,
slipped by with quiet regularity. Each nun was assigned her own
work to keep the abbey functioning, but everything, even sleep,
came second to prayer. Matins, lauds, prime, terce, sext, nones,
vespers, and compline were divine duty, prayers that marked the
passage of the hours and gave meaning to each day. When the bell
sounded its sonorous peal, the abbey, like a beast with one single
heart and mind, fell at once into worship.

Sister Marjorie approached one of the other nuns in the cloister.
They murmured quietly, the taller nun bending to hear, their veils
drooping together, hiding their faces. Sister Marjorie pointed at
me and then beckoned me to approach. The other nun had a round
face, and her smooth cheeks dimpled when she smiled at me. "My
name is Sister Marjorie also," she said. "That will make it easy for
you to remember. The sisters call me Marge. What is your name,
dear?"

"My name is Agnes, Sister."

"That is a lovely, holy name. Sister Marjorie tells me that I am to
take you to meet Mother Elfilda in the chapter house." She looked
at me appraisingly. "Do you know proper manners for an audience
with the abbess?"

"No, Sister." I swallowed nervously.

"Come with me. We shall wait in the vestibule of the chapter
house, and I shall explain what you need to do."

We crossed the cloister to a faceted round building with a
vaulted roof. It was nearly as ornate as the church, with towering
stained-glass lancets and decorative moldings. The nun ushered
me into a dark, cool anteroom and indicated that I should sit on a
stone bench that jutted from the wall. Low voices from the inner

chamber drifted toward us, but I could not make out any words. While we waited, several laymen wearing country clothes arrived and sat in patient silence across from us. I recognized one of them as the reeve from Aviceford Manor; he must have had a special petition for the abbess.

Sister Marjorie bent her freckled face toward me and instructed me in a barely audible whisper. "When you enter the chamber, kneel in the doorway, and then progress to the middle of the chamber, where you must kneel again. Do not move unless Mother Elfilda beckons you forward. When the prioress tells you to stop, kneel again and wait until you are spoken to. When you are requested to speak, always begin with a greeting. Bow on each occasion you are asked to speak. Do you understand?"

I felt a stab of doubt; I was not sure that I had followed what she had said, and it was all foreign to me, but I nodded anyway.

"Now, sit quietly," she whispered. "Someone will come for you when they are ready. The prioress is fitting you in between appointments, so it will be a quick audience." She smiled at me encouragingly and then crept away, leaving me alone.

It felt like hours before the heavy chapter house door swung open and a group of sisters swept out, their white veils billowing behind them. One of them signaled to me that I should enter, so I edged uncertainly toward the door as they filed past. When I reached the threshold, I knelt and looked up. I had a fleeting, fanciful idea that I had entered a jeweled forest. Colors from the stained glass mixed with shadows in a way that reminded me of light filtered through a canopy of trees, and the ceiling was so distant and dark that it might not have been there at all. At the far end of the room was a dais, and upon the dais, in an ornately carved chair, sat the abbess. The prioress stood stiffly next to her, vigilant and obedient. Over the top of a brass lectern in the shape of an eagle, the tip of a quill bobbed; the nun who wrote with the quill was short enough to be invisible to me.

Mother Elfilda motioned to me with her hand, and I moved to the center of the chamber and knelt again as I had been told to do. The prioress clucked impatiently and said, "Come here, girl! You are not a tortoise."

I approached the dais, kneeling for the third time. Mother Elfilda was tiny and delicate, like a child pretending to be king on her father's throne. Her exquisite features might have been carved from alabaster, so white and still was her face. She wore the same gray habit and spotless wimple as the other nuns, though her veil was longer, and a heavy gold cross hung from her neck. I could tell from the fine, pale arches of her eyebrows that she was fair, and her eyes were the color of robins' eggs.

"Who might this be?" Mother Elfilda's voice had the pure timbre of a Sanctus bell.

I was not sure whether she had addressed me, but as the prioress glared at me with her close-set dark eyes, I croaked a nervous reply. "God bless you, my lady, I am Agnes come from Aviceford Manor to work as a chambermaid."

"Chambermaid? But there are no ladies' maids at Aviceford. Oh—you must be the one sent to help Mary with Rose House. You know how to clean properly, I hope? The work at Rose House is not heavy, but you can help in the laundry if you have spare time."

That I was not to be a lady's maid felt like a truth I had known all along but had been too stupid to acknowledge. Of course the laundress had exaggerated the desirability of the post in order to make me feel worse for not being able to take it. Why had it not occurred to me before? She would have wanted the post for herself if it had truly been so good. I had come to the abbey to do the same sort of work that I had done at the manor, and the laundress would know it. The cow.

"Take her to Mary so that she can be settled. God be with you, Agnes."

I bowed and took several steps backward before another nun grasped my elbow and escorted me outside. Why had I made such a stupid presumption? Worse, why had I made my presumption known? The abbess seemed to have disregarded my ignorant comment, but I wanted to reach back through time and snatch my words from the air. I cringed when I imagined Fernan discovering my mistake, and then I cringed again when I realized that he had already known the truth when I boasted about being a lady's maid. He had, after all, been the deliverer of the message.

Humiliation is felt most sharply in youth, and it is hard for me now to understand why Elisabeth's deception was so painful to my young self. I did suffer. Eventually, I consoled myself that I was out of the manor, and the abbey was near to paradise itself. I decided that humiliation was my punishment for the sin of pride, which I should tear from my soul by its roots.

ROSE HOUSE

Mary was in charge of maintaining the residential building, otherwise known as Rose House, one of many outbuildings in the abbey's compound. Due to its isolation, the abbey had to be self-sufficient, and the outbuildings included an infirmary, a guesthouse, a bakery, a brewery, workshops, a laundry, and, of course, barns, stables, a henhouse, and a pigsty. Beyond those buildings lay vegetable gardens, orchards, modest grain fields, and a mill where the nuns ground their own wheat.

Rose House could accommodate up to four residents, and it was usually populated by affluent pensioners. During the time that I worked at the abbey, however, the whole building had been turned over to the abbess's mother, the dowager countess of Wenslock. Lady Wenslock was cousin to the former king, and she was exceedingly wealthy in her own right. It was gossip among the servants that she chose to live at the abbey in order to atone for whatever sins had led to her eldest daughter's madness. Providence had marked very different fates for the two living fruit of Lady Wenslock's womb. Abbess Elfilda had become a powerful instrument of

God, a mystic and philosopher, whereas Lady Alba had fallen prey to the devil, descending into lunacy and delirium. Had I foreseen the hand that Lady Alba would eventually play in my own fate, I might have listened to the gossip with more interest.

While Rose House was beneath the means of its noble denizen, it was not rustic. Each of the four apartments boasted a sizable hall decorated with tapestries, carved panels, and moldings, and Lady Wenslock had brought furniture, statuary, and silver with her. There were separate solars for sleeping and sitting, and the garderobes were comfortable. Because Lady Wenslock had claimed the largest apartment and made annexes of the other three, she dedicated chambers for music, embroidery, reading, dining, and receiving guests. Many times each year, visitors made the trip from the city to stay with her and enjoy a quiet retreat. For the wealthy, this was a pilgrimage to a holy place, as Ellis Abbey was a sanctuary where God's presence could be felt most powerfully.

Although Lady Wenslock did not live like an anchoress, she did not have all of the comforts customary to a woman of her rank either. Her needs were attended to primarily by Mary, a young woman who had graduated from the nunnery's school. Mary, in turn, had but one servant working exclusively for her—the position that I would fill—though she could borrow from other parts of the abbey when necessary. Visitors to Rose House brought their own servants, and all of the cooking took place in the abbey's kitchens, but due to the fluctuating number of visitors, the amount of work necessary for upkeep of the residential building was unpredictable from week to week.

I met Mary in the main hall, which, despite its grandeur, was almost cozy, as it was crammed with draperies, decorative furniture, artwork, and bagatelles. I wondered whether Lady Wenslock had tried to stuff the furnishings of an entire castle into Rose House.

Mary herself was a far less interesting sight. She was angular and thin, with a wan, pinched face and furrows between her brows that belied her years. Her gray frock flapped loose, and the way her pointed chin jutted forward on her long neck made me think of a chicken. She greeted me politely enough and asked about my experience.

"I did all manner of work at Aviceford Manor," I lied. "I can do whatever is needed, be it cleaning, polishing, provisioning, tending the fires, smoothing or repairing her ladyship's garments, or running errands." Anything Mary asked me to do would be better than working in the laundry.

"My lady countess is exacting. She has requested a new servant from Wenslock Castle; the girl will come next month when her ladyship's niece visits the abbey. In the meanwhile, I expect you to do the cleaning, keep the buttery and woodpile stocked, and tend the fires if the evenings and mornings become cooler. I tend to my lady's person and wardrobe." She sniffed. "Your duty is to stay out of her ladyship's sight."

Mary stiffened as the dowager countess herself entered the hall. Despite a slow and faltering step, she looked like a galleon, her ample bust leading the way, her gauzy white wimple tented on both sides of her face like sails. She wore a green velvet gown embroidered with gold thread, but no jewels save a brooch in the shape of a cross. To my astonishment, she made straight for me. I knelt hastily, bruising my knee. Lady Wenslock took a wheezy breath, saying, "You must be the one come to fill in for poor Lizzie. I hope that you will find Rose House to your liking. Mary will help you."

As I stared with round eyes, Mary said, "I was just going to explain her chores, my lady." Her expression was sour.

The countess lowered herself carefully into a chair, deflating like a bread loaf taken out of the oven on a cold day. "First, fetch my Book of Psalms, and bring that stool closer so that I can raise my feet." She looked at me and smiled, the wrinkles on her face rearranging themselves; tiny sunbursts appeared in the corners of her eyes. "Stand up, child. What is your name?"

"My name is Agnes, my lady. God bless you, my lady," I added quickly.

As Mary left to find the psalter, Lady Wenslock sighed, saying, "I don't suppose that you can read, young Agnes."

"No, my lady."

"Mary can read, but she has no feeling for it. She makes prayers sound like an accounting of the wheat harvest. I have asked my niece to find me a girl who understands the words she reads. Of course, such a girl would refuse to work for Mary, and Mary is such a good girl."

I shifted my weight from one foot to the other, wondering what I should do.

"I believe that girls should be taught to read and write. My daughter's treatise on the spiritual weapons required to defeat evil is considered as wise and important as any recent written work. Perhaps even divinely inspired. Imagine what ideas are locked up in the hearts and minds of women who simply lack the tools to express them."

Mary had returned, carrying the book.

"Do you not agree, Mary?"

"My lady, your most holy daughter is a marvel and a gift to us all straight from God," Mary said with sudden passion, "but I know my place at your feet and at Mother Elfilda's feet as sure as Agnes knows hers."

"Your humility does you credit, Mary. True nobility comes from being humble, benign, and courteous. Without these key qualities, all other virtues are worthless." She took the psalter from Mary and opened it, holding the book at arm's length and tilting her head back. We waited several moments, but she ignored us, so we curtsied and Mary led me away.

"My lady countess is most devout."

"She is kind."

"Yes," said Mary acerbically, "he that hath pity upon the poor lendeth unto the Lord. This is one of her many favorite sayings."

"What happened to Lizzie? The girl who was here before me?"

"Lizzie got herself with child."

"Lady Wenslock must have been greatly aggrieved!"

"Quite the contrary. It was Mother Elfilda who threw her out. Lady Wenslock would not throw a stray dog out of the house."

I had the impression that Mary did not approve of Lady Wenslock's lenience. She showed me the rest of Rose House, which was equally crowded with furniture and decorative objects, some beautiful, some strange. I wanted to pause to admire each one, but Mary kept a brisk pace.

The room that impressed me most was the library. Mary explained that the countess had collected over two hundred books in her lifetime, a sum that was incomprehensible to me. She had donated most of the books to the abbey's large library, but she kept some of her favorites at Rose House, heavy leather-bound tomes chained to lecterns. The library was the brightest room in the building and also the most spare. White damask embroidered with *W*'s encircled by gold crowns draped the lecterns, and the walls were lined with matching simple white tapestries, showing what I assumed to be the arms of the late Count of Wenslock and edged with the same crowned initial. The room was otherwise bare of furniture and art.

"Can you read those books?" I asked, delighted by the romance of the room.

"Nay!" She looked shocked. "I am not allowed to touch them! And you may not enter the library except to dust."

She pointed out the buttery, and then we left Rose House to visit the brewery and the kitchen where I would fetch Lady Wenslock's meals. Mary explained that the nuns took their meals in silence, and the countess preferred to eat alone or with her guests when she had visitors. I would have to bring the tray of food to Rose House and then dash back to the dining hall so that I could partake at the servants' table. Although not bound by vows, the servants were not allowed to break the silence either. This sounded dreary to me, but Mary did not seem to mind. I suppose that she was used to it from her years at the convent school.

I came to find out that Mary was the daughter of a baronet, and she had been sent to the abbey as a child, biding her time until her parents could find a suitable husband. Since the baronet was not exceptionally rich, and since Mary did not possess beauty or charm to overcome her lack of a fortune, eligible men proved elusive. As the bloom of youth fell away, her prospects dimmed further. She was content to become a nun, but her father had not yet given up his ambition of finding a match that would elevate the family's fortunes, and so she waited patiently, caring for Lady Wenslock.

Though Mary was gentle born and austere by nature, she did not treat me unkindly. To my relief, even though I sometimes finished my work early, Mary never sent me to help in the abbey's laundry. I discovered in those first weeks that she preferred me to do my work without consulting her, and as long as we did not have guests, she did not mind me visiting the cloister or the rose garden if I had time.

Rose House was named for the adjacent rose garden, and I had a favorite spot, a sun-warmed stone bench facing a bowered path to the fishpond. I liked the chatter of birds and shimmer of water through the tangled vines. As summer drew to an end, there were few blooms left, but the air still held the lingering scent of roses. Sometimes I collected fallen petals for the sisters who made aromatic water and salt paste. To this day, the smell of roses transports me back to a time when the breeze, the sun, the reflections of water on a bowered path were an unspoken promise from God.

One day Fernan's silhouette blackened the arch of the bower; I recognized him by his broad shoulders and easy lope. The gravel crunched under his heavy boots as he approached, flashing his bright smile.

"How goes the life of leisure for the new lady's maid?"

I colored, remembering my mistake. "You know perfectly well that I am not a lady's maid. But I am doing fine, thank you."

He threw down his satchel and sat beside me on the bench. "I am very glad to hear it. You look well. Now I can see your pretty face without the soot. You look rested. And your hands are no longer blistered." To my shock, he took my hand from where it rested on the bench and stroked it lightly. I snatched it back without thinking, as though his touch burned. He paid no attention.

"How do you find life at the abbey?"

My mouth was dry. "It is heaven. Mother Elfilda is a saint. Lady Wenslock is too." I wanted to slide farther away from him, but it seemed like an awkward thing to do. The flesh on my hand tingled.

"Have you figured out yet how to make your post permanent?"

"No. A new girl is supposed to come next week." I had managed to put out of my mind the knowledge that I would be sent back to the manor. I did not want to think about it. Frustration rose like gorge to my throat. "You are so fortunate! You can come and go as you please. I . . ." I lowered my voice. "I am not free."

Fernan looked at me thoughtfully. "Maybe it is unjust that my father was a knight and yours is a peasant. But you were born with some advantages. You are smart and pretty. And resourceful. Your life is only beginning."

Nobody had ever described me as pretty before. I looked at him to see if he was making fun of me, but his eyes were serious.

"You really don't know that you are beautiful, do you," he said.

I looked down at my big hands and long, tapering fingers. "My father always called me an ox. He told me that I wouldn't need a dowry because I could pull a plough as well as any team."

"Being strong does not disqualify you from being beautiful."

"Beautiful for a plough-beast." I ducked my head, but I felt a flush of pleasurable warmth, along with a tangle of feelings that I could not identify. "I have to get back to work."

I stood abruptly, but he rose at the same time, very close to me, so that my eyes were level with the opening of his collar and the hollow at the base of his brown neck. I could not breathe until he stepped away with a small bow. He picked up his satchel and adjusted the strap across his chest. "I hope to still find you here after next week. I shall look for you here in the garden whenever I pass by on my way from the stables."

As I watched him walk away, I resolved to never linger in the rose garden again. A moment later, I wondered how often he visited the abbey.

Mary and Lady Wenslock attended Mass daily, and Mary did not mind if I did too, as long as we were not too busy. Mary and the countess set out much earlier than I, for Lady Wenslock walked slowly, and she preferred to arrive and settle herself before the gray flock of sisters rushed silently into the church.

Mass was my favorite part of every day. The church building itself was enough to induce rapture; I believed that no heathen could enter it without being compelled to fall immediately on his knees and praise God. The sheer height filled me with awe. The walls ascended like cliffs to the dizzying apex of the vaulted roof, the columns virtually disappearing into the shadowy reaches. Gold stars had been painted between the ribs of the vaulting, adding to the illusion of infinite distance, and jeweled rose windows floated mysteriously in the blackness, seemingly without support. During the Latin Mass, I would gaze at the paintings of the stations of the cross, or at the scenes depicted in the lancet windows, their brilliant images arranged in panels one above another, and try to imagine what it would have been like to have lived in the time of Christ.

The part that I loved most was the sermon by the abbess at the end of Mass. After the priest said *"Benedicamus domino,"* Mother Elfilda would climb the spiral stairs to the pulpit, regal and light as an angel, to address the congregation. She held us in thrall, her command so profound that no cough or rustle could be heard until the last word dropped from her mouth. Her voice would rise, clarion clear, echoing through the nave and choir, and then it would fall to a hush so intimate that I felt she was speaking only to me. It was not only her otherworldliness that held us spellbound, but the wisdom and dazzling truth of her words. When she reached the most stirring parts of her sermons, her white hands would sometimes lift from the lectern like doves taking flight, but her pale face always remained still and saintly, like the image of the Virgin in the manor's chapel.

In one of the sermons I remember best, Mother Elfilda compared the Virgin Mary to an onyx, the precious stone that opens up to receive a drop of dew when the sun shines on it. After nine months it opens again and another onyx falls out, leaving the original stone unchanged. Mary remained pure, untouched, even as God forced Joseph to wed Mary.

Mother Elfilda did not dwell on Joseph's reluctance, a story I had heard many times, but rather on Mary's reasons for needing to wed Joseph. Marriage was protection against being stoned for adultery, and she needed help for the birth and flight into Egypt. A painting in the church depicted a beatific Mary and baby Jesus on a donkey, the baby's tiny fist clutching at her cloak, and Joseph walking beside them with an expression of grim determination. He was a guard for the Holy Family and a decoy to prevent the devil from identifying Christ.

Another of Mother Elfilda's sermons that affected me deeply was a reminder to the sisters of the symbols that their ordinary clothing represented. Even more than paternoster beads represented prayer, a habit represented contrition and confession, a kirtle trust in God, boots two desires, to amend and to abstain from evil, a girdle restraint of one's will, a wimple abstinence, and a veil obedience. Every part of the sisters' lives perfected the bending of human desire toward God.

Although I was not allowed to quit my duties in order to observe the liturgy of the hours, I began to observe them in secret.

As long as I was alone, when the bell tolled, I knelt wherever I found myself, usually on the cold stones. The ache in my knees caused me to stagger when I tried to stand. At matins, when the sisters slipped quietly from their beds in the dark of night to go to chapel, I rose and knelt beside my mattress, in winter shivering so violently that my teeth knocked together. I willed my soul to forget about its cage, unleash itself, swell past the boundaries of my flesh, and open itself utterly to the Holy Spirit. Sometimes I felt an answer, a warmth blooming deep inside me, a soft unfolding of unspeakable tenderness. When the susurrus of leather-clad feet in the arcade warned of the sisters' return, I was reluctant to crawl back into the cocoon of my blanket.

I did worry that God would be displeased with my unorthodox observance of the hours, or that someone would catch me kneeling alone and accuse me of Lollardry or some other form of heresy. Yet my devotion suffused me with peace and quiet joy, a bright clarity of mind. I began to see tiny pieces of the Kingdom of God all around me, and something as ordinary as the song of a lark could bring tears to my eyes.

ENLIGHTENMENT

A few days after my conversation with Fernan, Mary informed me that Lady Wenslock's niece had delayed her visit until after Michaelmas. I rejoiced in my reprieve, and I did all that I could to make Mary happy. I did not know whether she had any influence over my staying or leaving, but it would do no harm to have her on my side. I made sure that she always had ale on hand from the most recent batch, and I strewed fresh herbs or made bouquets every day. I anticipated where the countess and Mary would sit in the evening, and I prepared a fire ahead of time. In every way, I tried to be helpful but invisible.

Mary spent most of her time with the countess, scribing letters, helping in the dressing room, or, most often, reading to her. She was also responsible for taking her ladyship's gowns to the laundry and arranging her wardrobe. She devoted little time to inspecting my work and even less to telling me how to do it. I liked to plan my own days and keep my own counsel.

One day, when Mary was away, I came upon Lady Wenslock sitting alone. She wore a glossy marmalade gown that swallowed the chair beneath her, and her hair was covered as usual by a wimple that flared like wings, maintaining its complex structure by means I could not fathom. I was hoping to leave unnoticed, but she looked up from her book and beckoned to me.

"Come here, come here. I need someone to read to me." Her loose jowls trembled when she spoke.

I curtsied, bowing deeply. "I beg your pardon, my lady, but I cannot read." I wondered if she was touched.

"No matter, come here."

I walked to her side and stood obediently.

"Do you know what book this is?"

I had heard Mary reading to her from it many times. "Your psalter, my lady."

"Very good. What psalms do you know?"

"I know several by heart, my lady. I do not know the numbers."

"Recite one now for me."

I began with the first one that came to my mind. "'By the rivers of Babylon, there we sat down, we wept, when we remembered Zion. We hanged our harps upon the willows.'" I relished the words that tumbled from my tongue, a long string of ancient and perfectly polished phrases that belonged to other people, in other times, and yet lived somewhere inside me. As I spoke the last line, a chill trickled down my spine: "'Happy shall he be, that taketh and dasheth thy little ones against the stones.'"

"Wonderful! That is not a psalm for the faint of heart. You have remembered nearly every word correctly, and you spoke them with feeling. Well done. Now, that is Psalm 137 . . ." She opened the book to a page illuminated with angels, trees, flowers, and a river of turquoise and purple.

"These are the words you spoke. Do you know this letter?" She pointed to a bulbous, richly colored rendering of the letter *B* encircled by gold filigree. The figure of Christ crouched in the emptiness created by the top half of the letter, and he reached down to men in the lower half, while they raised their arms longingly toward him.

"That is the letter *B*, my lady." My brother had learned his alphabet at church, and he had taught me most of the letters.

"Good!" Under her drooping lids, her eyes were bright and clever as a raven's. "Then what does this first word say?"

"By?"

"Yes, of course! By. And the next?"

"The."

"Yes!"

"Rivers."

"Yes! Now, if you know your letters, you can tell when you have a word wrong, because you will know that the sound at the beginning of the word is incorrect."

My heart beat like a rabbit's. She smiled at me, pleased. "Go to the solar with the blue canopy and hunting tapestries. You will find several old psalters in the chest there. Bring one to me."

I flew to the room and opened the chest. Something made of gold brocade lay on the top, but when I lifted the folded cloth, I found five books beneath. The covers were worn and undecorated, and when I leafed through the first one, I found the inside plain as well. I brought it back to Lady Wenslock, and she nodded with satisfaction. "I shall mark the pages of the psalms you know so that you may study them. Hand me my embroidery, there."

I lifted her embroidery from the floor, and she cut several lengths of thread. "This first long one marks Psalm 137. Which other psalms do you know?"

"'In the Lord put I my trust. How say ye to my soul, flee as a bird to your mountain . . .'"

"Ah, Psalm 11. 'Upon the wicked he shall rain snares, fire and brimstone, and a horrible tempest: this shall be the portion of their cup.' Very good." She marked another page with a shorter thread. "One more?"

I could not think of another in that moment and shook my head, looking at the floor. "No, my lady."

"No matter, no matter. Take this psalter, child, and study those two psalms. When you have made out all of the words, come back to me, and we shall find two more."

I took the book from her, and she patted my hand; her wrinkled skin was surprisingly soft. Gratitude welled in my heart. *A price far above rubies*, I thought. I could not recall what those words described, but I knew that what she had given me was precious beyond measure.

From that day, I took my psalter with me to the rose garden at every chance. The last blooms had fallen, and the purple lavender was gone, but the trees were beginning to dress for autumn, and the sun on the pond seemed even more brilliant through the thinning vines. I studied the psalter and listened for Fernan's step on the gravel, and after some days, I heard it again. I felt an irrational urge to hide at the sound of his boots. I steadied myself, and he joined me on the bench.

"Agnes, I am glad to see that you are still here."

"Her ladyship's niece delayed her trip until after Michaelmas."

"And what do we have here?"

"A psalter. Of course."

"Of course? But I thought that you could not read!"

"Nor can I. I am learning."

He leaned over my shoulder to look at the page. He smelled of woodsmoke and something foreign, not disagreeable, but earthy. "'For the righteous Lord loveth righteousness; his countenance doth behold the upright.'"

"Can you read it for me? I want to be sure that I have the words right."

He smiled and read the psalm to me. His voice had a pleasant timbre, and his light accent made the words exotic. Desert, mountains, rain of brimstone, tempests of fire, he made these as real as the garden around us.

"Shall I test you? What does this say?"

He pointed to words on the page and I read them. I had been studying the psalm for some time.

"You are a scholar, cinder girl." He regarded me warmly. His eyes were a deep amber-flecked brown, fringed with long black lashes that would be the envy of any woman. "Do you want me to help you with your reading?"

I nodded.

"I shall give you a parchment," he said, removing a sheet no bigger than my hand from his satchel. "You must find a quill and ink. We shall make it a game. As you learn words from your psalter, you can use them to write a letter to me. When you have filled this parchment, give it to me, and I shall check it for errors." He leaned close, and I could feel his warm breath as he murmured, "Write something nice. At your core, you are soft and sweet." He ran a fingertip lightly over the gooseflesh on my neck before getting up to leave.

I stayed rooted to the bench, clutching the parchment in my lap, as the crunch of Fernan's boots grew fainter. My stomach tumbled. I could not tell dread from longing. The sliver of space that had separated his shoulder from mine as we sat together on the bench had pulsed with warmth, and just as when a cat jumps down from your knee, the cold that replaced it was made more profound by its emptiness.

I did not move for a long time, letting the chill of the autumn breeze blow away the memory of his touch. I wanted him to come back; I wanted to lean against his broad chest, feel his warmth surround me. I wanted him to never return. Something about him sickened me. He made me feel as though I were descending to a dark place, as though he were choking off the light and air above me.

After more than an hour, the church bell tolled for none. I rose stiffly from the cold stone bench to kneel on the gravel. I closed my eyes, welcoming the cleansing pain. I let it wash over me, purify me. Roiling excitement and disgust thinned and parted like clouds revealing a patch of blue sky. With growing clarity of mind, I realized what I had to do.

The Holy Spirit was telling me to devote my life to God. This was why I had been sent to the abbey, why the countess was teaching me to read psalms, and why Fernan filled me with confusion. My heart yearned for the pure, celestial element of air, not the base, dark element of earth. Every sign pointed in the same direction, toward God, only I had been too blind until now to see it.

I would become a bride of the Lord, a maidservant, allow myself to be absorbed into the body of the church. I would never be parted from Mother Elfilda, who was as beautiful as an angel and as wise as a saint. I would do anything she asked of me. Being near her was more worldly reward than I deserved.

My heart grew wings as I thought about spending my life at

the abbey, learning, praying, devoting my body and soul to God. When I stood again, I felt a new peace and sense of purpose. I tucked the parchment into my pocket and returned to Rose House.

September passed swiftly. I did not spend time in the rose garden anymore, but I continued to study my psalter when time permitted. I convinced Mary to teach me new psalms; though I was too timid to admit to her that I was trying to learn how to read, Mary soon found out. Lady Wenslock had me recite psalms to her on occasion, and she marked new ones in my psalter, which slowly filled with colorful embroidery thread. The more words I learned to read, the easier it became for me to memorize new psalms, and the countess was pleased with my progress.

I told no one about my plan to join the nunnery. I was most frightened of telling Mother Elfilda, but the idea of returning to the manor was unthinkable, and so I requested an audience with the abbess. I received no response, and as Michaelmas approached, I became increasingly nervous. I prayed and prayed. The Holy Ghost whispered to my heart: an audience would come.

On the eve of Michaelmas, I had to accept that I was not going to have the opportunity to speak with the abbess. I told myself that I should not have expected an audience; Mother Elfilda had great responsibilities. She had authority not only over the convent but over the abbey's vast holdings, which meant that except for the king and the bishop, there was no higher ruler, judge, or spiritual guide for the souls occupying the abbey's lands. A request from a domestic servant was doubtless of lowest priority on a long list of petitions she received daily. Still, I had been so certain of an answer. It had seemed like divine will.

It was with great heaviness of spirit that I readied Rose House for Lady Wenslock's guests. After days of preparation, only the finishing touches remained. I found bright yellow hawkbit growing near the fishpond, and I mixed these with lacy hogweed to decorate the bedchambers. I put fresh linens on the beds, replaced every candle, and burnished the countess's silver ornaments one last time. Finally, I fetched barrels of fresh ale from the brewery and arranged them in the buttery.

The outriders arrived near noon and alerted the grooms to be ready to receive the horses. Mary ordered me to fetch four more servants from the abbey to help with unloading. I was taken aback, because I had been told to expect only three guests, the countess's niece and two other ladies. Mary smiled cynically. "An honorable life may not consist in the abundance of one's possessions, but status certainly does. You are not used to the ways of the wealthy. Next to her peers, my lady countess lives like a pauper."

I could not imagine any pauper living like Lady Wenslock, but when I saw the packhorses, carriage, carts, and wagons, I understood the need for many hands. A uniformed guard opened the door of a peculiar bulbous carriage emblazoned with the royal arms, and three ladies in rustling silks stepped down. Six other guards waited idly for grooms to take their horses, while the ladies' servants and I bustled in and out of Rose House, carrying chests, trunks, carpets, and trundles, listening carefully for Mary's instructions. I looked around, wondering which of the women was to be my replacement.

The week after Michaelmas was a blur for me. There was much to do to keep the guests comfortable, and I was busy from dawn until long past dusk. I could not even take time to attend Mass, and I was tortured by the thought that I was missing Mother Elfilda's sermons during my last days at the abbey. Even when I had time to eat, I hardly touched my food. I receded from the world like a wave sliding back along the shore.

Then, one day, the guests departed, and life at Rose House returned to normal. Nobody told me to leave, and no new servant appeared. When I asked Mary about it, she merely shrugged and said, "I told you that my lady countess would not put a stray dog out of the house."

This was how I learned that I would be allowed to stay on at the abbey. I would like to say that I felt overwhelming relief, but for some time I felt only disorientation. Never before had the complete absence of an event changed my life so profoundly. It was as though I had prepared for a blow that never came, but I was unable to let my body unclench. I went about my life as before, not quite believing that any of it was real.

I immersed myself more than ever in my psalter. To supplement my reading, I began to write on the parchment that Fernan had given me, using a quill and ink that the younger Sister Marjorie took from the abbey's scriptorium. I told her that I was copying psalms, and she said that God would approve of that use of the abbey's writing supplies. I wrote slowly and awkwardly, sometimes hunting for days for a single word. My choice of words was limited to those that appeared in my psalms, and I had only a small piece of parchment to record them, so I had to choose and scribe with care.

I did not see Fernan anymore, and I had no intention of showing him my work. Nevertheless, I would be lying if I said that I had not been writing for him. In a childlike way, I imagined him finding the parchment. He would read the painstakingly selected words, and his eyes would widen in wonder. He would shake his head in disbelief that an uncouth maid like me could produce such radiant sentences. Sometimes in my imagination, I would be standing before him, and he would take my hand and tell me that I was clever. The image caused a pleasurable flutter, but I never imagined him doing more than taking my hand.

Autumn grew colder and darker, and the first snow fell. I found it difficult to sleep at night, for even with the shutters closed, the frigid wind whistled through the paneless windows of the dorter. There were moans and grumbles throughout the long night, as the nuns also slept poorly. In the gray dawn, our breath became fog, and sometimes our coarse wool blankets were white with hoarfrost. Nature compensated for its cruelty, however, when the sun rose full on pristine snow. I liked to kick the glinting powder in the air on my walk to Rose House, keeping my cold fingers tucked under my arms and thinking about the fires I would soon have crackling. The countess spared no expense when it came to keeping our woodpile stocked.

During Christmastide, the nuns spent less time attending to their duties and more time in church. After nones, the sisters forewent their usual administrative meeting in the chapter house and met instead to sing. Music wreathed through all twelve days of Christmas, culminating in a service on the Feast of the Epiphany. No words could describe the music. The voices of the sisters rose toward heaven, revolving around one another in a slow dance, echoes weaving back through the original melody to create sound that was both complex and ineffably pure. When Mother Elfilda sang alone, the beauty of her voice pierced me like the sword of Saint Michael.

The food of Christmastide was less wonderful than the song, but far richer than the usual fare at the abbey. We ate goose cooked with butter and saffron, and after the Mass of the Divine Word, we even ate roasted swan. The king sent venison from his hunting lodge, and of course there was mince pie and frumenty with cinnamon, nutmeg, and dried currants. I was sorry to return to our usual bland diet when the holidays were over, but that was a reminder to me of how blessed my life had become. I did not like to think of my sister cooking pottage over a meager fire, worried that the barley might not last the winter.

It was not until the eleventh day before kalends of February that the prioress finally granted me an audience with Mother Elfilda. I felt less urgency for the meeting than when I had first requested it, but that did not diminish my nervousness. In fact, the long wait for an audience made it seem even more important and valuable.

I had not returned to the chapter house since my first meeting with Mother Elfilda. Before entering the foyer, I stomped the snow from my shoes. My throat had been sore since morning, and now my stomach hurt as well. I pushed back my hood and fidgeted with my coif, rehearsing for the thousandth time the words that I would say to Mother Elfilda.

I watched the other petitioners as they were ushered one by one into the chapter house, wondering what business brought them to the abbey. After some time, the door opened again and a sister motioned to me silently. The chapter house looked just as it had when I was last there, with Mother Elfilda on the dais and the prioress standing at her side. I knelt in the doorway, and the prioress said brusquely, "Come here, child."

Kneeling before the dais, I was closer to Mother Elfilda than I had been in months. I was struck once again by the abbess's small stature and icy fragility. Her face was unlined, though she must have been nearly beyond childbearing age, and her features were perfectly still, barely inhabited. She turned to the prioress, who looked down at her scroll. "This should be Agnes, Mother, the girl who works for Lady Wenslock. She came from Aviceford Manor after that problem with the other servant. Lady Wenslock asked that she stay on. The girl requested this meeting."

Mother Elfilda looked back at me. "Yes, Agnes?"

The words that I had practiced for months caught in my raw throat. The solemnity of the chapter house, the regal bearing of the abbess, the impatient stare of the prioress, these brought the abbey into clear focus, as though I were seeing each stone and glass pane in detail for the first time. It was like waking from a gauzy dream to see the mold and soot stains on the ceiling, reminders that snapped me sharply back into the real world.

"God save you, Mother." My voice sounded strange to me.

"Yes?"

"I have prayed . . ."

She gazed at me blandly.

"I have prayed, and I think . . . I think that perhaps . . . perhaps the Holy Ghost is guiding me toward a new fate."

"Ah." Her voice was clear and brisk. "You would like to get married, and your father is not free. You should return to Aviceford and arrange the terms with Emont. We shall find a replacement. What are you, sixteen?"

"Nearly fifteen, Mother. But I do not wish to marry. I wish to be a nun!" There, it was said.

A crease appeared between her brows, and she pulled her head back as though she had smelled something foul. "You are a servant. You are not even free."

The prioress scowled and banged her staff on the wooden dais. "You are wasting the abbess's time with your nonsense!"

I lurched forward, holding my stomach. I could not catch my breath. Seeing the expression on Mother Elfilda's face, I realized with horror the extent of my delusion. To the abbess, I was a packhorse, an animal that has value as long as it can work, nothing else. She would no more invite me to become a novice than she would invite a horse to the dinner table. I had made a fool of myself a second time, only this time, the humiliation was nearly too much to bear. A nun tugged at my hood. The door creaked as the next petitioner entered. I managed to croak some sort of blessing, though the abbess and prioress were already conferring about the next meeting, and they did not turn to see me go.

Once I was out of the chapter house, I could no longer control the waves of sickness. I ran out of the cloister, and the vomit came up, burning my sore throat, staining the snow an ugly yellow. I wanted to run to the woods and keep on running. I wanted the earth to swallow me. I wanted to lie down and never rise again.

Instead, I covered up the dirty snow as best I could and went back to work. When the church bells rang, I did not stop to pray, not then and not ever again.

THE ROYAL COURT

Do the peasants who wait by the side of the road for a glimpse of Princess Elfilda feel about her the way I felt about her godmother, the abbess? My worship was a cousin to the love knights-errant profess for damsels in unbreachable towers. Mother Elfilda was the epitome of feminine beauty and grace, and she possessed enough wisdom and influence to rival any man. I would gladly have been her champion in one thousand metaphorical quests and battles had she only deigned to ask.

Had I been allowed to serve the abbess, my infatuation would doubtless have waned as I aged——all passions are strongest in youth——but she was and still is an admirable person. My present antipathy is at war with the esteem I cannot help but feel. Though her cold beauty has faded, Mother Elfilda remains a superb philosopher and skillful leader. She has made Ellis Abbey the second-most important center of religious power in the kingdom.

It is perhaps because of the abbess's influence that her role in Ella's marriage to Prince Henry is spoken of so often. It is quite true that the couple might never have met had it not been for Mother Elfilda. Still, it was not the abbess's intention to marry her goddaughter to the prince, and if it had been, she would have arranged the union in the normal fashion. Marriages are not made by throwing young people together in a ballroom, and it is romantic foolishness to suppose that a person of the abbess's stature would leave something as important as matrimony to serendipity.

Last week, Matilda related outlandish tales about Mother Elfilda. We were keeping watch in Ella's antechamber; now that the princess has entered her confinement, she must be closely attended day and night. Though we happily anticipate the baby's arrival, we are nervous, because the princess is so small and the birth may be dangerous.

Matilda sat next to me on a bench outside the door to Ella's chamber. She leaned close and whispered so as not to disturb the princess. "You will not believe what Isabella Florivet had to say."

Her breath tickled my ear. I liked the conspiratorial closeness and the way she tucked her arm around mine.

"She heard the servants talking," Matilda continued. "They said that Mother Elfilda turned rags into a ball gown for Ella by waving a wand and chanting a spell!"

I had heard strange versions of Ella's history, but this one in particular took me aback. Quite apart from the blasphemy and the impossibility of conjuring finery from thin air, it beggars belief that the reverend mother of Ellis Abbey would need to resort to magic to procure a gown.

"Nonsense! Do they dare to call the abbess a sorceress?" I asked incredulously.

"No, Mother." Matilda stifled a laugh. "Apparently, she's a fairy! A *good* fairy, of course, not one of those baby-snatching sorts." She covered her mouth with her hand and glanced guiltily toward Ella's chamber, worried that she had invited bad luck.

I patted her arm and said, "Not to worry, dearheart, we won't let any fairies near our princess."

I suppose it is easy to believe that the otherworldly abbess is not a mere mortal like the rest of us. I used to take her for an angel, but I too would now rather prefer to think of her as a sprite.

9

FERNAN

The abbey never lost its beauty for me, but once I no longer felt a part of it, the beauty turned cold. Timeworn saints with storm-blurred faces stared blindly from arches and doorways, and stone after pale stone climbed mutely toward the sky, monuments to dead days, refusing to divulge their secrets. I thought of the hands that had raised the buildings, carved the stone, assembled the stained glass. I wondered how many workers had died during the construction of the church and how they had been paid for their labor.

I continued to attend Mass, but I sat as far from the pulpit as possible. When Mother Elfilda climbed the spiral stairs to give her sermon, I opened my psalter to read. She was not addressing me, so I was not obliged to listen.

Despite my disillusionment, my feelings toward the countess did not change. She might have been eccentric in the attention she paid to a servant girl, but I remained grateful. We did not speak often, and Lady Wenslock never offered me the same familiarity she did to Mary, but she treated me with the respectful condescension of a superior, not the disregard of an animal husbander.

Spring breezes caused the snowdrifts to round and slump, wearing them thinner until yellow grass and mud showed through. The longer days tempted me back to the rose garden, where buds were beginning to form. Bright green haloes softened the skeletal angles of branches, and then one day, the trees burst into full leaf. Swallows darted and swooped in the fresh-scrubbed spring air.

I had not seen Fernan since early autumn, and I did not doubt that he had given up looking for me in the garden. One day, however, he appeared, whistling through his teeth and looking as carefree and handsome as ever. I had been walking toward the fishpond, and he joined me on my stroll.

"Well, well, if it isn't Miss Agnes. I thought that you had gone back to Aviceford, but I didn't find you there either."

Although not even a year had passed, my decision to avoid Fernan seemed to belong to a much younger version of myself. I could not explain the reason for my absence without also exposing my callowness, and so I merely told him that I had been busy.

"I am glad to see that they have let you out for some sunshine, finally," he replied. "You look well. You seem to have grown even taller, and it suits you."

I kicked at the gorse beside the pond.

"You wear the most dismal clothing though. You look like one of the nuns."

"Well, I'm not. Anyway, you are hardly in a position to throw stones."

"True enough," he said, looking at his coarse, mud-flecked cloak. "I don't want to call attention to myself. Besides, I'm not as pretty as you."

I made a face.

"Tell me, what is the news at Rose House?"

I informed him about the latest visitors, and about Lady Wenslock's health. She had not much appetite, and her cheeks were hollow. "I am worried that she is ill, although she complains of no fever, nor cough, nor stomach trouble. She is more fatigued than she used to be."

"Well, she is a very old woman. Frailty is to be expected. How goes your reading?"

I blushed and looked down at my psalter full of threads. "It is improving."

"Did you write me a letter? I have been waiting for it."

I had the parchment tucked into the back of the book, but now I was too shy to show it to him. "I could think of nothing to say. Anyway, I don't know how to write very many words. I just copied down some things. It isn't for you."

"Let me see it anyway. I told you that I would correct your writing. I don't mind if you had nothing nice to say to me."

"It wasn't that! It was hard to find words."

"So show me what words you managed to learn."

He stopped walking, and I realized that he would not take no for an answer. Reluctantly, I handed him the parchment, and he read aloud:

"'When I consider the silver face of the moon that waxeth behind thick clouds of night I ask if she knoweth any thing seeth she a man on a horse a shadow small as dust driven by the wind or the foolish young woman who looketh upon her in wonder the light of her countenance revealeth all that liveth what then thinketh the moon of man and woman who dwelleth in her light joined by her regard from the heavens.'"

His voice trailed off at the end. He read it again, in silence, and then he looked at me as though I had grown donkey ears. "Did you write this?"

"Yes . . ."

"By yourself?"

"Well, I copied the words . . ."

"This is not from any psalm."

"No, no, I mean that I took words from different psalms."

"I cannot believe that you wrote this. Are you a witch?"

I laughed, and after a moment, he laughed too. I wondered about his hesitation. He handed the parchment back to me and frowned. "You should be a nun, not a servant."

"Well, I am not."

As we completed the loop of the pond, he motioned toward the stable.

"I should be going."

"I didn't hear your news."

"I shall come back tomorrow. Can you meet me? Same time?"

I nodded.

"Very well. Good evening to you, witch, or marvel, whatever you may be."

The following day, I found myself looking forward to seeing Fernan again. My thoughts about him were no longer darkened by queasy apprehension; whereas before he had seemed foreign or unwholesome, our stroll around the pond had made him seem quite ordinary. I was in need of a friend, and I did not see why that could not be Fernan. The churnings of my mind had unnecessarily complicated what should have been simple. I decided to be more blithe, more like Fernan. I finished my work quickly so that I could get to the rose garden on time.

Fernan was already waiting for me when I arrived at the garden. He was not wearing his usual traveling clothes, but a white shirt that contrasted sharply with the deep bronze of his skin and a neat, fitted doublet. For once, he was not carrying his satchel. He gripped a drooping bunch of bluebells in his hand. When he smiled and waved, my heart made a sudden leap.

Fernan offered the flowers to me with an exaggerated bow and suggested another stroll around the pond. I liked that his long stride matched my own, and I was reminded again of two wolves loping through the woods. We tarried by the water while he told tales from his travels. One story about a hare that got loose in an alehouse caused me to laugh until tears streamed down my cheeks. We saw the occasional worker or servant pass by, but they were far away and paid us no heed. It seemed as though we were alone in the world.

Except to hold my elbow on a muddy incline, Fernan did not touch me until we said good-bye. He tucked a bluebell under the edge of my coif and asked me to meet him again the following afternoon, which was to be his last day at the abbey for a fortnight. I savored the memory of the warm brush of his fingers on my brow as I returned to Rose House with a light step.

I woke, crestfallen, to the sound of rain. In the fog of sleep, the reason for my heavy heart was at first elusive. It had something to do with dark leaves shaking under the assault of raindrops in the empty rose garden. Fernan would not come.

All morning, I watched the sky anxiously; by dinnertime, the rain had stopped, but the clouds had not lifted. My chores stretched to eternity. When Mary asked me to restock the wood bins, I could

not hide my impatience. "Can I not do it later? I would like to go
out for a bit."

Mary looked at me suspiciously. "Why are you so eager to go
out on a day like this?"

"I want to take a stroll before the rain returns." I knew that she
found my preference to be outdoors peculiar but not objectionable.

"Restock first. Then you may go out."

Though I resented the delay, her question had awakened my
guilt. Was it appropriate for me to spend time alone with Fernan?
I wondered what Mary would think if she knew that I was not taking my stroll alone. I did not want to think about it, and I swatted
the worry aside with annoyance. The wood made a satisfying clatter as I released it into the metal bins. I liked the sharp smell of pine
on my hands.

The rain held off until I got to the rose garden, although the sky
was eerily dark. Fernan did not remark upon my tardiness. He had
brought bluebells again, and he carried a cerecloth cape.

Perhaps because of the weather, or Fernan's imminent departure, or Mary's question, I was in a somber mood. Fernan first
tried to jolly me, but I resisted. Finally, he said, "What is wrong?"

I shrugged. "I guess that I am not much good at conversation
today."

There was a slow beat of raindrops, and the tempo quickly increased. Fernan lifted his chin toward the sky, letting fat drops
splash against his face, and then he opened his cape, pulling the
hood over my head and wrapping the cerecloth around both of us.
He snaked his arm around my shoulder and pulled me toward him.
"A little rain won't hurt us, will it?"

Rivulets were beginning to form under his glossy black curls, and water dripped from the tip of his nose. His smile was fierce. "There is shelter close by. We can wait out the worst of this torrent."

He led me not toward the stable, which was closest, but to a barn just beyond the pond. By the time we reached it, the rain was hammering hard, and it was a relief to find refuge. Fernan pulled the heavy door shut behind us, leaving us in the dark, surrounded by small piles of hay, withered dregs of the winter supply. Rain beat thunderously on the roof. I shivered with cold. I thought about running back to Rose House, where the fires were lit.

"Take off your wet cloak," Fernan said. "I shall cover us both with the cape, and you will feel much warmer." I could not make out Fernan's features well in the dim light, but I could hear affection in his voice.

I dropped my sodden cloak on the floor and hesitated.

"Come on," he said, patting the hay beside him. "I promise not to bite."

I crouched next to him, and he put his arm around me again, pulling the cape up to my shoulders.

"There, isn't that better?"

I was warmer, but my body still shook, echoing the pounding of rain above us. I tried to calm myself by counting the slats in the door.

Fernan tugged at my coif. "You should take this wet thing off and let your hair dry." He jostled my shoulder playfully. "I won't watch."

Out of vanity more than anything, I welcomed the suggestion. I had beautiful hair like my mother's, mahogany and thick. I had taken to sprinkling it with rosewater, and the scent was lovely when I let my hair down. I pulled my plaits from their crisscross and shook them loose. My tresses fell nearly to my waist, brushing against the hay at our backs.

Fernan whistled. "Who knew that the cinder girl had such a magnificent mane?" He ran his fingers through my hair, and I did not pull away. "So soft too." He continued to stroke my hair meditatively, and after some time, his hand caressed my face as well. "You are so beautiful, Agnes." His voice sounded tight, constricted.

I was used to the dark by then and could see Fernan better. He gazed at me with great concentration. I thought it strange and wonderful that such a strong, handsome, intelligent man should be interested in me. It made me feel powerful and weak at the same time.

When Fernan bent to kiss me, I lifted my face toward his. I was shocked to find myself melting into him; I was a candle that had never known a flame, and now that the flame was lit, I softened and glowed in a way I had not known was possible. Our lips touched gently at first, and then more forcefully. I put up no resistance when he pushed me back into the hay, nor when he nuzzled and touched every part of me, lighting fires wherever he went. I should not have been surprised when I felt him pushing between my legs. I tried to sit up, but he leaned heavily on my chest, murmuring my name, telling me that everything would be fine. I struggled feebly against his weight, but he entered me with a tearing flash of pain.

It was as though I had been struck hard across the face. I woke from my languorous torpor to find a man jerking and jiggling on top of me, an ache between my legs, sharp bits of hay poking my bare skin. I had been bewitched, and the spell was broken. Fernan was lost in his own world, panting, eyes shut. After some time, he moaned loudly and collapsed over me.

I watched the brightening light between the slats of the barn door and listened to the rain slow and stop. Fernan's breathing eased. He seemed to have fallen asleep. When he did not move, I tried to shift him off of me. This woke him; he smiled and tried to kiss me, but I turned my head.

"Oh, Agnes, it is too late to be reticent now. Kiss me."

I refused, so he rolled away. "It is not always so nice for maidens the first time. You will get used to it." He smiled. "You were sublime." He stroked my hair, but I cringed. "You should not feel guilt. You are not a nun, after all."

Everything he said only made me feel worse. I stood and pulled down my skirts; something sticky oozed down my leg. There was blood on the floor. My only thought was to get out of there, back to something familiar, back to Rose House.

Fernan escorted me as far as the garden. I did not want him to come any farther, lest we be seen together. I had not worried about being seen the day before, but everything seemed different now, dirty.

"I shall be gone for a fortnight, Agnes, but I shall look for you when I return." He picked up my hand and kissed it gently. "Do not break my heart, lovely lady."

Before returning to Rose House, I walked to the stream. I was still sore, and every step was a reminder of what had transpired. I followed the brook into a small thicket where I could be concealed, and there I cleaned myself in the frigid water. I lifted my skirt and knelt in the water until I was numb. I wanted to wash away the last hour of my life, go back to a time when I felt whole. I knew that something fundamental within me had changed, though I did not yet know what.

I lay sleepless all that night, buffeted by warring emotions. I did not want to think about what had happened, but I could not put it out of my mind. I felt sick when I remembered Fernan on top of me, his eyes closed like a newborn kitten, making sounds that were not quite human. It was an unholy fire that he had awakened in my body, but my heart quickened as I remembered how deliciously it had licked the marrow of my bones. His stories by the pond, the sunlight on his face, his soft kiss on my fingers, those were memories that did not belong to the dark barn, the smell of damp wool and moldering hay. One Fernan I loved, the other revolted me.

In the days that followed, I could think of nothing but Fernan. I changed my mind one hundred times about whether I would return to him, but long before a fortnight had elapsed, I began to frequent the rose garden again.

Fernan reappeared on a summery afternoon. He was as cheerful and jocular as ever, and we fell easily back into conversation. He did not act as though anything had changed between us, and I wondered whether I had dreamt the time in the barn. He remained at the abbey only two days, and on the second day, he brushed his lips softly against mine, telling me that he would return in one week.

I waited eagerly for his return. This time, Fernan brought me a gift, a dark green gown that he had bought in the city. I gasped with pleasure when he unfurled it and held it against my shoulders. The fabric shimmered, and there was gold embroidery over the breast. It was nearly as beautiful as one of Lady Wenslock's gowns.

During our stroll, Fernan linked my arm with his, so that I held his forearm. When he covered my hand with his, I felt safe. Under the bower in the rose garden, he pulled me to him and kissed me tenderly. Then he looked earnestly into my eyes, caressing my neck with the tips of his fingers, and asked me to sneak away in the night to meet him in the barn. To my surprise, I agreed.

The moon rose nearly full that night and peered into the dorter, illuminating the long row of sleepers with eerie yellow light. I lay awake, studying the stars in the nearest window, my chest thrumming with the pounding of my heart. Sounds of coughs and shifting bodies gradually quieted. Once I judged that everyone was asleep, I rose and removed my nightcap. I had hidden the gift from Fernan beneath my bed during evening services, and now I slid it out, folded it over my arm, and crept silently toward the arcade. In the shadow of the pillars, I pulled the gown over my thin shift and shook my hair loose. I did not pause to think again, but flew barefoot over the darkly lit paths to the barn.

Fernan opened the door when he heard my footstep. Yellow pools of candlelight flickered where he had arranged candles on the floor, and the hay had been moved to one side of the barn and covered with a blanket. Fernan smiled broadly and took my hand, guiding me over the threshold. "You look like a princess, my sweet," he said, kneeling to kiss my hand. "Will you dance with me?"

"I do not know how to dance."

"I shall teach you." He stood facing me. "You will move past me so." He put his hand on my waist and guided me across the rough floor. "Turn away, now spin and face toward me."

I did as he asked.

"Now take my hand and we shall take one turn together."

My hand felt small in his. He looked happy. Soon, I was happy too. As we danced without music, he drew me close at every opportunity, making a game of kissing me when we passed each other. After some time, we were not dancing anymore, only kissing, and I did not want him to stop. Like a plum, I had ripened as spring turned to summer. I was filled with sweet nectar, heavy on the branch, loosening for the fall. He had only to cup me in the palm of his hand and pull ever so gently, and I was his.

There was nothing logical about the way I behaved that summer. I knew that Fernan would never marry me, but I continued to meet him at the barn when he asked. I had no hopes for my future, and that made me reckless. Deep down, I knew that I was careening on the brink of a precipice, but loneliness, love, and the impetuousness of youth drove me on.

It was simple to slip away at night, because anyone who saw me would assume that I had failed to properly take care of my needs at the rere-dorter before bed. The ease of our trysts lulled me into complacency. During daylight hours, Fernan and I rarely met anymore, so my life was sliced sharply in halves by the setting of the sun. In my real life, I was a dutiful servant who was increasingly worried about her ailing mistress. In my dream life, I was the desirable young lover of the handsome, charming son of a knight. I saw myself reflected in the hunger in his eyes, and I liked what I saw. I admired the creamy whiteness of my skin against his, the perfection of my pear-shaped breasts in his hands, the coltish sleekness and strength of my body under him, my long legs wrapped around his waist. Fernan was the blank parchment upon which my dream self was illuminated, and his desire made me wondrous.

Like all idylls, ours had to come to an end. In early autumn, Fernan's mood changed. He became distracted, testy, and his teasing took on an edge of cruelty. At first, I did not understand what was wrong. I tried to please him, but that only made him withdraw further. He spent less time at the abbey, and our trysts became rarer and more brief. As I felt him slipping away, my desperation grew. My dream life had become the only life I wanted to live, but it was not mine to choose. Only Fernan had that power.

One night, Fernan was late coming to the barn, and when he arrived, I rushed to him and threw my arms around his neck, crying, "What happened? I was so worried!"

He peeled my arms away and then released me. "I am here now."

"But why are you so late?"

"Why do you pick at me like a villein's slut?" He began to pace.

"You kept me waiting. I was not sure that you would come."

"I should not have come!"

My desperation was unbearable. I took his hand. "Lie down, my love, and I shall stroke your brow. I did not mean to upset you."

"Is going to bed all you can think about? As though you were a common whore?"

"I love you, Fernan!"

"You are not going to trap me by speaking of love or by having that child. You came to me willingly. You threw yourself at me!"

I was bewildered.

"You mean to tell me that you do not know that you are with child, with your swollen belly and breasts like melons? You can hardly fit into your shift!"

It was true that I had grown rounder and that I had not felt well. I was vaguely aware that I had not had a monthly bleed in some time. My hands instinctively covered my belly. As the truth revealed itself, I began to sob.

"Come on now. Stop your crying." Fernan's voice softened. "Come here, Agnes. Come here."

He put his arms around me, but I could not stop my pitiful

display. Convulsions shook me as I tried to keep from making a sound. I cowered in his arms.

"I did not mean to be so cruel. Perhaps there will be a miscarriage. Such things happen."

I pressed my face into his shoulder and tried to shut out the waves of panic. I had felt trapped before, and I had thought that the world could take nothing more away from me. I now understood that I had been mistaken.

The months that followed were bleak. I was fatigued and sore, and I battled an agitation that kept me from sleeping and eating. I had been so blinded by the metamorphosis of my body from child to woman that I had not recognized the signs of pregnancy, but now that I knew I was with child, I could not ignore the relentless swelling of my belly. I wondered how Fernan had noticed the change when there was only a modest hillock below my waist, but now the bulge was undeniable. I did not imagine a babe within, but a tumor or bubo. If I could have sliced my belly off with a knife, I would have done so.

Lady Wenslock's health continued to worsen. A physician now resided at Rose House, and nuns from the infirmary had been brought in to tend to the countess at all hours of the day. She rarely rose from bed, which meant that I did not see her anymore. It was whispered that Lady Wenslock would soon die.

Whereas the prospect of her death used to cause me worry about my own security, now I only felt sad that she suffered. Lady Wenslock's death could no longer alter my fate. Once it became apparent that I was with child, I would be forced to leave the abbey. I had nowhere to go.

I had no more trysts with Fernan, and I mourned him. There were times when I hated him, to be sure, for the part he played in my predicament. Yet I also remembered moments of great tenderness. His eyes had shone when he gazed at me, and I had felt safe in his arms. I thought that he loved me, even while I understood he needed to marry a person closer to his own station.

I believe that it was Mary who made the abbess aware of my condition. She asked questions about my ever rounder figure, and then I was told to report to the chapter house. I was seized by a foolish impulse to run away, but I set it aside. In any event, I was not sure that I had the energy to do such a thing. A terrible lassitude had entered my body, turning my limbs to lead. Even my heart was invaded by metallic coldness. I imagined myself transfigured piece by piece into a statue of dull gray ore, my heartbeat slowing until it stopped altogether and I remained frozen, a parable for future generations, an eternal warning.

Two nuns were sent to escort me to the chapter house. Like a condemned prisoner flanked by guards, I walked with my head bowed in shame. The first snow of the year had fallen earlier in the day, and a few stray snowflakes still floated down. I marveled at the perfection of a delicate flake that landed on my sleeve. Why had God made nature so perfect and humans so flawed?

One sister entered the building ahead of us, presumably to announce our arrival, and there followed an exodus of nuns and laypeople. My remaining attendant then guided me into the nearly empty chamber. I could not look at the prioress or abbess as I approached. Once I was kneeling before her, Mother Elfilda spoke to me in a cold voice. "Is it true what I have heard about your condition?" Her face was a mask.

I could not speak, but I nodded.

"Speak louder. We cannot hear you."

"Yes, my lady."

"You are aware that fornication is a mortal sin."

"Yes, my lady."

"Did you commit this grievous sin with full knowledge of the gravity of your offense?"

"Yes, my lady." No amount of blinking could prevent my tears; they splashed onto my bodice, leaving ragged blotches on the gray wool.

"Were you coerced into this sin?"

"No, my lady." A loud intake of breath, an aborted sob, escaped my throat and echoed like a thunderclap in the silence.

"Did you commit this sin more than once?"

"Yes, my lady."

"This is a very grave matter. Your soul is not merely weakened, but dead to God. Your bond to God's saving grace has been most monstrously ruptured."

I focused on her white slippers, willing my breath to slow.

"With whom did you commit this sin?"

My gaze snapped to her face, and fear replaced self-pity. I had not thought about what this would mean for Fernan. Mother Elfilda's face remained expressionless.

"Mother . . . I . . . I do not know his name."

A flash of anger contorted her lovely features momentarily. "Do not play games with me! What is his name?"

"My lady." I swallowed hard. "He did not tell me, my lady."

"Nonsense! Is it not enough that your soul is in mortal peril? Must you compound your shame with dishonesty? I shall discover who committed this grotesque sin with or without you. Tell me his name!"

"Fernan, Mother."

"I cannot hear you! Speak louder."

"Fernan, Mother."

"I thought as much." She sighed, then turned to the prioress and spoke irately. "This cannot continue. My abbey cannot be responsible for situating every servant girl he beds and gets with child!" The abbess then lowered her voice, and I could hear no more of what she said.

The prioress waved my dismissal as she bent to catch the words of Mother Elfilda. A gray veil dimmed my eyesight as a nun escorted me out of the chapter house and into the gathering dusk. She left me in the cloister, which was crowded with sisters hurrying to supper. The dusting of snow on the ground was now crisscrossed with lines of dark footprints.

After some time, the cloister emptied, and darkness drew closer. The night was moonless, but stars appeared through rents in the scudding clouds. My dizziness passed, leaving emptiness in its wake. I sat on a snow-covered bench, waiting for tears to blur the stars and set them swimming. The sharp pinpricks of light remained, distant and immovable.

10

OLD HILGATE

Like a prisoner, I was outwardly passive, but my soul could find no peace. I had fooled myself into believing that I was important to Fernan, that he loved me, that his love elevated me beyond what Abbess Elfilda could see: an ignorant, cringing servant, a stain upon the earth. I blamed myself for my situation more than I blamed Fernan. My self-deception had been willful. Even then, as I waited to be cast out of the abbey, I recalled the tenderness in Fernan's voice and touch, not the way he discarded me once his desires were satisfied.

I would be sent back to my village, and Emont would ask the reeve to find a husband for me. Every child was a potential asset for the manor, and if I could not be put to use as a servant, I would be put to use as a breeder. The pregnant daughter of a penniless villein is not a wife any man desires, however. I would be given to someone with no better prospects. Someone poor, probably an old widower who needed a woman to raise his children. I hoped that he would not be cruel or violent.

At least I would see my sister again. Lottie would never turn her back on me. In the past, I had felt sorry for her, but now she would feel sorry for me. Her husband was poor, but he was young and decent. I wished that I had never been sent to the manor, that my father had found a husband for me as he had for Lottie.

I did not want to think about feeding someone else's starving children with the scant, spoiled remains of winter oats, or giving birth to my child on some stranger's dirt floor amidst rodent and chicken droppings. Still, that fate would be better than finding no husband at all.

My purgatory ended when Fernan himself came to Rose House and asked to speak with me. Mary looked as though she might faint. I was taken aback, but days of stewing in dread and remorse had dulled my feelings. When I asked Fernan to follow me to the library, Mary was too astonished to raise an objection. I knew that she would not bother us there.

The white draperies and tapestries were blinding in the sunlight that poured through the arched windows. I adored the library, and I had cleaned it until it was as spotless as a shrine. In all that time, I had never dared to do more than hover near the mysterious leather-bound tomes, inhaling their musty odor. The books now reminded me of the whole world beyond my petty heartache, and that thought made me calm.

Fernan was unshaven and subdued. He seemed smaller than the last time I had seen him, as though he had shrunk, or I had grown. For the first time, I noticed that his thin wrists dangled foolishly from his too-short sleeves, and his face contorted in an unattractive grimace when he was distracted by thought.

"You wish to speak to me?" The coldness in my voice was foreign to me.

"Yes, I . . ." Fernan looked around, disoriented. "Mother Elfilda is displeased, as you might imagine."

"I am aware of Abbess Elfilda's displeasure."

"She has threatened to end her patronage of me if I do not take responsibility for the baby." He winced as though the words caused him physical pain.

After a long pause, I threw my words at him. "You have to marry me?" I meant to hurt him with my sarcasm, but the words hurt me instead.

"I have to take you away from here."

"And leave me?"

"No . . ." He looked miserable. "The last girl, Lizzie . . . They found her a husband. Mother Elfilda refuses to do it again."

At the mention of Lizzie, I felt a surge of disgust. It was doubly humiliating that I had been lured into the same pitfall as the girl before me. "Where do you plan to take me?"

"Old Hilgate. I shall rent you a room at the alehouse."

"What about you?"

Fernan narrowed his eyes. "I am a messenger for the church. My life is on the road. I shall give you the money you need, but do not expect me to keep you company."

I searched his face for some trace of the old Fernan, the man who had teased me, stroked my hair, taught me to dance. This Fernan looked sullen, like a child denied his supper. It struck me that he had always been like a child. He was charming and flirtatious when he wanted something, but frustration made him petulant. He had scooped my heart from my breast to use as his plaything, but now he was tired of it, and he was angry that he could not move on to other entertainments.

"I understand, Fernan. I shall impose on you as little as possible."

He looked relieved. "We leave at noon."

After packing my few belongings, including the green gown that could no longer stretch over my tumescent belly, I left the abbey as I had come, riding pillion behind Fernan on his pretty rounsey. The air was cold but still, the sky a flat, featureless gray that portended snow. I did not look back until we rode through the gate in the outer wall. There, I glanced at the words carved so deeply into the weather-worn stone at the apex of the arch. I could read them now: *Ecce ancilla domini.* Behold the handmaid of the Lord.

Fernan brought me back to the market town, Old Hilgate, and there he rented a room at the alehouse. The building was as grim and filthy as I remembered, and the room above the brewery was draughty and dark. The first night, Fernan slept beside me, his arm around my thick waist. The wind whistled through cracks in the daub, and our blankets were rough and foul smelling. I lay awake long into the night. The warmth of Fernan's body against my back and the soft rumble of his snore made me feel lonelier than I had ever felt before.

In the morning, he was gone. Fernan left a bag of coins next to the bed, and I was grateful for it. Downstairs, I found the alewife sleeping by the fire, and I roused her to ask for a drink. She had grown gaunt since I had last seen her, and her cough was ominously deep, a wet rattle. The woman gazed at me blankly with bloodshot eyes but did not stir. I told her to go back to sleep and helped myself to the bitter ale.

Snow had fallen in the night, and the sky was an empty blue. I ventured out for a walk and found the town to be more pleasant than I remembered, if only because its squalor was tucked neatly under a clean white blanket. Flags of bright blood on the snow advertised the fleshmonger's shop; a gabble of trussed poultry floundered nearby. Chimneys puffed cheerily, and children tromped through fresh snow in the streets, shouting to one another as though every one of them were deaf. It was near Christmastide, and doors were decorated with pine boughs and bright ribbons. Few townsfolk were out, but those who were greeted me civilly. I took a deep breath of the wintry air. I could make a fresh start in Old Hilgate for myself and for my child.

When I returned to the alehouse, a plump, ruddy-faced woman was plying the alewife with a bowl of stew. She paused with the spoon in midair and squinted at me. "Good day to you. Are you the renter Alice was telling me about?" Her gaze swept from my head to my toes.

"Yes, my name is Agnes, Goodwife." The woman was dressed in costly velvet, and I was acutely aware of my rough woolen dress and ratty cloak. At least the cloak hid my swollen belly. I was about to duck my head and curtsy, begging her pardon, when it occurred to me that she knew nothing about me. I stood tall and lifted my chin. "My husband and I just arrived. Forgive my appearance, I have not yet unpacked." I gave her what I hoped was a charming smile.

The alewife turned her head, refusing the spoon. She moaned softly and slumped back into her chair, closing her eyes. The other woman set the bowl down.

"Welcome, then. I am Henny, the blacksmith's wife. I am trying to get Alice here to eat a little dinner. Will you be staying long in Old Hilgate?"

"I am not sure how long." I hesitated. "My husband is a messenger, and we were just married, so we have not yet decided where to settle."

"A hearty congratulations on your marriage, and God bless! From where do you come?"

My heart raced. "Ellis Abbey, most recently. My husband is a ward and agent of Abbess Elfilda."

Her broad face lit up. "Oh, were you a pupil at the abbey, then? That would explain it," she said, presumably referring to my attire. "And you fell for the abbess's ward!" She winked at me. "How wonderful! Who are your parents, dear?"

The woman had unwittingly helped with my deception, but I did not have a ready answer to her new question. I said the first thing that leapt into my mind. "They are Sir Roger Thorpe and Lady Thorpe of West Chillington." These were Mary's parents.

Henny's eyes widened, and her hand flew to the base of her throat. "Oh! So you come from nobility, then!"

I blushed at my poorly chosen falsehood. "Nay, Goodwife, my father is but a baronet, so I am an ordinary commoner." For good measure, I added, "My parents will not acknowledge me now that I have married in secret without their consent. They have cut me off entirely."

"Oh, my poor dear, that is terrible!" She bustled over to where I stood and took my hands, looking at me earnestly with her watery blue eyes. "You are such a dear, modest girl. Look at you blush! If you need anything at all, you just ask me. You are most welcome in Old Hilgate!"

I squirmed and endeavored to direct her attention away from me. "How is the alewife?"

Henny shook her head somberly and dropped my hands. "Alice does badly." She returned to the alewife and stroked her cheek. "You are going to eat the last few bites for me now, aren't you, sweeting? We need to get you stronger."

Alice opened her eyes and mumbled something that I could not hear, and Henny let out a barking laugh. "There is the spirit! We shall have you back on your feet by next week."

Alice was not, in fact, destined to get back on her feet. Henny told me later that Alice had a wasting illness, consumption. The woman's misfortune was compounded by the loss of her business, for the aleconner had barred the sale of Alice's thin, vile-tasting brew. Worse, her only daughter had died the year before from drowning in the river, so she had no family to care for her. Without income from food or ale, poor Alice relied on the charity of her neighbors and the occasional room rental for her living.

Henny brought daily meals for Alice, though she had a large brood of her own to feed. George, her husband, was the only blacksmith for many miles, and he did a brisk trade. They were one of the wealthier families in Old Hilgate, and George was both an alderman and a leading delegate of the parish guild. Both husband and wife were respected in town for their acts of charity. I came to know Henny as a genuinely good and generous person, and it pains me to remember that her knowledge of me was based in a lie.

I used most of the money that Fernan left me to buy three new gowns and a cloak. There was not much to choose from at the weaver's shop, but I found serviceable wool. I instructed the tailor to create long, vertical seams and wide necklines, the sort of cut favored by guests at Rose House. The wool fabric was wrong for that style of dress, but the townsfolk of Old Hilgate knew nothing of the latest fashions. I paid for rabbit-fur trim on the hood of the scarlet cloak, which was an extravagance, but it seemed like the sort of thing a well-bred woman would do. Looking back now, from my place at the royal palace, I know how rustic I appeared, but at the time, I thought the clothes exceedingly fine.

To complete my transformation, I learned to wear my hair like the ladies from the city who visited Lady Wenslock. I folded my plaits on each side of my face and tied them with ribbons, or sometimes I bound them with crespinettes. Of course, unlike the ladies at Rose House, my crespinettes were unadorned by jewels. When I went out, I always wore a plain wimple, as would any respectable married woman.

By the time Fernan returned, I had already been introduced to a number of townsfolk as the newly married, estranged daughter of a baronet.

"My, my," he said, dropping his snow-dusted cloak on the floor of our room. "I hear that you have come up in the world!"

"I did not intend to deceive everyone. It just came out that way."

"Really, now, you just couldn't stop yourself from lying?"

I felt my face grow hot.

"I don't care. It makes things easier for me, actually. Where did you get the gown? It is rather . . . unusual." He put his hands on my shoulders, forcing me to turn in a circle. He flipped the plaited loops of my hair playfully as I spun.

"I had it made. I couldn't afford better fabric."

"*You* couldn't afford? It isn't your money, is it? How much did you spend?"

"Not much. I needed clothing."

"Don't think that you have landed in the lap of luxury. The coins I gave you must last the month. Use them to feed yourself, not to buy fripperies."

I had only a few pence remaining, not enough to get by for weeks longer.

"What do you care about appearances anyway?" he continued. "The only reason the townsfolk believe you is that they are cloddish louts. I could pass off Perla as the king's finest warhorse here. You have aspirations to climb to the lofty heights of Old Hilgate society? I suppose that *is* a grand aspiration for a laundry girl."

I chafed at his harshness, but there was no advantage to provoking him.

"Have you had supper?" I asked.

"Yes, and I am spent." Fernan sat heavily on the bed and flopped back, his arms outstretched. He hadn't bothered to remove his boots, and dirty meltwater dripped from his heels, collecting in brown puddles on the floor.

"I shall bank the fire then and help you to bed."

Fernan lay with his eyes closed while I readied the coals. Flickering tongues of the dying fire illuminated his handsome profile and lent his skin the rich luminosity of polished bronze. Whereas once his appearance would have stirred up a whirling cloud of trembling butterflies in my belly, I couldn't help but notice that his top lip was too thin, the angle of his jaw too soft, his brow too prominent.

After undressing, I brushed my hair with lavender water and loosened my shift so that my swollen breasts swayed and strained against the sheer linen. Fernan did not open his eyes when I removed his boots, but when I pulled at his breeches, he propped himself up on his elbows. In the dim light, I thought that I detected hunger in the gleam of his eyes, and when he reached for my face and pulled me toward him, I knew for certain.

His desire ignited my own lust briefly; the response of his body to my touch was affecting, and his gaze told me that he wanted me. Still, his rough hands hurt my breasts, tender with ripening milk, and when he closed his eyes, he receded from me like the sun slipping below the horizon. It was not long before he gasped in a helpless spasm and lay heavily over me, panting, his breath hot against my skin. I pushed him away before he fell asleep. He left me slick with his sweat; I shivered and pulled the blanket to my chin.

When Fernan left again the next morning, there was a new bag of coins by the bedside.

After I whitewashed the walls of our chamber and bought a trunk to store our few belongings, I had little to keep me occupied. At first, I was elated. I had not often been bone-weary at Rose House, but my time had not been my own. Like the stones in the church walls, the sheep that gave wool, and every blade of grass under-foot, I had been the property of the abbey. To wake in Old Hilgate with no master, no duties, to be entirely unaccounted for—it was a miracle.

The joy of idleness wore thin after a few lonely weeks. I spent some time with Alice, helping her to bathe, emptying her bedpan, laundering her linens. The woman's caustic humor and lack of self-pity appealed to me, but she hadn't the strength for company. I couldn't even interest her in my cooking, which was understand-able, since my pottage was barely edible, and Henny brought such delicious food.

Restless one day, I decided to visit Henny at her home, a half-timbered house remarkable for its large size and costly tiled roof. She greeted me at the door with a child on her ample hip and a sword in her other hand.

"Oh, Agnes, come in!" Henny said. She had to raise her voice to be heard over shrieking children and clanging from her husband's smithy, which was located directly behind the house. A wave of heat spilled from the doorway into the wintry air.

I must have looked startled by the sword, because Henny held the blade out for me to inspect the decorative work and said, "I do the etching for George. Isn't this coming along nicely? This is meant to be a vine of roses here, around the feet of the lion. Come in, come in!"

Shyly, I stomped the snow from my boots and stepped inside. Fires crackled in two hearths at opposite ends of the expansive hall. The warmth was welcome after a frigid morning above the alehouse. Alice's fires often died, and I did not want to spend money to keep one lit in my chamber.

"We are always in the midst of shambles," Henny said. "It must seem like a sty, but our humble home welcomes you. Here, sit!" She dropped the sword on a table with a clatter and patted the bench. It had apparently been her workstation before I arrived, for there were bowls of acrid liquids, rags, brushes, sharpened sticks, and globs of half-melted wax crowding the table's surface.

"Take off your cloak," Henny said. "You may leave it anywhere."

The tot on Henny's hip patted and poked at her mother's large breast.

"You had your milk for today," Henny said, though the child was too young to understand. "It's time you learned to eat meat!" To me, she said, "I'm too old for babies. Thought little Tom was the last, then this one came along. But you are the sweetest faunt-kin, aren't you, lovey?" Henny kissed the girl's plump cheek and sat beside me with a sigh. "You look like you've got one on the way. Say good-bye to that pretty figure. This is what a dozen childbirths will do to you." She pointed at her broad waist. "Have you had dinner? Stay, and I shall feed you with this horde of savages."

"You are too kind," I said. "You have enough mouths to feed."

"So one more makes no difference. Besides, you should enjoy Bessie's cooking. She's my eldest. Deaf and dumb, but cleverness in the kitchen will get her a husband someday, I don't doubt. Her black pudding is the best you will ever have. She is such a good girl. Marion, have you met her? From the house on the corner? Her daughter is Bessie's age and gives her no end of grief. Lazy as an old sow. An old sow in heat. She goes snuffling after boys when she should be minding the shop."

"It seems that everyone in town has a shop."

"A body has to make money. I suppose you have a dowry and your husband's income." She lifted a reddened, chapped hand and examined her broken nails. "I wish I could be a noble lady, just for a day."

I folded my own hands in my lap so as not to draw attention to them.

Three little children dashed into the hall and chased one another around the table, yelling and laughing.

"Quiet!" Henny shouted. "Charlie, I will box your ears if you knock over my supplies!"

They continued to yelp but ran away again. Henny sighed. "Savages, truly."

"Do you have a stall on market day?" I asked.

"No, dove, my Georgie works on commissions," Henny said proudly. "I miss shop work sometimes. My father was a fishmonger, and I liked seeing customers. Father said a blatherskite like me was bad for business; I kept people chatting too long. I have always had a mouth on me. You seem like the quiet sort, dignified. Sometimes I wish I were like that too, but you can't change how God made you."

"Perhaps I should open a shop." A thrill ran through me as I said the words. The idea of making my own money was intoxicating.

"It's not easy work, child," Henny said doubtfully. "And there isn't much a lass can do. Become an alewife like Alice, that's about the only choice. Mind you, we miss having a real brew house in town. There's old Hal's place, but he just brews on the side, and he charges a king's ransom for the stuff. I'd rather make my own. Or rather, Bessie and Meg make our own. Such good girls." Henny absentmindedly shifted the whining baby to her lap and bounced her. "There was a young widow, years ago, who made a delicious brew. Alice, bless her heart, never came close to as good. She always charged a fair price though. Alice may speak sharply, but she is virtuous, and under her rough ways is a heart of pure gold. The widow I told you about, well, she was a pretty one, and the men nursed their ale all night and mooned after her. Now that I think of it, you look something like her, though you are much taller, and your hair is more of a mousy color. She ran away with a carpenter from the city. It was quite a scandal, for they said he had another wife. You should have heard the gossip! The wives here were happy enough to say Godspeed to that little vixen. Though I don't know. Wasn't her fault she was so pretty."

I let the subject fall, but the thought of making money consumed me after our conversation. Brewing could give me freedom.

When Fernan returned, I presented my plan casually while I bathed his feet. "How would it be," I asked, "if I earned a few shillings while you travel?"

Fernan's leg jumped involuntarily as I scrubbed a sensitive spot on the sole of his foot. He liked me to scour his callouses, but he was ticklish.

"What?" he said disinterestedly.

"I thought that perhaps I could convince Alice to let me revive the idle brewery and regain the license to sell ale."

"Mmm." He closed his eyes, and after a pause he murmured, "Brewing is bad business. Prices are fixed by the king. When the cost of ingredients gets too high, brewers lose money."

"Alice made it work."

"Barely, by the look of things."

"I wish to give it a go."

"Hire yourself out. That would be secure income."

"My labor would pay mere pennies. If I had my own shop, I could make this a real home for us."

Fernan snatched his foot from my hands impatiently and sat up. "If Alice wants to put you to work, that's fine with me. Just don't expect me to subsidize your little adventure."

I remained kneeling, expecting him to return his foot to the basin, but instead he looked at me in silence for a moment and then grabbed the hair at the back of my head. With a firm hand, he dragged my face close to his. "Don't look at me like such a worried rabbit," he said with a smile. He bent closer and kissed me. Even as I felt smothered by his wet, demanding mouth, his familiar scent drew me in. I was not sure that I wished to be free of him.

Alice was easily convinced to let me try to reclaim a license to sell ale. Her life had become a trial, and she relied on the aid of friends and neighbors to get through each day. A tenant who could keep a roof over her head was welcome. "The work is unpleasant, unblessed, and unprofitable," she told me, "but I am exceedingly glad to have you pay the rent, lass." There was fondness in her voice if not in her words.

The difficult part of my scheme was learning how to brew. Even with instructions from the alewife, it took me some time to make a passable batch of ale. The malted grains left in the brewery had gone to rot, and she did not have a kiln, so I was forced to buy expensive barley that had been malted at Cothay Manor. Fernan would be angry, but I planned to make the money back. I could not rebuild Alice's business without spending some money first.

When I tried the hand quern, it took me a whole day to grind enough grain for one batch, and then Alice told me that I had damaged the husks too severely, so I had to begin again. The mashing, however, was the hardest part. Knowing how much scalding water to add to the mash and how long to continue mashing is something that can only come from experience. The first four batches I made tasted nothing like ale, and the fifth was oversweet. By the sixth batch, however, I had a decent drink.

Through my trials and failures, I began to understand why Alice's brew had been so unpalatable. The ingredients for ale were not cheap, and her equipment limited her production to small batches. Since the royal assize set the price for ale so low, Alice chose to cut corners in order to increase her profit. She added oats to the barley, and she saved fuel by not boiling and skimming her wort. Then she added extra water to the grain, making three or four infusions, which she mixed together to produce a dilute ale that soured quickly.

I decided that a new approach was needed. After the aleconner declared my drink to be fit for sale, I swept and scrubbed the alehouse, cleared out the filthy rushes, polished the flagons until they shone. I replaced the alestake and made merry garlands of holly to decorate it. I had already spent most of Fernan's money on barley, so I decided that there was little additional harm in spending my last shillings to buy a large stack of firewood from the woodmonger and replace the rank tallow with fine beeswax candles. The plaster on the walls was still blackened and grimy, and the window could not be opened in winter because it lacked glazing, but the room was nonetheless transformed. The sight even coaxed a faint smile from Alice. "You have worked a small miracle here," she said. "A pig would no longer feel at home!" Speaking brought on another paroxysm of coughing, and she spat dark blood onto her sleeve.

Despite her weakness, Alice wanted to be in the thick of things as the alehouse reopened, so I bundled her in blankets and sat her by the fire. She had lost so much weight that I could lift the tiny woman as easily as I could lift a child. As time passed, I grew large and rosy with new life, while Alice dwindled. Sores appeared in those places where her sallow, sagging skin was an insufficient cover for the sharp bones beneath. Her breath smelled of rot. I did my best to make her comfortable, but I could see that she suffered.

On the first day that the alehouse opened anew for business, I made only two sales, and I began to panic. The next morning, I brought gourds of ale and cups to nearby shops and offered free drinks to anyone who would try. Most of the townsfolk had tasted Alice's ale previously, and they said kind things about the quality of my brew. I also visited the homes of townspeople I knew, including Henny, and I invited them for a free drink that evening. I could not afford my generosity, but I had to do something to bring in customers.

That night, the alehouse was full to overflowing, and everyone seemed to be in the mood for a wassail. The crowd was raucous; men joked and guffawed loudly, and spirited songs broke out within and without the building, as some revelers even sat in the snow to drink their free ale. At one point, someone stumbled or was pushed into a table, and all of the flagons landed on the floor with a mighty crash, provoking uproarious laughter. Alice sat serenely by the hearth in the midst of the tumult, her eyes closed, a slight smile on her lips. The fire and the warmth of many bodies made the room so hot that I felt faint; I welcomed the blasts of cold air that swept in every time the door was opened.

Henny and George arrived toward the end of the evening. They knew all of the townspeople, and they made a point of greeting each and every one of them heartily, infusing the room with even greater cheer.

"We always liked to come here when poor Alice was brewing," Henny told me, "though I confess we liked the kidney pies better than the ale." She wrinkled her nose. "Look at this crowd! It is so nice that you have brought good ale to Old Hilgate. We will stop brewing our own now! It must be hard for you, raised as you were, to do the work of an alewife. It is good, honest work, and I greatly admire you for not being above it. It does nobody credit to be all high and mighty. Christ Himself associated with the lowliest of people. I met Mylla Ainsley on the way, and she said that you should quit your husband and go home if he is so poor and your parents are so rich. I told her she knows nothing of young love! Not to mention Christian humility. Where is that husband of yours?"

I escaped Henny's patter to check my stores in the brewery. Only a few gallons remained. Though I had started to charge customers after their first drink, the income was not enough to buy all of the new brewing supplies I would require. I shuddered, realizing that I would have to ask Fernan for more money.

As though he had been conjured by my thoughts, Fernan was at the door when I exited the brewery with the last of my ale. He looked around the crowded room, startled. I grabbed a flagon and threaded my way to him.

"Would you care for a drink?" I did my best to smile flirtatiously.

"What is this?"

"An alehouse."

"Yes. I know."

"We spoke about this. I got the license. I thought you would be pleased to see me earn a few shillings."

A slow smile spread across his face. "Really? Is that so?" He tipped the flagon as though examining the contents. "Let me taste your wares, then." He drained the flagon in one long draught. "Not bad! Not bad at all. A refill!" He handed me the empty flagon and pushed even closer to me than was necessary in the crowded room. "You look lovely tonight. A little plumpness suits you." He patted my round belly.

I hurried to fetch more ale. When I turned away other requests, explaining that the stock had been drained, the alehouse began to empty. I kept Fernan's cup full, however. Henny was kind enough to put Alice to bed, and George clapped Fernan on the back before leaving, declaring Fernan to be a right lucky fellow.

There was much cleaning to be done, but I left it for morning so that I could go with Fernan to bed. I brought up one of the new beeswax candles and helped Fernan to undress. He sighed as I stroked his back. "How much money do you expect to make from your new enterprise?" he asked.

"If I sell my regular ale at two pence per gallon and spiced ale at three, I could make two or three shillings each day easily. It costs twelve pence for a bushel of malted barley, but I can malt my own come summer. After I pay for firewood and sundries, I could earn more than a crown each week." I was making most of this up, because I did not know how much I would sell each day, nor whether I could continue to get away with charging more than the one and a half pence for ale allowed by law.

Fernan whistled between his teeth. "That is a tidy sum. How much did you make tonight?"

I would have to ask for more money eventually, and he was in a good mood. I decided to seize an opportune moment. "I had to give drink away in order to get word out about the alehouse. I need to brew even faster, and I am almost out of barley. I shall need another couple of shillings, but I promise that this will be the last time."

The words had hardly left my lips when his fist slammed into the side of my head. The floor tilted ominously. I had not regained my balance when he hit me again, and I fell to the floor. There was a loud ringing in my ear, and though he shouted something at me, I could not make out the words. I crawled to the door, and he did not try to stop me.

I spent the night by the hearth in the alehouse. At dawn, the clomp of Fernan's boots on the stairs woke me. He was dressed in his cloak, and he carried his satchel. I feigned sleep, so when his footsteps stopped near me, I do not know whether he looked down at me or merely paused to adjust the strap of his satchel. After I heard the door slam, I rose and began the long task of cleaning up from the night before.

I managed to borrow enough money from Henny to get me through the next week, and after that, I did not have to ask for money again. I created new spiced ales, using combinations of juniper, apples, laurel, cinnamon, and lavender, and these were enormously popular. Increasingly, townspeople bought their home supplies from me rather than brewing ale themselves, and I had trouble keeping up with demand. I hired a girl to help with cleaning and serving so that I could devote all of my time to brewing. I knew that soon I would have to find ways to increase my production. I would also have to think about what would happen when Alice died. I could not afford to buy the alehouse from her, and as Alice had no living kin, Ellis Abbey would repossess the alehouse, and I would be without a home or source of income.

The next time Fernan came home, he acted as though nothing had happened between us. He had, after all, merely disciplined his wife. He did leave me an allowance when he departed, so perhaps he meant to make amends, but I did not want his offering of peace. I bided my time, and when I had saved enough money, I filled two bags with coins and placed these, along with the unopened sac he had given me, on a trencher meant for his supper. The alehouse was busy that evening, and some eyebrows rose when I placed a plate full of money in front of my husband. Fernan said nothing about it, but he never offered me another penny of allowance.

MOTHERHOOD

As weeks passed, I became increasingly aware of the babe that grew inside me. When I lay still, I felt a queer fluttering, as though a creature covered in softest eiderdown were circling, trying to settle itself for sleep in my belly. In those quiet moments, joy would thrill in little waves from my heart to my fingertips, sweeping away foreboding about the birth. A restless excitement grew in me too. For the first time in my life, it seemed that something important would belong to me.

Fernan spent more time at the alehouse as the baby's time drew near; he seemed intrigued about the idea of becoming a father. I had not forgiven him, but I decided that it would be better for me to keep him close than to push him away. I fed him, washed his feet, encouraged his self-pride, and made myself available and receptive to him in the night. He began to tease me sometimes as he used to do, and he joked about how strong our son would be—for he was sure the child was a boy—given the mighty kicks he could feel when he rested his hand on my belly.

Despite his more frequent visits, Fernan was away the evening my lying-in began. When the cramping started, I wondered if I had eaten something gone foul, but at the iron-fisted grip of the first real pain, I knew to send the neighbor to fetch the midwife.

The midwife arrived at dusk to find me crouched in a corner, gasping with each new paroxysm of pain. She was a frail woman with a stooped back and chilblains on her crooked fingers, and I wondered if she was fit for the task. She got me into bed, gave me vinegar and sugar to drink, and opened the window to let in the frigid air. I was grateful for the cold, as it took my mind away from the pain. When I lay back in bed, I felt a warm gush of fluid on my legs and cried out with fear. The old woman clucked and brought some rags.

"This is good, very good. Now that the water has broken, things will go quickly."

"How quickly?" I squeezed my eyes shut as another wave of pain flowed over me.

"Who is to say, dear girl? It is up to Saint Margaret. Before sunrise, I am sure. Let us say a prayer to Saint Margaret now."

She placed an amulet on my belly and began to murmur and chant. I closed my eyes between the pains. When she finished her prayers, she rubbed my flanks with strongly scented rose oil. My throat constricted as the image of the rose garden at the abbey floated unbidden to my mind, but a fresh wave of cramping overpowered the remembrance.

The midwife's granddaughter arrived near the middle of the night and started a fire to heat some water. The midwife napped in a chair as her granddaughter took over the vigil. She was a pretty girl, younger than me, but obviously used to attending at births. She tried to get me to drink more vinegar with sugar, but I could not. I felt as though a beast had clamped its jaws around my middle and was shaking me, trying to tear me in two. Just when I thought I could bear it no longer, the girl called to her grandmother. The old woman sprang up surprisingly swiftly.

"Is the babe come to meet us finally?"

The girl pointed to what must have been the evidence between my legs.

"Bring more rags, and warm the water. Good, good. I can see the head. Your babe is behaved. Coming out just right. It will be over soon, and you can rest."

There was a slither and another rush of fluid, and then the midwife held a slimy, dark creature in her hands. She deftly flipped it over her forearm and swept her finger in its mouth. A loud wail ensued, and the midwife heaved a sigh of pleasure. "You have a big, healthy baby girl, dearheart. Thank Saint Catherine. She is a dark one, but babies lighten up. I bet this one will turn out as fair as my Maggie here."

The midwife severed the cord, and then she helped her granddaughter to wash and swaddle the baby snugly in strips of linen. She set the cocooned bundle on my chest and busied herself between my trembling legs with a new mess of sticky afterbirth.

The babe's eyes were shut behind swollen lids, and her black hair was matted to the top of her skull, where her skin fluttered and pulsed. She seemed alien, a pupa that had pushed her way out of her casing. I lifted her so that I could see her face better and found that my arms were shaking too. Though her skin was flush with blood, I could tell that her complexion was nut brown, like Fernan's. Her lips were a delicate bow, tiny and perfect. I traced her mouth with my finger, and she opened her eyes, little slits filled with the softest glisten of black, a gaze that was placid, wise, distant. She stared at me as though she could see through me, or as though she knew me entirely. I could scarcely believe that this strange creature belonged to me.

"There now, mostly clean. Give your bantling aught to drink. We are going to get some sleep, but Maggie will come back at sunrise. Here is a pitcher of ale and a bowl of fresh water. Maggie, dearheart, close the window and bank the fire."

"I have already finished with the fire, Grandmother!" Maggie pulled the shutters closed, and they departed.

I had seen women feeding their babies in the village, but I felt awkward and uncertain. I pulled up my shift and held it bunched around my armpits, exposing my breasts to the cold air, and I brought the baby's face toward one of my puckered nipples. Immediately she parted her lips and clamped her warm velvet mouth on my breast. Her dark cheek pressed into my pale goose-flesh; she sucked with controlled urgency, as though drinking were the only thing in life that mattered, and she was the master of this important task. It was a marvel that she knew exactly what to do. I was not expecting the shock of pleasure, nor the wonder I felt then. After some time, her rhythm slowed, and the grip of her mouth loosened. Her lips made a soft smacking sound as she released, and all of the tension left her little body. Her head lolled back as sleep overcame her.

As I watched her drowse, tears filled my eyes. I was seized with the fear that she would die, that I would lose her. Angels are not meant to dwell in the world of men. I was never meant to have anything so good.

Through the night, the baby woke me with her cries, and each time I pulled her close, I felt a queer sorrowful joy. She was a piece of me that had broken free to become her own person, a stranger. We did not know each other, and yet in the instant I first beheld her, she became everything to me. As long as we both lived, I would never truly be alone again.

When Maggie came again the next morning, she was as cheerful and energetic as she had been the night before. She brought with her a cradle that she had borrowed from the Dryver family; it had been well used by their six babies, but Sara Dryver was not expecting another soon. Maggie fed me bread and milk, and I felt well enough to get up. I was tired and sore, but much of my strength had already returned.

Fortunately, I remained healthy, and I went back to brewing and cooking. Though new motherhood prevented me from sleeping well at night, my heart and my step were light. I swaddled the baby and carried her everywhere with me. When I had to serve drinks in the alehouse, she stayed in her cradle by the hearth. Customers took turns picking her up when she fussed, even a few of the men. Some commented on her dark complexion, but most just cooed and smiled.

I looked up every time the door let in a gust of cold air, hoping that Fernan had returned and we could have the baby christened. When he finally did arrive, he was in a foul mood, for he had heard from one of the townspeople that the baby was a girl. It was evening, and the alehouse was crowded. In winter, there was little to do after the sun set, and the men liked to gather together by the fire and drink spiced ale. Fernan took off his cloak and found a spot on one of the benches nearest the door. I brought him a tankard, and the fleshmonger sitting next to him made a joke about new parents.

Fernan just scowled and swallowed a long draught. He thumped the tankard on the board and did not meet my eye.

Later that night, I brought the baby to him and placed her in his arms. Fernan did not smile, but his expression softened. He put his smallest finger in her mouth, and she sucked eagerly for a moment before she realized that there was no milk to be had. She cried and waved her arms in wide, uncoordinated jerks until her tiny paw found Fernan's finger, and then she settled again.

"We have to choose godparents and have her christened."

Fernan shrugged irritably. "You choose."

"I want my sister to be the godmother."

"Don't be stupid. A peasant sister would ruin your story. Anyway, I shan't travel half a day for a christening. You should ask Henny and George to be godparents."

I knew that he was right. It was impossible for my sister to be the godmother. Even if it were not for the fiction I had created about my life, it would have been an unwise choice, because Lottie had nothing to offer our daughter, whereas Henny and George had wealth and influence in Old Hilgate. I longed for my sister though. The bonds that had closed around my heart when I left the abbey had sprung open again at the birth of my daughter, and I felt the ache of Lottie's absence as though for the first time.

"We can make George and Henny godparents, but I want to name her after my sister, not after Henny."

Fernan sighed loudly. "Henny will be offended, but do what you want. It is on your head."

I lied to Henny, telling her that my sister had died years before, and that I wanted to name my child in honor of the only family member who had ever truly cared for me. Henny, God bless her, was a sentimental creature. She looked as though she were going to weep over my long dead sister. George grumbled about the irregularity, but Henny told him to mind his own business. Her large extended family lived in Old Hilgate or the immediate environs, and she pitied me for my isolation. The least she could do was to not make a fuss about her goddaughter being named for my dear departed sister.

A dozen parishioners joined us at the church door for the christening. They gathered in the thin midwinter sunlight, stomping their feet and flapping their arms to keep warm. It was a bitterly cold day, and the priest's words hovered in a fog above his head as he muttered his blessing through frozen lips. Father Michael placed salt in the baby's mouth, provoking an indignant howl. George and Henny quickly recited the paternoster and credo, while the priest snuffled and wiped his red nose on the edge of his stole.

We were relieved to proceed to the baptismal font; it was no warmer inside, but at least we were sheltered from the wind. Henny undressed the wailing infant and handed her to Father Michael. Watching my naked child tremble and shriek with panicked incomprehension caused my hands to shake; I willed them to be still. The priest plunged her into icy water for one brief, cruel moment, and then it was mercifully over. Henny wrapped the newly baptised Charlotte in a white gown and delivered her to my waiting arms.

We threw a party for the christening at the alehouse, but Fernan did not even stay until the celebration ended. He said that he had to return to the abbey before sunrise, but I suspected that he wanted to avoid another night of broken sleep. After everyone left,

I banked the fire and took the exhausted Charlotte to bed with me, tucking her little body into the crook of my arm and covering her with warm blankets. Charlotte was my family now.

Alice died quietly one night during Pentecost, and most of the townsfolk attended her funeral. Despite her sharp tongue and bad ale, Alice had been well liked. She had always been willing to help a neighbor in need, and she had provided free food to those who could not pay. I too had developed an affection for Alice, but during her funeral Mass, I was preoccupied by my own fears.

I looked around the church and reflected that I now recognized most of the parishioners. Children shifted from foot to foot, their faces masks of boredom. Some of the girls wore bright ribbons and daisy chains. It had been a long winter, and everyone was grateful for spring.

I rested Charlotte against the swell of my belly, an early sign of the new baby already on its way. It was too soon. My Charlotte would just be learning to walk when this second one arrived. I wondered how many children my sister had, and how they fared. Then I began to worry again about how I was going to manage with Alice gone.

I had to appeal to Fernan for help. I was not sure that he could afford to buy the alehouse back from Ellis Abbey, and even if he could, how would I convince him to do so? He was miserly, and he would think only of the risk of losing money. My roaming gaze slid past the altar and paused on the back of George's balding pate, which dipped slowly forward and then jerked upright as he struggled to stay awake through Mass. His family took up the whole front pew; Henny hissed like a mother goose at their wiggling, whispering children. George was a businessman. I decided to approach him for advice when church let out.

George set a time to visit me the next morning, but he surprised me by arriving earlier than planned. I was just finishing Charlotte's feeding, and I hastily laced my gown. He did not apologize. Instead, he took a seat atop a table and planted his dirty boots on the bench in a wide stance. George was a short, thickset man, but he took up as much room as a man twice his size.

"So, you want to buy Alice's alehouse?"

I lowered the sleeping Charlotte into her cradle. "Yes. I need to convince Fernan that it would be a sound investment. Business is good, and I am making nearly a pound each month after expenses. What do you think it would cost to buy this building?"

George looked around, frowning. "The alehouse is in poor condition. It needs work. The steward could probably be talked into selling it for twenty pounds."

"If I am careful with my money, I could pay that back in three years."

"I can offer you the money at an interest rate of fifteen percent."

I had not expected this. "Usury is against the law."

George laughed. "Nobody gets arrested for loaning money. Anyway, it would be between you and me. Nobody else need know. And if you cannot make a payment on time, you can find other ways to compensate me. It must get lonely with your husband away so much of the time." He jerked his hips forward suggestively, and his potbelly jiggled. Then he smiled down at me as though he had made a funny joke.

I felt a wave of nausea, then anger. I had not expected this from

George either. "I shall consider your generous offer of fifteen percent interest," I replied evenly. I looked him in the eye, unsmiling.

George pouted about my coldness, but he made no further
advances. After he departed, I scrubbed away the muddy footprints that he had left on the bench and floor.

Despite the unpleasantness, George had been helpful. I had an
estimate for the price of the alehouse, and he had given me the
idea of offering to pay Fernan back with interest. When I made my
proposal to Fernan, he did not blink at the price of twenty pounds.
I realized then that I had underestimated both his wealth and his
desire to be free of me.

In the end, Fernan managed to negotiate a price of fifteen
pounds for the alehouse with the abbey's steward, and I was elated.
Though I knew that Fernan had helped me with his own best interest in mind, I felt a new warmth for him. He had negotiated
skillfully, and he had taken on the encumbrance of purchasing the
alehouse without complaint. He was not a toad, like George, and
he had remained faithful to his promise to Abbess Elfilda to support me. He did not love me, and I did not love him, but after Fernan purchased the alehouse, I found the burden of being a good
wife less onerous.

In spring and summer, my ale sold more quickly than ever because of frequent market days, but regular evenings were slow.
Long hours of sunlight kept people at work, and cold did not chase
them indoors at the end of the day. When it was quiet, I liked to
open the window upstairs and lie in bed with Charlotte, watching
the colors of the sky change with the sunset. The night winds that
sent inky clouds scudding across the square of pink sky framed
by our casement also breathed delicious cool air into our chamber, waking orange tongues of flame in the fireplace, billowing the

makeshift bed curtains I had hung from one of the ceiling's rough wooden beams. The breeze flowed over our bare skin with a caress that was both voluptuous and pure. Sometimes Charlotte nursed lazily, twining her little fingers in my hair, pulling soft strands against her cheek and holding them there with surprising force. Other times I rocked her in my lap, singing to her. She would look at me with a serious expression, a tiny furrow in her brow, as though she were trying to understand the words of the lullaby. Some nights, she cried inconsolably, though I never knew the reason. When that happened, I walked with her, bouncing, telling her stories she could not understand. Charlotte's wailing would fade to mewling and then snuffling, and if I nuzzled and kissed her smooth skin, she would smile. After she fell asleep, I watched the rapid rise and fall of her tiny chest and drank in her sweet milk scent, wishing that I could see inside her dreams.

Fernan warmed to Charlotte as she grew. Along with his coloring, she inherited his bright smile and liveliness, though not his gregariousness; as a baby, just as now, Charlotte was cautious with strangers. I think that Fernan saw his own reflection in his daughter's face, and that made him happy.

Just before Matilda was born, Charlotte learned to totter around on her sturdy legs, and Fernan liked to chase her with a feather or fuzzy blade of golden sedge, tickling the back of her neck until she laughed with delight. When she lurched too close to fires and hot cauldrons, he snatched her back, but one afternoon he was too slow, and she knocked into a boiling kettle that I had left on the hearth. She burned her arm, and her neck was scalded by water that sloshed from the spout. She still has a rose-colored scar that snakes from the base of her throat to the edge of her jaw, which is why she wears only high-collared gowns.

Charlotte's shrieks reverberated through the kitchen; Fernan scooped her up in his arms and plunged her into an open barrel of ale to cool her skin, but her agonized cries did not abate. I dashed across the room more swiftly than I would have thought possible in my ponderous state, and when I reached out to help him hold the thrashing child, I felt Fernan trembling.

We wrapped Charlotte in soft cloth, and Fernan paced in circles, cradling the whimpering baby, a look of anguish on his face. When she finally settled, I sat beside Fernan and leaned my head against his shoulder. He laced his fingers through mine, and I whispered a prayer as we watched our injured daughter drift into a fitful sleep.

It is said that mothers' remembrances are all about the firstborn, and that is true for me. My memory of Matilda's infancy is a warm-hearted haze punctuated by fleeting images: her downy head nestled against my neck, her clinging to my chest, naked and froglike, in the last warm days of early autumn, her snuffly breathing when she nursed. Matilda was a sweet, quiet baby who never demanded much.

Fernan was unhappy that I bore another girl, and he hated to be kept awake by crying, so he stayed away from Old Hilgate for increasingly long stretches of time after Matilda's birth. I do not doubt that he kept another woman, or women. When he was home, Fernan was mostly cheerful. I paid my debt to him regularly, with interest, and I made him comfortable at the alehouse. He sometimes cuffed the children, but he did not hit me again. I was grateful that Fernan mostly left us alone, and I prayed that I would not become pregnant again for some time.

We chose Matilda's godparents well. John and Matilda Lothrop ran the town's mill, and after they became her godparents, they crushed my malted barley at no expense. John adjusted the grinding plates to just the right distance apart, so that he did not turn my grain to flour. I gave them free ale in return, but the better end of the bargain was mine, as they saved me many hours of hard work with the hand quern.

It took me two years to repay Fernan, and then I had a third story built on the alehouse, replaced the old daub, plastered the walls, and added glazed windows. The building became one of the finest in town. Old Hilgate was not a great center of commerce, but it had its own bourgeoisie, and I was welcomed into their ranks. I solidified my social position by offering help to merchants with simple reading or writing; I even sometimes helped with accounting. They thought that I had received a rarefied education at the abbey, but in truth, I had only a small amount of knowledge; it was just that their knowledge was even less than mine.

Once Matilda learned to walk and talk, the girls became thick as thieves. Charlotte was practical and inventive, whereas Matilda was both soulful and fierce. Between the two of them, they concocted elaborate schemes, such as the time they created dyes from berries, flowers, and mud, and they used them to paint pictures on the outside wall of the alehouse. They looked nothing like sisters, as Matilda was fairer, with a tawny complexion, hazel eyes, and auburn hair, whereas Charlotte had her father's brown skin, big dark eyes, and a mass of glossy black curls that sprang out from the tight plaits I wound around her head. Yet the two were always together, like peas in a pod, arms circling each other's waist, whispering little-girl secrets in each other's ears.

At the end of each day, Charlotte and Matilda tumbled like puppies into bed with me and demanded a story. I have never possessed much imagination, but I made up stories as best I could. They only liked happy endings, and their favorites involved castles. I talked or sang to them until they fell asleep, their small limbs draped over me. Even at the time, I knew that those were the happiest years of my life.

12

MISFORTUNE

Although the four years following Matilda's birth were golden, they were not perfect. There always seemed to be some problem with the brewery; rodents eating the grain, the ale spoiling too soon, the abbey's sergeant imposing unreasonable fines. What made me most unhappy during that period, however, was watching Charlotte awaken to the fact that she was ill-favored.

It is said that beauty is in the eye of the beholder, and while I believe that to be true, it cannot be denied that society has strong opinions about what is beautiful and what is not. My Charlotte was unacceptably dark skinned. It did not matter that she was strong and lithe, or that her shining brown eyes were large and soft as a doe's. It did not matter that she had inherited her father's dazzling smile. To other children—and to many adults—she was ugly, and to them, her outward appearance reflected darkness in her soul.

In her sixth year, at midsummer, Charlotte was attacked. The Saint John's Day celebration was just getting under way in a meadow outside of town. It was a hot day, and I was helping to move a food table into the shade of a tall oak when little Matilda came pelting over the riverbank at a furious pace. She grabbed my wrist and pulled me away with all of her strength, sobbing. I could not understand what she was trying to tell me, but she pointed toward the river, and I ran in that direction, terrified.

When I crested the riverbank, I saw that a half dozen girls had surrounded Charlotte, shouting names like "witch," "blackie," and "devil's daughter." Their voices were shrill and edged with spite. I recognized three of them as Mylla Ainsley's children, our near neighbors. Charlotte's gown was torn and covered in mud; she had fallen or been pushed to the ground several times. Blood trickled from a gash in her forehead and another on her arm. The girls picked up stones from the bank and launched them forcefully at Charlotte, pushing her farther and farther into the river. Charlotte, wild-eyed, struggled to keep her footing in the rushing water while raising her hands to deflect the stones.

Fury swept me down the bank with such speed that I might have been flying. With strength fueled by rage, I seized the nearest girl by her shoulders, lifting her high into the air. She seemed to weigh nothing at all. I shook her much harder than I intended, and her head wobbled and snapped back and forth as though she were a dead rabbit in the jaws of a dog. The other girls stood frozen, staring. I wanted to throw the evil child into the river, but I released her instead and let her fall to the ground. Charlotte whimpered and waded unsteadily toward me through the current. I scooped her from the water and held her tight, murmuring soothing words, wiping the blood from her brow until she quieted. By the time I looked again, the girls had fled.

Charlotte was afraid to go outside after that. The Ainsley brood lived in our row; there were seven or eight of them, and they roamed like savages. John Ainsley was a master carpenter, and though he provided well for his family, he traveled for work, leaving his wife, Mylla, alone to manage their children. Mylla was a pious and opinionated woman who could not keep her own home in order, but she always had time to pry into the affairs of other people.

I called on Mylla to let her know what had happened and to enlist her help in making sure that it never happened again. She came to the door wearing a prim gown with an unfashionably high collar. Her face was still lovely, but there were deep creases between her brows, made permanent by age. Her graying hair was pulled back severely and covered by a veil, though her bare feet indicated that she had no immediate plan to leave the house.

"Yes?" She eyed me suspiciously.

"Good morning to you, Goodwife. I have come to tell you about something that involves your girls and my Charlotte."

"The darkie?"

I flushed. "So your daughters called her. They threw stones at her and tried to push her into the river. She could have drowned."

"My girls would know when to stop. They would never have let her drown."

I bit my lip, trying to keep my temper in check. "Stopping just shy of murder is not a demonstration of Christian charity. Your girls were not only calling names, they were throwing stones. Charlotte was terrified."

Mylla glared at me. Her eyes were green and gold, beautiful, but filled with hostility. "True Christians are not just fair of face but fair of spirit. I was not there to see what happened, but I know my girls would never hurt any good Christian girl who was minding her own business."

"Well, I was there, and I am telling you that your children attacked my Charlotte."

"That seems unlikely to me."

"I saw it with my own eyes!"

Mylla shrugged her angular shoulders. "I don't know anything about it."

I stood helpless before her, trembling with fury. Mylla's lips twisted in a smug smile. I yearned to remove the smile with a sharp slap across her face. Instead, I did the only thing I could, which was to bid her good-bye and walk away.

After Saint John's Day, Charlotte clung to my skirts, refusing to go out. I had hoped to tell her that the Ainsley children would leave her alone, but I could not even offer that assurance. I tried to convince her to go out anyway. I did not want my daughter to live her life in fear, and I did not believe that children would bully her too badly in town, where adults were watching. Matilda joined me in trying to convince her, tugging on Charlotte's hair and scampering about, teasing, but Charlotte still refused. Matilda would go outside alone, her head hung low. She was a quiet girl, but determined, and she was not going to let her fearful sister keep her cooped up indoors.

I put Charlotte to work in the brewery; she helped me to sort through the old barley or stir the mash when I had to tend to customers. She was diligent and focused for such a young girl, and I was proud of her. Still, I could tell that she was wistful; she wanted to be in the sunshine with her sister, and I wanted that for her also.

One day, Matilda succeeded in convincing Charlotte to leave the house to play. God help me, I encouraged her to go. I knew that something was amiss when I heard the screaming. Children were always shrieking outside, but this was a sustained keening, a formless wail of distress. I rushed into the street in time to see that the noise came from one of the Ainsley girls; she ran past me, a flurry of pale blue petticoats, her face contorted in a howl. I did not see Charlotte and Matilda, so I ran in the direction from where the girl had come.

As I passed the first alley, I spotted my daughters. Matilda was helping Charlotte to stand; it looked as though she could bear no weight on her right foot. Charlotte's hair was disheveled, standing out in a wiry halo around her head, and her dress was completely torn from the neckline to the waist. Both girls looked grim. Matilda was muttering something to her sister, and Charlotte was crying.

I stopped in front of them, panting. "What happened?" I asked. My voice sounded too sharp; I had not meant to bark at them.

"They hurt Lottie." Matilda was nearly four, but she still lisped like a baby. There was a smear of blood on her chin.

"Who hurt Lottie?"

"The girls."

"What girls? The Ainsley girls?"

"And others," said Charlotte.

"They said she was a witch. They pushed her."

"My ankle is twisted."

"They said witches get pulled on a rope, and they are naked. And people throw stones."

"Why did the girls run away? Why was the girl screaming?"

Matilda looked at me slyly. "I bit her."

"You bit her?"

"Tilly jumped at the big girl and knocked her over too." Charlotte wiped her tears, leaving a long streak of dirt across her cheek. "Then she bit her. Hard. The girl tried to get away, but Tilly hung on with her teeth. The girl got mad, and then she got scared because she was bleeding and Tilly wouldn't let go. I was scared too. I thought Tilly would kill her. Then she got her off and ran away, and the others ran too."

Matilda tilted her round face toward me with an expression of defiance mixed with apprehension. She set her mouth in a grim line, waiting for the blast of my anger and her punishment. I wanted the girls to have the appearance of being high born, and they were used to me reacting furiously when they behaved badly. I was not qualified to teach the nuances of manners, but I routed out coarse behaviors by whatever means were necessary.

Matilda held Charlotte's brown arm protectively over her narrow shoulders. A dark bruise was blooming under her eye, and I realized that the blood on her chin belonged to the girl she had bitten. She looked fierce, barbaric. As I watched them, these mysterious creatures who came from my womb, I felt my determination, my certainty, sag and collapse. I did not know what was best for my daughters.

I lifted Charlotte; she was heavy, but I was big and strong enough to cradle her in my arms still. I kissed her forehead. She still had a raw scar there from Saint John's Day. I sighed and said, "We should go home, girls."

This time, it was Mylla Ainsley who called on me. She never frequented the alehouse as a customer, and she looked about the empty room awkwardly, as though she had entered a foreign country. It was clear that she did not want to be there. She wasted no time in getting to the point; her voice crackled with anger. "Your beastly urchin bit my Ann. If I *ever* see either of those animals again, I shall personally whip them to a bloody pulp. We are God-fearing citizens in this town! You don't belong here. None of you. Not you or your heathen husband or your heathen children. Go back to where you came from!" Her eyes bulged, and taut cords appeared on her neck.

"You cannot come to my home and threaten my children."

"Home? This is no home. This is a nest of sinners!" Her eyes were wild. "I shall threaten if I like. My family has been in Old Hilgate for five generations, and we do not tolerate heathens here, or witches."

My blood turned cold. It was one thing for children to call one another witches, but it was something else entirely for an adult to use that word. Although I had never heard of a child being put to death for being a witch, it was a dangerous accusation.

"What do you mean, 'witch'?"

A glint of triumph shone in Mylla's eyes. She had seen my fear.

"You know exactly what I mean."

"Take that back, or you will regret it."

"Take what back? That your ugly daughter is the result of congress with the devil? That she is marked?" She said this with a sneer, taunting me.

"If you say one more blasphemous word about Charlotte, you will regret it."

"Ha! Who knew that you could be so funny? *You* listen to *me*. I shall say whatever I want. If your brats come within fifty feet of any of my children, I shall flay them. Nobody would stop me, not after what happened to my Ann today. They are animals. You keep them away, or *you* will be sorry!" She left, slamming the door behind her for emphasis.

With trembling fingers, I poured myself a cup of ale, and then another. I could not rid my mind of the image of myself as a young girl, helpless, unable to defend myself against the laundress who mocked me. I felt the full force of my hatred for Elisabeth, but she now wore the face of Mylla Ainsley. It was worse that the victims were my own daughters; I would have suffered any injury or indignity if my suffering could have spared them theirs. I could not stand having failed Charlotte and Matilda.

After some time, and yet more ale, I grew calmer. My girls were healthy, and they were fortunate to have been born into better circumstances than me. Snot-nosed bullies would not determine their fates. The extent of Charlotte's success in life would be the true measure of whether she had won against Mylla Ainsley and her ilk. In the meanwhile, I would find a way to shut Mylla up about Charlotte. I was determined to give her a taste of her own medicine.

My plan proved easier than I had anticipated. While I chatted with customers in the alehouse, I mentioned that Henry, the itinerant tinker, had seen an unusually large black cat on Mylla's roof, and I asked whether anyone had noticed a strange number of dead rodents and birds on our street. Townsfolk disliked Mylla; some were envious that she had been a great beauty in her youth and had married well, others resented her sanctimoniousness, but all seemed eager to see her brought down a peg. Soon, gossips were asking why the smoke from Mylla's chimney had a greenish tinge, and why she always kept her shutters closed. There were sightings of a mysterious cloaked figure slinking toward the river at night; I even heard claims that a naked woman was seen in the embrace of a shadow at the edge of the woods. It was not in the least believable that a woman as pious and rigid as Mylla would turn to witchcraft, but the story was titillating enough to spread like fire on a thatch roof. To encourage the conflagration, I reported that Maggie, who had taken over most of her grandmother's midwifery practice, had noticed an unusual number of miscarriages in Old Hilgate. I had even suffered two miscarriages myself.

Eventually, the rumors made their way to Mylla's ears. She did not have to be shrewd to realize that I had something to do with the gossip, and she paid me another visit. This time, I was ready for her.

Mylla threw the door open with a bang, startling a party of travelers who were supping at the alehouse. I was in the brewery, but if I had any doubt about who had slammed the door, it did not last long. Mylla shrieked, "Agnes! Agnes, you rump-fed hag, get out here!"

I straightened my skirts and went out to meet her. "Why, Mylla!" I said. "What a pleasant surprise. What can I do for you? I have some new lavender ale that is fresh and not too sweet if you would like some."

She flushed even more deeply. The travelers had stopped eating and watched with interest, doubtless hoping for an entertaining catfight.

"I know that it is you spreading scurrilous rumors about me!"

I raised my eyebrows. "Rumors? What sort of rumors? You know that I am too busy for gossip."

"You are trying to get me accused of heresy!"

"Oh my. Such a thing would be very dangerous."

Her eyes flashed murderously. "Nobody will believe your villainous lies. Everyone in Old Hilgate knows the godly life I have lived!"

"Oh. Well then, you have nothing to worry about."

"Do not pretend to me that you are not behind this!"

"Maybe if I did hear such a rumor, I could try to squelch it the way you try to squelch lies about my children. You know that all of Old Hilgate drinks and sups at my tavern. They listen to me. Or maybe you could spend some time here yourself. Get to know people better. They find it strange how much you keep to yourself."

Mylla glared at me, breathing hard. She must have realized that it was a fight she could not win, for she picked up a full flagon from the table and threw it in frustration. It clattered on the sideboard, splashing an arc of ale onto the wall. The man whose ale it had been yelled "Ho!" but Mylla paid him no heed. She spat on the floor and left without saying another word, but I knew that things would get better for Charlotte after that day.

Although Charlotte's troubles caused me pain, we had plenty to eat, a comfortable home, and a community that mostly welcomed us. Fernan remained distant but constant. We had no more children for a time, partly because Fernan was so often absent and partly because of my miscarriages. Fernan still hoped for a son, but I eventually gave him another daughter, which was when our real misfortunes began.

Matilda was four years old when I was pregnant with Catherine, so I was glad to welcome a new baby. She was born healthy, but Fernan came home with a fever one day, and the baby sickened a fortnight after he left again. In the beginning, Catherine was colicky and restless, and she refused to nurse, but this was soon followed by a high fever and flux. I called on Maggie, who gave me some poultices. It seemed at first that Catherine was improving, but then, to my horror, I noticed small reddish spots in her mouth and on her forehead.

Maggie brought her elderly grandmother to see the baby, but by then the rash had spread over Catherine's entire little body, forming flat, velvety patches. Matilda also developed a fever. I did not need a midwife to tell me that this was the pox.

I sent Charlotte to stay with her godparents, and I asked Maggie to fetch medicine from the apothecary. It was of no use, because Matilda vomited every hour, and she could not keep the tonic down. I closed the alehouse so that I could tend to the children day and night.

Catherine whined and fussed, but Matilda's suffering seemed worse. She heaved and choked when there was nothing in her stomach left to come up, and she drifted from fitful sleep to confused delirium. The shivering that racked her body was so violent that her teeth chattered. She sat up in bed once, her eyes open but unseeing, and cried out. Most of the time, I lay helplessly beside her, stroking her back or singing softly. I could not understand how she shivered when her skin was as hot as a cauldron on the fire.

I wondered how Fernan fared, and too soon the news came to find me. A pounding on the door woke me just before dusk; I had nodded off beside the children. I left Matilda sleeping and carried Catherine with me to answer the knock. Catherine had become quieter, and I did not know whether to be glad or worried. She slept most of the time, and I had to rouse her to nurse. The rash on her skin did not seem changed.

At the door stood a burly young man who introduced himself as Ralf, the sergeant for Ellis Abbey. He took a step back when he noticed the rash on Catherine's face.

"Sorry to bother you, Goodwife, but I have brought bad news. The man who owns this alehouse has died, and I am here to evict any tenants."

"Fernan is dead?" My head hurt, and my heart began to pound.

"Was he a relation?" The sergeant asked this reluctantly, not wanting to hear the answer; he had already guessed that I was not a renter. He scuffed the dirt with his toe. The weather had been dry, and a cloud of fine dust rose.

"He was my husband . . ." I was used to Fernan being gone, and we had shared little genuine intimacy, but the knowledge of his death brought real grief. I thought of the day before his fever, how he teased Charlotte and Matilda, dandling them on his knee just as he had when they were babies. He bounced them high into the air, much to their delight. I couldn't imagine his powerful limbs stilled, his eyes sightless globes, his familiar face a mask of death.

"I am sorry to hear it, madam. I am also sorry to tell you so, but you will have to leave." He looked embarrassed.

"But it is my alehouse! I own it. I have paid every cent for it."

"I don't know anything about that. I was told to come here and make sure there are no squatters."

"How did Fernan die?"

"Pox. He was at the hospital at the abbey, but the nuns could not save him." Ralf crossed himself quickly.

Tears rose to my eyes. I was so tired. "I need to tend to my children, and when they are better, I shall visit the abbey to sort this out. The alehouse is mine."

He looked at me dubiously, unsure what to do.

"Please. I need to go back to my daughter. Tell the reeve, or the steward, that I shall come as soon as I can to sort this out."

The sergeant hesitated. He looked at Catherine, and then he glanced over his shoulder to where his horse was tied. When he looked back at me, his expression was troubled, but he said, "Very well."

I waited on the threshold until he unhitched his horse and left. Matilda continued to sleep. The vomiting seemed to have ended, and she felt less feverish to my touch. I searched her face and breast anxiously, hunting for the first red spots, but her tawny skin remained flawless. My lips moved in a whispered prayer to Saint John that Matilda be spared.

I lay back down and arranged Catherine beside me. Her eyelids fluttered faintly, but she did not otherwise stir. I wondered whether I should wake her for a feeding, but she seemed so peaceful that I did not want to disturb her. I watched her little face in repose until the last light from the window died. In the gloom, the rash hardly showed. Her breath came quick as a rabbit's. I settled my head next to her so that I could feel her little belly press up against my cheek with each rapid breath, and I fell back asleep.

In the morning, I woke to find Catherine's body cold. Her lids were open, and her glassy eyes stared sightlessly at the ceiling. As though falling from a height, I watched the pain rush toward me without feeling it. When it hit, the breath left my body soundlessly, surging from my mouth like my soul escaping. My baby was dead. My Catherine.

No tears came, and my body ached with the effort to expel some part of my agony. I dug my fingernails into my arms until bright spots of blood appeared.

I could not leave Matilda, who still slept, so I cradled Catherine's body all morning, kissing her cold brow and praying for her soul. I told myself that she was already with the angels. But who in heaven would comfort her when she was alone and frightened? At the thought of Catherine forsaken and afraid, my tears finally came in great racking sobs.

Matilda woke, and I struggled to compose myself. She looked at me, confused, trying to make sense of what was happening. "Mama, what is it?" Her voice was weak and thick with sleep.

"It is nothing, sweetheart. I am just worried for Catherine." I hid the baby's face from Matilda. "You must be thirsty! I shall fetch you a cup of water."

I went downstairs and placed Catherine's body in her cradle, covering her entirely with a blanket. I felt sick. I wished that Fernan would come home. As soon as the wish flitted through my mind, I remembered that Fernan too was dead, and a new wave of grief threatened to overwhelm me. I could not think about that now. I had to tend to Matilda.

Matilda drank the water I brought, but she ate nothing. "Where is Catherine?" she asked.

"In her cradle. I thought that she would be better there."

"Where is Lottie?"

"With Henny and George. She will come home soon. I have to go out for a little bit. If Henny comes by, tell her to wait for me. I shan't be gone long."

I carried Catherine's body to the rectory and found Father Michael. He had been eating bread and cheese, and he wiped crumbs from his black beard with a bony wrist. I told him numbly about Fernan as well. He blessed the bundle in my arms and said that he would pray for both of their souls, and he would prepare a funeral Mass for Catherine the following day. I am sure that he pitied me, but I could not help but feel that it was only another day's work for him.

When I returned to the alehouse, I saw a pot of steaming stew on the table by the door, and I knew that Henny had come to visit as she did nearly every day. I found her upstairs, laying fresh blankets on Matilda and piling the soiled clothing for washing. When she saw me, she looked concerned; I shook my head, warning her not to ask in front of Matilda.

"We are enjoying having Charlotte with us," Henny said cheerfully. "She is a helpful child. She misses you though. She would like to come for a visit. Might do all of you some good!"

"I am not sure, Henny. This air is corrupted. Let her bide with you a bit longer."

"I am glad to see that Matilda looks better!"

"She does. I pray that . . ." My voice trailed away. I avoided meeting Henny's eyes.

"Well, now that I have tidied up here, let's get you some supper. You are too thin!"

Downstairs, I told her about Fernan and Catherine. She embraced me warmly, exclaiming, "Oh, you poor dear girl! You poor, poor dear!"

Her kindness provoked a new flood of tears. When I could speak again, I said, "Henny, I could not manage without you. You are an angel."

"Tut, tut, no talk of angels. Someone up there might hear you. Your job is to care for your little one. Charlotte is fine, and I shall see to the funeral arrangements. All you need do is show up. I shall fetch you tomorrow. Now eat up!"

I thought about Alice sitting in the same spot while Henny spooned food into her mouth, and how strange it was that I had taken her place. I had become an alewife, and like her, I had lost a daughter and a husband. Henny now brought dinner for me as she used to do for Alice. Like the seasons, the cycle of life and death rolls relentlessly forward, grinding our selfhood, those treasured sentiments and aspirations that distinguish each of us, into a handful of dust. Once I am dead, nobody will remember Catherine. Apart from a faint echo in the depths of her sisters' memories, it will be as though she never existed.

※

Spots appeared on Matilda's face the following morning. Though I knew to expect the worst, I had allowed myself to hope that she would be spared, exposing myself anew to the grip of despair.

Matilda looked deathly ill. Although her fever had not returned, she whimpered that her whole body hurt, especially her head. She lay unnaturally still, her limbs limp, her eyes closed. I held her hand, not knowing what else to do. Her fingers did not grip mine in response, and her skin felt clammy and cold.

I left Matilda briefly to attend Catherine's funeral; I do not remember the Mass, for while I mourned one daughter, I battled the terror that I was about to lose another. Even after that short absence from home, I was shocked by Matilda's appearance when I returned. Her face was entirely covered by angry pox, now swelling into discrete mounds, as though a horde of red insects swarmed over her skin. Her eyelids were thick and purple, and her mouth hung slack.

I propped Matilda against my arm and tried to feed her broth, but it trickled down her chin. She was not asleep, but profoundly lethargic, and she seemed unable or unwilling to swallow. Most of the bowlful soaked into her shift.

To quell my rising panic, I kept busy. I brushed Matilda's soft hair, rubbed her skin with ointments from the apothecary, gave her sips of water when I thought she could manage. I washed her clothes and blankets, and I changed her shift. When Henny brought supper, I tried to get Matilda to eat, but it was no use.

For eight days, Matilda languished. Horrific pustules on every part of her body grew to the size of berries, then burst, releasing a foul fluid. Her features became distorted beyond recognition. I plied her with broth and water, but she wasted before my eyes. I cradled her in my arms and prayed to God and to every saint in heaven to heal my daughter, my fierce, loyal, clever Matilda. I begged God to take my life instead, to let innocent Matilda be raised by her godparents, good people who had lived a better life than I had. At night, Matilda twitched and moaned and kept me from sleeping, but I held her close, wishing that I could somehow bring her spirit inside me, so that I might shelter her and give her a new birth.

On the ninth day, Matilda sat up in bed and asked for a cup of water. My heart leapt with joy; I would have walked all of the way to Saint Augustine's well to fetch her a drink if she had asked me. Matilda's strength returned quickly after that, though her skin remained hideous. The pustules turned purple and black, and some became open sores. The apothecary made new ointments to soothe her pain and promote healing.

I brought Charlotte home, and although I tried to forewarn her, she cried out when she saw Matilda's face. Charlotte quickly regained her composure and kissed the top of Matilda's head, telling her sweetly how much she had missed her, but Matilda began to sniffle. "Does my face look so bad?" she asked, her voice trembling. She looked at the macerated skin of her hand, doubtless wondering if her face looked the same. In truth, it looked worse.

"No!" Charlotte and I said in unison.

More softly, I said, "No, sweetheart. You are my beautiful princess."

Journal Entry

THE ROYAL COURT

We are sunflowers that cannot resist Ella's radiance; we are compelled to turn our faces to bask in her incandescent beauty when she is near. As she entered the chapel this evening, though she was shrouded in black for the queen consort's funeral Mass, her face half-hidden in the shadow of her veil, every eye was drawn to her. She glided beside her husband to their pew near the altar, her alabaster hand resting on his arm; before she knelt, she pushed back the black lace of her veil, and a golden ringlet slipped free. The escaped curl danced in the torchlight, glinting as though shot through with gold thread, before she tucked it away.

No doubt I will hear murmuring tomorrow about the scandal of the exposed hair, which, I concede, could be construed as disrespectful to the queen's memory. In the moment, however, nobody looked discreetly away.

Which is more profane, a loose lock of hair or a church filled with subjects who have more interest in gawking than in mourning their dead monarch?

Our fascination with feminine beauty is elemental. It is said that men wish to possess the princess and women wish to be the princess, but I believe that is only part of the truth. We are drawn to extraordinary beauty mindlessly and purposelessly; we flutter on dusty moth wings toward the effulgence with no understanding of why we do it. Perhaps when we see a woman with the aspect of an angel, our souls are tricked into following her, mistaking her for a guide to paradise.

The opposite, of course, is also true. I have watched ladies whisper to one another and detour to the far side of the fountain court to avoid crossing paths with Matilda, and I have seen how a crowd of courtiers parts to give her a wide berth. Her face is infinitely precious to me, yet I understand the impulse to avoid her. The pox scars have distorted her features, so that one eye cannot open fully, and her nose is bulbous and cratered. When I run my fingers over the cragged surface of her skin, an odd pain courses up my arm and lodges its fangs in my heart. I can only imagine the jolt of pity and revulsion a stranger might feel when beholding her for the first time.

It upsets me when my daughters are referred to as Princess Elfilda's "ugly stepsisters," but in Matilda's case, the label is sadly accurate. Charlotte is not homely, if one discounts the unsightly scar on her neck, but I understand that she lacks the fine features, fair coloring, and silken hair that our nobility so treasures. I can accept that nobody admires my daughters, but if God bestows beauty according to His inscrutable plan, there should be no shame in being uncomely or even ugly. Yet the "ugly" in "ugly stepsisters" is not mere description but moral repudiation.

I had hoped that Charlotte and Matilda could participate in the care of young George, Ella's son, but his nurse is frightened of them. She seems to believe that their ugliness will contaminate the little boy, or that their appearances are the result of inner corruption, an indication of wicked intent. She refuses to let Charlotte or Matilda hold their nephew, and when they try to play with him, the nurse hovers nearby, squawking and interfering. When George visits with his mother, my daughters have more freedom to engage with him, but those occasions are rare.

I am not ungrateful for our miraculous good fortune, but this is the sort of injustice that makes me wish that we could flee this gilded cage, just the three of us, to live in peaceful seclusion. Despite our rarefied circumstances, we have no control of our destinies.

13

RETURN TO AVICEFORD MANOR

Workers from the manors traveled to Ellis Abbey every autumn to harvest the grain, and I decided to take advantage of their migration for an escort on my way to petition the abbess. The road to the abbey passed through Old Hilgate, and near Michaelmas each year, workers flocked to the alehouse for a drink. I hungered for tidings of my family, and whenever I discovered that one of the workers came from Aviceford, I plied him with free ale in exchange for news. In this way, I learned about my father's death and about my brother's modest success. Thomas had inherited our father's half-virgate and had painstakingly expanded his landholdings, first through hard work and clever alliances, and then through marriage to his second wife, who was a daughter of the reeve.

Few women traveled for the harvest, and the men knew nothing about Lottie, except that she was still alive, as was her husband. They could not tell me how many children she had, whether she had enough to eat, or whether she was happy. Such details do not interest menfolk.

I did not recognize most of the villagers from Aviceford, and none of them recognized me. My transformation into the daughter of a baronet would not have fooled gentry, but the villagers doffed their caps and called me "m'lady." They gave me curious looks when I asked after Lottie and Thomas, but they were too respectful to question me. It was not that they had heard the false tale of my parentage, but that I dressed in silks and imitated the diction and conduct of my betters. Rose House had provided my first template of gentle manners, and I had learned to emulate Fernan's court-bred speech and bearing. Even though I worked as an alewife, the peasants assumed that I had been born into a respectable family.

When I requested an escort to Ellis Abbey, a group from Cothay Manor accommodated me willingly. I left Charlotte and Matilda with Henny, promising to return within the week. The workers made space in their cart and laid down rough woolen blankets so that I would be comfortable. To reward their kindness, I brought loaves of bread, cheese, and two cold legs of mutton to supplement their suppers.

As we pulled away from the alehouse, I examined its familiar facade; the upstairs windows looked back at me like a pair of consoling eyes. I had known that building in so many moods. The old hunched thatch roof, damp and disheveled in gloomy drizzle, had given way to a smart new slate roof that the alehouse wore like a jaunty hat. In autumn, crimson ivy wrapped the walls in flame, and in summer, misty clouds of miniature white roses climbed the trellises. I had lifted the children on my shoulders to pluck gnarled icicles from the lintel and sweep away the snow that crouched plumply above our heads, waiting to drop. It did not seem possible that we could be evicted from our home.

The villeins had been on the road since first light, but they maintained a good pace; we left Old Hilgate in the late morning and arrived at our destination before dusk. When the white spires of the church came into view, time melted away, and I felt the same awe that I had a decade earlier. We made our way up the tree-lined avenue to the road that led to the stable, and when we passed the rose garden and the pond, I had a fleeting urge to jump from the cart and run to Rose House. I wondered what had become of Mary since the countess's death and whether anyone lived at Rose House now.

The party left me at the guesthouse and went on to the barracks at the edge of the compound where they would spend the night. I could not find an empty room, but a woman from Healdshead Manor offered to share hers. It was a tidy, narrow chamber with two simple pallets and a basin, a palace compared to the housing for the workers.

I could not sleep that night. It was not only that the other woman snored and that I was away from my daughters for the first time. It was that I could no longer shut my mind to the worry that the abbess could deny my claim to the alehouse. What future could I offer to Charlotte and Matilda if my living were taken from me? It would not be easy to find Charlotte a husband even with a dowry, and it would be even harder for Matilda if her pox did not heal well. Without either money or beauty, they would have to become servants or settle for a husband nobody else would want.

Lying awake, I thought of my stone collection. The stones had sat for years on the lid of a chest at the alehouse, where the girls liked to sort them by color and size or arrange them in patterns. Though I was a grown woman, a stone in my palm would have calmed me that night.

I had to wait two days for an audience with Abbess Elfilda. The overcast sky sent down a constant, halfhearted drizzle, but I spent my time outdoors, walking restlessly around the compound. As I passed close to the fishpond, sleek frogs leapt from the grass by my feet and splashed into the jade water. The lavender had gone to seed, but there were frowsy blooms left on the rosebushes, nodding their heavy heads in the wind and rain.

I had been little more than a child when Fernan and I had strolled through those grounds and flirted in the garden. I had allowed his brown eyes to become the whole of my world, allowed myself to believe that I would be there to witness the blooming of roses every spring and to collect petals from their fading coronas every autumn. Since then, eight years had passed, more than a third of my life. I was a mother, a widow, an alewife. I felt incomparably older, but the gardens that had bloomed in my absence still beckoned to me. My romantic vision had shifted: I wanted to hold my daughters' little hands and show them the frogs and flowers, hunt for wild strawberries, recline on the grassy banks of the pond to sing songs. The nobility imagine that we peasants are too brutish for fanciful dreams. They should ask themselves why, then, are fairy tales so popular with the masses?

I saw Sister Marjorie, and a few other familiar faces, but they did not recognize me. My sorrow made me shy and apathetic, and I could not bring myself to approach them. Besides, I did not want to answer questions about my years in Old Hilgate. I had built my life on lies, and I was not proud of it.

The sun broke through the clouds as I made my way to the chapter house on the third day, and I chose to see the change in weather as a good omen. I fiddled with my veil, hoping that I had selected the best clothing to project competence and respectability.

Although my name was toward the end of the list of petitioners for the day, I arrived early, having nothing else to keep me occupied. I watched the anxious faces of other petitioners in the anteroom, wondering who would leave successful that day. The expressions on their faces as they left the chapter house told me who had received a favorable response and who had not. I prayed silently that I would be smiling when I left. The afternoon stretched on. My stomach grumbled and I felt light-headed, for I had been too nervous to eat.

When my name was called, I squared my shoulders and forced myself to walk with a firm step. The chapter house had not changed, except that there was now a desk beside the lectern, and this was occupied by an officious-looking nun with a scroll and quill. Jeweled light splashed momentarily across her parchment as the sun darted from behind a cloud and disappeared again. She read out my name and the reason for my visit as I curtsied to Mother Elfilda. I did not recognize the new prioress who stood next to her on the dais. She was younger than the prioress I had known, but she had the same rigid posture and stern face; doubtless she also had the same talent for enforcing discipline.

The abbess was even slighter than I remembered. She could not have been much taller than my Charlotte, and I doubt that she weighed as much. She turned her tranquil gaze toward me. "You are the girl who left with Fernan." It was not a question.

"God be with you, Reverend Mother." I noticed fine lines at the corners of her eyes, radiating like spiderwebs. It struck me as an odd placement of wrinkles, since I had never seen her smile.

"And you are here because you claim that his alehouse belongs to you."

"I bought the alehouse from him, Mother. I paid every penny."

"I suppose that you have brought the new deed?"

I flushed. "We did not sign a deed, my lady. He was my husband."

"Then according to our documents, the alehouse belonged to Fernan. After his death, the property reverts to Ellis Abbey."

"But I am his widow! I am at least due my piece of the inheritance, my lady!" I curtsied low to apologize for the forcefulness of my statement.

The abbess beckoned to the prioress, who stooped toward her. They conferred in low voices, and then Mother Elfilda said, "I am told that we have no record of your dower either. In fact, we do not have a record of your marriage."

"God bless you, Mother, it is true that I had no dower. I was penniless. There may be no record of the marriage, but that is not uncommon. We lived together as man and wife. Surely, my lady, the abbey's court will recognize the law of inheritance for widows!"

The abbess's blue eyes were cold. "The law specifies no such thing. It may be customary for widows to inherit, but in a case where there was no dower—and I suspect no wedding—nothing is owed to you by law. *Vir caput est mulieris.* Man is head of the woman."

"Forgive me, Mother, but I have two young children. What will become of us?" My voice shook with frustration and fear.

"You will return to Aviceford, and Emont will find you a new husband."

"No! Pardon me, my lady. I cannot. Please. I am begging you. Please give me the opportunity to buy back the alehouse from the abbey. I can pay for it in less than two years!"

Abbess Elfilda looked to the prioress, who asked sharply, "What can you offer for it now?"

"I have two pounds in savings. I shall have more soon!"

"This girl is wasting our time, Mother!"

I thought of George and his offer of a loan. "I can get twenty pounds!"

The prioress sighed impatiently. "Where will you find such money?"

"A friend."

She narrowed her eyes at me, but Abbess Elfilda held out her hand and spoke mildly. "Usury is prohibited, and I weary of this discussion."

Not knowing what else to do, I prostrated myself on the stone floor. "Mother, I am begging you, in the name of Jesus our Lord, please help my daughters! They are innocent. I have raised them to be courteous and godly, and their father was the son of a knight. Surely God's plan is not for them to be the wives of coarse and brutish peasants!"

"Get up!" the prioress snapped. "Mother Elfilda is finished with you!"

"No, it is all right, Eleanor." The abbess sounded tired. "They are the daughters of my ward, after all. What do you request on their behalf?"

Much as I had hoped to keep the alehouse, I had prepared myself for rejection during my lonely walks around the pond. I knew what to ask next. "My lady, Charlotte and Matilda would be ideal students for your convent school. They are good girls. They are clever, obedient, and devout."

"How will you pay for their education?" demanded the prioress.

"With respect, Mother Prioress, the abbey's coffers were enriched once when Fernan bought the alehouse, and they are being enriched again now because of his death. I have improved the building, and it will fetch far more than the last time. These monies, along with Fernan's savings, will pay for his daughters' educations many times over."

The prioress seemed unaffected by my words, but I detected a softening in Mother Elfilda's voice when she said, "This is a just argument. It would be the right and Christian thing to do to bring the girls into our school."

I sagged with relief. All was not lost. "Thank you, my lady! You will find them to be excellent students."

"You still must return to Aviceford."

"Yes, my lady."

She looked at me steadily. "You have genteel manners and speech. You might make a fine lady's maid. My sister now lives at Aviceford Manor, and she is expecting her first child. I shall send you to help."

The days following my audience with the abbess were an agony. I was frantic to return to Charlotte and Matilda, but once I arrived home, I was equally frantic at the thought of losing them. I lay awake at night, listening to their snuffly breaths, resting my fingers lightly on their slender chests to feel their warmth and the movement of the sweet bones beneath their skin. To please them, I made their favorite foods, and though queasiness and the lump in my throat kept me from eating, I watched hungrily for their bright smiles. At times my despair overwhelmed me, and I slinked into the brewery and muffled my sobs in a towel. I tried to feel grateful for their opportunity to attend the convent school, but I was too absorbed by my own selfish pain. When my daughters left my body at birth, their roots remained behind, entwined in the flesh of my heart, wrapping tighter and deeper as they grew tall and strong in the light of the world. The blood in my veins sang their names with each heartbeat, and I did not know how to survive being torn from them.

Matilda's pox had blackened and were beginning to heal. Scarring was inevitable, but I still prayed back then that some of her beauty would return. Her health had certainly been restored, as had her spirits. It broke my heart to see how happy it made her to have me home again. She gamboled about the alehouse like a spring lamb.

Charlotte, on the other hand, sensed my distress, and she followed me everywhere with a furrowed brow. I knew that I had to tell them of what would come to pass, but I put it off, hoping that I would think of some new solution. When the abbey's sergeant returned with a notice of eviction, however, I knew that I could delay no longer.

I sat with Charlotte and Matilda on the bed and told them that they were to go to school. While they looked at me with wide eyes, I described for them the beauty of Ellis Abbey and the wonder of the library and scriptorium. I told them about the rose garden and the fishpond. When I finished, Matilda said, "But, Mama . . . we want to stay here."

"Yes!" Charlotte agreed. "We never want to leave!"

"I would also like to remain here in Old Hilgate," I replied. "We do not have a choice in this."

They looked alarmed, and Matilda asked, "But why?"

"Because your father is gone, and we are not allowed to live here anymore."

"Where will you go then?"

"I must go to Aviceford Manor."

"Where is that?"

"Not far," I lied. "I shall visit you as soon as I am able."

"But I cannot bear to be without you!"

I sensed Matilda's rising hysteria. Though I had tried to keep the sorrow from my voice, I had not done well. To distract them, I gathered the stones from the chest and handed half of the collection to each girl, saying, "When you miss me, take one of these stones into the palm of your hand, like so. Then close your eyes and concentrate on one of your happiest memories from Old Hilgate. When you do that, God will whisper in my ear, and I shall send you the softest kiss on your cheek. You will feel it, I promise."

The girls were not mollified and would not be turned back from their grief. They were so desolate that I nearly changed my mind in that moment. If I accepted a new husband, no matter what deprivations they would suffer, we would at least stay together as a family.

I knew that their only opportunity for a life of peace and comfort lay in the church. As nuns, they would have a far better life than I could give them. I held my daughters as they wept long into the night.

I sent Charlotte and Matilda to Ellis Abbey with Mylla Ainsley's husband, John. Much as I loathed Mylla, John was a good man, and he was kind to my daughters. He needed to lug his carpentry tools to the abbey, and he was glad of an excuse to ride in a coach.

After we loaded a trunk full of clothing into the carriage, the girls would not say good-bye. Charlotte clung to me and refused to let go. I kissed the top of her head; the frizz of hair that had come loose from her braids tickled my chin. Her familiar scent, like spring grass and fresh-baked bread, brought more tears to my eyes. I knelt awkwardly, still holding Charlotte, and I begged

Matilda to kiss me, but she clutched her doll and turned her face away. Finally, John had to pry Charlotte from me and force them both into the coach; Charlotte tried to twist away, so he cuffed her sharply, and she stumbled into the bench with a dazed look. John swung himself up and gave the horses a smack with the reins. As they pulled away, Matilda watched me with frantic eyes, her arms outstretched, wailing "Mama! Mama!" until her voice was mercifully drowned by the wind.

I told myself that I had done the right thing, that my daughters would be happy, but I was plagued by doubt and by my own excruciating loneliness. Nothing gave me comfort, and I could find no respite from the emptiness. I drank ale to excess, hoping that it would usher in oblivion, and so it did, for a brief while. Then I would wake, dizzy and sick, staring into blackness, startled by a scrabbling rat or wind-rattled shutter. More tankards could hurry the endless blank hours of darkness before dawn, but morning brought nothing but more sickness and another long string of creeping, desolate hours until dusk.

By the time I returned to Aviceford Manor, I had wrung out all of my tears, and I felt as insubstantial as the dry autumn leaves that drifted and crunched underfoot. I paid little attention to the exterior of the manor. Ivy grew thicker than I remembered; the gargoyles were draped with creepers, and inky stains of lichen nibbled at their heads. They leered blindly at me through broken eyelids as I passed through the front entrance. I noted with numb indifference how much the interior had been altered. The austerity of the manor had given way to jumbled, extravagant domesticity. Even the corridors were choked with a hodgepodge of rugs, tapestries, carved furniture, and statuary. As the new chamberlain led me through the foyer, I recognized one of the statues, a bronze cerf that held its head cocked to one side, as though listening. My fingers remembered the contours of the smooth flanks and sharp antlers that I had once dusted at Rose House.

In my absence, Emont had taken a wife, Lady Alba, the daughter of the late Count and Countess of Wenslock and sister of Abbess Elfilda. Emont's wife had apparently inherited not only her mother's belongings but also her mother's taste for miscellany and tolerance for clutter.

I had heard tales of Lady Alba when I lived at Ellis Abbey; it was said that she was even more beautiful than her sister, but that she had caused her mother much heartache. As a young woman, Lady Alba had visions and heard the voice of God, and it was said that she was destined to become a great mystic. While her older sister rose in the church to the position of abbess, however, Lady Alba's behaviors became increasingly strange. She stopped eating because she believed that her food was poisoned, and nobody could convince her otherwise. She became so thin that her clothing hung off of her like rags, and she wore the same loose gown every day and night until she smelled like a beast of the woods. After she proclaimed herself to be the Virgin Mary, she was sent to the archbishop for a cure of the evil spirits that had invaded her body. It was even whispered that she bore a demon child.

When Lady Alba reemerged into society, near the time that I moved to the abbey, her mind and beauty had been restored, but her mother could not find her a suitable husband. According to Mary, Lady Wenslock was greatly aggrieved by this problem. She died without seeing her youngest daughter wed, but somebody else had succeeded in finding a match, probably Abbess Elfilda. Emont could not have been the first choice, but then the trouble of find-ing a husband grew worse with time. Lady Alba must have been at least a thirty-year-old bride, what Fernan used to call "winter forage."

The new chamberlain introduced himself as Wills; he appeared to be far more pleasant than his predecessor. When I asked what had happened to Geoffrey Poke, Wills replied merely, "He died." Wills had a large round face topped with ginger curls that made me think of a pumpkin, and though he was twice my age, approaching fifty years, his manner was oddly hesitant. I wore fine clothing, my best scarlet silk and a lace wimple that Henny had pronounced per-fect for setting off my fair skin and brown eyes. I spoke with a cul-tured accent, affected a stately bearing, and stood a full head taller than Wills. I expect that he did not quite know what to make of me.

Wills led me through the great hall, which was brightened by white tapestries brought from the library at Rose House, the ones showing the arms of the late Count of Wenslock. I was so used to seeing the tapestries in the smaller chamber that they seemed dwarfed by the great hall. The effect was vaguely comical, like seeing a grown man dressed in clothing meant for a child.

We mounted the stairs to the family's quarters, and Wills knocked lightly on the door to Lady Alba's chambers. A young woman with a worried expression and dark circles under her eyes answered the door. She looked at me suspiciously, and then asked, "What is it that you want, Wills?"

"Not even a hello, Joan? I have brought a new maid sent by the reverend mother. Her name is Agnes."

"You are a maid?" She looked shocked.

"Yes, I am. I am pleased to meet you, Joan."

The woman gaped at me, and then she recovered and smiled

shyly. "Between Gisla and me we've got our hands full, so I'm not sorry to have you join us. Why don't you come in and meet Lady Alba and her new babe. Gisla will figure out how you can best help."

Wills left us, and Joan stood aside to let me into the anteroom that adjoined the main chamber. There was a canopied bed on one side of the room and an imposing armoire on the other. On the wall beside the armoire was a painting of a pretty blond girl seated on a horse. Except for a braid encircling her pale forehead, she wore her hair loose, and it cascaded nearly to her booted foot. I wondered if it was a portrait of a young Lady Alba.

When we entered the large inner chamber, it took a moment for my eyes to adjust to the gloom. Though there were two large windows, the shutters were closed fast, making the room airless and dark. Narrow strips of sunlight squeezed through thin cracks, illuminating dust motes but little else. An enormous bed hulked in the middle of the room; it was raised on a platform beneath a frame draped with hangings. Thin bands of moted light slashed the drapes with the radiance of a cloudless afternoon. As my eyes grew used to the shadows, I could make out the *W*'s encircled by gold crowns embroidered on the canopy and bed curtains. A silvery voice called from behind the drapes. "Joan! Did you fetch my wine?" The familiar clear timbre of the voice made me shiver.

"No, my lady, I am going to fetch it now. I have brought a new maid sent for your comfort by Mother Elfilda. She is called Agnes."

"My sister sends a maid; should I be afraid? I think not, she has brought ought that is sought. That is a new . . . thought? . . . Spot?" There was a long pause and then a giggle. "What rot!"

Joan pulled back the curtain as Lady Alba made blowing sounds with her lips. She lay sprawled on the feather bed, dressed only in a gossamer shift, her back resting against a pile of satin pillows. Like her sister, she had the delicate features of a doll, and her skin was so pale that she glowed like the moon in the dim light. Lady Alba did not otherwise share the abbess's ethereal quality, however. She was plump, with dimpled cheeks and a jiggling bosom that overflowed her bodice. Her teeth were discolored, giving her a slightly sinister air when she smiled, but it was easy to see why she had been considered such a beauty when she was younger.

An elderly woman—Gisla, I assumed—sat on a stool next to Lady Alba, holding the ends of her corn-silk hair in one hand and a brush in the other. "Welcome, Agnes." Her voice creaked like a door on ancient hinges. "We will be glad of your help."

I was startled by the wail of an infant; only then did I notice the cradle beside the bed. The cry wrought its work on my breasts; I felt a painful tingling, and then milk gushed from my stiffened nipples, soaking through my gown. Gisla's eyes widened.

"You have milk! Where is your baby?"

My arms ached for Catherine as though she had just that moment been torn from me. "She is dead."

"I am so sorry, dear. But I must say, you have come at a good time! We are looking for a wet nurse for the little one."

I did not know what to feel. The infant's cry had made the pain of Catherine's death fresh and sharp, but at the same time, I longed for the comfort of a baby in my arms.

Joan picked up the crying infant and rocked her gently. Lady Alba paid no attention; she flicked impatiently at some invisible lint on her sheet and asked Joan again to fetch her wine. Gisla rose stiffly from her stool and shuffled around the bed. "Hand me the babe, Joan. You go and fetch the mistress her drink." She turned to me. "Come with me; let's see if you can quiet this little thing."

I followed Gisla to the anteroom, where she bade me to sit on the edge of the bed. "It would be a shame for your milk to go to waste. And you will feel better to get rid of some of it." She handed me the baby, who weighed nothing at all. My daughters had all been big and sturdy; Lady Alba's baby was a mere wisp by comparison.

"What is her name?" I asked.

"Elfilda, after her godmother. But we call her Ella."

14

ELLA

Ella and I had problems from the beginning. Nursing was difficult for both of us, because Ella could not abide the rapid flow of milk, and yet she was hungry. She latched eagerly to my breast, but within moments she would begin to thrash her head from side to side, pulling painfully on my nipple. She would then release with an angry cry, jerking her fists in the air while my milk sprayed against her reddened cheek. I would settle her by walking and singing, but the sequence inevitably repeated until my milk had been drained to a slow trickle.

I worried about Ella's feedings because she was so tiny. I could cradle her head in one hand and easily support her entire body on my forearm. By her age, Charlotte had already weighed a stone, but Ella must have weighed less than half that. She was slim and long limbed, with skin so translucent that I could see the blue veins snaking across her scalp. Her little body thrummed with nervous energy, and her voice was high pitched and eerie, like a lute strung too tight. She had the alert look of a wary bird, and her eyes were a dark slate; it was only later that the color faded to the peculiar shade of violet she is so famous for now.

Lady Alba did not like to be woken by the baby, so I slept in the anteroom with Ella and Gisla, while Joan used the trundle in the main chamber. Ella woke every two hours through the night, and I passed my days in an exhausted fog. Remembering the sweet, idle first months of my own daughters' lives made me miss them all the more. My babies had nursed with calm earnestness, their eyes unfocused, their expressions entranced, as though they were gazing into the heavens. My milk made them drowsy and content, and they drifted into sleep like a skiff pushed along by a light breeze.

With Ella, feeding was a battle that was never won nor lost, only punctuated by armistices when both sides were too spent to continue. I got to rest when Lady Alba took the baby, but that was often only once each day. Sometimes Lady Alba played with her daughter's fingers and toes and spoke to her in singsong nonsense rhymes. Other times, she placed her in the cradle and ignored her completely. Whenever Ella cried, Lady Alba gave her to me to take away.

Because my entire responsibility was to care for the baby, I enjoyed far greater freedom than I had during my previous time at the manor. I was not officially permitted free rein of the house, but in practice nobody checked my movements. Lady Alba left her chambers only for supper, and sometimes not even then. If she was not in the mood to dress, she would have Joan bring her food on a tray.

When Ella was awake, I swaddled her and carried her with me to wander the corridors and grounds. She liked to be walked, and I found Lady Alba's chambers suffocating, so I was glad for an escape. Though I usually skirted the great hall by taking the outside staircase and reentering by the back foyer, on a particularly rainy autumn day, I decided to stay indoors.

The great hall seemed to be unoccupied. A fire roared in the giant hearth, its crackling drowned by the torrent of rain that battered the windows. The air was chill, and though I disapproved of the wastefulness of a large fire, I was tempted to warm my hands for a moment.

Two imposing high-backed oak chairs flanked the fireplace, new additions since the arrival of Lady Alba. I had almost traversed the long shadow of the nearest chair when I glimpsed a hand on the armrest. I froze, realizing that the room was occupied after all. I meant to creep along the wall and leave undiscovered through the screens passage, but fate would not have it so. A puddle of water had formed at the base of one of the windows, making the floor slick. My fall was swift and silent. Instinctively, I twisted my body in midair, so that my back struck the floor, followed by my head. My ears rang from the thud of my skull against the stone, but I succeeded in holding Ella away from my body, unscathed. For a moment, we remained an inert tableau, my back to the floor with Ella suspended above me, her face toward the roof. I wondered if she miraculously still slept, but then came a piercing shriek. The cry continued until she had squeezed every shred of breath from her tiny body; she fell silent as she choked and struggled to fill her chest anew, and then she let loose another shrill wail.

I rose awkwardly to my feet, hushing the baby. My head throbbed. Standing before me was Emont, arms crossed, frowning. I curtsied and apologized for the intrusion.

"You must be the nurse." His words were rounded by a soft slur. From his silhouette, I could see that he had grown heavier.

"Yes, sir." I jiggled Ella, whose cries had begun to subside.

"How is my daughter?"

"She does well, sir." On an impulse, I added, "Would you like to hold her?"

He looked at his child dubiously. I thought that he would say no, but he surprised me by reaching out his arms. His hands were steady. I gave him the little bundle, and he retreated to his chair by the fire, murmuring. I followed him, saying, "She knows her father. She is quiet in your arms."

He smiled up at me, pleased. Age and paunch had not improved his looks, but his smile was charming. "You seem familiar. What is your name?"

"Agnes, sir."

"Agnes. Do I know you?"

"I worked here years ago. As a laundry girl."

His gaze swept over me quizzically. "You were not the girl who looked after me when I was ill?"

"I was, sir."

"My. Yes, I recognize your eyes. You were always so grave."

"My cow eyes, sir? I believe that is what you called them."

Emont snorted. "Yes, I recall that you were always direct too. I see that you have grown up. You seem quite . . . elegant." In the firelight, I could see that his coppery hair was now streaked with white. He had pouches under his eyes, and one of his lids drooped, but the irises were a more startling blue than I remembered.

"I had the benefit of some education, and I married well."

"What happened to your husband?"

"He died of the pox."

"Ah." He looked down at Ella, who had fallen asleep again. He rocked her gently. "I am sorry."

My throat tightened in response to his solicitude.

"What is that by your ear? Are you bleeding?"

I lifted my hand to my temple, and my fingers came away sticky with blood. Emont rose and handed Ella back to me. I realized that I had grown taller than him. He pulled an embroidered handkerchief from his pocket and reached for my face. I flinched as he leaned close and dabbed softly. His breath smelled strongly of wine. I stood stiff and ill at ease, but he seemed to find nothing strange about the situation. After a moment, he gave the handkerchief to me, saying, "I think that the bleeding has stopped, but keep this in case you need it."

"Thank you." I stepped away from him.

"You must bring Ella to see me every day."

"Yes, sir."

"I am glad that you are back, Agnes."

"Thank you, sir."

He smiled at me and then sank back into his chair, closing his eyes wearily.

It became my routine to bring the baby to the great hall each day at dawn, after her morning feeding. Ella and her father were both early risers. Emont was occasionally surly, but he took only ale before noon, so he was not drunk in the mornings. In the hour or two before the chamberlain or the reeve arrived to discuss manorial business, Emont held his daughter, cooing like a grandmother. I was beginning to notice how peculiar he was, how bumbling and unrefined, something that I could not see as a child. He paid little heed to social convention, but I do not believe that he rebelled against it; he was simply oblivious.

Emont conversed with me as though I were his equal. He asked about my experiences, and he was particularly interested in my time at the brewery. The first morning, he asked how I learned to brew ale.

"Alice, the former alewife, gave me lessons."

"Was it difficult?"

I laughed. "Yes, sir. The first six batches were awful! I thought that I would go out of business before I even got started."

"What did you do wrong?" He sounded genuinely curious.

"Well, first I damaged the husks of the barley, and then I ground it to too fine a flour. Then I mashed too long, then too short, then too hot, then too cool. Then I boiled it too soon and the head fell." I smiled. "There are so many ways to ruin a batch of ale!"

Emont handed me his cup. "Taste this and tell me what the brewer could do better."

I took a dainty sip. "Better is a matter of taste, sir. I find this overly sweet. I would have added more gruit. I would have let it stand longer before straining."

Emont looked delighted, as though I were a juggler who had performed a difficult trick. After that, he made me taste his ale nearly every day and give him a critique. It became a sort of game for him to predict what I would say when I did my tasting.

As the time for manorial business approached, Emont became restless and irritable. He complained about the difficulties of administration and the demands of the abbey. He particularly disliked court days, when he had to preside over disputes and disciplinary actions for wrongdoers. On those days, he yelled for more ale, and the serving boys could not bring it fast enough. By the time the first petitioner arrived, Emont was often soused and completely ineffectual.

One morning, when I prepared to take Ella away, Emont requested that I stay. The baby had fallen asleep, so I remained in my chair. Emont fidgeted with his cuffs and pushed stray hairs back from his brow. His hair had thinned, and he wore his curls pulled back in a scraggly tail. He rose and paced by the fireplace. When the bailiff arrived, he scowled, saying, "I was rather hoping you might have found something else to do with your morning."

The bailiff, a bearded bearlike man with a gruff demeanor, did not look amused. He carried a roll of parchment under his arm, and his face became grimmer when he saw me. He turned to Emont. "Sir. What is the woman doing here?"

"I asked her to stay."

The bailiff opened his mouth to reply but then seemed to change his mind. He shook his head in disapproval as he spread the parchment on a trestle table, weighing the edges down with Lady Alba's bronze candleholders. "We have some problems, sir."

Emont shrugged impatiently. "We always have problems."

"We could barely make our payment to the abbey. But now the mill needs a new millstone, which is probably coming at a good time, since one of the horses that's used to run the mill is lame. We have brought in no new fines this month, and we have lost three villeins to fever."

I shivered as I thought of Lottie and Thomas, hoping that they were not among the dead. I was anxious to visit the village, but there was not enough time between Ella's feedings.

"Also, we are losing our second girl this year to Cranfield Hall. We need to make these girls marry Aviceford boys or raise the price for leaving. We are short enough of hands as it is."

"What is the fee that we have levied?"

"One ox."

"That does not seem too low a price."

"And yet it is, apparently, because they keep leaving." The bailiff's tone was biting.

"Who decided that it should cost an ox?"

"You did, sir."

"Well, what should it be?"

"Is it not up to you to decide, sir? An ox does not seem to be sufficient."

The exchange continued in this manner for some time, with both men becoming increasingly frustrated. When Emont ended their meeting, it seemed to me that nothing had been resolved. Emont flopped heavily into his chair and bellowed for some wine. A serving boy scurried in, carrying a carafe and a cup.

"I hate this place." Emont rubbed his eyelids and blinked. I wondered whether Ella would inherit his long lashes. "It gives me a headache."

"Why do you use horses to run the mill?"

"Why not?"

"Because oxen are cheaper. They eat less and do not need to be shod. But the way the abbey's mill works, using wind, is cheapest of all. You do not have to feed a windmill."

"The mill has always been run by horses."

I shrugged. "That does not mean that it must always remain so."

Emont looked annoyed. Perhaps my presence had been a comfort to him, but it was not anymore, so I prepared to leave.

"Good day to you," he said wearily.

I tucked Ella closer and curtsied.

"I shall see you in the morning, sir."

"Yes, see you in the morning."

I took most of my meals in the family's quarters, along with Joan and Gisla. They were pleasant companions, though Joan could be testy when Lady Alba was giving her trouble. The mistress was capricious, and she sometimes made unreasonable demands. On one occasion, she got it into her head that we were all living inside her looking glass, and that the image in the looking glass was the real world. She had Joan turn everything in her chamber backward, including the bedclothes.

On a more frightening occasion, Lady Alba decided that Ella was a changeling. I had left the baby in her mother's care, and Joan caught her dangling the squalling Ella by her legs over the fire, shrieking, "Tell me your name! Tell me your name!" After that day, we made sure that Lady Alba was never alone with her daughter, although to my knowledge, she never mentioned fairies or changelings again.

Rarely, I took a meal in the kitchen with the other servants. The atmosphere was more relaxed since Wills took Geoffrey Poke's place as chamberlain; seating by rank was no longer strictly enforced, and the chatter was louder and more jovial. Many of the servants were new to me, but the one person I would gladly have missed was still there. The laundress had grown even fatter since I had last seen her, and the lines on her face gave her an expression of perpetual sourness.

The first time that I noticed her, my heart quickened, and my palms began to sweat. I forced myself to walk slowly to her table and take a place across from her, where I sat with my hands neatly folded until she looked up. I expected her to be startled, but she merely narrowed her eyes suspiciously.

"Huh? What do you want?" As she spoke, she opened her mouth wide, affording me an unpleasant view of the food she was chewing.

"I just stopped by to say hello, Elisabeth."

"Do I know you?"

"You don't recognize me?"

I was gratified to see her eyes widen.

"What are you doing here?"

"I am the nurse for Sir Emont and Lady Alba's baby."

The laundress looked around uncomfortably. "You have come up in the world, haven't you?" She gave me a treacly smile. Her teeth were rotting.

"Yes, I have." I reached across the table and took the bread from her plate, and then I smiled back at her. "It is so lovely to see you again."

I walked away. Elisabeth was worried, and that was enough for the moment.

It was not until Saint Crispin's Day that I had an opportunity to visit Aviceford Village. Both Sir Emont and Lady Alba had fallen ill with flux and vomiting, and I offered to keep the baby away for the day. Joan and Gisla were so busy caring for the mistress that they did not ask what I would do. I doubt that they would have approved of my plan to take Ella to the parish church with me, so I did not mention it.

Ella was a fussy baby, but she was most settled when we walked. Her watchful eyes stayed open, and I chatted to her along the way. I pointed out a squirrel and a sparrow, and I sang a song about a robin that my mother used to sing. I could only remember a single verse, which I repeated over and over, but Ella did not seem to mind. She frowned at the sky or stared at my chin with a serious expression on her face.

Arches of crimson and gold branches over the road were made brighter by vivid patches of cerulean sky. There was not a breath of wind, but the occasional leaf came loose and floated down. One landed on Ella's head, and she responded with such wide-eyed shock and consternation that I had to laugh.

We came upon the bridge by the church far sooner than I expected, for I remembered the walk as being much longer. The river was no more than a stream, and the span of the bridge was so short that I could cross it in five strides.

When the church came into view, I was seized by shyness. Clusters of villagers sauntered down the lane opposite me, collecting in the churchyard; over the hubbub of conversations drifted the laughter and shrieks of young children. The church, which once seemed so magnificent, looked dingy and inconsequential to me now. Some of the villagers glanced at me curiously.

I had not seen my sister and brother since they were youths, but I recognized Thomas in the crowd right away. His head was uncovered, and he wore his wavy brown hair the same way he had as a boy. Though his shoulders had broadened, he still slouched as he used to. He was engaged in conversation with an older man when I tugged on his sleeve.

"Yes?" He took a step back.

"Thomas! I am your sister Agnes!"

"Agnes?" A look of surprise came over his face. "Not little Nessie who went off to the manor house?"

He regarded me from head to foot, and I realized that my fashionable wool dress and wimple were foreign in the village. I touched the edge of my veil self-consciously. "I am. I went to Ellis Abbey for a time, and then to the town of Old Hilgate. I worked as an alewife."

"You sound mighty fancy. Where did you learn to talk like that?"

"The abbey, I suppose."

My brother was like someone from a dream. He was both familiar and entirely alien. His placid brown eyes were the same, but his face was bronzed by the sun and deeply creased, ancient. Like the bridge over the stream, and the church, he had shrunk. I remembered a strapping youth, clever from his lessons at church, seasoned and wise from his work in the fields. Before me was a tentative, uncouth peasant with stooped shoulders and gnarled hands, a gap where his front tooth had gone missing, cheeks hollow from privation.

Thomas turned back to the man whose conversation I had interrupted. "Can you believe this is my little sister?"

"I would've guessed she was lady of the manor!"

"Where are you living now, Nessie? Look at your sweet babe!" Having recovered from his surprise, Thomas seemed pleased to see me. He peered at Ella.

"Oh—" I felt disoriented and unaccountably miserable. "Nay, this here is the daughter of Lady Alba. I am her nurse."

"So you are back at the manor!"

As Thomas spoke, a small, meek woman approached. She had a purple bruise on her weather-worn cheek, and she held the hand of a boy of about three years.

"Lottie! Would you believe it . . . Here is Nessie!"

The woman stiffened and looked at me warily.

"Lottie?" My voice caught in my throat. She looked nothing like the sister I remembered. "Why— Why, I wouldn't have recognized you!" I had tried to sound cheerful to cover my confusion, but I realized that my words might have been hurtful. I paused lamely, searching my tumultuous mind for better words. We both remained rooted in place.

"Nessie was just telling me that she is the nurse at the manor. This is the new baby."

"Her name is Ella," I volunteered, my voice too bright.

As though woken by her name, Ella began to wail. I jiggled her while Thomas and Lottie stood awkwardly by.

"Do tell me your news, both of you! Thomas, I have heard that you are doing well. And, Lottie, how many children do you have? Where is your home?"

"I've got three. This one's Hugh. I lost four. My Margaret drowned last spring."

I could barely hear her over Ella's crying. "Oh, Lottie, I am so sorry. I hope the others are well?"

"Well enough."

"How is your husband? Aldred?"

Thomas crossed his arms and frowned. "His name's Aldrich."

Lottie shot a worried look at her brother.

Ella continued to cry, and little Hugh pulled on his mother's arm.

"What celebrations are planned for Saint Crispin's Day?"

Thomas gestured to women setting out food on a table next to the church. "Mass. Then we eat, as usual. That woman on the end with the green hood, she's my wife, Matilda."

"Matilda! That is the name of my daughter." I looked at Lottie expectantly, but she did not ask about my children. She swatted her son to stop him from tugging on her. Her gaze darted around the crowd.

"A well-chosen name," Thomas said.

We all fell silent except for Ella. I groped anxiously for something to say, but my mind had been swept clean. The baby's piercing cry nettled me. Finally, Thomas said, "Looks like time to go in for Mass. You coming, Nessie?"

"I'll try to settle the baby, and then I may come in."

"Well, sure is a surprise to see you. I hope we shall see more of you, now that you are back. We heard that you left, but then nothing more. I feared you died." He looked to Lottie. "Are you coming in?"

Lottie nodded to him and gave me a weak smile. "There has been a Christmastide celebration at the manor since Lady Alba came." A bit of warmth entered her voice. "Maybe we shall see you there."

I watched until they disappeared through the church door, but Lottie never looked back. I walked back over the bridge as quickly as I could while comforting Ella, ashamed by how relieved I felt to be returning to the manor.

15

MANORIAL BUSINESS

Christmastide was a sad time for me. I longed to return to my life in Old Hilgate with Charlotte and Matilda, or even to hear news about how they fared at Ellis Abbey. I consoled myself by remembering the roasted swan and pudding that the nuns had served at the Feast of the Epiphany. I could imagine the delight on my girls' faces when they tasted the first succulent bites. Charlotte would nibble daintily, luxuriating in new delicacies, while Matilda would wolf down her meal and then sneak her little fingers onto her sister's plate, crawling her hand forward like a clever spider. I imagined them hale and smiling; I could not bring myself to consider any other possibility.

Lady Alba worked herself into a state of high excitement before the holidays as she planned for banquets. She usually lost interest in new pursuits within hours, but Christmas held a particular fascination for her. She emerged from the cocoon of her chambers to give servants orders and supervise their preparations. It was the only time of year that she undertook any of her duties as lady of the manor, and she did a poor job of it, not knowing how the manor functioned. Some of her dictates were nonsensical, and some resulted in needless waste, but nobody was brave enough to gainsay Lady Alba when her blue eyes were flashing and her rosy lips were parted in a fierce smile. The servants grumbled, and Emont was even more mercurial than usual. In the mornings, when I brought Ella to him, he bellyached about his wife's intention to invite every soul in Aviceford for Twelfth Night.

"It is good for you to be charitable," I told him. "Loyal villagers make better workers than unhappy ones."

"Maybe it is good to be charitable when you are rich, but it is a right foolish thing to be when you cannot afford it!"

I had sat through enough of Emont's business meetings to know that his statement was true. "Perhaps you could reason with Lady Alba? Tell her to bring some provisions to the parish church instead?"

"Reason?" Emont snorted scornfully. "One does not reason with Lady Alba."

It was not proper for him to speak to me so familiarly, but it was not unusual either.

"Why not hunt for venison?" I was still thinking of Christmastide at the abbey.

"I have no license, and this land is all royal forest hereabouts."

"Lady Alba could ask her sister. The king is generous with the abbey. And he would not deny a license to his cousin, particularly not at Christmas."

"Second cousin. You do not see us getting visits from the king," he said dryly. "But it is a good suggestion. That might suit my lady very well. She is an excellent horsewoman." Emont smiled for the first time in days.

✳

Lady Alba did organize a hunting party, and I observed their return through the warped glazing of a window in the great hall.
I was taking advantage of the master and mistress's absence by
walking with Ella through the empty house when a wavering
blotch of color crested the brown hills near the orchard. A frag-
ment of scarlet streaked away, and quite suddenly Lady Alba was
galloping toward me at full speed, a mere stone's throw from the
window. She pulled her horse up sharply just in front of the manor;
the bay mare reared, beating the air like a charger in battle. Ten-
drils of pale hair whipped in the wind, and the lady's red cloak
billowed and fluttered behind her. Her face was flushed, and her
smile was wild and triumphant.

When Emont plodded into view, he looked stodgy and grim in
comparison. His wife tossed some words to him over her shoulder, and then she threw her head back in laughter. Emont's countenance soured further.

I did not wait to see what quarry they had caught, because I
had no invitation to be in the great hall, and I did not want to be
discovered. I later heard that they had killed two small red deer.
Much of the meat was preserved for Sir Emont and Lady Alba, but
there were plenty of leftover innards to make pies for the villagers.

The banquet at Aviceford Manor was a strange affair. The great
hall was decorated with garlands of holly, ivy, and bay, and scores
of candles glowed in the wall sconces and on the tables. These,
along with a hearty fire, made the room festive and welcoming. The
people of Aviceford were not used to such finery, however. They
entered bashfully, hesitating before taking a place at the long tables, and then they whispered or sat in silence, as in church.

Lady Alba wore a green silk kirtle of a hue that flattered her
milky complexion; jewels sparkled at her throat and on the gold

net caul that bound her fair hair. She swept through the aisles that divided the long tables, loudly commanding the villagers to eat more and be merry. Every man, woman, and child paused with head bowed as she passed by, in direct opposition to her bidding. She continued to bawl cheerfully, unobservant, stopping every now and again to take some wine. Emont sat alone at the oak table on the dais, sipping his drink and pecking at his food, ignoring his wife's behavior.

I left Ella with Joan in the solar so that I could find my brother and sister. After taking in the scene from the top of the stairs to the great hall, I descended nervously. My mind had recoiled from thoughts about Thomas and Lottie since our awkward exchange at the church, and I was reluctant to touch a wound that had not yet healed. Though we were bound by blood, we had grown so far apart, as though we no longer spoke a common language.

I closed my eyes to be rid of the image of Thomas and Lottie walking away from me, but the devil played a trick. Behind my eyelids, I saw not my brother and sister, but Charlotte and Matilda, their backs to me, receding in the distance. My heart pounded and my hands grew slick. My children were younger than I was when I left home. Would they become estranged from me too? I had feared never being reunited with my children, but to lose our attachment would be a worse fate, one I could not bear.

I found Lottie when I reached the bottom of the stairs. She was sitting halfway across the room, her head bent low over her plate, eagerly shoveling food into her mouth. Next to her sat a tall, spare man, her husband. He was feasting with as much determination as Lottie; I could not make out his features well, except for a beaklike nose that pointed toward his trencher. A skinny girl of about six years sat next to him, and while I watched, she dropped her spoon on the floor. The man cuffed the back of her head so hard that her chin crashed against her breastbone. She did not cry out, and the man resumed eating.

I looked back at my sister. What did that sallow-faced woman have to do with me, or with the Lottie I remembered? She had been depleted, used up by the exigencies of her family and the costs she had paid for mere survival. Her life had unwound too quickly, and there was nothing left to look forward to other than the gnawing hunger of winter and more children who would die before they were grown. The same would have been true for me had I stayed.

I made my decision swiftly, strangling a nascent bloom of horror. I ran back up the stairs, knowing that I would not see my brother or sister again.

Joan sat in the anteroom to Lady Alba's apartment, braiding her hair by the light of a guttering candle. She was surprised that I returned so soon. "Did your family not come?" she asked.

"Nay, they did not come. You should go down now and eat some food. I shall watch over the baby."

"She will sleep now through the night, I expect. You could come too. I heard that there will be a minstrel after supper."

"I am tired, and I have heard minstrels before."

Joan, who was still a little bit in awe of my former life, did not attempt to persuade me further. She finished braiding her hair and left for the great hall. I checked on Ella in her cradle and then sank onto the bed in the anteroom. By the light of the candle, I could dimly make out the painting beside the armoire. Gisla had confirmed that the portrait was of our mistress as a child, seated on her favorite horse. The girl in the painting had a serene expression, so different from Lady Alba's today. I wondered whether the demon that had possessed her as a young woman had been only partially exorcised, whether the shadow still lived within her.

My mind pulled at its traces like a stubborn mule, trying to turn my thoughts back to Lottie or my daughters, but I would not allow it. I carried the flickering candle into Lady Alba's chamber, treading cautiously in the weak aura of light cast by the flame, for there were often unexpected obstructions where the lady had tossed some garment or bauble on the floor. A movement by the bed startled me, and I spilled a blob of hot wax on my wrist; as I choked back my cry, I realized it was only a looking glass that had been propped against the trundle. At the bedside, I found the object of my search, a carafe of wine that was still half full. She would not remember in the morning how much had been left. I poured myself a large cup and then settled back on the bed in the anteroom, pulling a blanket over my shoulders. A strain of flute music drifted up from the great hall below. The minstrel had begun the evening's entertainment. I gulped the wine, hoping to escape into sleep. Ella would be up before dawn, demanding her breakfast.

When the door swung open, I knew that something was amiss. Even Lady Alba would not bang the door so loudly, for fear of waking the baby. Emont stood on the threshold, swaying slightly.

"Won't you invite me in?" His voice had a bitter edge that he had not used with me before.

"Of course, my lord, you are at home," I said soothingly, rising from the bed. "But your lady has not yet returned."

"I know. She is dancing with the whoresons she invited into my home."

"It is not unusual for the lady of the manor to organize a Christmas feast for the villagers."

Emont raised his voice. "She is debasing herself and my na
by mingling with rabble and scum!"

I did not point out that he was associating with a servant.

Emont stepped close to me after closing the door behind him.
He smelled of cloves and sweat and the bilious sour-sweetness of
drink. He pushed his flat, leonine face nearer to mine. "You are
beautiful," he said more softly. He reached for me and wrapped his
hand around my neck, trying to pull me to him. I resisted, stepping backward, which caused him to stumble sideways into the
armoire. There was a loud crack as his shoulder struck the door of
the armoire heavily, and then he heaved himself upright again. I
held my breath.

Emont glared at me with his fists clenched. Though I had heard
nothing from Lady Alba's chamber, I said, "I think I hear your
wee daughter crying. I must see to her."

I took the candle and ducked into the other room. My breath
came quickly, and my hands were shaking. I had the urge to smash
my fist into Emont's face, but that would cost me my position, and
I had nowhere else to go. Acceding to his advances could be just
as disastrous for me, and the idea of letting him paw me was revolting.

I went to the cradle, where Ella still slept. Resentment surged
as I looked at her. She was so scrawny and strange. She turned her
head away from the light and mewled. I would take her with me,
because Emont would not trouble me if I was holding his precious
daughter.

The moment I picked her up, Ella began to cry. I brought her
to Emont, and I was surprised to find him sitting on the edge of
the bed with his head in his hands. His tangled hair hung forward
and hid his face from my view. When he looked up, his expression

was sorrowful, and a little bewildered, and I pitied him. He was the same awkward Emont who begged for my company daily. I sat beside him and shifted the baby onto his lap. She reached for the tips of his curls and quieted.

"You see how she adores her father. She is always content with you."

I could hear the trace of a smile when he answered, "She is an angel come down to earth to comfort me." He caressed his daughter's cheek. "You take good care of her."

I thought guiltily of how roughly I had just pulled Ella from her cradle. "I do try."

"Her mother is not suited to the task." He paused, and then sighed. "Neither am I suited to be a father."

"You are more devoted than any father I have known! You visit with her every day."

"Her mother is busy spending Elfilda's dowry on silk gowns and trinkets, and I can barely furnish the food for a Twelfth Night celebration from the money we bring in for the manor. What kind of life am I going to give my daughter?"

Emont was so wealthy by the standards I had known that I was appalled by his self-pity. "Your daughter has her mother's beauty, the good name of her father, the blessings of her godmother, and she will never want for food," I said curtly.

He looked up at me, blinking, as though dazzled by a sudden light. "I must seem ridiculous to you."

"Oh! Not at all, sir, not at all."

"You know what it is to be hungry, don't you? To work for your living. Not to be free. You must think me so ungrateful."

I squirmed, not knowing how to respond. Emont took an eccentric interest in my brewing experience, but I had never before had the impression that he viewed me as a fellow mortal. No master does.

"I hope you don't think me a drunken popinjay. I suppose I'm not dressed well enough to be a popinjay. And I am drunk." He snorted softly. Emont kept his head bowed for a moment and then handed Ella back to me, saying, "I should go."

When I took the baby from him, she began to cry again. I bobbed in a shallow curtsy. "Good night. I shall bring Ella to you tomorrow."

On his way out, Emont staggered and took a bruising knock against the door frame. As I closed the door behind him, I felt a measure of disgust, but I also had an urge to call out to him, to say something that would ease his mind or provide some small comfort as he fell asleep.

The next morning, Emont did not acknowledge our meeting in Lady Alba's chambers. The pouches under his eyes were pronounced, and he was more disheveled than usual, but he chatted as though nothing had happened. I had expected him to be embarrassed and to treat me coldly, but the opposite was true. From that day forward, Emont took me into his confidence more than he ever had, sharing his frustrations with the manor and the demands of the abbey. I came to understand that he relied entirely on the information and advice of the chamberlain, the bailiff, and Mother Elfilda's steward, and that he did not review the books himself. He was like a boy who had not memorized his Bible verse and hoped nervously that the priest would not call on him. Although he had authority over all but the steward, he lacked the confidence to gainsay their decisions, possibly because he feared being discovered as ineffectual. He pretended to grasp the details of the manor's finances, but he had never applied himself to learning them. I wondered whether he had the capacity to learn them even if he was willing to try.

I knew enough from running a brewery to be able to understand household accounting, and I was frustrated with Emont's lack of insight. I asked him to show me the books, and he seemed eager to accommodate my request. Days went by, however, and the chamberlain did not bring the accounts for me to review. I asked Emont again, and he told me that he would remind Wills. Finally, I grew tired of waiting, and I approached Wills myself.

I found the chamberlain in the kitchen, upbraiding a scullion. I waited until the end of his harangue, and then I called to him. Wills's eyes narrowed when he saw me. "Yes?" he asked.

"Sir Emont has asked me to review the household books."

His round face colored. "What business is it of yours? Since when does a nurse review household accounts?"

"Since our master asked me to do so," I replied mildly.

"I don't have time right now."

I stepped closer, so that he had to lift his chin to look up at me. "If there is something that you would rather I did not see, then it is not a good idea to play games with me now. I shall see those books sooner or later, and when I do, you may wish for me to be pleasantly disposed toward you. I suggest that you get them now."

The red in his face spread to the roots of his ginger hair. He glared at me and then turned away. "Very well," he said, "I shall bring you the scroll for the past year."

It took me three days to finish combing through the accounts while Ella took her naps. The pattern that emerged was of incompetence more than petty thievery. While Wills had probably padded some of the expenses in order to set aside an income for himself, his greed was not the biggest problem. There was obvious waste in purchasing items that could have been produced at the manor, overstaffing the kitchen, failing to make use of animals that had been confiscated from tenants or collected as heriots. There were senseless extravagances, most likely at Lady Alba's behest. Taxes and fines were not being consistently levied, and when they were, they were not always being collected. I did not have details from the bailiff about sales of grain and produce, or about fees collected for use of the mill or ovens, but I could see from the income column that whatever it was, it was not enough.

I spoke to Emont about my findings, and he asked me to join his meeting with the chamberlain and the bailiff, who was known among the villagers as Black Bear, or simply Black, for his large size and dark hair. They were already at the table when I arrived carrying the scroll; Wills shot me a glance that was both worried and hostile, and Black tipped his head almost imperceptibly in greeting. A woolly beard partially concealed the bailiff's expression, but there was no mistaking the coldness in his eyes.

"I invited Agnes to point out some unnecessary expenses she discovered in our accounting," Emont said apologetically.

"How could she possibly know what is necessary and what is not?" Wills said.

I opened the scroll and smoothed it over the table. "Let me show you some ways you might save a few shillings," I said briskly. "Then you can get on with more important matters."

The bailiff grunted, and Wills crossed his arms, frowning at the parchment.

"You see what you have spent on flour just for December?"

"We had the whole village here at Christmastide," Wills said, "of course we needed flour!"

"Look at November, then. It was no better." I turned to Black. "How often do we accept promise of payment for use of the mill?" I knew from Matilda's godparents, who ran the mill in Old Hilgate, that debts did not always get paid.

"What does that have to do with anything?" Wills asked peevishly.

I ignored Wills and kept my gaze on Black, who shrugged his broad shoulders and said, "I don't know. Perhaps four or five times each month."

"Those people haven't the money to pay. What if they don't have money the next month either? Do you let them use the mill?"

The bailiff glanced uncomfortably at Emont. "Sometimes."

"They have no money, but they do have wheat or barley. What if you took a portion of their milled flour?"

"The villagers already harvest grain on manorial land."

I pointed to the ledger. "And this is what you spend to buy your grain back from the abbey. If you take flour as payment from the villagers' allotments, you can bypass the abbey altogether." I turned back to Wills. "How much flour do we lose to mouse infestations and rot?"

Wills reddened. "I don't believe that is a problem."

"Have you not seen how much the scullions throw away? If you had mouse-proof containers built and kept them nearer the fire, where it is dry, you would suffer far less waste."

"Even if we eliminated the cost of flour altogether, it would make no real difference to our monthly expense."

"I beg to differ. Every line on this sheet is important. What about this one? Twenty crowns for ale? A royal fortune! We could make our own for a few shillings. Why do we not make our own soap too? And why do you have so many kitchen staff? You have three paid servants and a half dozen villeins who must be fed from the manorial larder. They sit idle when there are no guests, which, as far as I can see, is nearly always. They could be working the land instead of sitting on their thumbs."

It was the first time I saw the bailiff smile. "The lass has some sense in her pretty head," he said to Wills. "I could use some of those idle hands to repair the church roof."

A loud snore caused me to start. Emont had fallen asleep beside me, sprawled on the table. He stirred, and his arm flopped over a portion of the parchment. I stood over him, unsure how to proceed. He let out a long, whistling breath that ended with a comical vibration of his lips, not unlike the sound of escaping flatulence. The bailiff chuckled, and when I looked at Wills, he was having trouble suppressing his own smile.

"I suppose this concludes our session," I said.

"Yes," Wills said stiffly, his smile snuffed out. He tugged the ledger from under Emont's arm. "We cannot continue without the master."

The bailiff bade me good-bye politely, but Wills left without a word. I found him later, in the kitchen.

"Would you like me to show you the problem with the flour?" I asked.

"I have eyes in my own head."

"I am not your enemy, Wills. I would like to be of assistance."

Wills looked at me skeptically.

"I cannot say why I have the master's ear, but I have it—"

"Yes, why?" he interrupted. "I bet you lift those fancy skirts for him."

I stared at the chamberlain until he began to shift uncomfortably and dropped his gaze. "You have not only insulted me grievously, you have insulted the lord and lady of the manor," I said. "Would you stand for any of your staff to say such a thing?"

"I shall look into the grain and flour storage," Wills said by way of apology. "You had best get back to work."

Though he said no more about it, Wills did follow my advice about the flour. I became a regular attendee of business meetings, and Wills grudgingly accepted some of my suggestions. Once the resistance of the bailiff and chamberlain had worn down, Emont began to wander away partway through meetings, leaving me to finish for him. As the lord's tacit representative, I took over, in one small way, the duties of the lady of the manor.

THE ROYAL COURT

The seasons slip by as I scribe my history, and while new events keep the court gossip mill turning, there is a sameness to every day that obscures the passage of time. Mornings, afternoons, and evenings unspool torpidly at the palace; life here is a tedious string of aristocratic social rites overlaid by idle chatter. The brightest moments are those spent with family, though today our precious time together was marred by tears.

We joined Ella in the green solar, where she has been receiving well-wishers and their gifts for baby Princess Phillipa, named for the new queen consort. Little Prince George came for a time too, with his nurse. He is a delightful boy, and now that he can talk, it is evident that he is as clever as a wren.

Ella was radiant in a simple satin gown, her tresses

adorned with pearls. Flanking her on the settee were two ladies-in-waiting, Cecily Barrett and Isabella Florivet. Both women wore elaborate gowns and had their hair sculpted into fashionable cornettes, but though they are not unattractive, they were like a pair of common mules browsing next to a majestic destrier. The elegant line of Ella's long neck, her graceful bearing and lustrous golden mane would put any thoroughbred to shame. It is rumored that the Barrett girl has found her way into Prince Henry's bed, but I don't believe it. What man who owns the kingdom's best horse would consent to ride a mule?

Chairs had been arranged for the attendants, and George's nurse had wisely chosen one close to the door, positioning herself to escape when the little boy began to squirm. I kissed the crown of his fair head as I squeezed by, and he rewarded me with a smile. We are accomplices in mischief, Georgie and I, which is why his nurse looks so sour whenever she sees me.

Charlotte and Matilda had saved me a spot beside baby Phillipa and her nurse. I asked to hold the baby, and Isabella sniffed sharply. I don't care that it is uncouth; I am not going to pass up the opportunity to cuddle my granddaughter. Phillipa is a placid little thing; she favors her father, with dark eyes and hair. When I stroked her creamy cheek, her perfect little rosebud lips twitched with dreamy contentment.

When Charlotte asked to hold the baby, Cecily said in her wheedling voice, sweet as honey, "Is Lady Charlotte feeling broody?"

Charlotte pulled Phillipa closer as though to protect her.

Ella was occupied with a subject, an elderly woman who winced arthritically as she curtsied low. Cecily whispered, "Don't squeeze the little doll, or you will have puke on your . . . Where *did* you get that gown?" Her smile was counterfeit. "It is so . . . rustic."

Isabella giggled and said, "I have heard that a certain courtier has taken a keen interest in Lady Charlotte. Perhaps there will be babies in her future after all."

I was surprised to see a faint flush in Charlotte's cheeks. She is usually dismissive of these cruel girls, but her look was one of embarrassment tinged with self-conscious pleasure.

"What sort of interest do you mean?" Matilda asked sharply. She put her arm around her sister.

"Oh, well, you should ask Charlotte, shouldn't you? Perhaps I have said too much." Isabella lowered her chin and widened her eyes, parodying a child caught in a fib.

"What is she saying, Lottie?" Matilda asked.

"It's . . . It's probably nothing."

Charlotte's discomfiture was difficult for me to watch.

"Your 'probably nothing' seems to be provoking a good bit of amusement," Matilda said dryly. She is never afraid of speaking her mind, which may be a silver lining to her disfigurement. She doesn't care a whit what anyone thinks of her.

"There have been letters . . ." Charlotte's voice was so low that I could barely hear her. "And a gift. A trinket, really." She pulled a ring from her pocket. It was cheaply made and obviously too small for her fingers.

"Oh how adorable!" Cecily said. "She carries it with her!" She winked at Isabella behind Ella's back.

"Who sent the letters?" I asked cautiously.

"I have not met the gentleman," Charlotte responded, her eyes downcast.

"Do tell us his name!" Isabella said.

The well-wishers had cleared out, and Ella turned to face us. "What is so funny?" she asked.

"Charlotte has a secret admirer!" Cecily said. "Tell us his name!"

"Sir Blakely Snoodgrum," Charlotte whispered.

Isabella tittered and Cecily covered her mouth with her hand. Ella looked from one to the other with her lovely violet-blue eyes. "Isn't that what you call his majesty behind his back?" she asked.

Cecily frowned.

"See, now you've ruined their fun, Princess." Matilda's voice was harsh, and Ella flinched.

"They were making sport of Charlotte," I explained. "Tell me, Cecily, how many marriage proposals have you received? And you, Isabella, you must have been heartbroken when the baron married Lord Geraint's daughter. Her fortune is so much smaller than yours! I wonder why he chose her?"

Matilda snorted, Charlotte blinked back tears, and Ella watched us with a puzzled frown. She is bright, but she has never been able to discern oblique messages concealed behind ordinary words. Cecily opened her mouth to deliver what I don't doubt was to be a nasty retort, but Matilda cut in, saying, "Isn't Phillipa lovely? It brings tears to my eyes just to see her so happy in your arms, Lottie. She is a sweet lamb and beautiful like her mother." She made as though to brush away a tear, and Charlotte glanced at her gratefully, her eyes brimming.

"Our poor princess looks exhausted," I said. "Would you two ladies be so good as to inform the chamberlain that she needs to rest and see her back to her chambers?"

Ella looked relieved.

"You have no standing to tell us what to do!" Isabella said crossly.

"Of course, it was only a suggestion. Your Highness, are you weary?"

"Yes, very much."

"So, I shall find the chamberlain myself. Come, Charlotte, give Phillipa back to her nurse and help me to find Aleyn."

We left Matilda to contend with the other two ladies-in-waiting, which I am sure she did ably. I wish that our lives were not filled with people such as these, that we could live like a real family. I miss the intimacy, the warmth, the simplicity that we captured so fleetingly in those tender days that are more dream than memory for me now.

16

VALLEY OF THE SHADOW

By the age of three, Ella had become a child of breathtaking beauty. Every time I glanced at her, I found her even more exquisite than she had seemed the moment before. Her hair grew in silken curls like her father's, but the color was pale gold, like her mother's. She had eyes too big for her small head, liquid pools of amethyst fringed by long, sweeping lashes. While most children have sturdy, chubby limbs, Ella's were the slender and graceful limbs of a fawn. Lady Alba dressed her in light-colored satins that suited her fair skin, but the gowns were impossible to keep clean. I took to dressing her in serviceable wool whenever I knew that her mother would not see her.

Like other children, Ella learned to walk on her first birthday, but she did not begin to speak until her third. Until then, she had been able to follow instructions, but she mainly got by with pointing, grabbing, or crying to communicate what she wanted. Emont worried that his daughter was simple, and he sighed with relief when, seemingly overnight, she learned to chatter and sing. Her

voice was pitched high, the droll but charming warble of a sparrow. When she shrieked, however, her voice pierced like a dagger.

Ella did not like stories or pretend play. What she liked best was
sorting and arranging. I remembered how much I loved collecting
stones as a child, and I tried to interest her in searching for a new
collection with me, but she did not care for the outdoors. Gisla
suggested that I try buttons, and that was more successful. Ella
could sit for hours, lining up the buttons in neat rows from largest
to smallest or sorting them by color and shape.

Emont was smitten with his beautiful daughter, and he denied
her nothing. He requested treats from the kitchen every morning,
so she was anxious to go to him as soon as she woke. Ella still slept
beside me when she was three, and she would prod me awake with
little kicks and pokes, telling me to hurry. It was a struggle to get
the child properly clothed and her hair brushed; she squirmed and
complained, and if she saw an opportunity to escape before her toi-
lette was complete, she would invariably take it. Emont seemed not
to care whether her hair was a squirrel's nest, and if Ella managed
to elude me in the morning, she would peer at me triumphantly
from behind the safety of her father's legs. Gisla was the only one
who could convince the girl to sit docilely for a brushing; the old
woman had infinite patience and a soft touch.

Once Ella was clothed, she would race downstairs singing
"Treats! Treats!" Emont hid the sweets, pretending that he had not
brought any. Ella searched the hall and Emont's pockets until she
found her reward, and Emont allowed her to curl in his lap like a
cat while she nibbled.

Ella preferred her father's company to anybody else's, I believe
because he demanded nothing from her. He did not insist on good
manners, like I did, or dress her up like a doll, like her mother. He

did not try to draw her into conversation like Joan and Gisla. He simply let her abide in his presence, and she was content.

Toward the end of Ella's third year, Lady Alba changed in some fundamental but inexplicable way, as though a part of her went missing. She had never gone out much, but during that period, she withdrew almost entirely from the world. She refused to leave her chambers, and I never saw her fully dressed anymore. A light within her was snuffed out. Whereas she used to vacillate between fevered intensity and the charming whimsy of a mischievous child, she became listless and indifferent. Her eyes were dull and her face slack. Night and day, she huddled on her bed wearing the same dirty shift, refusing to let Gisla or Joan bathe her.

I often found Lady Alba muttering to herself when I brought Ella to visit. She paused with her head tilted to the side as though listening for a response, though nobody else spoke. If I tried to get her attention, she usually ignored us or feigned sleep. Ella sang little ditties, hoping that Lady Alba would join in as she used to. When she got no response, she settled for lying next to her mother on the bed, playing with her limp white fingers. The sun burned through the shutters, laying stripes across the accumulation of discarded toiletries on the floor. The rosewater that Joan sprinkled on the bed could not hide the stench of Lady Alba's unwashed body, but Ella did not so much as wrinkle her little nose.

Emont had been a rare visitor to his wife's chambers, and after one particularly bad evening, he stopped visiting altogether. Ella was asleep when Emont knocked on the door; Joan vacated the chamber to give the master and mistress their privacy. After a silence, we heard an incoherent scream and then loud cursing from Emont. He banged the door open, holding the palm of his hand over his eye. Streaks of blood ran down his face. He lurched rapidly through the antechamber, like an injured hart fleeing from hunters. That was the last of his nocturnal appearances.

Gisla wrung her knobby hands, worrying for Lady Alba's soul. She brought the priest to give her mistress communion and hear her confession, but Lady Alba turned mute as a stone. Gisla told me that when the priest blessed her forehead with holy water, the lady recoiled from his touch. This convinced the loyal servant that the devil had invaded her mistress's body, and she resolved to speak with Sir Emont about sending Lady Alba to the bishop.

Whether the bishop could have saved Lady Alba, we cannot know. What transpired was so dark that nobody has spoken of it since. One day at dawn, as I floated in the shallows of early-morning sleep, Joan burst from Lady Alba's chamber, wailing and sobbing. Gisla was already out of bed, and she asked sharply, "Whatever is the matter, girl?"

"The mistress!" Joan wailed. Her face was a mask of anguish.

Gisla's eyes widened in alarm. She marched briskly into Lady Alba's chamber to investigate. Ella, who sat up straight in bed beside me, stared after the old woman, her face blank. I pulled the child protectively toward me, and though she did not resist, she did not yield either. She remained silent and inanimate as I kissed the top of her head.

Gisla shouted my name, and Joan collapsed against the wall, mewling helplessly. My legs refused to run. Fear and duty struggled for control of my limbs, and though duty won, I moved toward Lady Alba's chamber with leaden footsteps.

I could not make sense of the sight that greeted me. Gisla, her wrinkled face red with strain, gripped Lady Alba's thighs, holding her aloft as though she were tossing her into the air. Lady Alba slumped to one side; her corn-silk hair cascaded over her shoulder, dancing slowly back and forth over the top of Gisla's black nightcap. She swayed gently, like a stalk of wheat in a light breeze.

"Come here!" Gisla wheezed. "Take her legs!"

Lady Alba's face turned slowly toward me like the moon waxing. It was purple and swollen beyond recognition. I swallowed the gorge that came to my throat and relieved Gisla of the task of supporting our mistress's weight. My strength fed on fear and revulsion. I lifted Lady Alba effortlessly, high into the air, so that the cord around her neck slackened, and she slumped farther sideways. Her cold body pressed against my cheek; the foul smell sickened me. Gisla righted the overturned footstool and stepped up to untie the noose from Lady Alba's neck. This attempt was unsuccessful, but she retrieved a knife from the side table to slice through the silken tie. Lady Alba must have used the same knife to cut a length of cord from the bed hangings.

I laid the body awkwardly on the bed. Joan still moaned in the anteroom. I went to the door and saw that Ella was on the bed where I had left her. She watched her hands intently as she waved her fingers sinuously in front of her eyes, something she did to calm herself. I closed the door softly, hoping not to disturb her.

Gisla worked to remove the noose from Lady Alba's neck. It had bitten deep into her flesh, and the swelling nearly swallowed the cord, leaving only a thin sliver visible in the channel it had cut. Lady Alba's eyes were slits between her puffy, violaceous lids, and the whites had turned a satanic red. I tried to close her eyes, but they would not remain shut.

"Agnes, try this knot. My old hands are no use." Gisla's voice shook.

I worked on the cord until I loosened it, and then I pulled it as gently as I could from the furrow in Lady Alba's neck. It was dark with blood, but nothing fresh oozed out.

"She has been dead some hours."

Gisla nodded and winced as though it hurt her. "The stupid sow slept right through."

"It was not Joan's fault."

Gisla did not answer. When she looked at me, there were tears standing in her eyes. "Help me to wash her. Fetch some water."

"No amount of water is going to hide what she did."

Gisla struck me across the face with shocking ferocity. I brought my hand to my stinging cheek.

"Fetch the water."

The slap woke my anger, but I also saw too late how traitorous my words had sounded to the old woman. I did as she bade me.

We stripped away Lady Alba's shift and gave her the bath that she had so badly needed but refused. It was a strange intimacy with her body, greater in death than it would have been in life. She could not flinch or pull away, and we could not mount a wall of words between us. The absence of her soul made her nakedness stark, and I did not want to touch her. Gisla tended to her with a quiet tenderness that made me feel ashamed.

The color drained from Lady Alba's face as we cleaned, leaving her pale except for delicate blooms of red on her cheeks and nose. The whites of her eyes remained discolored, but as the swelling subsided, we managed to close them. In silent collusion, we dressed her in a high-necked gown that hid the wound on her neck. Gisla's hands trembled as she fastened the buttons.

Gisla took her mistress's jeweled brush and worked through the tangles in Lady Alba's hair as she had done so many times before.

She looked at me, her face grim, and spoke for the first time since we began the bath. "You had better go and tell Sir Emont."

I dressed quickly in the anteroom. Joan had ceased her moaning, but she remained crumpled against the wall. I asked her to stay with Ella before I left.

Emont was still in his bedchamber; as he did not like to have an attendant sleep with him, he answered the door himself. His reddish curls hung in greasy ropes from beneath his nightcap, and his white, hairy legs poked out from beneath his gray undertunic. I would have felt more comfortable delivering bad news in the great hall, when he was fully dressed, but I could not delay. I took a deep breath. "I am sorry to bring you bad news, sir, but Joan found Lady Alba dead this morning."

Emont's expression did not immediately register the shock, but his polite smile dissolved with painful slowness. "What happened?"

Gisla expected me to deceive him, but I had not taken the time to invent a convincing lie. I feigned bewildered confusion, saying, "I . . . I don't know. Joan said that she did not wake."

"Has someone sent for the priest?"

"Not yet." Given the circumstances of Lady Alba's death, I had not considered calling the priest, though of course I should have, or people would begin to ask questions. I looked at my slippered feet to hide my burning cheeks. My great toe poked through a hole in the upper.

Emont closed his eyes and rubbed his forehead. In a strangled voice he gasped, "Oh, my God!" He calmed himself and said more firmly, "I shall have to let her sister know. Show me to Lady Alba."

I led Emont to his wife's quarters. Joan had not moved, but Ella was nowhere to be seen. We passed into the dim and airless

chamber, where the strong scent of rosewater greeted us, a loud
note that failed to obscure the pungent undertone of accumulated
odors. Gisla was gone. Slanting shafts of morning light filtered
through the shutters. Nothing seemed out of the ordinary, except
for the silence.

Gisla had arranged Lady Alba's hands so that they lay folded
over her velvet-clad bosom. She looked so angelic, her pale face
smooth and expressionless, her golden hair spread out like a halo,
that I nearly believed my own falsehood. Emont went to the bedside and touched his wife's hand.

It was then that I saw Ella. She crouched in the shadows behind
the bed, still as a statue, her eyes watchful. I did not want to disturb
Emont, so I approached the child carefully, as one might approach
a feral creature. Before I got within arm's reach, Gisla appeared,
announcing that the priest had been summoned to anoint Lady Alba's corpse. Ella took advantage of the distraction to dart away.
Her father, who was asking Gisla for details, did not notice.

Ella hid from me for several hours; I finally found her sitting
behind the curtains in the solar reserved for guests. She wrapped
her arms around her legs, resting her little chin on her knees. Her
expression was blank and her eyes were dry. She did not look at me
as I crouched beside her and stroked her back lightly.

"Ella."

She did not respond.

"Ella, your mother has gone to heaven to be with God. Jesus has
welcomed her home."

Ella seemed unaware of my presence. I was used to Charlotte
and Matilda's occasional stony silence, their quiet, fuming resentment, but this was not the same. Ella was simply absent. I shivered.

"We have to get ready to go to the abbey, sweetheart. There

will be a Mass for your mother. She will take her place among the saints."

I could get no response from the girl. I wondered queasily whether she knew that I was not telling the truth. That was impossible; the child had seen nothing and knew nothing of heaven's rules. I gave up trying to talk to her and picked Ella up in my arms. She stiffened, her eyes flashed with hostility, and then she became passive again. She did not fight me when I dressed her and braided her hair. I packed a trunk for both of us, and then we joined Emont in the carriage.

The trip to Ellis Abbey lasted an eternity. Emont stared fixedly out the window; the countryside that crawled past was brown and drab after a long winter, and the sky a dull gray. I worried that he would ask me questions about Lady Alba's death, but he said nothing. If he had any suspicions, he kept them buried, where they belonged.

Ella reclined on her father's lap, dozing or simply looking at the roof. At times, she hummed tunelessly. We had bread and cold chicken for supper, and I peeled an apple that was spongy from months in the cellar. I sliced off small pieces for Ella, and she took them absently from my hand. Sickness from the morning's events and my nervous excitement about seeing my daughters again made it impossible for me to eat. As the hours dribbled by, my heart pounded on my rib cage like it was trying to get free.

We arrived at the abbey as the bell rang for vespers. The sky was orange and pink in the west, and the air held the freshness of early spring. Grooms met us and helped us down from the carriage just outside the church, and Mother Elfilda herself appeared from the door to the cloister. She was attended by two nuns, one of whom I recognized as the prioress. Their veils glowed in the fading light and fluttered behind them like banners. The abbess held out a small, pale hand to Emont, saying, "I am sorry for your loss."

Emont bent to kiss her hand and replied, "It is your loss as well, Your Reverence."

Mother Elfilda bowed her head in assent. "You may use the bishop's chambers tonight, Emont. Sister Margaret will show you to them, and a manservant will meet you there." She looked to Ella, who was clinging to her father's leg, and to my astonishment, the abbess stooped to speak to the child directly. "I am your godmother, Elfilda. I shall help to care for you now that your mother is dead. We shall celebrate the ascension of her soul into heaven tomorrow."

Ella looked up at her with huge eyes, saying nothing. The abbess smiled faintly. I wondered if Ella reminded her of herself as a child. The resemblance was striking.

"Are you the nurse?" Mother Elfilda showed no sign of recognizing me.

"Yes, Mother."

"You may take Elfilda to the guest quarters. Sister Margaret will come for you when she has shown Emont to his rooms."

Servants were already unloading our trunk from the carriage.

"I know the way, my lady."

The abbess and prioress had started back toward the church without waiting for my reply, so I took Ella by the hand. She did not want to let go of her father. He kissed her head and bade her go with me, and she relented to do so as long as I carried her.

I let Ella ride on my back, holding on to her little hands so that she did not grab too tightly at my throat. She seemed to have recovered from her earlier torpor, and she chattered about the animals that she had seen during our trip to the abbey. As she seldom went outdoors, and as there were no animals within the inner gate of the manor, even sheep were a novelty for the girl.

Although it was out of our way, I went first to the cloister in the hope of seeing Charlotte and Matilda. The sun had set, which meant that vespers was ending, and the children would soon be on their way to their dorter. I lingered in the arcade in the deepening twilight, trying to entertain Ella by watching the sky for the first stars to appear. She grew bored and cold, and guilt crept over me when I heard her kittenish yawn. Reluctantly, I left the empty cloister and brought Ella to the guesthouse. Our trunk had been delivered to the large chamber at the front of the building, where I put Ella to bed, relieved that she had returned to her normal three-year-old self. I settled beside her, knowing that sleep would be elusive. I yearned to go to my daughters; they were so close, and my mind filled in every detail of their appearances as they slept. I could see the rise and fall of their breathing, the fluttering of their eyelids, their loosely curled fists flung wide. I could feel the warmth of their brows as I kissed them good night ever so softly.

The next morning, Ella was up with the sun, and I took her to the abbey's kitchen to fetch her some milk. I planned to wait in the cloister until Charlotte and Matilda passed through, so I brought Ella's buttons on a small tray to keep her occupied. On the day that poor Ella would see her mother buried, I was as nervous as a young girl on the way to her wedding.

We did not have to wait long for the convent school girls to finish morning prayers. I watched them file out of the chapel, all garbed in the same gray frock that I had worn at Rose House so long ago. The older girls walked quietly in pairs, and the younger ones spilled out after them, jostling one another and stifling giggles. My heart was in my throat as I searched the faces for my daughters.

When I saw Charlotte, I caught my breath. She had grown so tall! Her raven hair and dark skin stood out among the fair children like a black sheep in a flock of white. Soft contours of baby fat were gone, giving way to the hard lines of her jaw and graceful bridge of her nose. Without thinking, I stood, spilling the tray of buttons that Ella had been playing with on my lap. Ella shrieked, and I bent to comfort her, promising to gather the buttons. I did not have time to straighten before Matilda crashed into me crying, "Mama!" We fell backward onto the grass, still dead from winter, and Matilda covered my face with quick pecking kisses. When she smiled, I could see that she was missing two of her teeth. Behind her, wavering through my tears, Charlotte looked down on us, beaming.

Ella was so surprised by the commotion that she stopped crying. A nun scolded the girls sharply, and Matilda let go of me and brushed the yellow blades from her skirt. Her face was still badly scarred from the pox. Though her skin was no longer discolored, it was distorted by pits and jagged ruts. My heart ached as I remembered her smooth, perfect baby face nuzzling at my neck.

"What is the meaning of this behavior?" demanded the stout nun. Some of the younger girls lingered and stared.

"Forgive us, Sister. This is our mother," said Charlotte.

The nun raised her thin eyebrows. "Is this how a lady behaves?"

"No, Sister," the girls replied in unison.

"You must each pray a novena so that you will remember next time."

Charlotte groaned.

The nun turned to me. "I did not know that their mother had come. Are you taking them home?"

Charlotte and Matilda watched me with shining eyes, childish hopefulness written clearly on their faces.

"No, Sister. I have come for Lady Alba's funeral. This is her daughter, Elfilda. I am her nurse."

Matilda's chin quivered.

"I would like to visit with my daughters while I am here. I have not seen them in more than three years. We could spend this morning together. I must leave tomorrow to bring Elfilda home."

The holy lady looked doubtful. It was difficult to reconcile my appearance and speech—and my daughters' positions as convent students—with the fact that I was a servant. She was probably unsure of what to make of me or how to address me. Finally, she said to my daughters, "Meet us for prayer at terce. You may stay with your mother until then." The nun herded the remaining girls to the dining hall like a mother goose, leaving Charlotte and Matilda behind with me.

The girls became shy once everyone was gone, but I asked them to help me to pick up Ella's buttons, and that seemed to put them at ease. They examined Ella with fascination. With her long, graceful limbs and dainty proportions, Ella looked like a golden-haired Bathsheba shrunk down to the size of a doll. Next to her, my daughters were giants.

Charlotte, who had always been nurturing, tried to play with Ella. She made a game of counting the buttons, which made the tiny girl laugh, but when Charlotte tried to pick her up, Ella screeched and hid behind my skirts. I proposed that we go for a walk around the pond to look for frogs, and my suggestion was met with enthusiasm from the older girls, but not from Ella. She avoided water like a cat. I promised that her feet would not get wet, and she agreed to come as long as I carried her.

On the way to the pond, I peppered Charlotte and Matilda with questions about their lives at the abbey, but they were not interested in talking about it. They skipped around me, chattering about a girl who had fainted during Mass, how angry the prioress had been, what they hoped to eat for dinner, and how much they loved Ella's blue gown. I managed to gather that they were both good pupils, and that they liked some teachers and loathed others. I suppose that I got the only answer I needed, which was that they were not unhappy.

The ground around the pond was muddier than I had anticipated. I tried to herd the girls away from the edge and onto more solid ground, but they were carried away by their excitement; when the frogs tried to escape into the rushes, Charlotte and Matilda followed. I warned them that they would be punished for dirtying their shoes, but they did not care. After a while, I did not care either. I followed their movements hungrily. Their delight nourished me, and their laughter brought color back into the world.

Ella was not tempted to join the older girls, but she watched their activity with interest from her perch on my back. When Charlotte trapped a frog in her hands, Ella leaned precariously low to peer into the darkness between Charlotte's fingers. As she could see nothing, Charlotte opened her fingers wider and wider, until the frog saw its chance for freedom and sprang into the air. Ella started and I nearly lost my grasp of her, but then she giggled happily. Charlotte laughed too and promised to find her another frog.

As the time to part grew near, Matilda grew quiet and sidled closer to me. She pulled at my arm, but as I needed both hands to hold on to Ella, I could not embrace her. I tried to set Ella on some dry ground, but she squirmed and refused to get down. Matilda then whined plaintively that she did not wish me to leave, and she tried to hook her arm around my waist, but Ella was in the way. I am not certain whether Matilda hit or pinched her, but Ella sent up a wail of fury and indignation.

"Matilda!"

She looked at me sheepishly.

"Shame on you!" I shifted Ella so that I held her against my chest, and I kissed her golden hair. "You apologize to Ella right now!"

Matilda's expression darkened as she watched me cuddle the whimpering Ella. "I'm sorry."

"She is just a wee girl. You should know better!"

"Yes, Mother."

Matilda had never called me Mother before, only Mama. Her tone was more sad than cold, and I had the urge to drop Ella and gather my own daughter in my arms. Instead, I called Charlotte over and said, "I shall help you both to get clean. The bells will ring shortly, and we should go back."

Charlotte looked stricken, and I did not know how to comfort her. I struggled to keep the tears from my own eyes. On the road, Ella consented to walk, and I gathered tufts of grass to clean the girls' shoes. They plodded silently back to the cloister with me as the bells rang for terce. When we reached the arcade, Charlotte turned to me, her eyes glistening. "When shall we see you again, Mama?" Her voice wavered.

"I don't know, my angel." Ella pulled at my skirts, and I yanked them away in annoyance.

"Shall we ever live with you again?"

"I wish it with all my heart."

"Me too."

Ella whimpered, but I ignored her. I embraced Charlotte and Matilda quickly and told them to hurry, for they were late. They

left reluctantly. As they neared the chapter house, Matilda looked
back over her shoulder. I had just picked up Ella, but I managed to
raise my hand to wave. Matilda turned away again without returning the gesture.

The funeral Mass was not very different from any other Mass I had
witnessed at the abbey. All of the sisters were in attendance, but
there were few other guests, and as far as I could tell, nobody shed
a tear. The richly dressed men and women in the front pews likely
came to curry favor with the abbess, whether they belonged to the
Wenslock family or not. I am not even certain that Lady Alba's
sister mourned her passing.

Ella and I sat in the pew behind Emont. He did not look well; his
face was sallow and bloated. I had dressed Ella in her finest velvet
and brushed her hair until it shone, but he did not remark on her
beauty in his usual manner. He merely patted her cheek and then
knelt to pray.

After Mass, the abbess led a procession to the burial ground, but
Ella and I did not follow. The little girl had fallen asleep with her
head on my lap, so I remained behind in the church and let her rest
until we had to join the others for the abbess's reception. Though
she had shown no outward signs of grief, I pitied the child for the
loss of her mother. Lady Alba had been inconstant, but Ella must
have loved her dearly.

Lady Alba's body was a feast for worms, but I wondered what
would become of her soul. Hers was the gravest of sins, one that
could not be repented. It did not seem right that murderers could
go to heaven after confession, but Lady Alba would not be afforded
such a chance.

I twined the ends of Ella's pale curls around my fingers as she slept. Her hair was soft and fell in perfect ringlets around her fair, heart-shaped face. I felt a shiver of wonder, just as when a huge harvest moon floats silvery bright on a purple horizon, or when the church fills with song at Christmastide.

Sadness pressed down upon me when I thought of my own daughters. Nobody would ever find them beautiful.

As the sun dropped low in the sky, the western windows glowed and cast their brilliant colors over the floor and the pews. I tried to feel grateful for my good fortune, telling myself that Charlotte and Matilda had a comfortable life. I could not help but worry that just as Ella had lost her mother, my daughters were losing theirs too.

17

BETROTHAL

After Lady Alba's death, Joan moved to Cothay Manor, and Gisla became a maid to Ella. The child did not need two servants to care for her, but I was glad for the help, and Gisla was glad for the ease of her new position. I hardly needed to justify the expense to Emont and Wills; I had by then taken over most of the household accounting, and they seldom questioned me anymore.

Black, the bailiff, was not as imposing as he first seemed. Though big and gruff, he was a reasonable man and respectful to women, most particularly to his wife, who, according to Black, was the most admirable person in all of Aviceford. Had he been a less broad-minded, thoughtful sort, it is unlikely that the bailiff would have worked with me on the idea that ultimately made the manor profitable.

The population of the village had been in decline for some years. Young men escaped to the towns, hoping to gain their freedom and learn a trade. Young women married into more prosperous manors or ran off to town with their beaux. As Aviceford was the least lucrative of the abbess's holdings, other manors poached workers.

A lord stronger than Emont or a bailiff tougher than Black might have staunched the bleeding, but as it was, the shrinking population pinched Aviceford ever tighter.

"We haven't got the men for harvest," Black complained at one of our meetings. "The grain will freeze on the stalks if it don't rot first."

It had been a wet summer and autumn, which pushed harvest back into the arms of winter. We had already had a frost and a hailstorm; yield was bound to be poor, and Black was in a rush to get whatever grains were undamaged safely into storage.

"Surely the manor can spare a few more able bodies," I said.

"I have already given as many as I can spare," Wills snapped. He disagreed with me about reorganizing labor at the manor. I was bothered by the inefficiencies, but I had no authority to tell Wills what to do with his servants.

"A few more able bodies would scarcely be enough in any case," Black said. "I asked for help from Cothay, but they claim they're just as hard up."

"A bunch of loiter-sacks is what they are," Wills said.

"The shortage gets worse every year," I observed.

"Aye."

"What if you quit planting and let grass grow for sheep?"

"We cannot feed our people with sheep alone," the bailiff said.

"You could let most of the people go. They are leaving already."

"And how can we survive without rent money and fines?"

I thought about how to respond delicately. I did not want the bailiff to think that I was accusing him of laxity, though in truth, he did a poor job of collecting payments. "Many a virgater is delinquent at one time or another," I said. "They say they will pay with eggs, but the hens won't lay, or they will get you the money after they sell an ox. The income has never been enough to sustain the manor, and the situation is only worsening. As more villagers leave, the land becomes less productive as well. There is no way out except to change the entire arrangement."

"Your plan is to trade peasants for sheep?" Wills said. "I would sure like to see the sheep till the fields."

"Turn the fields to pasture," I said. "Sheep don't pay rent with coins or eggs. They pay with valuable wool. They never miss a payment. They rarely run away. For each virgate farmed by a peasant, we could raise whole flocks of sheep. When too many sheep are born, we need not feed them. They will feed us instead."

The bailiff was not immediately persuaded to my point of view, but over the span of three years, he turned an increasing portion of Aviceford's lands over to pasture, and the manor's fortunes improved considerably. We had no trouble paying our debts, and we were able to put villagers to work constructing new barns and helping to repoint the outer walls of the manor house. Those who lost their land and did not want to help with construction left to work at one of the abbey's other manors or to one of the nearby towns. I suppose that Lottie and Thomas were among them, as I never saw or heard from them again.

When Ella was eight years old, her godmother came to visit. This was an extraordinary event, because the abbess seldom traveled, and after the death of Lady Alba, the manor almost never received visitors. Previously, Abbess Elfilda had shown interest in her niece by sending gifts, which included a superbly rendered portrait of the Virgin and child that we hung by Ella's bed. Ella loved the painting, perhaps in part because the beatific Madonna resembled her own dead mother.

Ella had taken over Lady Alba's chambers, and I still shared the anteroom with Gisla. As these were the largest and most richly appointed rooms in the house, we moved out in favor of Abbess Elfilda. Ella slept with me in the attic, and Gisla slept by the hearth in the kitchen to keep her old bones warm. Emont was so concerned for the abbess's comfort that he had a new feather bed and quilt brought from the city, though Ella's were still perfectly serviceable. He pestered Wills about preparations for the visit until the chamberlain was quite beside himself. Wills had grown a long ginger-and-white beard, which he yanked when he was anxious. I thought that he would pull it right off his chin in the days leading up to Abbess Elfilda's arrival.

The abbess traveled with a retinue of ten people, three of them nuns. I did not witness their approach myself, but when Gisla came to fetch Ella, she told me breathlessly that the holy lady had ridden in a gilded carriage that bore the insignia of the House of Wenslock. Upon arriving, the abbess asked to see her goddaughter. Gisla joined us, as she did not want to miss a rare bit of excitement at Aviceford Manor.

The abbess perched on one of the high-backed chairs by the blackened maw of the fireplace in the great hall, and Emont sat opposite. Two nuns flanked Mother Elfilda, surveying the room as though they expected barbarians to leap from behind the tapestries. Gisla and I nudged Ella toward her godmother. I had trained Ella to curtsy and to kiss the abbess's hand, and she carried out my instructions flawlessly. Although she was a quiet girl, Ella had not a shred of shyness, and she was good about following rules. She was tiny, which made her look much younger than her real age, giving her the appearance of being precociously clever and poised. The abbess was charmed.

"What lovely manners!" Mother Elfilda said. Her voice was clear and lightly resonant. "How old are you now?"

"I am eight, Mother."

"And do you know your prayers?"

"Yes, Mother."

"What are the seven holy virtues?"

"Faith, Hope, Charity, Justice, Prudence . . ." Ella paused and furrowed her brow. She could become upset when she failed to remember something that she had learned. As Gisla and I watched from across the room, I held my breath.

". . . Fortitude and Temperance." Ella looked pleased with herself.

"Quite right. And can you recite the paternoster?"

Ella rattled off the Latin words to the prayer in her singsong warble.

"Such a clever girl!" The abbess looked at Emont. "Who teaches her lessons?"

"Her nurse, Agnes."

"This must be a remarkably learned nurse to teach her prayers in Latin."

"I believe that she learned her letters at your abbey, my lady."

"She was our student? Then why does she work as a nurse?"

"Not a student, my lady. Agnes worked for your mother. She married your ward." In our years together, Emont had learned nearly every detail of my past.

Mother Elfilda squinted into the shadows where I stood. "Of course. I sent you as a lady's maid to my sister. I thought that Emont would have found you a husband by now."

I moved into the light and curtsied, saying, "Your Reverence."

"Are your daughters still attending our school?"

"Yes, Mother. I am very grateful."

"I suppose it is fitting that since you have been teaching my god-daughter her prayers, I have been teaching your daughters theirs." She turned to Emont. "Elfilda will need a proper tutor soon. She is no longer a baby."

"Yes, of course, Mother."

The abbess turned back to Ella. "You have done well to remember your paternoster. Tomorrow I shall teach you the fifteen rosary promises. Your father is going to find you a real teacher from the city now that you are a big girl. Now go to bed, and I shall speak with you again tomorrow." Mother Elfilda waved her hand in my direction. "You are dismissed."

That night, Ella and I slept in the garret at the southern end of the manor house, where there were several narrow pallets raised on sagging wood-and-rope frames. The attic had housed the servants of visitors, but had fallen into disuse after the death of Lady Alba. Rodents chewed through the beds and pulled out the stuffing, leaving straw scattered over the rough floorboards, and all was blanketed by a layer of fine dust. Only one bed had not yet caved in upon itself, so I made that one up to share with Ella. When I shook the mattress, the dust rose in a great cloud, and as it settled, the last rays of sunlight captured the slowly moving motes. Ella watched with fascination, reaching into the beams of light to close her little fist around vanishing firmaments.

Despite the mischief by rodents, the garret was cozy. It smelled of pine, and there was no trace of mildew; it was warmer and drier than many parts of Aviceford Manor. Ella did not mind ceding her chambers to the abbess or sleeping in the attic, but she grumbled about sharing a pallet with me. I tried to give her space on the bed, but we kept slipping into the valley in the center of the mattress. Fortunately, the girl's drooping eyelids were soon too heavy for her to lift, and she fell into slumber.

Ella squirmed and rolled in her sleep, wrapping herself in a cocoon of bedclothes. Each time she turned, her long braid writhed across the pillow like a golden snake. I lay awake, chilled by the cold night air, plucking at the blankets when I had the chance to steal some back. The hunchback moon crept slowly across the window, and an owl hooted in the distance. A lonely moth trying to escape whirred softly and thumped against the glazing, dashing its body repeatedly into the unyielding glass in its bid for freedom. I tried to picture Charlotte and Matilda asleep at the abbey with moonlight on their faces. Of course, at that time of year, the shutters would be closed, allowing no more than a thin blade of light to pass through.

Ella's face in the moonlight was ineffably beautiful. I turned toward the wall and closed my eyes. After what seemed an eternity, I too fell asleep.

Abbess Elfilda remained at the manor for one week, during which time Emont succeeded in maintaining the appearance of sobriety. The abbess met with Ella daily to further her religious education. On the morning of her departure, she joined Emont's meeting with the bailiff and chamberlain. When it became clear to her that I meant to join too, the faint creases on her brow deepened. She turned to Emont, saying, "Why is she here?"

Emont cleared his throat. "Agnes has been helpful with accounting, my lady."

Mother Elfilda raised her pale eyebrows. "Your child's nurse is minding the books for you?"

"Well, not exactly minding." I could tell that Emont was cursing himself for not having foreseen her reaction. Hers was no different from the bailiff's reaction years before, but we had all grown so accustomed to my role that we forgot how unconventional it was.

"What, then, if not minding?"

"She is clever with numbers, my lady. She points out mistakes."

The abbess seemed to consider this for a moment. She leaned back in her chair and waved her hand impatiently. "Get on, then. I am listening."

The meeting was routine and uneventful; Mother Elfilda asked some questions, but she did not seem to be particularly interested in the answers, and business was quickly concluded. After the bailiff knelt and bade her farewell, the abbess requested that I remain behind with her and Emont. She folded her small hands in her lap and looked at me placidly. "You have been a good nurse for Elfilda, but she has grown too old for a nurse. It is time that Emont found a husband for you. You are still young enough to have more children."

The dread that I felt was mirrored on Emont's face. He had come to rely on me not only for administration of the manor, but as his only company. The self-doubt that plagued Emont made him uncomfortable with peers and distrustful of servants; he was bewildered by manly conventions and wary of feminine artifice. As I was straightforward and uncritical, and as Ella loved him unreservedly, Ella and I were the only people he wanted to have near him.

Emont's voice was tight when he replied, "I am sure that we

can find work for Agnes here at the manor house when Ella gets a tutor. The girl is attached to her, Mother. It would be a shame to separate them."

I had not seen much evidence of Ella's attachment to me. Regardless, Emont's statement did not mollify the abbess.

"All the more reason to find a husband for her. It is not natural for children to form too strong a bond with a servant."

"Your Reverence?" I paused, waiting for an invitation to speak.

"Yes?"

"I believe, my lady, that you have been pleased with the income from Aviceford Manor these past two years?"

"That is true."

"My efforts have helped to raise that income, my lady, and I would be pleased to continue to contribute where I am needed."

The abbess shrugged irritably. "I appreciate your service, but that is the work of a lady of the manor. We shall find someone suitable soon, I am sure." Abbess Elfilda gave Emont a disapproving look and then stood, indicating that the conversation was over. "You may stay with Elfilda until her tutor arrives. I shall have one sent from the city."

After the abbess and her retinue departed for Ellis Abbey, Emont sought me out. I had settled Ella into bed in her own room and was reading my psalter by the light of a candle in the anteroom. Gisla was already asleep in her bed when Emont opened the door and beckoned to me to follow him. Someone who knew him less well might not have noticed his unsteadiness; he had evidently made up for his week of relative abstinence at dinner.

Emont led me down the corridor toward his chamber. The door

was open, and the flickering firelight guided our way. Once inside, he closed the door and sank heavily into his chair by the hearth. The room was warm, so I loosened my shawl.

"That woman should stay at the abbey and leave manorial affairs to the lords of the manors. I shall find a way for you to remain here with me."

I watched the flames dance on the hearth. The charred skeleton of a log collapsed, sending up a shower of orange sparks.

"You will stay until a tutor arrives, anyway. Then we shall find a new position here for you. Abbess Elfilda needn't know." His tongue was thick with drink.

"It would be no secret if I continued to help with the books."

"You could tell me what you think in private. Nobody else need know."

"You do not think that the servants gossip? That the abbess's steward will report the gossip back to his mistress if she asks about me? And she means to find you a new wife. What wife will tolerate my interference?"

Emont groaned and leaned his heavy head on his hands. "What would you have me do?"

I was heartsick. Everything good that I had wrought in my life was torn from my grasp. I had raised both the alehouse and the manor out of ruin, and with a heedless flick of her wrist, the abbess had taken them both from me. I blamed her for the loss of my daughters. I hated her.

"There is nothing to be done," I said hollowly. I was too dispirited and hopeless to even shed a tear.

Emont pushed the veil of hair back from his face. His gaze glittered with hectic intensity.

"You could work in the laundry."

"And what? Drink ale with you in the morning? Become your whore?" Memories of Elisabeth's degradation turned my stomach.

"I . . . I can't bear for you to leave." His expression was anguished.

A bold thought crept into my mind. Perhaps there was a way for me to stay. I needed a husband, and Emont needed a wife. My breath quickened as I imagined the impossible, and before I could snatch back the words, I heard myself say, "You could marry me."

Emont tipped his head back and laughed with a mixture of drunken amusement and bitterness. "Marry you? I could sooner marry my horse."

"Why not?"

"Why not? Are you out of your mind? You are a servant, and I am the son of Lord Henry Vis-de-Loup."

"I was married to the son of a knight. I am already functioning as the lady of the manor, and a good one at that. I am not young, but I have at least a decade of childbearing years still ahead. Besides, who will you take for a wife otherwise?" I knew that he did not want a new wife. Most women unnerved him, and he was too ashamed to let a stranger into his life. He wanted me by his side.

"The abbess would be outraged. You are not even born of gentry."

"It might ruffle her feathers, but what would she do? You are the father of her dear niece and goddaughter. She will not take the manor from you. She cannot hurt you without hurting Ella."

"You are completely mad. This idea is mad."

I knelt down before him and reached out to brush my fingertips across his lips. My shawl slipped from my shoulders, leaving my arms bare. Emont gazed down at me with an expression of confused longing. Emboldened, I placed my hands on both sides of his face and pulled him toward me until his lips touched mine. His breath was hot, as though he had a fever, and stank of wine. I concentrated my senses on the prickly heat of the fire at my back. A bead of sweat slid between my breasts.

Whether in a moment of decisiveness or loss of balance, Emont lurched forward, pressing his mouth hard against mine. Our teeth clashed dully before I teetered backward, my head landing a fingersbreadth from the hearthstone. Emont slid from his chair and crawled on top of me. He straddled my waist. There was hunger in his eyes, but also pleading. His weight squeezed the breath from me, and I was relieved when he shifted forward to lay his chest against mine. As he was too short to reach my mouth, he shimmied clumsily, like a boy climbing a tree. His movement dragged my shift until it bunched around my thighs. I lay still while he planted sloppy kisses on my mouth, but when he grasped my breast, I turned my face away, saying, "No, Emont."

He grunted but sat up again, crushing my ribs beneath his hips. "Come to bed." His voice was hoarse. He staggered to his feet and held out a hand to help me up, but I didn't trust his balance. I stood on my own, brushing down my skirt.

"You will only make things worse for both of us." I stroked his arm lightly with an affection that was only partly feigned. For all of his drunken, awkward advances, he did care for me, and for all of his privilege, he was deeply unhappy.

Emont leaned forward and kissed me again. I pressed my lips briefly to his, and then I pushed him away again. "No. Please. Why don't you lie down on the bed? I shall untie your boots. It is late and time you slept."

Emont looked at me hopefully. He tried to take my hand, but

I placed my hands on his shoulders instead and guided him to the bed. When we reached the bedside, he grasped both of my wrists and searched my face intently. His eyes were lucid; perhaps he was not as drunk as I had believed. I felt a queasy flutter and could not meet his gaze.

"Agnes, you are unlike anyone I have ever met. You are so clever and kind. I . . . I wish . . ."

The naked sentiment in his voice made me uncomfortable. I did not like to hear him describe me as kind. I cut him off, saying, "Perhaps you should meet more women." I had meant to sound wry, but the words were bitter even to my own ears.

Emont held my wrists a moment longer, and then he flopped down resignedly and closed his eyes. I unlaced his boots slowly, telling him a story about Ella from earlier in the day. Before I could finish, he began to snore.

In the weeks that followed, Emont twisted and strained against the bonds of circumstance. He did not want to risk angering Abbess Elfilda, but he could not bear the thought of marrying me to another man. He made untenable proposals to hide me at the manor, but even he understood that the abbess would soon hear if he were consorting with an unwed servant.

I encouraged Emont's attachment by being warm and solicitous, hoping that he might cave in and marry me, but my attentions inflamed Emont without pushing him closer to a decision. He drank more heavily than ever, and he was intolerant of his daughter, which he had never been before.

One morning, while we sat together in the great hall, Ella squirmed on Emont's lap and knocked over his cup of ale.

"Get off me, you clumsy mimmerkin!" he bellowed and pushed Ella forcefully from his lap.

The girl landed on her knees, and she remained still for a moment, stunned. Then Ella's lovely eyes widened and she let out a shriek, an uninterrupted keening. Emont grasped her long hair, which she wore loose that day, and he hauled her to her feet with a sharp yank. He pushed his face close to his daughter's and shouted, "Take your sniveling elsewhere!"

This ended Ella's shriek, but she began to sob. Shaking, she pulled away from her father. I rose to help her, but Emont roared, "Stay!" so I sank back into my chair, and the girl ran crying to Gisla by herself.

Emont gripped the arms of his chair. I waited for his breathing to slow before daring to speak.

"You should go to her and soothe her spirits with a few kind words," I said.

Emont closed his eyes and knocked the back of his head against the carved headrest. He sighed. "I know," he said. "I will go to her."

"You are a good father."

"I am a weak father."

"Most fathers do not show so much affection to their daughters."

"She is all I have." He sounded miserable.

"She can certainly be trying at times."

Emont opened his eyes and looked at me curiously. The color of his eyes was the same arresting violet-blue as his daughter's, and it occurred to me that his gaze shared something of her innocence as well.

"You find Ella difficult?" he asked.

His words took me by surprise, for I had assumed that everyone found Ella difficult. "She is quick to tears," I said, "and she is a fussy child."

"She is sensitive."

"Yes, I suppose that is true," I murmured. "Can I fetch you more ale? Would you care for a blanket?"

"Do you not like her?"

I had never posed such a question to myself. Ella was my labor, my duty, just as the laundry had once been. She was peculiar, certainly, a solitary woolgatherer who did not engage in play like other children. She was a stickler for quiet and rigid in her likes and dislikes. Still, she was a good girl, rarely defiant, and as fastidious about following rules as she was about routines.

"She is a dear child," I said.

"The dearest," Emont agreed. "An angel. Perfection itself."

I smiled politely.

"I do believe that she is the brightest and most beautiful girl in the kingdom."

"Undoubtedly," I said. "Certainly the most beautiful I have ever beheld. And she is clever."

After a pause, Emont said, "You would be a good mother."

"I *am* a mother."

"Of course, of course. You had daughters once too."

"I have daughters still." I had not seen my children in five years. I did not know if they remembered me. I only knew that they were alive because I begged the abbey's messenger to inquire for me.

"I hope that I did not offend you," Emont said. "I only meant that you are good with Ella."

"I shall fetch that ale for you." I left for the buttery, my eyes burning.

✹

The days dragged on, and Emont made no decision. He was cornered, frantic for an escape but unwilling to run toward the danger he perceived on every side. He was simply unable to act.

I tried to speak about a plan for me to return to Old Hilgate. I thought that he might give me the money to make a new start; I had guided the manor out of debt, and he could afford to be generous. From Old Hilgate, I could visit Charlotte and Matilda at the abbey.

Emont refused to discuss any of this with me. He pounded his fist and told me to keep quiet and allow him to think.

Ella caught a fever, and she was sick for several days. Soon I too began to cough and ache, and then it was my turn to be confined to bed. My fever subsided, and I thought that I was improving, but the cough worsened. I had paroxysms that left me gasping, and then the fever came roaring back, worse than before. My phlegm turned putrid, then to blood, and I was frightened.

Gisla sent for the apothecary, but the medicine did not help. Troubled dreams leaked into waking hours until I could no longer distinguish sleep from wakefulness. My breathing was labored, and I had nightmares about drowning in a pond covered by gray scum and dead rushes: I sank and sank into lightless depths. The muddy bottom of the pond was as soft as eiderdown and just as yielding, and as I descended, it enfolded me until it closed over my mouth and nose. Then I would wake, heaving and struggling to catch my breath.

Often when I woke, I saw Emont's concerned face hovering over me. He rubbed my back or sat me up to ease my panic. Though I do not remember it, Gisla told me that a physician came to bleed me, and when he left, he told them not to expect me to survive.

Emont took up a vigil at my bedside. He prayed, and Gisla said that he wept when he saw how my lips turned blue as I gasped for breath. He gave up food and drink, though when Gisla saw how his hands trembled, she convinced him that he should at least take some ale.

I was ill for two weeks and wobbly as a newborn kitten when it was over. Emont insisted on feeding me broth by his own hand, and he supported my arm on his shoulders as I tried to walk again. I had never seen him so gentle, not even with Ella.

Fasting had made me gaunt; my gowns hung loose, and I was startled by the angularity of my face in the mirror. It suited me—at the end of my third decade, the soft contours of youth had given way to more sculpted features. The hollows beneath my cheekbones and sharp angle of my jaw were too austere to be beautiful, but, coupled with my large brown eyes, the effect was still pleasing.

Emont seemed to be enchanted by me. He watched me so intently that I was embarrassed and found it difficult to meet his gaze. Much to Gisla's disapproval, he gave me one of Lady Alba's necklaces, and he insisted on fastening the clasp himself. Once he had properly arranged the jewels, he held me at arm's length and told me that I was dazzling.

Though I was the servant and he the master, Emont was happy to fuss and coddle me, bringing cups of cider and tucking blankets around my knees. My infirmity seemed to give him new purpose. He was never more cheerful—or more sober—than during my convalescence.

On a sunny afternoon, Emont bundled me in one of Lady Alba's fur cloaks and took me outside for a walk. The snow had melted, leaving behind puddles and mud, but the breeze carried the loamy promise of lilies and lilacs. My legs were still weak, but the sunshine lifted my spirits.

"It is good to see some color in your cheeks again," Emont said.

We walked in companionable silence for some time, his arm brushing against mine, and then Emont stopped. He tapped his walking stick against the cobblestones. "You do know how much I value your company, Agnes?"

I watched him tug at his tunic where it wrinkled over his belly. When his eyes met mine, I was embarrassed by the vulnerability I perceived in them.

"I value your company also, sir," I replied.

"Sir? You haven't called me that in a while." He cleared his throat and smiled nervously. "You had suggested that we get married."

I suppose that I must have looked as uncomfortable as I felt, because he laughed and said, "Don't tell me that the formidable Agnes has become a blushing maiden!"

My heart beat almost painfully against my ribs. "It is only that I was not expecting you to speak of marriage."

"I have had time to consider."

"You are reconciled to the impediments?"

"It is not so much that . . ." He twisted his walking stick for a moment. "I have discovered that I cannot live without you. It is a ridiculous idea for me to marry you, but I don't see any other way. I . . . I know that you do not feel about me as I do about you. I do hope that you have some affection for me. I believe you do. Of course, the marriage would be a great advantage to you, as you know . . . And of course to me, because you are the best manager anyone could hope—"

When I could no longer stand for him to go on, I placed my hand on his and said, "Emont, it would be my honor to be your wife."

With a sharp intake of breath, he clasped my hand in his and bent to kiss it. He smiled at me, his eyes glistening, and said, "Thank you, Agnes. I will endeavor to be worthy of you."

The unnatural transition from servant to betrothed of a lord did not progress smoothly. There are no signposts for such an over-throw of convention. It is said that Ella rose from rags to riches by marrying a prince, but in truth, she was a high-born lady, even if her father was not wealthy by royal standards. Ella's marriage was only unusual. Mine was unthinkable.

It is fortunate that we were isolated in the countryside and that visitors had become rare, or Emont might have lost courage in the face of censure from his peers. As it was, in lonely Aviceford Manor, crouched atop a hillside and surrounded by no one but unlettered peasants, we heard objections only from Gisla and, of course, Ella.

I told Gisla the news myself, after we put Ella to bed. She looked dumbfounded. "What is this you speak of?" she asked, not trust-ing her own ears.

"I am to be married. To Emont."

"No! That cannot be!" She covered her mouth with a gnarled fist.

"It is. We are betrothed."

"The master must marry a lady! Marry a servant? Foul——" She searched mutely for words to express her outrage and finally spat out, "Scandalous!"

I set my candle down and lit a second one in a wall sconce. The room Gisla and I shared lacked its own hearth, though the fire in Ella's adjoining chamber kept us warm.

"I have done a great deal to right this sinking ship," I said. "The manor has never been so profitable. Emont has never been so well. You know that I do him good."

"You do, that is true, but marriage? To a nobleman?"

"Are you not happy for me?"

Gisla crossed her bony arms. "You have always acted above your station. I lay no blame on you for that. You are educated. I lay no blame on you for catching the master's eye either. 'Tisn't your fault you were born handsome. But there is right and there is wrong, and a servant marrying a master is wrong."

"Even if it will be good for the master? Good for Ella?"

"What Ella needs is a mother with proper standing. She is the granddaughter of a count and a baron. She cannot have a villein stepmother! It would ruin her reputation. How would her father find a husband for her?"

"You really doubt that Ella will find a husband?" I said teasingly.

Gisla's indignation did not prevent her lips from twitching with a smile. It was obvious that only a blind man could be unaffected by Ella's enchantment. She pressed her lips back into a thin line and said, "'Tisn't proper," but the disapproval in her voice had lightened.

"I understand your objection," I said. "This is terribly unconventional. I do not deserve Emont's love. He is likely to change his mind. If he does not, the abbess will doubtless interfere before we can be wed, and you will be gratified." I knew that Gisla disliked the abbess for her cold treatment of her sister, Lady Alba. "There is only the slimmest chance that we will arrive at the altar, but in the meantime, I beg for your compassion. You and I have always been friends and allies to each other."

Gisla waved me away irritably. She was not ready to capitulate, but she had a soft heart and did not hold out for long. A few days later, she told me how touched she had been when she saw Emont sitting vigil at my sickbed. A few days after that, she compared me with Asneth, the poor orphan who was clothed by an angel so she could wed Prince Joseph of Egypt. Perhaps unintentionally, Gisla constructed a romantic narrative around my marriage to make the unpalatable more agreeable to her strict sensibilities. The stories we tell ourselves have great power.

I was far less successful with Ella than with Gisla. The problem may partly have been my approach, for I was unaccountably nervous. I brought gingerbread to sweeten her mood, but as Ella nibbled her treat, perched on a high stool, I was at a loss for how to broach the matter. I paced awkwardly around the girl and then blurted, "Your father and I are to wed!"

Ella stopped eating and looked at me warily. "Who are you both to marry?" The detached tone of her fluting voice was disconcerting.

"Each other."

"You are to marry my father?" Ella sounded doubtful, as though I had told her that I had sprouted wings and was going to fly to the moon.

"Yes. I am to be your stepmother."

Ella's gaze was cool. She went back to nibbling her gingerbread. Perhaps I ought to have left her alone, but I wanted to be sure that she understood. She was such a quiet child; I never knew what was going on behind her pretty eyes.

"We will be a family," I said brightly, "and you may call me Mama if you wish. Gisla will still care for you as she does now."

Ella ignored me. She munched and brushed the tips of her hair against her cheek in a circular motion.

"I shan't mind if you would rather call me Mother. You are a big girl now. I suppose that 'Mama' sounds babyish to you. I forget how old you are, since you are so small." I felt foolish, running my mouth, but her silence unsettled me. I plunged on, "This is no great change, not like your father marrying a stranger. We will all continue to live together, only now as a family."

A tear trickled down Ella's alabaster cheek, followed quickly by another.

"Oh," I said, "no, dearheart, don't cry." I put my arm clumsily around her shoulders, but she shrank from me. I removed my arm and watched helplessly. Ella stared at the floor; tears made silvery paths down her face and beaded on her long eyelashes.

"Would you like your poppet?"

Ella did not acknowledge me, but I fetched the doll anyway. Guilt and annoyance followed me as I rushed through the corridor. A part of me wanted to comfort the poor child, but another part wished nothing more than to be away from her.

When I returned with the poppet, a clay doll with a fancy gown and coronet, Ella had brightened.

"Shall we find beads to sew on her train?" Ella asked. She was always improving upon the poppet's garments with bits of lace and embroidery.

"Certainly," I said. "We can snip some from your mother's old clothing."

Ella's expression wobbled, but she recovered her equanimity.

"Even though your mother lives in heaven now, she will always be queen of your heart," I said. "Death does not diminish a mother's love. Not a whit. She cherishes every hair on your head, and she sings your praise to the angels."

Ella jumped down from her stool and brushed crumbs from her lap. "Help me find some beads," she said.

Though Ella did not speak of the marriage, she clung to her father even more than usual. She sat in his lap like a tot, ate from his plate, climbed into bed with him in the morning.

Ella had always resisted lessons from me, but as her nurse I had insisted. The betrothal changed our relationship: I lost my narrow authority as governess, but I had not yet been granted the broader authority of a parent. I looked on in frustration as Ella squandered her days in idleness, and Emont colluded with her, encouraging his daughter to lounge against him hour after hour.

"She is just a small child," Emont told me.

"Eight years old," I said. "Nearly nine. I was not much older when I worked in the laundry. If a tutor is coming, she had best learn to read her prayers, not just rattle them off."

Ella yawned and pressed her face into her father's shoulder.

"She will eventually learn to read," Emont said complacently. "Let her be a child. She will have time to be a lady when she grows up. She will have little use for reading anyway."

I bristled but answered pleasantly, "Lady Wenslock is frowning from heaven."

"Abbess Elfilda does the frowning here on earth. She will ensure a tutor. That family has a fixation with educating girls."

"Idleness is to the soul as rust is to iron."

"Idleness is Ella's birthright." Emont smiled and stroked his daughter's hair as though she were a pet.

"Ella may become the lady of a great house," I said stiffly, "but no manor runs itself. She will have duties, and it is best that she does not learn to expect leisure."

"You hear that, lambie? You had best listen to Agnes. She is to be your stepmother soon."

"I don't want you to marry, Father," Ella said, her eyes wide.

"But you love your nurse!" Emont responded.

Ella wound her arms tightly around Emont's neck.

"She is worried about the change," I said.

"I shall not call you Mama!" Ella said.

"There is no need for you to call me Mama."

"I shall not call you Mother either!"

I waited for Emont to reproach her for being disrespectful, but he did not.

"Manners, Ella, mind your manners," I said mildly, knowing that my words fell on deaf ears.

Ella peered at me from over her father's arm. As was so often the case, her face was inscrutable.

It was Gisla who eventually found a way through the girl's defenses. Ella had a fascination with women's clothing that went beyond the usual childlike interest in dressing up. She sorted her mother's gowns by style and then by shade, and she made small alterations, such as pinning a skirt into the semblance of flounces, to surprisingly pleasing effect. Gisla suggested that Ella might design her own gown for the wedding. This project was a double blessing, for it both occupied the child and distracted her from the significance of the day.

I pushed Emont to have a wedding within the month, as I did not want to give him the chance to lose courage. As we planned to wed quietly in the chapel at the manor, there was no need for a formal betrothal or the posting of banns. We informed the manorial staff of our intent, and though there was some outrage, there was also a communal sigh. Not everyone was happy to have a new lady of the manor, but at least they were familiar with me and my ways. They did not miss Lady Alba, and they had feared that her replacement might be worse.

Emont and I married in early spring with only Ella and Gisla in attendance. Ella was resplendent in a rose silk gown with her mother's emeralds around her neck. Gisla coiled her hair into cauls, provoking squirming and complaints, for Ella was not used to wearing her hair dressed. Still, she bore herself proudly and simpered happily when we told her how beautiful she looked.

Emont was pale and stiff, but he showed no signs of regret. He gave me a lovely gold ring, which I had not expected, and he smiled as he slid it onto my finger.

Although the marriage was more than I could have hoped for, my heart still ached. I longed to return to Old Hilgate, to the merry alehouse and my daughters. I even missed Fernan, who had been strong and wholesome, for all of his flaws. The same could not be said of Emont, nor of his strange daughter, who watched the world through limpid eyes but kept her thoughts secret. They lived in silent passivity and gloom, like soft-bodied creatures that dwell beneath stones in the forest floor.

On my wedding night, I ate supper in the great hall for the first time, and Ella joined us for the special occasion. Servants glided quietly around us, carrying enough food for a party many times larger than ours. Emont said little; he looked tense and unhappy, and he gulped his wine for solace. Ella gazed absently into the distance, picking at her food.

After supper, Emont retired to his chambers, and I retired to mine. I could have taken Lady Alba's solar, but I did not wish to evict Ella from her bed. Instead, I chose the more modest guest solar as my sleeping quarters. I did not yet have a maid to undress me, so I removed my own gown and put it away. I waited until I was sure that Emont was undressed, and then I made my way down the corridor wearing only my shift. Emont was waiting for me in bed. The fire had already burned to embers; when I held my candle aloft, I could see Emont's eyes gleaming in the darkness. I fumbled with the bedclothes to get under the covers. For a long time, Emont lay with his head propped up on his hand, gazing at me and stroking my hair tenderly. He ran his fingers over my ribs and told me that I was too thin, but he said it so warmly that I knew he was not disappointed by my body. Just as I began to wonder if he was too tired to consummate our marriage, he tugged at my shift, signaling me to remove it. I obliged. His member was soft from too much wine, and it took some effort to accomplish our coupling, but when it was over, Emont sobbed with relief.

After I crept back from Emont's bed and into my own, I lay awake, staring into the dark. I would never be a servant again. I was Agnes Vis-de-Loup, the lady of the manor of Aviceford.

18

UGLY STEPSISTERS

M y first act as lady of the manor was to gather all of the servants together in the kitchen at dawn. From that day, they were accountable to me, and I wanted to make certain of their obedience. I also wanted to establish my own discourse with the servants. Having observed firsthand the relationship of chamberlains to both underlings and master, I knew that truth frequently fell victim to expediency, self-interest, or sycophancy. I did not want to have to rely on Wills for all knowledge about what transpired in my own manor.

Scullions put out bread and ale while Wills played the reluctant shepherd, herding sleepy servants into the kitchen. Wills was unhappy about my request, which he viewed as both eccentric and a threat to his authority.

The servants gathered in silence against the back wall by the fireplace, yawning and shuffling their feet. Their eyes glinted suspiciously in the dim morning light that filtered through the grimy skylights. Those who had come in from outside were still damp from rain, and steam coiled from their cloaks along with the scent of wet wool. The laundress tried to hide herself at the back of the group, but her effort was unavailing. It made me think of a groundhog grown too fat to scurry into its hole in the ground.

"Welcome." My voice echoed from the high ceiling. "I know some of you better than others. I am Agnes Vis-de-Loup, your new mistress."

Several of the men glared at me with hard expressions. My resolve faltered, but I took a deep breath and continued.

"I intend to make Aviceford the most profitable of Ellis Abbey's manors. You can benefit from the manor's wealth through improved living conditions, but nothing can be accomplished unless you all do your part."

The yawning stopped, and they watched me intently.

"I shall demand that you work hard, and I shall hold each of you accountable. Today, I shall release anyone who chooses from his obligation to the manor. Leave unfettered and find your fortune elsewhere. Those who choose to stay will be given a wage, be they serf or free, and that wage shall rise or fall in proportion to our manor's fortune. Work hard and you shall be rewarded. If you will not do your part, then leave. I shall extend amnesty until the week is out."

The silence was profound. Some of the servants looked confused, and some looked angry. I resisted the temptation to wring my hands nervously. Doubt gnawed at me. I had counted on the self-interest of these men for my scheme, but I had not taken into account how hidebound they were. Why had I been so proud to think that I could change the way the manor had always functioned? If I loosened Will and Emont's grip on the servants too much, I risked rebellion. Until the day before, I had been a servant myself, and they were unconvinced of my authority.

I opened my dry mouth to break the terrible silence, and a burly man stepped forward, saying, "How much will you pay us, and what will you expect of us?"

I noted the absence of deference in his words. "Jack, isn't it? Pay will depend upon each man's position, between two and six shillings each year for most of you. An extra shilling at Christmastide in a good year. What I shall ask is that you assist with building projects, transportation of goods, harvest, shearing, or whatever other tasks need to be accomplished once you have finished with your own work. Gardeners will not be idle in winter, and scullions will not be idle when we have no guests. You will work hard, but you will be rewarded. The more profit comes to the manor, the more you will earn in your wages, the better the living quarters will become, and the more meat we can afford to feed you."

A low rumbling passed through the crowd. My breast shook with each heartbeat. Jack grimaced and wagged his head indecisively, causing the sinews of his thick, short neck to bulge. Then he nodded slowly and said, "That sounds fair. I have never been afraid of hard work." He turned to his fellow servants and said, "What she says seems fair. She is our mistress."

Another servant stepped forward, a scowling young man with a rust-colored beard. I did not recognize him. He said, "This is just a trick to get us all to work our fingers to the bone. She tricked the master into marrying her, and now she brings her sorcery to bear on us." Several others murmured in agreement.

I had to assert myself, or I would lose control. I squared my shoulders with confidence I did not feel, and I raised my voice until it rang clear in the cavernous kitchen, using a tone that I had so often heard Abbess Elfilda use from the pulpit. "You have one week to leave quietly. But make no mistake. Insubordination will not be tolerated. Hard work will be rewarded, but if you make trouble, you will be flogged until your back runs with a river of blood. I shall have no mercy on anyone who threatens the security of my manor."

As the echoes of my voice died, the sun cast its first rays through the windows and skylight, banishing the gray pall of dawn. I held my ground, staring down anyone who met my eye. The red-bearded servant clenched his fists and snarled, but he said nothing. Most of the others looked at the floor. I decided to count it as a partial victory. If they insisted on being sheep, at least they would be my sheep. I raised my hands as though in benediction and said, "You may go."

The laundress scurried for the door, but Wills stopped her as I had instructed. He also detained the only other female servant, a wiry young woman with a ruddy complexion, ashes on her apron, and blisters on her fingers. After all of the men filed out, I approached them. Elisabeth eyed me warily from beneath the graying curls that escaped her shapeless bonnet. The laundry girl quivered like a rabbit.

"Wills tells me that you have to do more of your share of the work in the laundry now, Elisabeth. That must be hard for you."

The laundress pursed her small mouth. Fine lines now radiated from her lips, and her chin was framed by deep grooves. "I have always been a hard worker."

"I have a different memory. I see that your hands are still white and soft, not chapped and blistered like this girl here. What is your name, young woman?"

"Beatrice, my lady."

"Beatrice, do you agree that the laundress does her share?"

The woman glanced at Elisabeth's face and then mine with panic in her eyes. "Why yes, my lady." She stared fixedly at her shoes.

"Then I suppose that she can manage on her own without you for some time?"

Beatrice looked even more agonized.

"You do not need to answer. I know that she will manage fine. I do not have a chambermaid, and until I find one, I would like you to work for me."

Beatrice stared at me with dumb surprise. The laundress began to complain, but Wills cut her off sharply.

"How long will you keep her from her proper duties?" Elisabeth asked, trying to hide her frustration.

"As long as I please," I replied.

"I shall leave!"

"You haven't the courage to leave. In any event, you are not allowed."

"You just said that anyone could leave!"

"Is this how you address your mistress?"

"You said that anyone could leave, *my lady*," she said, barely moving her lips.

"That is for everyone else. You will have to earn your freedom if you wish to leave." I would gladly have been rid of the woman, but I could not ask one of the men to do laundry, and it would take some time to find a replacement.

"I cannot keep up with the laundry without help!"

I raised my eyebrows.

"My lady." She choked on the words.

"You will do your best. I believe that you remember the punishment for sloth. You set it yourself."

The laundress's face turned bright red, but she said nothing further.

"You are dismissed," I said sweetly. "Wills, show Beatrice to my chambers and make sure that she knows her duties. She will return to the laundry when I decide. Perhaps she will get a promotion to chief laundress if she does her duty well."

In the end, only two servants left Aviceford Manor. The rust-bearded one, who worked in the kitchen, departed that same day, and the boy who kept the pigs left the next. There was resistance to change, but when the servants received pay, some for the first time, they softened. We managed the manor better with fewer staff. They became more vocal, and when we had meetings at dawn, the servants gathered gladly around the table for bread and ale. Wills grumbled that it was not properly respectful for the servants to speak with the lady of the manor, but even he had to admit that the added income was welcome.

Not long after the wedding, Abbess Elfilda sent a messenger with the news of her displeasure. Emont fretted and drank himself into a stupor, but I was too joyful to care, for the abbess also sent a gift far greater than any I could have dreamt of: Charlotte and Matilda were returned to me. Since I had vexed the abbess, she refused to continue my daughters' education. When Wills brought the news, I flew down the stairs, barely touching my feet to the ground. The girls were dark silhouettes against the bright blue sky, standing on the threshold on either side of the messenger. In the years since I had last seen them, they had grown tall; Charlotte was nearly the same height as the messenger. Matilda had not lost her old habit of standing with arms akimbo, her head tilted to the side.

When I reached the bottom steps, I burst into tears, which caused them both to hesitate in confusion, but when I called to them, they rushed into my embrace. I had never been so happy as in that moment, holding their narrow, sturdy bodies against mine, Matilda's face buried against my breast, Charlotte's strong arms around my neck. I held the girls so long that Matilda began to squirm; I let go reluctantly and looked at them. They both wore the rough woolen frocks issued by the abbey, and their hair was entirely covered by modest veils. Charlotte was more willowy than I remembered, which emphasized her doelike quality. Matilda, not yet teetering on the brink of womanhood like her sister, was sturdy, and her hazel eyes were still bright, but her pockmarked face had lost its roundness. I stood with my hands clasped, tears streaming down my face, until Charlotte wiped my cheek with the tips of her fingers and said teasingly, "Mother, we would never guess that you are happy to see us!"

After Wills put the girls' little bundles away, I gave Charlotte and Matilda a tour of the manor house. I told them that I had been a little younger than Matilda, ten years old, when I first arrived at Aviceford Manor. The girls were polite, but unimpressed by the building; compared with the abbey, Aviceford was rustic and small. They were more interested in the sleeping quarters, particularly Ella's chamber. Matilda ran to the canopied feather bed and threw herself on it with a delighted squeal, while Charlotte mused aloud about how enchanting it would be to sleep on a soft mattress next to a warm hearth.

I instructed the cooks to serve meat pies for supper, and as a special treat, I had the gardeners forage for early strawberries to serve with honey and clotted cream.

Emont was already at the table drinking wine when we arrived in the great hall for the meal; he greeted us pleasantly, but from the vagueness of his smile, I could tell that he was drunk. Ella sat shyly next to him with her head bowed.

"Ella," I said, "these are your stepsisters, Charlotte and Matilda. You met them several years ago, but you may not remember."

Charlotte stepped forward and knelt down next to where Ella sat on the bench. "Hello," she said, pitching her voice to a register friendly to young children. "I see that you have a lovely purple necklace."

Ella had tied a satin ribbon around her neck as a makeshift choker, an adornment that seemed odd then but would one day become a signature flourish. She touched the ribbon self-consciously and glanced at Charlotte with a timid smile.

Matilda joined Charlotte and put her arm over her sister's shoulders, saying, "I am Matilda. I played with the frogs with you."

At the sight of Matilda's scarred face, Ella started and squirmed backward along the bench. Matilda stood gracefully and stepped away, while Charlotte turned sharply to look at her sister. Matilda flashed her a smile that said "I am not troubled," and Charlotte's expression softened. It made me sad to realize that such reactions to Matilda's appearance were a common occurrence.

"Sit, please," I said to the girls. "I see that the food has arrived!"

We arranged ourselves on the bench opposite Ella and Emont, with Matilda farthest from her young stepsister. Servants placed a steaming meat pie in front of each of us; the aroma made my mouth water as Emont mumbled through grace.

"I recall that you both love this meal," I said.

"Oh, we do!" Matilda said. "At the abbey, we had one made all of venison, with dates and ginger spice."

"That was delicious, but remember the pork pie with almond milk?" Charlotte said. "That was my favorite."

Crestfallen, I said, "I am afraid that we haven't got venison or almond milk here at the manor."

"No matter, no matter," Charlotte said quickly. "This is lovely! Thank you, Mother."

Emont drained the carafe into his cup and signaled for more wine to be brought. "How is the battle-axe?" he asked Charlotte.

Charlotte was mystified. "I beg your pardon, sir?" she said.

"It is so wonderful to have you both home," I interjected.

"The old shrew, the old harpy," Emont said, slurring the last words together.

I knew that he meant Abbess Elfilda, but I feigned ignorance. "Ella," I said, "Charlotte and Matilda can tell you about some of the lessons they learned at the abbey."

"Oh yes," Matilda said. "We wouldn't torture you with Latin, but we know some jolly songs."

"Tilly was the best of all the girls at Latin," Charlotte said proudly. "I got the birch for botching my conjugations."

"You did fine, Lottie," Matilda said. "Edeline was the one who never knew her lessons. Sister Anne grew tired of birching her, because no matter how much she hit her, she forgot what to say. Poor Edeline."

"Remember when you wrote the answer on her hand for her? Sister Anne nearly fell over with surprise when Edeline got the right answer."

Matilda laughed.

I felt as though I were observing my daughters from a great distance. "We shall have to get you new gowns," I said. "Those gray ones are dreadful. I remember how uncomfortable they were."

Charlotte shrugged. "We are used to them."

"Oh, may I have new gowns also?" Ella asked.

"You have plenty of gowns," I said.

"I have no new ones."

"Because you have yet to outgrow the ones in your wardrobe."

"It isn't fair," Ella said.

"Let the little angel have a new gown," Emont said. He kissed the crown of his daughter's head and stroked her hair with an unsteady hand.

"I shall consider it," I said tersely.

"I shall make sure that you get the prettiest new frock," Emont whispered loudly to Ella. He smiled down at her.

"Would you like to speak with the seamstress, then?"

Emont slammed his fist on the table. "I will not be argued with! It is your fault that this has happened! That they have been sent here!"

A cold sweat prickled my brow. I knew that he was upset about the message from the abbess, but I did not want him to make Charlotte and Matilda feel unwelcome on their first day back with me. They both watched him with wide eyes, unsure of what to think.

"This will all blow over, Emont," I said. "If it does not, you may rely upon me to set it right."

"What do you know about setting things right?"

"A good deal. I do not believe that I have ever failed you."

Emont looked like he was groping for a response, but I cut him short, saying, "Ella, you should tell Charlotte and Matilda about the beautiful gown you designed. Please, Emont, do have some strawberries. They are the first of spring!"

The strawberries and cream were a distraction, and my prediction did prove true. The abbess had banished Charlotte and Matilda from the abbey as punishment for my marriage, but she took no other measures against us. Her message exhorted me to be a proper guardian for her godchild and contained a veiled threat of reprisal in the event that we caused her further displeasure. She did not want to take Ella from us, however, nor did she wish to inflict upon herself the task of finding new management for Aviceford Manor, particularly after I had made the manor profitable. The abbess vented her spleen, but she was a practical woman. I understood her, for I was practical too.

After supper, Matilda and Charlotte taught Ella a song with an elaborate accompaniment of hand claps and finger snaps. They giggled at the lyrics and the mistakes they kept making. Ella had trouble following along, but she joined the merriment; her shrill laugh was like the call of a shrike, humorless and louder than was warranted.

I helped Emont to bed, and when I returned, Ella asked if Charlotte and Matilda could sleep in her chambers. I was pleased to see the three getting along so well, but also sad that my daughters were more eager to share Ella's quarters than mine.

I had Beatrice put the extra feather bed in Ella's chamber for Charlotte to use; Matilda took the trundle beside Ella's bed. While I helped Gisla with the bedclothes, Ella showed her stepsisters the pearlescent hairbrush she had inherited from her mother, and Charlotte volunteered to brush her hair. I expected Ella to say no, because she never let anyone touch her hair except Gisla, but to my surprise, she happily accepted. She sat cross-legged and serene on the bed while Charlotte gently untangled and smoothed one long golden lock at a time. Matilda lay on the trundle, out of sight of the other two, telling amusing stories about the nuns and students at the abbey. I lingered so that I could hear the stories too. The candles guttered as they melted to stubs, and though I wished to stay and listen to more of their conversation, I told them that it was time to sleep and said good night. Charlotte and Matilda pulled me tight and embraced me fervently, but Ella ducked her chin and presented only her cool forehead to my lips. "Where is Gisla?" she asked.

"She was tired, and I sent her to bed."

Ella yawned.

"Good night, Mama!" Matilda said.

"Good night!" Charlotte chimed in.

As I closed the door, I could hear them already whispering to one another.

Even during our awkward reaquaintance, I was overjoyed to have my daughters home. Like an insecure lover, I tried to please them at every turn, serving favorite foods, purchasing new clothing, being solicitous to their needs. Despite my elation, however, worry gnawed at me. Had Charlotte and Matilda remained at the abbey, they might have become nuns, but that door had been slammed shut by Mother Elfilda. The only alternative was marriage. Emont would have trouble enough providing a substantial dowry for Ella; I was not sure that I could prevail upon him to settle dowries on my daughters. Without pedigree or beauty, I did not know what would become of them.

Matilda in particular was a concern to me. I coiled her hair in thick, lustrous braids behind her ears and gave her a gold chain to wear at her throat, but nothing could alter the fact of her disfigurement. Her intelligent eyes shone bright in her ruined face, and I tried to look only at her eyes, for without a reassuring anchor, my gaze slid and slipped from a sight that broke my heart.

Although Ella refused my lessons, preferring languid reclusiveness, Charlotte and Matilda did not resist being kept busy. Life at the abbey had been regimented and punishments harsh, so they were used to hard work.

Charlotte remembered little of Old Hilgate and Matilda nothing, but I told them stories of the alehouse and encouraged them to learn how to brew. They seemed to understand the value of acquiring such skills.

We were by then producing our own ale at the manor and selling the excess for profit. I brought the girls to the brewery, a new outbuilding designed expressly for the purpose of making ale, and introduced them to the servants who worked there. For several hours each day, Charlotte and Matilda learned the proper way to grind the barley, wet the mash, boil and skim the wort.

"These young lasses are quick to learn," the brewer said.

"Perhaps it runs in the blood. I used to make a nice lavender ale myself," I replied.

"Ye don't say, my lady. I would not have guessed it."

He meant this respectfully; he was new to the manor and had not known me as a servant.

When Charlotte and Matilda completed their first batch, I brought some to supper for a tasting. I handed Ella a cup, saying, "Try this, sweetheart. This is your stepsisters' first effort, and I believe it is quite good. You ought to join them in the brewery someday."

Ella took a sip and made a noncommittal sound.

Charlotte smiled and said, "Yes, you should join us!"

"It would be good for Ella to get out of her chambers," I said to Emont.

Emont made a vague noise very much like Ella's.

I persisted, saying, "It cannot be healthy for her to spend so much time alone."

"Her tutor will arrive soon."

"I promised the girls a share in the profits if they continue to brew. Ella, would you not like to earn your own money?"

Ella shrugged. "I have no need for money."

"Eat your carrots," I said.

Ella had picked all of the vegetables out of her stew. She poked them with her fork and said, "I hate carrots."

"It is wrong to waste food. Look, Charlotte and Matilda have eaten theirs."

"That's because they like them."

"No it isn't," Matilda said. "We were taught to eat everything in our bowls."

"We should be grateful for the bounty God has provided," Charlotte added.

"God had an idiotic idea when He made turnips and carrots," Ella said. "They are horrible!"

"Ella! Watch your mouth! Eat up, or there will be no supper for you tomorrow."

"Why do you always carp at me? You never yell at *them*!" She pointed across the table at her stepsisters.

I looked to Emont, but he just shook his head. "It harms nobody if she leaves a few carrots," he said. "And why should she work in a brewery like a servant? Let go of your ridiculous schemes, Agnes. Ella is happy. Why must you always be plotting?"

Because misfortune does not wait idly by until we are prepared for it, I wanted to say. *Because there may not always be enough money or food. Because the world may not always be kind to your precious daughter.* I wanted to say these things, but I held my tongue.

One day, Ella asked Gisla to open the cabinet where her mother's gowns were kept. Gisla's rheumatism was bothering her, so I sent her to lie down and opened the cabinet myself. The fabric still smelled strongly of lavender, and the scent transported me back to a dark and airless chamber, where Ella crouched in shadows, gazing at the corpse that had once given her life. Ella never spoke of her mother, and I wondered how much she remembered.

Ella chose a fancy gown for Charlotte to wear, and though Charlotte was nearly fourteen and too old for dress-up, she agreed indulgently to play along. Charlotte was so tall that the hem of her gown did not even graze her ankles, though it hung loose around her shoulders and gaped at the neck. Tiny Ella disappeared into the folds of her garment; Matilda and Charlotte found ingenious ways to belt the skirt high enough that she could walk and fold the sleeves back so that her slender fingers peeked out from the ends. Even dressed absurdly, Ella was beautiful. The girls had fun until Matilda asked for a gown to wear.

"You should dress as a boy," Ella told her.

"But I don't want to be a boy! I should have a blue gown so that we may all have different colors of nature. We can pretend to be three ladies, all sisters, who are imprisoned. You can be the baby sister who is small enough to fit through the window. We can lower you to the ground."

Ella furrowed her brow. She did not like stories or imaginary games. "If you like," she said uncertainly. "But you don't look like a lady. Your face is all lumpish and ugly."

Charlotte lashed out as quick as a viper, knocking Ella to the floor. She towered over the small girl, her dark face ablaze, roaring, "Never speak to my sister that way! You are a beast! For shame!"

Ella looked horrified. Her expression crumpled into one of misery, and she began to sob.

To separate the girls, I stepped between them. I should probably have tried to comfort Ella, but her abject prostration repelled me. I helped her out of her gown and sent her, still weeping, to find Gisla in the anteroom.

I rebuked Charlotte without much force. She should not have pushed Ella, but love for her sister was a cleansing fire. Ella and her father grew like mushrooms, soft. Charlotte had unsheathed something pure, a noble loyalty that was new to Aviceford Manor, and I was glad for it.

That night, Charlotte came to me complaining that Ella would not let her and Matilda sleep in her chamber as they had been doing. I had just gotten my drunken husband into bed with the aid of two servants, and I was in no mood to arbitrate the squabbles of little girls. I strode to Ella's chamber while Charlotte trotted behind me in an effort to keep up.

"What is going on here?" I demanded as I walked through the door. Ella was sitting on her bed with her chin on her knees, and Matilda sulked nearby.

"Ella says that we can't sleep here anymore!" Matilda was indignant.

"Don't be ridiculous, Ella! Where else are they to stay?"

Ella lifted her chin. Her expression was stony. "They can sleep in the attic."

"Ella! Charlotte and Matilda are your sisters now, not servants. You will have to learn to share."

"These are *my* chambers! They belonged to *my* mother!"

"That is true, but circumstances have changed. We are your family now."

Ella leaned her forehead on her knees for a moment; when she looked up again, her eyes brimmed with tears. She said, "Fine," almost inaudibly, and then she lay down, burying her face in her pillow.

I was relieved that Ella had capitulated so easily. I told Charlotte and Matilda to go to bed and returned gratefully to my own bed.

The following morning, Ella burst into my chambers just as Beatrice finished dressing my hair. It had taken an eternity and an excessive number of pokes and tugs for Beatrice to complete the task; she was uncouth and poorly suited to the work of a chambermaid, though she was diligent and kindhearted. Ella was crying again, and I could not make out what she was trying to tell me.

"Where is Gisla?"

"Fetch—fetching bread."

I sighed. "What happened?"

"Matilda hit me!"

"Why did Matilda hit you?"

"I don't know!"

I rose and sighed again. "Come, let's go and speak with Matilda."

Charlotte and Matilda, still wearing nightcaps, were huddled together and conferring in low, angry voices.

"What is it this time?" I asked impatiently.

Matilda jabbed her finger toward Ella. "She took our stones!"

"What are you talking about?"

"The stones you gave us! She took them!"

I had not thought about my stone collection in years. I couldn't help but smile. "You still have those?"

In unison, Charlotte and Matilda answered, "Of course!" Matilda added, "They are very precious to us."

Ella, who had by then stopped crying, said, "I was only looking at them! You hit me!"

"I did not! I barely touched you! Crybaby."

As though to prove Matilda's point, Ella began to cry again.

"Where are the stones now?" I asked wearily.

Matilda pointed to the bed and said, "There's one missing. The sparkly white one."

I looked at the rows of stones on the blanket. Ella had arranged them in a perfect square with the smallest at one corner and the largest at the opposite corner. I picked up the green stone and ran my fingers fondly over its smooth surface. "Where is the white one, Ella?"

"I don't know."

"You had better think about it some more!"

"Why am I in trouble? She is the one who hit me!"

"Matilda, you will apologize for hitting her."

"Sorry," Matilda muttered. "I barely even touched her," she repeated under her breath.

"Matilda!"

"Sorry."

"Now where is that stone, Ella?"

She pulled it reluctantly from her pocket. Charlotte said, "See? She stole it!"

"I did not steal it!" Ella said, blinking back more tears. "There was no room for it in the square. Anyway, it's just a stupid stone!"

Matilda jumped to her feet and stepped toward Ella menacingly. Ella shrieked and cowered behind me.

"Stop it, all of you! I am going to separate you. Ella, you can sleep in the attic until the three of you can get along!"

Ella stamped her little foot in fury. "It's not fair! Why do I have to sleep in the attic? This is *my* room! *They* should sleep in the attic."

"Because there are two of them and only one of you. Besides, you like the attic. We shall move up the feather bed, and I shall have Beatrice sleep there with you."

"It's not fair!"

"When you can get along, you can move back down."

"It's not fair!" Ella was by then yelling in her shrill voice. "I am going to tell Father that you are being mean to me!"

"Enough!" I thundered back. I knew that Emont would be sick in bed all morning from his excesses the night before. "Your father is still sleeping, and you will not disturb him! I shall hear no more about this!"

Ella sank to the floor, hiccupping and sobbing, as I walked out the door.

We moved Ella to the attic that day, and as it turned out, she never moved back downstairs. Like a magpie, she built a nest for herself out of colorful and shiny objects that she skimmed from her late mother's vast collection of statuary and miscellany. I was impressed by how comfortable and appealing she managed to make her garret.

Beatrice slept with Ella for the first few weeks, but as Ella preferred to have the space to herself, I returned Beatrice to sleeping in the kitchen. Once I found a more suitable chambermaid, I made Beatrice head laundress, much to Elisabeth's dismay. She was lucky that Beatrice had such a good heart, for Elisabeth deserved far worse. The young woman could not bring herself to force her former supervisor to work, and she lied to me about how the tasks were divided. Finally, I hired a new laundry girl and sent Elisabeth to look after the chickens and geese. I could count on the cook to keep her under a tight rein.

As Gisla did not like to climb the winding stairs to the attic, it became my habit to visit Ella in the garret at bedtime. I learned the location of every loose, splintering board and the warped lintel that sagged over the last turn of the staircase, so I could make my way up the narrow, dark steps without a candle. Crossing the threshold into Ella's domain was like leaving Aviceford Manor. A high, peaked roof covered the spacious southern wing of the attic, and though the windows were small, the entire space, including the rafters, had been whitewashed to a milky pallor that reflected the half-light pearlescent glow from the casements. Ella had draped her canopied bed with whimsical swaths of pastel silks, and she had strung a cascade of sparkling bits of glass and pieces of broken mirror between the posts; the effect was alluring and strange. Statues that had belonged to Lady Alba crowded the rough floorboards. Ella had chosen mostly representations of animals, and she dressed them with queer bits of clothing and jewelry.

I often found Ella singing or humming to herself, seeming to revel in her isolation. On one occasion, she was chattering merrily to the otherwise empty garret. It was midsummer, and the sun was just setting in a swamp of amber light. Ella's luminous skin was rosy in the dying rays of the sun, and her hair shone like spun gold.

"Who are you talking to, Ella?" I asked.

"Henrietta."

"And who might that be?"

Ella sighed as though she could barely abide my stupidity. "Henrietta the rat. She's right there."

I was startled to see that there was indeed a brown roof rat hunched in the corner. When I gasped, it scuttled under the armoire.

"I thought that we had closed all of the holes up here!"

Ella shrugged.

"They are disgusting." I shuddered, remembering how I hated to sleep on the floor of the kitchen. The rats would rustle in the corners at night, and in my nightmares they gnawed on my exposed flesh with their sharp yellow teeth. I loathed the furtive, hunchbacked thieves.

"Henrietta is nice. She keeps me company."

"I shall have Wills inspect for holes. It isn't healthy to have rats running around while you sleep."

Ella made a face and got under her covers. I kissed her forehead lightly and said good night. As I walked away, Ella said, "You won't hurt Henrietta, will you?"

"Don't be ridiculous, child. The world is overrun with rats."

"But you won't hurt her?"

"Even if I wanted to, I could never catch her. Rats are too fast and sneaky. Now go to sleep."

"Good night, Mother Bear." Ella had chosen this name for me from her favorite children's story. She rarely used it, but it warmed my heart when she did.

"Good night, Ella."

The next day, I told Wills to have the attic inspected for rats. They found some small cracks and sealed them, and Wills assured me that the problem was solved. I noticed rat droppings on Ella's bedclothes several weeks later, however, and when I visited her chambers in full daylight, I saw that there were crumbs and scraps of food scattered about. Ella had been feeding them. No wonder they were bold enough to climb onto her bed.

There were more droppings on the floor, some flattened to dark smears where Ella had stepped on them. I peered under the armoire. Nothing seemed amiss, though the pungent, nutty smell of rodents caused me to gag.

When I opened the armoire, the stench was overwhelming. A pair of black eyes gleamed at me from a scraggly nest on the lowest shelf. Around the nest were bits of rotting apple and other decaying lumps. The rat staggered to her feet, weighed down by a half dozen pink pups that hung from her teats. Their eyes were sealed shut, and their hairless skin looked raw and angry. The dam's feet rasped against the rough wooden shelf as she tried to scramble away. She twisted violently, knocking her pups free, and then she darted past me. For a moment I stood frozen, looking at the squirming heap of naked pups. They made impossibly high-pitched, eerie squeaks.

I sent a pair of servants to clean up the mess. They did not find the mother rat, but they cleaned out the nest, spoiled food, and excrement.

Ella must have discovered that the nest was missing just before supper, for she came to the table white-faced and trembling. She fixed me with a hard gaze and said, "What did you do to Henrietta?"

Charlotte and Matilda were already seated at the table, their hands folded politely in their laps. They looked at Ella curiously. Emont tipped back his wine cup and drained it.

"Ella. That is not the proper way to address me." She sometimes still spoke to me as though I were her servant. "And you cannot feed rats in your room! I do not understand how you can live like that."

"Henrietta is my *friend*. Did you kill her?" Tears filled her amethyst eyes.

"You are not permitted to feed rats! Your chambers were a revolting mess."

"Father!" Ella appealed to Emont. "Tell her to leave Henrietta alone!"

"Tell her to leave Henrietta alone!" Matilda mimicked softly in a lisping, babyish voice.

"She killed Henrietta!" An edge of hysteria had entered Ella's voice.

"Who is Henrietta?" Emont asked wearily. He had little tolerance for arguments and wanted peace to be restored as quickly as possible.

"Henrietta is a rat. Ella has been keeping it as a pet," I told him.

"That seems harmless enough."

"It is not harmless! Rats are a pestilence."

Emont rubbed his brow and refilled his cup. "Fine. Ella, apologize to Agnes so that we may have our supper."

Ella was outraged. "She should apologize to me!" Her cheeks flushed, and her chest heaved. "Henrietta was my friend!" She ran from the room, sobbing.

Emont called after her halfheartedly. He had no appetite for disciplining his daughter, and her tears invariably melted his heart. I shook my head at him with irritation. Ella's behaviors needed to be tamed, but Emont was no help.

Charlotte and Matilda exchanged a significant glance. I sighed and patted the back of Emont's hand. "Shall I call for supper?" I asked.

19

CINDERELLA

E lla did not enjoy having a tutor. She found the discipline of lessons tiresome; if it were up to her, she would have spent that
time sorting buttons or curled up in a corner, gazing at the ceiling.
Unlike most children, Ella did not often seek out playmates or di-
versions, but she never complained of boredom when she had the
leisure to daydream.

Despite Ella's dislike of lessons, she was an able and obedient student. She had a quick mind and a prodigious memory. She
became fluent in Latin and French, and she could rattle off the
names of every member of every royal family in the civilized
world. Her speech had a queer cadence back then, but that has
faded with age.

Ella's tutor, Frère Joachim, was handpicked by Abbess Elfilda.
He had a silver beard and merry blue eyes, and he usually took
dinner with us at noon. At the table, he shared lively stories about
biblical and historical figures. Charlotte and Matilda grew fond of
him, and for a while I had them sit in on his lessons with Ella.

"A riddle, a riddle!" the girls would say at dinner.

Frère Joachim would scratch his shorn head and pretend to be flummoxed. "I have no more riddles in this old head," he said.

"Please, Frère, one more!" Matilda pleaded. She was always the best at guessing the answer.

"One is dark, two are fair, one is small, two are tall, how many girls plague the poor old teacher for riddles?"

"Ha! You make fun of us, sir," Charlotte said. "Anyway, only two plague you, as Ella doesn't like riddles."

The monk's eyes were wreathed by wrinkles when he smiled at Ella. "Who is the fairest in the land?"

"That is hardly a riddle," I said dryly, "and perhaps it is not wise to teach children vanity."

Ella had the grace to blush. "I am no good at riddles," she said.

"You are good at many other things," Frère Joachim said kindly. "Let me see, a riddle. *I'm told a certain something grows in its pouch, swells and stands up, lifts its covering. A proud bride grasped that boneless wonder, the daughter of a king covered that swollen thing with clothing.*"

I felt the heat rise to my own cheeks and avoided meeting the tutor's eyes. I wondered if he teased me for my rebuke. Fortunately the girls were unaware of the double entendre.

"A seed sprouting?" Charlotte said.

"Bread dough!" Matilda announced triumphantly.

"Yes, dear child, bread dough. Now, one more: *On the way a miracle: water became bone.*"

"Ice," I said softly.

"Mother! You have ruined it!" Matilda said.

Frère Joachim looked at me with his piercing blue eyes. "Yes, my lady," he said. "Ice."

Deportment, music, and dance were taught by Ella's maternal second cousin, Lady Rohesia. She was a stern, matronly woman whose barrenness and widowhood were etched deeply into her sharp features. She visited the manor for one week every several months, making it amply clear that this duty was beneath her station. Lady Rohesia did not teach Ella out of charity, but because she relied on Abbess Elfilda for an income.

The deportment lessons made Ella the elegant creature she is today. Her famous gracefulness is not innate, but the result of diligent work. She had to master a tranquil air and erect carriage. No detail was too small; she even learned to lower her eyes to just the correct degree. It would surprise many people to know that dancing did not come naturally to Ella either, but she polished her steps through hours of reluctant practice.

It was Lady Rohesia who told the abbess that my daughters sat in on Ella's lessons. Frère Joachim received a letter forbidding him from taking time away from his pupil to teach her stepsisters. I tried to continue lessons for Charlotte and Matilda on my own, but their knowledge had surpassed mine. Happily, however, Frère Joachim brought several books from Lady Wenslock's collection at the abbey, and when Ella did not require them for her lessons, we read to one another. They were better readers than I, but I improved through practice. Listening to Charlotte's rich, clear voice, braiding Matilda's soft hair, watching the late-afternoon sunshine shimmer across the gilded cornice in the guest solar—those were sweet hours.

When Ella turned twelve, Lady Rohesia brought her to the city so that she might be introduced at court. They were absent for a month, which made Emont more restless than usual. He was uncommonly attached to his daughter, who still visited him every morning in his chambers. Ella liked to jump on his bed and snuggle against his soft, round belly; sometimes she told him about her lessons, but usually they just lay together quietly. I told Emont that she was too old for such behaviors, but he merely shrugged. Ella looked and acted far younger than her twelve years, and that suited her father fine.

Upon Ella's return, Emont had the cook prepare her favorite dishes, including pigeon pie. After we had all gathered around the table, Emont welcomed Ella home with a toast. Her stepsisters were excited to ply her with questions; Charlotte wanted to know about the people she had met at court.

"Oh, I met so many people," Ella replied vaguely.

"Were there foreigners?" Charlotte wanted to know if there were women in the city with complexions as dark as her own.

"There was a man with a funny accent. He gave me a basket of sweetmeats."

"Did you see the queen? Or Princess Anne?"

Ella took another bite before she answered. "I saw the queen. I don't know which princesses. I'm no good with names."

"What about the gowns?" Matilda asked. "They must have been magnificent!"

Ella had always taken a special interest in the design of gowns, so she answered with far more enthusiasm than she had shown up to that point. "I did see the most striking gowns," Ella said. "My favorite was blue with slashes in the sleeves that showed silver underneath and a gauzy little train. Also, so much velvet! Silk velvets with floral brocades and the most astonishing finishes. Also, many of the surcoats had patterns embroidered into the back gores with gold thread . . . Who would have imagined such a thing?"

"How was the food? It must have been divine!"

"Charlotte, let Ella eat her supper," I said.

Ella dug her spoon into her pigeon pie. "I missed regular food. I don't want to go back."

"You are mad," Matilda said. She leaned forward eagerly, the long loops of her plaits nearly dragging in her bowl. "I would give anything to go to court. Did you see any of the princes? Prince Henry is said to be charming and handsome."

"He is also said to be a rake," I interjected tartly.

The girls ignored me.

"You wouldn't be invited to court," Ella said to Matilda matter-of-factly. She had no sense of diplomacy. "Anyway, you wouldn't like it. It is the most boring place imaginable. All people do is talk, talk, talk."

"I should like to talk to people," Matilda said defensively. "I like company."

"Well, you would never fit in, and people would stare at you."

"Don't mind her, Tilly," Charlotte said. "Good company is wasted on her. The way she fidgets and stares off at nothing, they probably thought she was a half-wit."

"Charlotte! Apologize to Ella!" I could see the clouds of anger gathering in Emont's face, and I wanted to head off any further bickering.

Ella dropped her spoon with a clatter. "That is not true! Lady Rohesia told me that everyone said that I was the fairest and most delightful demoiselle they had ever seen. You're just envious!"

Matilda snorted and I lifted my hand saying, "Enough! You know how your quarrels upset Sir Emont. Remember your manners!"

Ella looked sheepishly at her father, and his frown vanished.

He smiled at her adoringly. "You *are* the most beautiful girl in the kingdom," he told her, "as well as the sweetest. Now tell me what you think of the pie. I had the cook make it just the way you like!"

Ella brought back from the city several fancy gowns commissioned by Lady Rohesia and bought by Abbess Elfilda. They were intricately ruffled and pleated, and some had lace at the bodice and cuffs. Cleanliness was not among Ella's attributes, and I worried that she would ruin the expensive garments in her carelessness. I instructed her to fold them neatly and keep them in her mother's armoire.

One morning, Beatrice passed me with a bundle of laundry, and I spotted one of Ella's gowns. It was a lustrous moiré, robin's egg blue, that shimmered like rippling water. I told Beatrice to wait and sent another servant to fetch my stepdaughter.

Ella skipped down the stairs, glad to have been freed from lessons, but her pace slowed when she saw my expression.

I pointed to the dress in Beatrice's bundle. "What is that?" I asked evenly.

"A gown, my lady mother." Ella remembered to address me politely, but she did not sound contrite.

"And what is your gown doing in the laundry? You have had no occasion to wear it."

Ella shrugged. "The laundress must have picked it up by mistake."

"Do you think that Beatrice spends her time riffling through the armoire?"

Beatrice began to tell us that she had found the gown on the floor, but Ella interrupted her. "How would I know how she spends her time? Anyway, the dress needs to be cleaned and pressed, and she can return it to the armoire."

"You see nothing wrong with leaving your dress in a heap on your dirty floor and then expecting Beatrice to clean, press, and fold it for you?"

"I should not have left the dress on the floor. I do remember now that you asked me not to. I am sorry, Mother Bear. But it is her duty. Why else do we have servants?"

"Do you not understand how hard Beatrice works?"

Ella shrugged and yawned.

"Come with me!" I grabbed Ella by her thin wrist, and her eyes widened. I dragged her down the corridor to the laundry.

"Let me go!" Ella whimpered.

The worried Beatrice trotted behind us.

The damp, acrid smell of the laundry room stung like a slap across my face. I had not been back since I was fourteen years old. The new laundry girl was up to her elbows in the basin; her bobbing white bonnet gleamed against the darkness behind her. She looked at us with curiosity.

"You may take the rest of the day to do what you like, Polly. Ella will do your work today."

The girl looked at me dumbly.

"Go on, Polly. Give Ella your apron and then off with you." I gave Ella a shove. "Put on that apron. You are going to learn how to do laundry."

Ella regarded me in disbelief. "You cannot mean to make me do the work of a servant! My father won't let you do this to me!"

I was too furious to answer her. I turned to Beatrice, who looked miserable. "Make sure that Ella does the bucking from the beginning. You have trained Polly well. Treat Ella the same way. She is your laundry girl today."

"You cannot do this to me!" Ella looked at me with tears in her eyes.

"Yes, I can. It's nothing more than what Polly does every single day of her life. You may come to supper tonight if you have finished your duties. I suggest that you start now."

Beatrice fluttered around Ella, looking concerned.

"Do not let her get away with shirking," I snapped at her. "If you do her work, you will have to answer to me."

Beatrice did not meet my eye but hung her head and nodded.

I rode the wave of my anger out of the laundry room, but as my emotion drained away, an ache set in around my heart. I plodded through my quotidian meetings and duties, finishing in the late afternoon, and then I stood cheerlessly by a window in the great hall and watched the snow fall. The flakes were downy, and in the absence of wind, they plummeted thick and fast. Snow accumulated on the windowsill, and before long, the gargoyles wore white veils.

Charlotte and Matilda sat by the fire, embroidering. They had brief, murmured conversations, but spent most of their time in companionable silence. Servants brought cider and took a pitcher of mulled wine to Emont, who remained in his chambers. He had been fatigued, and his skin had a dull, yellow cast; he had not been down for meals in several days.

I was restless and uneasy. As the shadows grew long, I resolved to fetch Ella from the laundry room. No sooner had the thought entered my mind than the girl appeared like a dark phantom in the doorway. She was covered in ash except where her tears had carved bright rivulets through the soot on her cheeks. To my surprise, she ran to me and buried her face against my breast. I recoiled from the filth, but when she sobbed, I twined my fingers in her silken hair and held her close.

I brought Ella near the fire and sat her in my lap as her father did. She left a smear of black on my bodice, but I did not chastise her. Charlotte and Matilda looked up from their work. I knew how it bothered them to see their stepsister behaving like a baby; they wanted me to force Ella to stop sniveling and accept her punishment bravely. In that moment, however, I felt nothing but pity. For all her beauty and cleverness, Ella had a deformed wing, which she hid by never trying to fly. Charlotte and Matilda, like common wrens, flitted competently about their business. They could not imagine that something so ordinary could be out of reach for their exotic and much admired stepsister.

"There now, Ella, it is all done now." As I stroked her hair, I could hear her muffled sniffles. I put my hand under her chin and tilted her head back gently. I could not help but smile at her black face. It reminded me of Fernan, how tenderly he had called me his cinder girl. I wondered how different my life would be if he still lived.

"You are the cinder girl now," I said aloud.

Ella snuffled and wiped her nose on her sleeve. Her chest heaved with a deep, ragged sigh.

"My little cinder Ella." I pushed the hair back from her forehead and kissed her brow. "I am sorry that the lesson was hard, but I do believe that you have learned it."

She nodded.

"Go, then. Run and tell Gisla to have a bath drawn for you. When you are clean, I want you to be sure that all of your gowns are put away properly. Then you may come down to supper. Ronald is stuffing some hens for tonight."

"Will Father come to supper?"

"I don't think so."

"He never comes to supper anymore!"

"He is not feeling well."

Ella huffed, and with an impatient flick of her skirt, she climbed the stairs. Matilda watched her go through narrowed eyes.

The Cinderella nonsense began with a squabble about horseback riding. The Wenslocks were a horse-loving family, and they took pride in their equestrian abilities. Abbess Elfilda insisted that Ella be taught to ride, and since Emont's health was failing, it fell to me to supervise her lessons when Lady Rohesia was absent. I did not know the first thing about horses, but I was qualified to make sure that Ella got in the saddle. This was no easy matter, because unlike her mother, Ella was frightened of horses.

I brought Charlotte and Matilda with me to the stables so that they might have a chance to ride also. As a young woman, I had dreamt of galloping through the countryside on the back of a noble white palfrey, my hair streaming in the wind. Plodding in tight, dusty circles near the fly-ridden stables at Aviceford Manor was a far cry from my youthful vision, but it still pleased me that my daughters had the opportunity to do something that I never could. I might have even joined them if I hadn't been concerned about looking foolish. My authority over the servants felt tenuous, and I did not want to do anything in front of them that might be perceived as undignified.

Ella took lessons on Tuesdays and Thursdays. Our manor was

too small for a real marshal, but Peter, who took care of the live-stock, was also the head of the stables. He was a kindly giant of a man who knew the animals well and could calm the most skittish colt with the soothing rumble of his voice and a gentle hand.

One sultry August afternoon, I brought the girls to Peter for a lesson. Black clouds threatened rain, and Ella dragged her feet in hope that a thunderstorm would force us indoors. I would have been happier indoors myself, for the air was close and oppressive, like the fevered breath of a sick child upon my face. Charlotte's gown had a dark sweat stain across the back, and Matilda's ker-chief was damp from mopping her face. Though Ella complained, she looked fresh under her wide-brimmed hat, her face a mask of serenity.

Peter met us outside, holding the bridle of Ella's caramel-colored pony, Lovely. Two docile old nags for Charlotte and Matilda were tied to the fence nearby. The older girls lit up when they saw Peter and quickened their pace to meet him, while Ella lingered behind.

"There are my three favorite young ladies!" Peter said with a grin. He stroked his silver-streaked beard with his free hand. "I have got Rosie and Copper saddled and ready for you two." He beckoned to Ella. "Come and give Lovely a snack! She misses you."

Peter held a carrot out for Ella while Lovely snuffled his arm and shook her luxurious white mane, stretching her neck toward the treat. Ella cringed and put her hands behind her back.

"Come now!" Peter leaned forward, proffering the carrot. "Your pony is happy to see you!"

Ella took the carrot and held it toward Lovely at arm's length, her face turned away as though she could not bear to watch. Char-lotte and Matilda rolled their eyes when the pony nibbled the end of the carrot and Ella snatched her hand back with a shriek, dropping it on the ground. Peter picked the carrot up patiently and fed the eager horse. He bowed his head to me in greeting.

"Good day, my lady. You are well, I trust?"

"Yes, Peter, thank you. Good day to you."

He turned to the girls. "Are you all ready for a ride? I thought we could walk together out to the back pasture." Peter whistled, and a boy emerged from the dark entrance of the stable.

"Help the young ladies onto their horses. Come, Lady Elfilda, show me how well you can mount your brave steed." Though Ella was twelve, people often spoke to her in a singsong voice they might use for a little child.

Ella shrank from the towering man.

"Ella!" I said sharply. "It is time to get on your horse!" I wanted them to leave so that I could find a cool place to sit.

Charlotte and Matilda were impatient also, as this would be their first time in the back pasture on horseback. Charlotte frowned at the dark clouds gathering overhead while Matilda hoisted herself onto her tired-looking nag without help from the stableboy.

Ella responded to my sharp tone of voice by approaching Lovely. Peter gave her his hand, but she pretended that she could not reach the stirrup with her foot. He guided her to the proper position, but she then made a show of not being able to balance or pull herself up. Peter attempted to steady her, but Ella miscalculated and tipped farther to the side than he could have expected. The kind man assumed that she was genuinely trying to mount the pony, not wriggle free. With a thud, Ella landed on the dusty ground. She began to cry, and then she rubbed her face with her dirty hands.

"Oh look," Charlotte said under her breath, "the cinder baby is back."

Matilda was less charitable and said loud enough for Ella to

hear, "What's wong, wittle Cinderella? Did the scary pony toss
you from her back?"

Ella let out an angry growl.

"Poor Cinderella. Her life is so hard."

"Stop it! Why are you always mean to me?"

"Matilda, enough." I wiped the sweat from my brow. "Ella, stop
crying and get on your horse."

Peter helped her to stand. I should have said something reassuring, but I was too annoyed.

The first fat drops of rain pelted down, raising tiny puffs of dust
around us. Ella pulled her hat low and made herself as small as possible by wrapping her arms around her shoulders and ducking her
head. She hated to get wet, and water on her face was particularly
abhorrent.

The patter quickened to a steady roar. There was no avoiding
getting soaked. The rain was not cold, and once we surrendered
to the drenching, it was pleasant. The clean water washed away
our grime and sweat, and for the first time in days, I felt cool and
refreshed.

Peter tried to shield Ella with his large hands, but it was useless.

"Turn your face to the sky and let the rain wash away the dirt,"
I said to Ella. "If you stop fighting it, you will find that the rain is
quite nice."

Ella shook her head and hunched lower. Lovely whinnied and
pulled at her reins, so the stableboy led her inside. The nags just
flattened their ears and tucked in their tails.

"Very well," I said to Ella, "we can go back to the manor and
get some dry clothes."

"There will be no riding lessons today!" Peter said.

Charlotte's brilliant smile was just like her father's. Water poured off the edge of her hood and dripped from her face. "More's the pity; it would have been fun to ride in the rain."

"We should take off our shoes and run through the back meadow!" Matilda said. "Come on, Ella. Join us! We are already wet, so why not have fun?"

Ella shook her head again.

"I shall keep calling you Cinderella if you won't come," Matilda teased.

"I don't care what you call me. I want to go inside."

"Suit yourself," Charlotte said. "Come on, Matilda!"

With that, Charlotte and Matilda ran away, laughing. Ella watched them go, her face vacant.

"Come along then, let's get you to a dry place," I said.

When she reached for my hand, I pretended not to notice. I adjusted her hat to better keep the rain off of her face.

"You look like a drowned mouse!" I said with false cheer.

Ella followed me home in silence, hunching her shoulders and skirting puddles.

20

GODMOTHER

The girls never did ride together, but discord did not always reign in our home. The holidays were merry, particularly Saint Crispin's Day, when we went into the village for the parade, and all three girls distributed gifts to the children. For weeks before, they toiled to make a basketful of simple toys, and their faces reflected the delight of the little ones as they handed out treats.

Christmastide was also a jolly time at Aviceford Manor; the girls looked forward to the feasts all year. We provided a Christmas meal for the villagers, and Charlotte, Matilda, and Ella always volunteered to help with serving food and drink. Ella was everyone's darling. "Such a beautiful angel!" they exclaimed. "She grows more lovely every year! She is even fairer than her mother, God rest her soul!"

On Sundays, when Ella had no lessons, she spent most of the day with her stepsisters. They chattered and braided one another's hair, or sipped cider, or sang songs. Sometimes Matilda read aloud from one of Frère Joachim's books. On such occasions, they were the picture of sisterly love.

My union with Emont had happy moments as well. When the

weather was fine, he sometimes took me for strolls through the orchards. He would tuck my hand into the crook of his elbow and tell me stories from his youth, such as how he learned to joust from his older brothers, or how he stole a bucket of honey from the beekeeper and dared his sister to eat it all. He had been fond of his siblings, and he was sorry to be estranged from them. I encouraged him to visit his family's estate, but he never did. I believe that he was too ashamed of his drunkenness and his failures, one of which was his marriage to me.

My husband visited my bed occasionally, and he was an affectionate if maladroit lover. Despite the rarity of his visits, he claimed to be attracted to me and praised my appearance; while I was never a great beauty, I looked youthful into my fourth decade, with a narrow waist, strong limbs, and a full head of thick mahogany hair. Emont was not appealing to me, but I did my wifely duty. No child resulted from our couplings.

Emont's health began to decline after the first five years of our marriage. He had always had gaps in his memory and poor balance caused by drinking, but I noticed that these problems became more of a constant for him, whether he was drunk or sober. He would give me a piece of news, and then moments later, repeat the same news to me again. After a conversation with Wills, he might say to me, "Where the devil is the chamberlain? I have not seen him all day."

When Ella was thirteen and still in the habit of visiting her father's chamber in the morning, she discovered him naked, trying to climb out of the window. She ran to fetch me, and when we returned, he was huddled against the wall, clutching a blanket to his chest.

"Emont?" I said softly.

He looked at me with frenzied eyes. "They are coming," he whispered.

"Who is coming, dearheart? We are here to help you."

Emont glanced at Ella. "Who is she?" he asked, still in a whisper.

Ella looked horrified. "Father! How can you not know me?"

"Agnes?"

"No, Emont," I said soothingly. "I am Agnes, your wife. This is Ella, your daughter."

Ella's face contorted as though she were about to cry. I touched her shoulder and said, "You should go. I will take care of him. He will be fine in a few moments."

Ella ran from us, and though her father recovered from the episode, she never visited his chamber again in the morning. She stopped seeking out his company during much of the rest of the day as well.

Despite his failing memory, Emont continued to drink heavily. Charlotte and Matilda learned how to deflect him; they understood when it was best to ignore him and when he needed to be pacified. Ella, by contrast, had little natural perceptiveness or sensitivity to moods. As she got older, she became increasingly upset by her father's behaviors, and her lack of calm made Emont worse. Ella kept Emont at arm's length, and the schism between father and daughter widened after an unfortunate conversation about Lady Alba. Charlotte had asked about the Wenslock insignia on the tapestries in the great hall.

"That is my mother's crest," Ella said. "The gold color represents virtue and generosity. The annulet is the symbol of fidelity."

Emont snorted. "Fidelity!" he said.

Charlotte paid no attention. "Do you remember your mother?" she asked.

"I remember that she was beautiful."

"Of course she was beautiful," Matilda said tartly. "We can all see that from the paintings."

"She was a lunatic," Emont said.

I placed my hand over Emont's. "I used to work for Lady Alba's mother," I said.

Charlotte smiled. "I know, in paradise. You always say that Rose House was like heaven."

"My mother was not a lunatic!" Ella said.

I squeezed Emont's hand, hoping to wake him to the trouble he was causing. "Now, Ella, your father didn't mean it," I said.

"She was stark raving mad," Emont mumbled.

"My mother was kind, generous, virtuous, and beautiful," Ella said with a quaver in her voice.

"She was a maniac," Emont said.

"It does not have to be one way or the other," I said. "People are not good or bad. God has created man in His image, but we are the inheritors of original sin. We each hold within ourselves both the dark and the light."

Matilda smiled at me sympathetically.

"You are vilifying my mother to make yourself feel better," Ella said to me.

"Why would I do such a thing?" I asked sharply.

"You want to make it seem like there was something wrong with her, because she was a noblewoman and you are a commoner. My mother was good and gentle!" She implied by her tone that I was neither good nor gentle.

"Lady Alba was a madwoman," Emont said flatly.

"Why do you always take her side?" Ella's chest heaved as she tried to keep herself from crying.

"He almost never takes Mother's side!" Charlotte said indignantly. It bothered her that Emont often interceded on Ella's behalf; she thought that her stepsister was spoiled.

"Girls, please," I said. "Let us speak of something else."

"If my mother were still alive, none of you would even be here," Ella said. "You are like great big cuckoo birds, taking over *our* home. If she had been here, none of this would have happened! All I have is my father, and he sides with the cuckoos!"

"You are agitated," I said coldly. "You do not mean to speak so disrespectfully to your father, I am certain. Perhaps you would like to take the remainder of your dinner upstairs, so that you may calm yourself."

"I shall! I shall take all of my meals in the attic. You want to lock me away up there, so you will have your wish!" Ella ran from the table, her silk skirts trailing prettily behind her as she dashed up the stairs.

Emont stirred from his lethargy; he looked confused and dismayed to see his daughter go.

"It will be fine," I said. "We will speak with her later and make peace. She misses her mother, that is all."

Ella calmed down, but I never did quite manage to make peace. She willingly abandoned her solitude for Charlotte and Matilda's company, but not for her father's or mine. Ella often ate meals in the garret, as she had threatened to do. I probably did not do as much as I ought to have done to draw her out. In the moment, it was always easier, and therefore seemed wiser, to let her alone.

After the decline in Emont's memory, he began to suffer from bouts of jaundice and lassitude; this was followed by slow but inexorable weight loss. The change was imperceptible from day to day, but over many months, his flesh melted away, leaving him gaunt. Skin sagged from his skeleton everywhere except over his belly, which protruded, round and taut, wreathed by dark veins. By the end, his face was unrecognizable, angular and sallow with sunken eyes and hollow cheeks. He lost interest in food and then lost interest even in drink. He slept most of the day and night, and I helped the servants to nurse him. One morning, shortly after Ella's fifteenth birthday, Emont simply did not wake.

Ella was inconsolable after her father's death. Though she had seen little of Emont in his last months of life, when she heard that he was gone, she threw herself onto his lifeless body and wailed. After an hour, I tried to draw her away, but she shook me off and clung to Emont's emaciated shoulders, her head against his cold chest. It was not until the moon had risen and Charlotte had plied her with an entire bottle of honey wine that Ella consented to leave. She glared at me as she stumbled off to bed, supported between her two stepsisters. It makes little sense, but I believe that she blamed me in some way for her father's death.

Though I had no great love for my husband, Emont's departure left a hole in my life as well. It was not a hole in my daily routine, for I was used to running the manor on my own, and Emont had rarely been good company. Still, after his death, something was conspicuously missing, like food that lacked flavor or a colorless sunset. When I passed by his empty chamber each night, to my surprise, my throat tightened and tears came to my eyes.

Worse than sadness was the fear that his death brought me. I lost my home when Fernan died, and I was sick with worry that my daughters and I would lose our home a second time. The manor belonged to Ellis Abbey, and while I was an able manager, Mother

Elfilda would not pass up the opportunity to bestow lordship of the manor on the son of a wealthy nobleman willing to make a donation to her abbey. I was approaching the end of my childbearing years, and though I was still vigorous, I would not attract a husband without money of my own. Marriage had saved me once, but it would not save me again.

I woke each morning from restless sleep, my head full of wool and my heart racing, imagining the clop of hoofbeats in the courtyard, fearing that the messenger had come. My only hope was that the abbess might wait to transfer stewardship of Aviceford Manor until she found a suitable husband for Ella. Ella was of marriageable age at fifteen, and the abbess would not expend the effort to situate Ella twice if she could avoid it.

I did not share my worries with any of the girls, but Charlotte and Matilda were more than usually solicitous; they must have felt my fear. Ella was, as ever, in her own world. In her initial throes of grief, she spent several days in bed, but she gradually emerged, taking up her old routines. She even began to join us for meals more often than not.

Dressing for mourning was, oddly, Ella's greatest hardship. To my eye, she looked no less lovely in black than in any other color, but she complained bitterly about her wardrobe. Fashion was a fascination for Ella; in scholarly soliloquies, she told us about silkworms, the cleverest materials for buttons, or the most famous shoemakers in the kingdom. It should have been no surprise that she did not want to be told what to wear, but I never understood Ella's passions. While she would lecture us enthusiastically about the warp and weft of satin fabric or the art of making brilliant dyes, she was silent on almost every other subject to the point of mutism. I thought that discouraging her obsession was good for her.

In addition, though Ella had never been a vain child, I worried that she might become overly enamored of her own appearance. Ella blossomed late into womanhood; around the time of her father's death, she filled out the bodice of her gowns for the first time, and the line of her waist curved sweetly where it had so recently been straight and unyielding. Perhaps she wanted to dress in a way that flattered her new figure, but I wasn't sure that was best for her. Besides, even beyond propriety, I had good reasons to insist that Ella observe the traditional mourning period.

Ella accused me of injustice. It incensed her that Charlotte and Matilda wore fashionable clothes while she could not. In truth, I battled my own sense of injustice every day, the nagging pain, like a rotten tooth, of having to compare my daughters to the kingdom's most beautiful girl. Even if it couldn't help Charlotte or Matilda one whit, it may be that I wanted to see Ella's radiance just the tiniest bit dimmed.

Our worst argument came in early spring, toward the end of her mourning. For the hundredth time, Ella asked, "When shall I be able to wear real clothing again?" She paced irritably and did not look at me when she spoke.

A light rain pattered against the windows in the great hall. Charlotte and Matilda were bent over a game of chess. The board with figures carved from white and dark stone belonged to Frère Joachim; the girls had convinced him to teach them how to play. Ella had no patience for the game.

"You *are* wearing real clothing," I said to Ella. "As to when your mourning will end, that will be on May Day, as I have told you many times before."

She pouted prettily. Ella was more beautiful than she had ever been. Her skin was luminous and unblemished, her eyes clear and lustrous. Although she had lost her childhood leanness, she remained delicate and slender, with dainty hands and feet. Her golden hair was her crowning glory, and even in mourning she often wore it loose, tumbling down her back in silken waves. I insisted that Gisla dress her hair when there were guests, but otherwise I let her wear it unbound and uncovered.

Matilda looked up from her game of chess to where Ella had stopped pacing before the fire. "Mourning dress suits you. You look like a sleek little raven."

"Exactly. Ravens are ugly."

"Don't be vain," Charlotte said. "Beauty is as beauty does."

"It's not vain to point out that this isn't fair! Your mother buys you new gowns but none for me! I have to wear these horrid black monstrosities. I look like a corpse!"

"Don't be ridiculous, child." I could not stand to hear someone so blessed be anything but grateful for God's gift. I would have given my right arm if that could have restored Matilda's face to even ordinary plainness.

"Why won't you buy me new gowns?"

"I have told you many times that I shall buy you new gowns when your mourning is over."

"I shall have Lady Rohesia bring new gowns for me even if you will not buy me any."

"You will do no such thing. This is not a time for frivolity, but a time to honor your father."

"If my father were still alive, he would make you act fairly! You only care about Charlotte and Matilda, and you give everything to them."

"Now you are being silly. You have everything that you could possibly need."

"You gave them my chamber and made me sleep in the attic!"

"You could have moved back downstairs anytime if you were willing to share."

With an exasperated sigh, Charlotte said, "You *like* having the garret all to yourself!"

"It's also not fair that I have to take lessons while Charlotte and Matilda sit around in fancy gowns playing stupid games, and anyway the gowns are wasted on them, for nobody ever sees them, and even if they did—well." She gestured toward her stepsisters.

Charlotte's voice hardened. "We can't all be as beautiful as Cinderella."

Ella's face flushed, and she said, "You are all mean to me! You treat me like a servant in my own home now that my parents are dead! You are glad that Father died and left you in charge!"

"How dare you say such a thing!" My voice shook with anger.

"Because it's true! You make me sleep in the attic like a servant, you make me wear these rags, you even made me do the laundry, which was the most horrible day of my life, one I can never forget, because everyone keeps calling me Cinderella!"

I took a deep breath, pushing my fury back down. To stop them from trembling, I tucked my fingers under my arms. I managed to calm myself, but an adamantine coldness filled the void where my anger had been.

"I shall forgive you, because you do not understand what you are saying. You should thank God for all that He has given to you—"

"I shan't thank *you*! You give me nothing!"

My hand shot out before I could stop it, and I cuffed the side of her head forcefully. Ella's mouth snapped shut, and her eyes widened.

"I do not want to hear another word. Get out. Now."

Ella glared at me with impotent rage, and then she fled.

Charlotte and Matilda sat frozen at the chessboard, staring at me.

"Mind yourselves!" I said.

Matilda raised her eyebrows impertinently, but they turned back to their game.

I retreated to the courtyard, where a listless drizzle pricked at dark, glassy puddles. A lone crow tore at a damp pile of kitchen refuse. The clouds relented, allowed weak rays of light to escape, and then smothered them again. I paced in circles and watched the dreary scene for as long as it took to convince myself that I had done nothing wrong.

Had it not been for these arguments with Ella, I might have been more sympathetic to her desire to attend the prince's ball at Cothay Manor. The gala was an unusual event. There had never before been a gathering of such scale and luxury within the holdings of Ellis Abbey, and the abbey had never before sponsored a social event. I am sure that Abbess Elfilda would have quibbled with the use of the word "sponsor," but everyone knew the ball would not have taken place without her initiative.

We first heard about the ball from Gisla, who was always abreast of gossip. Though she was frail and hard of hearing, she made it her business to know everything that went on at the three manors belonging to the abbey.

Gisla was still struggling out of her cloak when she found us in the great hall, where we were having dinner.

"Lady Agnes!" she called out in her reedy voice.

I was annoyed that she had let herself into the hall without speaking with the chamberlain, but from her eager expression and breathlessness, it was apparent that she could barely contain her news. She hobbled toward us quickly.

"What is it, Gisla?" I asked.

"A ball, my lady! At Cothay Manor!" She looked around the table at our puzzled faces with a gap-toothed grin. "The abbess is organizing it in honor of Prince Henry. And she's invited everyone from hereabouts."

"Everyone including us?" Matilda asked.

"Why, yes!"

"Whatever is the occasion?" I asked. "It is very strange for the abbess to host a party for a prince."

Gisla gave a wheezy laugh. She enjoyed being the messenger. "You would not believe the rumors! The goose girl at Cothay told me the abbess is trying to find the prince a wife. I hated to be the one to tell her that goose girls were not invited to the ball. Sweet thing."

"I thought Prince Henry was already betrothed?"

"There was a foreign girl, maybe a countess? I think she died. Prince Henry has so many older brothers in line for the throne, I don't doubt that it's hard to find him a fancy wife. But a king would not be looking to marry his son off to some country girl! That is just goose girl nonsense. No, I'm sure the abbess wants a favor from the king, and Prince Henry is just the one who got sent to visit Ellis Abbey."

"Is it true that he is so handsome?" Charlotte asked.

"I sure have never laid these old eyes on him, but it's said that he claimed the maidenhood of many a lady-in-waiting!" Gisla looked suddenly guilty and clapped her gnarled hand over her mouth. "I shouldn't say such things in front of Lady Elfilda."

Ella did not seem to be paying attention. She ate placidly, a dreamy expression on her face.

"This is so exciting!" Charlotte said. "We may go to the ball, mayn't we, Mother?"

"When is the ball?" I asked.

"The Saturday after All Fools' Day."

"Oh. You and Ella will still be in mourning," Matilda said.

I sighed. "Yes, that is true."

"Please, Mother, may we all go to the ball? Ella can plan what we shall wear!"

Ella lit up and joined the conversation. "We can have ball gowns made!" she exclaimed.

"Yes! Will you help us to choose fabric and designs?" Charlotte said.

"Of course! I already have some ideas. We will need to know our budget . . ."

"Ella, our mourning doesn't end until May Day," I reminded her.

"But I want to go to the ball!"

I sighed again. "It would be unseemly for you to go while still in mourning, and you are too young to go without a proper chaperone. Do you think it appropriate for me to chaperone you in my widow's weeds when all you want is a new gown? You hate crowds and parties."

Gisla glared at me. Ella's face clouded over, and for a moment I thought she would cry, but then she surprised me.

"I shall help Lottie and Tilly with their gowns, then," she said. "It will be such fun!"

"Mother, can't Ella come too?" Matilda asked.

I wavered for a moment, but I did not give in. I wanted Ella to learn patience.

※

One fresh April day, the abbess's messenger came to Aviceford Manor. I was surveying the herb garden when he crested the orchard hill. The apple trees were thick with blossoms; a breeze scattered pale petals like snowflakes around him. The gardener prattled on about sage and mint, not noticing that I had turned to stone.

The messenger dismounted and handed his reins to a boy. As he walked toward the door, I wondered how he would ask for me. Lady Agnes? The lady of the manor? Or was I simply Agnes again, the penniless and homeless mother of two unfortunate young women?

I excused myself to the gardener and walked stiffly to the front entrance. When I overtook the messenger in the foyer, my panic was like a hand around my throat, strangling me, preventing me from speaking. The messenger, a slender lad of no more than sixteen, bowed respectfully. He handed me a parchment from his satchel, telling me that it was from Abbess Elfilda.

Not wanting anyone to witness me reading the letter, I instructed the boy to find some food in the kitchen, and I took the letter to my chamber. My hands trembled as I unfolded the small parchment. There were only two lines written in a cramped, neat hand. *Elfilda will be excused from mourning to attend the ball. All necessary arrangements are being made.*

I fell back on the bed, laughing with relief. A reprieve! We were safe, at least for a time.

My next thought was one of annoyance. Ella had evidently sent a complaint to her godmother through Lady Rohesia. She was privileged by birth and would always have the upper hand. There was nothing I could do about it.

I put off telling Ella about her godmother's message for as long as I could. I suppose it was petty; I did not want to have to swallow my pride. We were expecting a visit from Lady Rohesia the week before the ball, however, and I had to tell Ella by then.

One evening at supper, I decided to get it over with. "Abbess Elfilda has requested your presence at the ball," I told her. "I imagine that Lady Rohesia will bring a gown for you to wear."

Ella gasped, and then she clapped her hands together. "How wonderful! I wish that I had some say in my gown though. This new fashion of lacing the sleeves at the shoulder is all wrong. I do hope Lady Rohesia won't bring one of those."

Charlotte rolled her eyes, but Matilda smiled, saying, "You see, I told you, dreams can come true!"

"I have learned all of the dances," Ella said. "I should teach you the steps!" She bounced in her chair.

"Nobody will dance with us," Charlotte said dryly. Ella's child-like mannerisms irked her.

Ella smiled. "Probably not, but you never know." She laughed. "Do you suppose that the prince will dance with me?"

"He will fall in love with you directly, like everyone does, I'm sure," Matilda said.

"I would not be too glad about dancing with the prince," I said. "Though he may be charming, he has no reputation for integrity."

"But he is so handsome," Charlotte said, winking at Ella.

"And rich!" Matilda added.

"Rich only matters if he marries you," I said grimly. "Handsome matters not at all."

Lady Rohesia arrived as planned, and she brought with her a gown that surpassed Ella's highest standards. The fabric was an opalescent water silk that shone like mother-of-pearl; glass beads sewn into the bodice glinted like diamonds. The shoes matched the extravagance of the gown, as they were encrusted with so many beads that they appeared to be made entirely from glass. Though the slippers were uncommonly heavy, Ella adored them. When Lady Rohesia was not watching, she danced across the great hall, fiery glitter scattering from her pretty feet.

Lady Rohesia told us dourly that the abbess would send a carriage for Ella, that she herself would accompany Ella to the ball, but that *she* would not act as chaperone. Tilting back her head, the noblewoman looked down her beakish nose at me. I gathered that I was expected to chaperone Ella, and that my daughters and I were to make our own way to Cothay Manor. This last part did not bother me, as I loathed the lady's company. I would wear my widow's weeds to the ball, and nobody would expect me to dance, or even to make conversation. Ella would soon tire of the noise and commotion, and then we would come home. Anyway, I was curious to see the prince. I had never met a member of the royal family before, and it didn't seem likely that I would have the opportunity again.

On the day of the ball, Lady Rohesia's maid dressed Ella's hair. It took two hours for her to weave pearls through a labyrinth of delicate braids, but the effect was breathtaking. Poor Charlotte and Matilda had only Gisla and my uncouth chambermaid to help with their hair. The well-meaning servants should have kept to the common hairstyles they knew best, but in an effort to do something special for the girls, they created oddly lumpy coiffures that lacked both sophistication and simplicity.

Charlotte wore a pale blue silk gown that set off her chestnut complexion and raven hair. In typical fashion, Matilda chose fabric as yellow as summer irises. Despite her ugliness, Matilda never hunched her shoulders or shrank from anyone's gaze. Both girls had learned at the abbey to carry themselves tall, and with the flush of excitement on their faces and joy in their luminous eyes, they looked lovely to me.

Even if Charlotte and Matilda had been true beauties, however, they would have faded like ghosts next to Ella, just as the moon disappears when the sun rises in all of its glory. The older girls gasped as they beheld their resplendent stepsister at the top of the stairs. Ella stepped carefully down to where we stood and twirled self-consciously so that we could admire her from every angle. It is said that no woman since Bathsheba has been as alluring as Ella on the night of the prince's ball, and I believe that to be true. She was so exquisite, so sublimely beautiful, that it was impossible to look away.

"Cinderella, you look like an angel!" Matilda exclaimed.

Ella blushed and said, "You look nice too."

"The prince will not be able to resist you!"

"I do not want to hear such talk," I said. "Ella will behave like the proper noblewoman she has been brought up to be. I want all three of you to stay near me tonight." I lightly tapped the tip of Ella's nose. "You in particular, young lady."

Ella nodded submissively.

"I do not want any of you to gorge yourselves on sweetmeats. Take small portions of any food offered to you, and eat it daintily. Do you remember all of the proper titles of address?"

"Yes, Mother," they answered together.

"Even if you are not yet tired, I do not want anybody to beg to stay late. It isn't proper for young, unmarried women to be the last to leave. We will depart before the mid-night repast."

All three murmured their assent.

"Ella, Lady Rohesia will meet you in the foyer; wait for her there. Charlotte and Matilda, our carriage is ready. Come with me."

I turned back to Ella. "You really do look magnificent, dear-heart."

She smiled at me sweetly and said, "Thank you, Mother Bear."

21

THE BALL

I had visited Cothay Manor twice before, but it looked different on this occasion. Short walls of lattice had been erected on both sides of the road leading to the manor, and these were decorated with flowers and woven grass. A great rose bower covered the arch of the gate, and torches lined the walkway and staircase to the entrance. Towering over the torches were flagstaffs; a soft breeze nudged the banners open, showing rich hues in the evening light. The vivid scarlet-and-gold standard of the royal family was interspersed with banners belonging to other families, and the royal flag was also draped over the imposing iron doors of the manor.

We alighted from our carriage well before reaching the rose bower. I instructed the driver, our head stableboy, to come back after the ringing of the compline bell and wait in the same place until we returned.

As we waited for Ella and Lady Rohesia to arrive, Charlotte and Matilda looked about in wonder. Horses broke into a smart canter as they approached the arch of white roses; when the coaches came to a halt, footmen jumped down to help the ladies descend. Brightly colored skirts peeked from carriage doors, then billowed like flowers unfurling their petals as the ladies stepped out, tugging layers of finery with them. In the light of the golden sun that hung low on the horizon, a glittering stream of guests mounted the stairs and disappeared through the dark entrance of Cothay Manor.

By the time Ella finally arrived, the stream of guests had ebbed to a trickle. Though we were not familiar with the approaching carriage, we recognized Ella's milky hand holding her favorite kerchief out the window; as it fluttered, she twisted it, flashing the green and silver sides of the fabric so that it looked like a minnow swimming through the air.

Abbess Elfilda had provided her goddaughter with a royal coach, a bulbous and heavily gilded contrivance with enormous, improbably slender wheels. Its pale sheen reflected the orange-and-pink sunset as the team of white horses pulled up to the archway. The footman helped Lady Rohesia down first. I waved, and the lady nodded slightly to acknowledge my gesture. She started up the staircase without waiting for Ella to emerge, letting me know that her duties as matron had been discharged.

Charlotte and Matilda hurried to the side of the coach; they reached out to touch its smooth surface and cooed admiringly as Ella stepped down. The three of them giggled at something Matilda said in a low voice and would have rushed up the stairs without me if I had not stopped them.

"Decorum, please, girls!"

Reluctantly, they quieted and adjusted their postures. We mounted the stairs and crossed the threshold into the torchlit screens passage. The din of voices and music greeted us, and Ella cringed at the noise. She was the first to reach the opening to the great hall, however, and she stepped boldly through. In the light of chandeliers and torches, the glass beads on her gown came alive with fire, and her golden hair shone brightly. Women standing under the minstrels' gallery turned to stare and poked their companions to do the same. I put my hand on Ella's shoulder and guided her toward the seats at the edge of the great hall. Heads swiveled in Ella's direction, while my daughters and I passed unnoticed in her wake.

We sat in the shadows against the wall. The great hall at Cothay Manor was at least four times as large as the hall at Aviceford, and much better appointed. Ivy and flowers decorated the walls, tables, and dais. Upon the dais, the high table was draped with scarlet cloth, and silver dishes were piled with breads and sweetmeats. At the center of the table sat a handsome young man; I presumed him to be the prince. He had dark hair, as Gisla had described, and an aristocratic nose. His black eyebrows were arched in an expression of boredom. He bent his head to speak with another young man to his right; they both laughed and raised their goblets to each other. A page clad in the king's scarlet and gold hovered nearby with a flask, waiting for his opportunity to refill their cups.

I had never seen a member of the royal family before. I expected to feel a thrill, a frisson of reverence when I beheld him, but he was just a man sitting at a table, nothing more. It surprised me to find him quite ordinary.

To the prince's left sat Mother Elfilda, her back rigid, her gaze resting politely on an object proffered by a bejeweled neighbor. In her black habit, the abbess looked small and faded. I wondered whether Mother Elfilda would gain the advantage she sought from the ball.

The nobility seated at the high table ignored the crowd as though an invisible wall separated them from the rest of the gathering. In the center of the hall, men and women bobbed and twirled in time to the music. I had never properly learned to dance, but I found it enchanting, the swirling silks, the graceful bows, the harmony of movement. I recognized few of the dancers; judging by their clothing, many guests had traveled from the city. Even the vast holdings of Ellis Abbey did not include enough wealthy families to populate a royal ball.

The girls tapped their feet and looked about eagerly. Charlotte and Matilda whispered to each other. The minstrels struck up a lively carole, and the dancers formed a ring.

"May we join, Mother?" Matilda asked, her eyes shining.

I smiled and nodded. Ella clapped her hands and jumped to her feet.

"Calmly," I said. "Remember your manners."

The three girls joined the merry circle. Ella seemed oblivious to admiring gazes; she hopped and skipped blithely with the chain of dancers, a bright smile on her face. When the song ended, several hopeful young men dogged her heels, but their schemes were interrupted by an announcement from the dais. The lord of Cothay Manor, a rotund, red-faced bull of a man, invited his guests to greet the prince.

A commotion erupted as women near the high table jostled to form a queue. The more elegant visitors watched the rush of locals with disgust. I put my arm out to signal Charlotte, Matilda, and Ella to stay seated beside me.

"But we want to meet the prince too!" Charlotte whispered.

"You may join the queue in time."

"Now?" asked Matilda a moment later.

"Wait."

Mother Elfilda had disappeared from the dais, leaving the chair next to the prince unoccupied. The lord of Cothay Manor stood behind the empty chair, tapping his fingers on the back, looking unsure about whether to seat himself or remain standing.

Matilda pulled on my sleeve. "Now can we go?"

The line of people waiting to greet the prince had settled, and the minstrels played a quiet tune.

"Very well. Come with me."

The queue snaked beside a table laden with ale, pastries, and bowls of exotic fruit. Ella picked up one of the strange-looking orbs and explained to Charlotte and Matilda that it was an orange from Aragon; she had eaten them during her visit to the royal court. Ella peeled the fruit and handed pieces to her stepsisters, who exclaimed that the flavor was marvelous. Matilda shared hers with me; the tanginess startled me, which caused her to laugh.

It did not take long for us to reach the front of the line. As the young woman in front of us curtsied low before the dais, the prince slumped forward and leaned his jaw on his hand as though it cost him effort to stay awake. The moment he saw Ella, however, his countenance changed. Like a wolf spotting a lamb, the prince smoothly lifted his handsome head, his gaze suddenly alert and hungry.

I began to introduce our party, but the prince interrupted.

"I know for certain that we have never met before, because I have never seen anyone so ravishing," he said to Ella. "What should I call you?"

Ella finished her curtsy, and when she stood, her cheeks were flushed. Her hands twisted behind her back. The heat and intensity in the prince's dark eyes caused me to squirm also, though for a different reason.

"Cinderella," she murmured, to my great surprise.

The prince smiled. "Cinderella, will you dance with me?"

I found the lack of formality in the prince's manner peculiar, but he seemed to put Ella at ease. She nodded happily. The lord of the manor, still monitoring the proceedings, called to the minstrels to play dancing music. Several people still waited in line to greet the prince, but he was blind to them. The prince did not even acknowledge Charlotte or Matilda, who kept their heads bowed respectfully. He jumped lightly down from the dais and kissed Ella's hand.

A stillness descended over the guests when the prince leapt to Ella's side.

"She is so beautiful!" they whispered, and, "Who is she?"

Ella and the prince danced, oblivious to their audience. While Ella was not the most polished dancer, her partner guided her expertly. She was pure light in his arms, a glittering, dazzling sliver of sunshine, a seraph. I was as transfixed as the strangers around me.

When the dance ended, the prince kept Ella for another, and then another. Guests joined the quadrille or returned to wine and conversation. Charlotte and Matilda waited in vain for another carole so that they might join the dancing without the necessity of a partner. None of the men approached them.

The evening wore on, and I thought that the prince would never tire of dancing, but then I saw him escort Ella through an opening in the screens passage. My heart thundered as I hurried after them. Ella would be easy prey for any man, and a prince would be used to taking what he wanted.

The air was fresher in the passage, and the torches wavered in a draught from the open door. Ella's warbling laughter drifted in on the breeze. The knot in my belly loosened as I realized that they had probably gone outside for some cool air.

When I approached the threshold, I could see the prince, facing away from me, leaning casually against a stone plinth. Ella's upturned face glowed in the torchlight. Strands of hair had pulled loose from her braids, and her cheeks were pink. The dishevelment only made her more beautiful. The adoration and elation that radiated from her lovely features stirred a dark memory.

I watched them uncertainly until the prince pulled Ella close and bent to kiss her, and then I coughed loudly. I stepped out of the doorway, feigning surprise.

"Why, there you are, my dear!" I pretended to have recognized the prince just when he turned around, and I curtsied reverentially. "Your Highness."

Ella glared at me, and Prince Henry regarded me blankly.

"We were just going back inside to dance!" Ella's voice was shrill.

Before I could say anything further, she ran through the door. The prince followed without a glance in my direction. I curtsied again anyway.

True to her word, Ella danced with Prince Henry. Every time the music stopped, the prince shouted for another quadrille. The couple was lost in their own world; they had no care for anyone else. The revelers grew restless, waiting for a more lively tune, and young women grumbled that the prince should not restrict himself to only one partner.

Watching a beautiful girl dance with the prince could not hold the attention of the crowd all night. Clusters of gossiping women and drunken men grew raucous and disorderly. The high table was abandoned, and the most fashionable guests melted away. Charlotte and Matilda shifted glumly on their bench or played word games. I sent them to fetch wine just to keep them occupied.

While the servants prepared the great hall for the mid-night repast, the minstrels took a well-deserved break. I saw my chance to extricate Ella when the prince bowed and walked briskly out the doorway behind the dais. Ella lingered in the center of the floor, no doubt waiting for her prince to return. I told Charlotte and Matilda that it was time to go home, and they looked relieved.

I knew that Ella would be unhappy to leave, but I did not anticipate the stubbornness with which she greeted me. She knew immediately why we were descending upon her, and before I said anything, she said, "I am not leaving!"

"We already talked about this, Ella. It is time to go."

"I am waiting for Prince Henry!"

"You have made a spectacle of yourself already. It is time to go home."

"I shan't leave without saying good night to Prince Henry!"

"You have had plenty of time to say good night, and you should have excused yourself long ago."

I grabbed Ella by the sleeve of her gown and pulled her toward the screens passage. Charlotte and Matilda complained that they were weary and ready for sleep. At first, Ella came docilely, but just as we left the great hall, she pulled roughly away, and her sleeve tore.

"Now see what you have done!" she said.

"Keep your voice down," I hissed. "We shall fix it later. Now come along."

"I shan't go with you!"

I wondered if she had drunk too much wine. Not knowing what else to do, I took Ella by the arm again and propelled her through the passageway and out the main entrance. Charlotte and Matilda trotted after us. I plunged gratefully into the chill night air, believing that the worst was over, but the cold reinvigorated Ella; she wrestled savagely from my loosening grasp at the top of the stairs, ripping another seam of her gown. One of her glass-beaded shoes fell off, and she picked it up in her hand.

"You don't own me!" Her voice cracked with the threat of tears. "I don't have to do as you say. You are not my mother! My mother is dead, and you took my father from me, and now he is dead too, and you are . . ." Tears streamed down her face. "You are simply wicked! I don't care if you are my stepmother, leave me alone!" She pulled her arm back in a swift motion and threw her slipper at me with startling strength. Fortunately, her aim was poor, and the shoe merely grazed my ear. It smashed into the glazed window behind me, and one of the panes fell out with a crash.

Ella's hand flew to cover her mouth in dismay, and then she fled, abandoning her other shoe on the staircase.

"What is wrong with her?" Matilda exclaimed.

"Just one of her tantrums," Charlotte said with disgust.

Both girls descended the stairs after Ella, but I remained rooted in place, shaken. Ella's tranquil disposition had always been complicated by uncontrolled outbursts, but I had never known her to be violent. My stomach turned as I thought of her mother's rages.

Crisp footsteps warned me of approaching men, but I did not turn until one of them spoke.

"Where did she go?" The prince sounded puzzled and disappointed. He was flanked by two pages clad in royal livery; in his hand, he held the shoe that had fallen to the stones behind me.

After the required obeisance I said, "She ran away, Your Highness."

He furrowed his brow. His features were patrician, but his expression vacuous. "Why would she do such a thing?"

I had interpreted the intensity of the prince's attention to Ella as predatory, but that did not match the guilelessness of his speech.

"I do not know, Your Highness."

"I must see her again. Where can I find her?"

An absence of wit or command in his words and bearing made his handsome face less appealing.

"Why do you wish to see her, sire?"

I was rude to ask the question, and I deserved a rebuke, but instead he said, "I love her, and I wish to marry her."

The statement was so outlandish that I nearly laughed.

"Can you tell me where to find her?" he continued, ignoring the incredulity that must have been written on my features. "I saw you with her earlier tonight."

There had been a cretin in our village when I was young, a man with a perfectly sound body but the mind of a child. The look in the prince's eyes reminded me of that man. I felt queasy and tired.

"She was an acquaintance of my daughter's from the city, Your Highness," I said with a curtsy. "I am sure that you will see her at court."

As I rushed down the stairs, the sparkle of Ella's abandoned shoe caught my eye, but I did not stop. I wished only to put the evening behind us.

I found the girls waiting in our carriage. Ella sniffled; her eyes were puffy and her skin blotched. Most of her hair had come undone. Charlotte and Matilda sat on either side of their stepsister, patting her arms soothingly. They muttered consoling words, but annoyance was evident in their voices and postures.

Ella refused to look at me when I climbed into the coach. I sat opposite, saying nothing. Her little hands, like white spiders on her knees, her dirty feet, her slumped shoulders, her blank face, these held no charm for me. My mind was in tumult, my heart a stone.

We rode in silence. As we neared home, I knew that I should

speak, but my tongue was lifeless. Weariness and sadness sapped my will. It would be over soon, one way or another. Mother Elfilda would find a husband for Ella, and I would be thrown once more on God's mercy.

My face grew hot and my eyes watered. I slid to the window and pretended to peer into the darkness. Charlotte and Matilda did not need to see my distress. I would find a way to protect them as I always had. I would beg the abbess to take them as novices, and if she would not, as servants. I might find a husband for Charlotte. The right sort of man might not mind.

As I gazed beyond the feeble light of our lantern, moonlit trees emerged from the dark. After a time, I could make out some details of the underbrush, like silver ferns and coltsfoot. I caught a movement in the shadows as some animal scurried into the forest.

I did not notice that Ella had moved to sit beside me until she put her head on my shoulder. I stiffened, resisting the impulse to shrug and pull away. I knew that she meant the gesture as an apology, and that I should accept it, even if her touch was unwelcome. I stroked her cheek lightly, and Ella sighed. Charlotte and Matilda were asleep, leaning into each other, swaying with the movement of the carriage. I remained as still as I could, and Ella was soon asleep too.

GLASS SLIPPERS

Everyone knows the story about Prince Henry's hunt for the beautiful girl he met at the ball, how he searched from house to house, asking every unmarried woman in five parishes to try on the glass slippers. That is a pretty tale. As usual, the truth is more mundane.

The prince easily discovered Ella's identity. After all, her godmother had been a host of the ball, and the lord of Cothay Manor knew Ella by sight. A simple inquiry would have turned up the information necessary for Prince Henry to gallop with his retinue to Aviceford Manor on a fine Sunday morning.

The men clattered thunderously into the courtyard, shouting and waving banners as though they were headed to battle, not to woo a naive young lady with golden hair. We all rushed to the windows, startled by the commotion. The prince leapt from his white stallion and strode to the entrance, not waiting for his escort. With a squeal of delight, Ella ran to greet him. I did not admonish or call her back.

It is true that the prince brought the glass slippers, for by the time I reached the foyer, Ella was already dancing in circles, her little feet flashing in the sunlight that poured from the open door. Her suitor watched with a besotted smile on his rosy lips.

My mouth was dry and my head ached. I curtsied low, remembering the lie I had told the night before. The prince did not acknowledge me.

Charlotte encircled my waist with her arm, and Matilda held on to my elbow. They both smiled at the scene before us. When Ella finished twirling, the prince dropped to his knees and took both of her hands in his. Members of his retinue crowded the door, casting shadows over the smiling couple.

"My lovely Cinderella," the prince said. "Come back to court with me and be my bride!"

Ella smiled happily. "Will you love me always?"

"I will love you until the stars in the sky no longer shine!"

"Will I have my own private chambers?" she asked shyly.

"You may have anything your heart desires!"

"Then my heart desires to go with you!"

The prince leapt to his feet and lifted Ella high into the air; he spun her around as though she weighed no more than a doll. While her peculiar laugh echoed through the foyer, her sparkling shoes fell off and struck the floor with two resounding bangs. After setting down the object of his admiration, the prince turned to me, beaming, no trace of recollection or resentment on his face.

"You must be Cinderella's stepmother."

Charlotte and Matilda's grips both tightened at the mention of Cinderella; I was not sure if they were cringing or amused.

I curtsied again, saying, "Indeed, Your Highness, I am Agnes Vis-de-Loup, lady of Aviceford Manor." Charlotte and Matilda curtsied with me.

The prince took a silk kerchief from his pocket and blew his nose loudly. "I assume that you do not object to my proposal to make Cinderella my wife?"

I hesitated for a moment, and Charlotte jostled me, mortified. Prince Henry did not seem to notice.

"Of course I do not object, Your Highness. We are honored. Have you spoken with her godmother, Abbess Elfilda?"

The prince shrugged. "She wants me to petition my father to give the abbey the rest of Ellismere Island. He will give it to me as a wedding gift."

Perhaps he was not so dull after all.

The prince took Ella's hand again. "We must go immediately. I shall send a messenger ahead to begin preparations for the wedding. I shall leave men here to gather your effects."

"Immediately?" Ella's smile disappeared. "Not immediately!"

"Why, yes, immediately! Why not? Do you not wish to be wed as soon as possible?"

"Of course . . ." Ella coughed, and when she began again, her voice quavered. "Can Mother and my sisters come too?" She looked at him beseechingly.

"They can come for the wedding, of course, but not now. We must be on our way."

"Will you not at least stay for dinner, Your Highness?" I asked.

"No! We have a full day of riding ahead of us and another to-morrow. We cannot waste more time!"

"Can I not stay here and follow later, with my family?" Ella pleaded.

"Do you not wish to come with me?"

Ella's violet eyes shifted uncertainly from the prince to where we stood, and then she nodded mutely.

"Then make haste! Tell your chambermaid to fetch what you require for the journey, and let us be on our way!"

Gisla had already left to make arrangements.

"Preparations will be complete soon, Your Highness. Please, enjoy a cup of wine in the hall while Ella changes her gown for riding."

"I shall wait outside." The prince kissed Ella's fingertips. "Be swift, my angel!" He strode out the door, and his escort fell in line behind him.

"Go, Ella, quickly! Do not keep the prince waiting!"

Ella threw her arms around my neck and buried her face in my shoulder. "I do not want to leave!"

Charlotte pulled her arm from my waist to make room for Ella. "I thought that you wanted to marry the prince!"

"I do!" Ella's voice was muffled against my gown.

"Well, it cannot be both. If you are to be his wife, you must do as he bids."

I felt her nod. "But I cannot bear to live so far from home!"

I sighed. "Aviceford Manor is not your home anymore, Ella. You will probably not even know the new lord and lady."

Ella looked up at me, her eyes wide. "What do you mean?"

"Abbess Elfilda will find someone new to manage the manor."

"But what will become of you, and Lottie, and Tilly?" She looked at each of us, distressed, while Charlotte and Matilda searched my face for clues about how to respond.

I had not expected Ella to be so concerned. Looking at her worried face, I felt a surge of self-pity, which I could have squelched had she not said, "I shall speak with Prince Henry. You will come to live with me at the palace!" She smiled merrily. "It will be lovely!"

I began to cry.

Ella looked even more alarmed. "Mother Bear!" she said. "What is wrong? Do you not want to live at the palace?"

I could not prevent myself from sobbing. All I could do was smile at her through my tears and pull her close. My heart swelled, straining against the bars of its cage. It was the happiest miracle of my life to hold Ella for no other reason than because I craved her nearness. She patted my back consolingly, as though she understood—I am grateful that she did not understand. She was my daughter, but that was the first time I allowed myself to be her mother.

23

THE ROYAL COURT

It is nearly five years since we joined Ella at court. We hoped for obscurity and prayed that the gossip would die down, but lamentably, the opposite has happened. After Prince George was killed in the jousting accident, Princes John and Hubert succumbed to bilious fever. Prince Michael, who is now heir to the throne, has always been sickly; he suffers from a sort of nervous prostration, and it is rumored that the king does not believe him to be fit to rule the nation even if he lives long enough. It is increasingly likely that Ella's husband, Prince Henry, will become the next king. Which means, of course, that my stepdaughter will be queen consort.

I do not know what to think of this situation as it pertains to Ella. She certainly has no desire to take on the responsibilities of a monarch, and she has no aptitude for politics. On the other hand, as queen consort, she could use her influence to create the sort of life she wishes, and Ella's lack of political acumen has certainly not prevented her from becoming the most celebrated member of the royal family.

While it is unclear whether or not Prince Henry's ascendency is fortunate for Ella, it is abundantly clear that it is unfortunate for Charlotte, Matilda, and me. At first, I saw no reason why my daughters were relieved of their duties to the princess and assigned to work for a visiting countess, or why we were seated in the last pew in chapel. When we were excluded from Ella's chambers—she was expecting her third child and had entered confinement—I asked the lady-in-waiting for an explanation. "I might ask why you are even at court" was all she had to say.

It was a foreign diplomat who finally explained the circumstances to me. I was walking in the garden when a man accosted me. Though he had a pointed white beard and a head of silver hair, he looked to be about my age, two score years. He was short and slight, and he had the sort of intense, direct gaze that is unfashionable at court.

"Pardon me, my lady," he said in an accent I did not recognize, "are you the mother of Princess Elfilda?"

"I am the stepmother, Lord . . . ?"

"Niccolò Barboro. Baron of the Most Serene Republic of Venice." The man tucked the book he had been carrying under his arm and took my hand. He kissed the tips of my fingers and looked up at me with a smile. "Forgive me. I did not know this word, 'stepmother.' I know that you are also a mother, for I have met your other daughters. Dama Matelda is most brilliant. You are too young to have children of such an age!"

"You flatter me, Baron Barboro."

"Please, call me Niccolò. We are both foreigners here."

"I beg your pardon? I am not foreign."

The man scrutinized my face, and then he smiled again. His teeth were unusually white and straight. "I believe that you understand me, gentle lady." He emphasized the last two words, but his tone was not nasty.

"How do you know my daughter Matilda?" I inquired.

"Ah, Dama Matelda is my tutor, and I am hers. She corrects my English, and in turn, I loan her books of Latin poetry. I believe that I have the better end of the bargain."

Though I did not get to speak with Matilda often, I was surprised not to have heard about the conversations or the poetry.

Niccolò laughed. "I see that your daughter has not mentioned me. Perhaps she thought that you would disapprove. I assure you, we have been well chaperoned."

"Oh, I . . . I did not . . ." I stopped, flustered. The need for a chaperone had not even occurred to me, as much because of the man's elfin appearance as Matilda's ruined face. To cover my embarrassment, I asked, "How are you enjoying the garden?"

"It is so cold!" He held out a delicate hand. "You see, my fingers are turning blue!"

I laughed. "But it is almost summer! How can you be cold?"

"Summer," he said grimly. "You know as much of summer as fish know of the desert. It is May, and I am still wearing my winter cloak!" He shivered dramatically.

"Then what sort of summer are you accustomed to?"

"Ah, balmy ocean breezes, the golden glitter of sun on water, the scent of oranges and jasmine mixed with warm salt air." He closed his eyes and breathed deeply, as though he could smell Venetian summer in the chilly garden air. "My home is paradise. I would never have left if I had been told that here it is always cloudy and cold."

"Why not stay inside by the fire, then? Surely the flowers do not draw you to the garden." I waved at the topiaries that had been pruned into severe, angular shapes.

The baron's voice turned serious. "I have heard that you come here most afternoons. I wished to speak with you. May I join you on your stroll?"

My heart beat faster. "Is something wrong with Matilda?" I asked sharply.

"No, no, not exactly," Niccolò said, stroking his beard. "Please, walk with me." He touched my elbow to guide me beside him down the path. "It pains me to tell you this, but I do not think that you and your daughters should remain at court. It is not safe."

"Not safe?" I tried to keep the alarm from my voice. "Whatever do you mean?"

"You are aware that Prince Henry is likely to become king one day?"

"Yes, of course."

"There is always some, ah, *fracasso*, when power changes hands. Some fight for who will be nearest the throne."

"But we are Princess Elfilda's family."

"Yes, this is the trouble. You are not her real family. And you are not one of them, the courtiers."

"We are lowborn."

Niccolò shrugged. "Our society is not so obsessed with lineage as yours. But yes, you are foreign here at the court. Like me." He smiled wanly.

We walked in silence for a moment, and then I asked, "How can you say that we are not safe?"

"Perhaps I spoke too strongly. I hope so. I have no knowledge of plots against you. But I hear what is said, and I know that there are some who would not mind if you disappeared into the tower."

"We have done nothing wrong!"

He sighed. "Do you know what they say about you?"

"I have heard these ridiculous tales about my daughters cutting off parts of their feet to marry Prince Henry, yes."

"It saddens me to tell you, but it is worse than that, my lady." He paused. "They call you evil. They say that you locked Princess Elfilda in the attic and spent all of her father's money on your own two daughters. They say that you forced the princess to do the work of servants. That you made her wear rags, and that you encouraged your daughters to persecute her."

My breath caught in my throat, and I blinked back tears. I had thought that I was impervious to uncharitable opinions, but his words breached my defenses. "There have always been rumors about us," I said.

"Now your king and queen are hearing the rumors," he said, "and they are persuaded that the presumptive heir to the throne should be distanced from you. I have become fond of your daughter Matelda. I would not want anything to happen to her or to those she cares about."

I tilted my face up to the bleak, gray sky to keep tears from sliding down my cheeks. A hawk soared high above us, its wings barely moving. When it crossed into the blurred edges of my vision, its flight looked erratic, as if it were underwater.

"I will find some remedy," I said into the wind. The lump in my throat was like a peach stone. For a moment, I despised the strange little man for bringing such dreadful tidings and for witnessing my humiliation.

Niccolò pressed his fingers lightly against my forearm. "I greatly apologize for interrupting your stroll. I shall leave you now."

I looked into his eyes as I said my thanks, and I saw nothing but kindness there.

The royal court is a harlot. The scarlet gown and painted face may look beautiful to a passing observer, but anyone who draws close enough can see cracks in the face powder and patched holes in the satin. She saves room in her heart only for the gold that lines men's pockets.

Once I realized how tenuous our position was at court, I saw peril at every turn. Charlotte, Matilda, and I had not done well at currying favor, and we had made powerful enemies of women like Cecily Barrett and Isabella Florivet by failing to prostrate ourselves before them. Foolishly, we had relied on our connection with Ella to protect us, but she was being swept along in the same river as the rest of us. She could ask for favors, but she had no say in matters of state, and she was unaware of the machinations of powerful cabals that determined who was invited to court and who was exiled.

Whispers and covert glances took on a sinister aspect. I was not permitted to visit Ella and her newborn son, and the chamberlain refused to seat me at supper, forcing me to ask for food from the kitchen like a servant. I did not believe that we would be thrown into the tower—we are not important enough to pose a threat—but banishment seemed increasingly likely.

Charlotte and Matilda were stationed in the palace wing closest to the river, where the less esteemed guests are housed. They attended to the foreign countess day and night, sleeping in a chamber adjoining hers, so our paths seldom crossed. As I did not trust the servants to deliver a message for me, I visited the southern wing myself at daybreak. I was afraid that I would be barred from entering, so I loitered outside, hoping that one of the girls would see me through the windows. Open ditches on that side of the palace carry waste to the river; the stench was terrible, but I did not have to contend with meddlesome courtiers or guards.

The palace stretched westward from where I paced; the looming walls were at first cloaked in shadow, then warmly tinted by the rising sun. The sweep of the roof was broken by a series of crenelated towers, spectral in the pale light. Details of stonework along the parapets and balustrades emerged as the sun grew stronger; the diamond-paned windows of the living quarters glittered.

Fortunately, I did not need to wait long. Charlotte ran through an arched doorway, holding up her skirts so she wouldn't trip. My heart swelled with a pang of joy when I beheld the flushed face I so adored.

"Mother," she said breathlessly, "why have you come?"

"I wish to speak with you and your sister." I had no plan, but Charlotte and Matilda deserved to understand our predicament.

"What is it? Is there trouble?"

"Not yet, darling, but we should speak. Can you leave for a brief time?"

Charlotte's dark eyes were solemn. She nodded and said, "Meet us in the usual spot in the garden after dinner. Tilly and I should be able to get away while the countess naps." She pecked my cheek and hurried inside, casting a concerned glance over her shoulder as she disappeared beneath the sweep of the arch.

I saw the girls approaching before they spotted me. They both wore dark gowns, which reminded me of the gray frocks they had worn at the abbey, and they leaned together conspiratorially, as they had when they were children. I could tell by Charlotte's tone that she was scolding her sister, though from afar, her words were mere song, like the call of a bird. Matilda laughed.

I greeted them, and Matilda said, "A secret meeting, how diverting, Mother!"

"You are in good spirits," I replied.

"Ah, but I can see that you are not. Tell me your troubles." Matilda linked her arm through mine, and we started down our usual path.

"I met your friend, Baron Barboro."

Matilda glanced at me warily. "A peculiar little man, is he not? His chambers are next to ours, so we see him often. He shares his books with us. He seems amiable enough, but there is something cloying about him."

"He certainly brought disturbing news."

Matilda squeezed my arm.

"What did he say, Mother?" Charlotte asked.

"He is concerned that we will be forced out of the court by those who believe us to be a liability to Prince Henry." I did not mention the tower. It did not seem necessary.

"Ella would never allow it!"

"When was the last time you saw the princess?" I asked.

"We have been busy."

"Have you met your new nephew?"

"No," Charlotte said uncertainly.

"It is not your duties that keep you away," I said. "You are not wanted there."

"But of course Ella wants to see us!"

I shrugged. "Perhaps. It does not bode well that she has not sent for us."

"Where would we go if we have to leave?" Charlotte asked.

"I am not sure. If we could secure a loan, we might start a brewery. You both have learned to brew."

Charlotte chewed her lip nervously. "What if the brewery failed?"

"I don't know."

"We could go to Venice," Matilda said in a small voice.

I stopped walking. "Venice?"

Matilda looked at me timidly. "Niccolò has invited me. I had said no, but I am sure that he would be happy if I changed my mind."

"But you don't want to marry him!" Charlotte said.

"Marry him?" I was incredulous.

"Why do you look so shocked, Mother? Did you think that nobody would ever wish to marry me?"

"I . . . No, of course not, it's only that . . . I was not expecting this."

"Well, it seems that Niccolò admires me despite my face." Matilda poked my side with her finger. "Who would have thought that such a thing could happen?"

"Oh, sweetheart, you are a treasure, and you know I think that you are one of the finest women ever to walk the earth. One of the finest two," I said, smiling at Charlotte. "One of the finest three," I quickly corrected myself.

"But, Tilly, you can't!" Charlotte said. She looked at me beseechingly. "She doesn't love him, and she does not want to live in Venice!"

"If Niccolò would allow you both to come with me, I could resign myself to such a fate."

"You cannot marry a man you do not love!" Charlotte said.

I was astonished at her naiveté. "Nobody marries for love," I said.

"Ella did."

"Your stepsister married a *prince*. Please do not tell me that you, of all people, are listening to these minstrel tales! These are the very reason we are being forced from the court!" I was outraged. "Prince Henry is not some heroic figure who saved Ella from a miserable fate, and Ella did not toss all reason to the wind to marry some pauper who stole her heart. She married one of the wealthiest and highest-ranking men in the land! You speak of *love*? Love is a sickness that causes men and women to do stupid things, the sorts of things that leave them sad and broken when the fever passes."

"And I suppose you think that anyone is a fool to fall in love with me?" Matilda said angrily.

"*You* are the fool if you do not realize that such fancies pass quickly when families raise the issue of inheritance!"

Matilda pulled back as though I had slapped her. The hurt in her face was wrenching. I drew a shaky breath and said, "I am sorry. I do not know how we got so cross. I love you so very dearly."

"I believe *you* are the one who got cross, Mother," Matilda said, "and isn't love a sickness?"

"Not the love I have for you!" I was perilously close to tears again. "You are my own flesh and blood and bones. You are my own heart!"

Charlotte put her arm around her sister's shoulders. "It is not right," she said, "for a woman to give her life to a man she does not esteem."

Her comment stirred my ire again. "You know little of the choices women must make," I said. "Do you suppose that most women get to live at liberty in manor houses and castles, eating stuffed pheasant off silver plates? That most women have any control over their own fates? Every woman serves a master, be it an overlord or a husband, and she is fortunate if he does not beat her and treat her cruelly. Everything you have, I got for you either through marriage or hard work. There is no alternative. Do you suppose that freedom was *ever* a choice for me?"

"We are grateful to you, Mother," Matilda said coldly, "and we are sorry that you have suffered." She said the word as though she did not quite believe in my suffering. "If marriage is to be my only salvation, then I too will suffer. We happen to have a sister who is a princess, however, and before any of us do anything foolish, I am going to speak with her."

Charlotte, ever the peacemaker, said, "Now, Mother was not saying that you must marry."

Matilda's eyes glittered. "I know perfectly well what she said, thank you, Lottie." Matilda spun and walked away, back toward the palace. Charlotte gave me a chagrined smile and then chased after her sister, calling her name. I sank to the ground and wept, oblivious to any prying eyes that might have been watching me.

A summons from Ella came the next day. I had spent the night awake, pacing in my narrow chamber, and I was not yet clothed when a messenger knocked loudly on my door and told me to report to the princess's quarters. I was surprised that Matilda had managed to arrange an audience so soon, but I dressed as quickly as I could and hurried to the royal apartments. As hostile glances had become commonplace, I wore a long veil and kept my head bowed in the dimly lit corridors.

An uncharacteristic timidity overtook me as I approached Ella's private chamber, but before I could hesitate, a stony-faced servant opened the door and ushered me inside. Ella sat on her daybed, wrapped in a purple brocade robe and flanked on each side by Charlotte and Matilda. As I curtsied, Ella asked, "Are you ill?"

I covered my eyes for a moment with my hands, realizing that they must be red from weeping. There was no looking glass in my chamber, so I had not seen the damage wrought by my sleepless night. I touched my eyelids gingerly with the tips of my fingers; they were puffed up like bread dough. "I am fine, Your Highness," I said. "It is nothing some rest cannot cure."

Matilda jumped up and rushed to embrace me. Her expression was anguished, and I could tell from her pink-rimmed eyes that she had also shed some tears.

"I am so sorry, Mama," Matilda said. "I was an ungrateful wretch yesterday. How could I treat you so horridly when you have done so much for us? Can you forgive me?"

I did not trust my voice, so I held Matilda tightly in my arms until the storm of feelings subsided. Then I said, "I hope that you will forgive me for my harsh words, my darling. I am not myself. I have been so worried—"

Matilda took my face between both hands and kissed me. Then she smiled and said, "Our princess has found a solution to our troubles!" She put her arm around my waist and turned to the others.

Charlotte and Ella looked pleased. Ella tucked a stray lock of glossy hair behind her ear and said, "My sisters tell me that you are unhappy at court."

Out of politeness, I began to protest, but Ella cut me short, saying, "I don't always like it here either. Sometimes I wish that I could get away. I like to make pilgrimages to the abbey, because it is always quiet and peaceful. I cannot choose to live there, but perhaps you should."

"But how can we live at the abbey?" I asked, confused. "We are not nuns, and we have no money of our own."

Ella laughed, showing her pearly little teeth. "Do you forget that the abbess is my godmother? She will deny me nothing." She cocked her head to the side and looked up through her lashes. "When my grandmother died, she left nearly all of her considerable estate to the abbey. My mother received some statuary and tapestries, a mere pittance. I was denied my rightful inheritance. Mother Elfilda settled some money on me for my dowry, but that was a tiny piece of what should be mine. If I tell her that I want the use of Rose House, she will gladly agree."

"Do not argue with her, Mother!" Charlotte said. She smiled happily. "You have longed to go back to the abbey. Think of how contented we should be there! Ella will visit often, and we can take the children to hunt for frogs around the pond without anyone telling us that it is not proper. We shall have all the books we wish to read and no awful courtiers. We shall be together!" Charlotte leapt to her feet and took my hands in hers. "Do say that we may go to Rose House, Mother!"

Ella stood also. She looked from one of us to the next with her big, luminous eyes. "If you have no objections, I shall make arrangements for the move."

I stepped forward and curtsied low. Charlotte and Matilda quickly joined me.

"I cannot properly express my gratitude, Your Highness," I said. "You are too generous."

"You are my family," Ella said simply. "We have had our differences, but I never doubted your love."

My soul shrank within me as I remembered shameful lapses in my love for Ella. My affections had never flown to her naturally; I had needed to push and shove my heart toward my stepdaughter, and I had, at times, turned a blind eye to my heart's obstinacy. I made excuses, telling myself that Ella was strange, and that anyone would find her difficult. That Charlotte and Matilda were more inherently amiable. That I was not Ella's real mother.

"Thank you," I said, bowing to Ella again. "You are far more kind than I deserve."

The perfumed air was suddenly oppressive. I could tell that Charlotte and Matilda wished me to linger, but I felt stifled and light-headed, so I excused myself. The feeling of suffocation did not improve in the corridor, however, nor could I stand to be alone in my dark chamber. I fled to the garden, seeking fresh air; when I burst from the door, bright sunshine dazzled my sore eyes, and I could draw an easier breath. Accusing glances and whispers still clung to me, however, feeding on the guilt that I had tried so long to hide, even from myself.

24

RETURN TO ROSE HOUSE

We moved to Rose House a decade ago, and I sleep in the same chamber my mistress, Lady Wenslock, slept in so long ago. Though there is plenty of room, even when Ella and her children visit, Matilda and Charlotte have chosen to continue to share a chamber. We take all of our meals together but keep busy with separate occupations for much of the day. Matilda teaches Latin to the convent students; she has become great friends with many of the nuns, and she sneaks them home for dinner whenever she gets the chance. Charlotte works in the scriptorium; she has great talent for illumination, and her volumes have gone to the best families in the kingdom. I have continued to write, mostly poetry. I don't know if anyone will read my work, but writing brings me joy. Our favorite hours are spent together in the library, where we know our favorite books by heart.

It has been a relief to escape the judgment and spitefulness we faced at court. I am certain that Ella has done nothing to promote stories about her ugly stepsisters and selfish stepmother, but she is so radiant, so simple and cheerful, and we are her shadows. In or-

der for her to embody beauty and goodness, we have to be darkness and perversity. This is the way of mankind, and it has always
been so, since God cast us out from the Garden of Eden. We can
only know virtue by understanding vice; we would be animals
otherwise, living, mating, breeding, and dying in a world without
righteousness or sin.

We did perhaps treat Ella too harshly when she was a girl, but I
know that Charlotte and Matilda truly wanted their stepsister to be
happy. So did I, though not nearly so much as she deserved. I am
still trying to make peace with my failures.

In a more complicated way, we also wanted Ella to be un-
daunted in the face of difficulty, thoughtful about the motives of
others, hardy in the face of God's small punishments. Charlotte
and Matilda's teasing, like my discipline, was meant to temper her
character, as fire tempers steel. It was perhaps not in Ella's nature
to learn these things, and stringency may not have been the proper
tool for teaching her, but we meant her no malice. It is only in old
age that I recognize that not all characters have a core of steel. Ella's character is made of something finer and less substantial, like
morning mist or the sparkle of sun on water.

Ella visits us every season and delights in the peacefulness of the
abbey. She usually brings some of her children. She has five little
princes and princesses now, two boys and three girls. The twins
were named Charlotte and Matilda, but little Charlotte died in the
cradle, so my daughters now share the duties of godmother to Millie. She is a sweet child, a ray of sunshine. Though she inherited
her father's brown eyes and dark hair, Millie's face is as fair as
Ella's. I am sad that Charlotte and Matilda will never know the joys

of motherhood, but they love their nieces and nephews, and they are grateful for the unusual freedom they have been granted.

Ella dutifully visits with Mother Elfilda, who is now abbess only in name. Her sight is failing, and she is frail. The prioress manages most of the daily functions of the abbey, and Ella ensures that we are well cared for.

The years pass quickly; of the half century I have been alive, the last decade has flown most swiftly. Every spring, I sit in the rose garden, where I watch the reflected light from the pond dance along the bower. When I hear the crunch of footsteps on gravel, I expect to see Fernan with his satchel slung over his shoulder, flashing his brilliant smile. Instead, it is my daughter. She takes her place beside me on the bench and strokes the back of my hand, smoothing down the blue veins that now worm beneath my spotted skin. I kiss her cheek. We may not deserve it, but we are happy.

ACKNOWLEDGMENTS

Years ago, I had a job interview with an imposing and revered chair of medicine. With passion, I described my heartfelt belief that the pursuit of science needs to be recognized as a team effort, and that the myth of the lone genius hampers progress. I thought that the gentleman would agree with what seemed a self-evident truth, but instead, he was appalled. "Why," he said, "that's like claiming that a great novel can be written by more than one author!" I didn't know how to respond at the time, but all these years later, I finally have my answer: Novels are created by teams of people too.

I am deeply indebted to all who have contributed to this book. To those who read early drafts and shared wise critiques and advice, including Jennifer Bird, Liese Schwarz, Lynn Stegner, Masie Cochran, and the astute team at InkWell Management, I am enormously grateful. Thanks also to the members of Pegasus 4, my physician writing group, for their perceptive comments and encouragement.

I am thrilled to have the opportunity to work with Jennifer Brehl and her team at William Morrow, members of the publishing pantheon that gave life to some of my most cherished stories. It is a dream come true.

Michael Carlisle, my agent, is the real Prince Charming in this story. He was determined to lift Agnes out of obscurity, and I cannot thank him enough for his unflagging faith and enthusiasm for this work. (He also happens to be a prince of a man, and most charming.) *Un grand merci aussi à* Alexis Hurley for introducing this book to the world beyond the shores of North America.

With all my heart, I thank my family and friends for love, inspiration, and support. Special mention goes to my daughter Claire, who has been a fierce champion for my writing aspirations; to my father, whose instincts for storytelling have been my guide; and to my wonderful husband, without whom this book would not exist.